AN ATLAS OF
IMPOSSIBLE LONGING

Anuradha Roy

AN ATLAS OF
IMPOSSIBLE LONGING

MACLEHOSE PRESS
QUERCUS · LONDON

First published in Great Britain in 2008 by

MacLehose Press
An imprint of Quercus
21 Bloomsbury Square
London
WC1A 2NS

Copyright © 2008 by Anuradha Roy

The moral right of Anuradha Roy to be
identified as the author of this work has been

a

All ⸱n
ma ⸱m
o

with⸱ ⸱her.

A CIP catalogue reference for this book
is available from the British Library

ISBN 978 1 84724 477 2 (HB)
ISBN 978 1 84724 478 9 (TPB)

This book is a work of fiction. Names, characters,
businesses, organizations, places and events are
either the product of the author's imagination
or are used fictitiously. Any resemblance to
actual persons, living or dead, events or
locales is entirely coincidental.

10 9 8 7 6 5 4 3 2 1

Printed and bound in England by
Clays Ltd, St Ives plc.

For Baba, still here

CONTENTS

PROLOGUE

The house in the picture is afloat on a river the innocuous colour of darkening sepia.

The house is a folly, a Roman-looking affair with tapering pillars soaring to its arched roof. Palm trees at its sides tousle the sky, leaning close and tall. Watery eddies frozen at the click of a shutter lick the pillars of its long verandah.

The river has been shifting and turning, spurning its ancient course, hungry for new soil. For years the little town – they call it a town, but it is only two or three brick houses and then fields and thatched huts – for as long as anyone remembers, the town has watched and joked about the indecisive river. Now they can see that the river is a little more daring each monsoon in its progress towards the house, claiming a foot, not the unintrusive inch any more. In my photograph it is still far away, held back by the wall of the ghat, lapping at the slimy stone the women stepped onto going for a wash.

Then the brown river in the picture begins to rise and the steps to the house become river and the verandah too becomes river. It rises until the verandah's windows open into water. I see people swimming behind the submerged windows, imprisoned by the drowned rooms as if in some abandoned Atlantis. I watch the palm trees come crashing down through the ornate roof. As the house dissolves, the flowering bakul tree on the left side of the picture flows boat-like into the water on a journey without end.

PART I

THE DROWNED HOUSE

ONE

In the warm glow of fires that lit the clearing at the centre of straw-roofed mud huts, palm-leaf cups of toddy flew from hand to hand. Men in loincloths and women in saris had begun to dance barefoot, kicking up dust. Smoke curled from cooking fires and tobacco. The drums, the monotonous twanging of a stringed instrument, and loud singing obliterated the sounds of the forest.

A man with a thin, frown-creviced face topped by dark hair combed back from his high forehead sat as still as a stone image in their midst, in a chair that still had its arms but had lost its backrest. His long nose struck out, arrow-like, beneath deep-set eyes. He had smoked a pipe all evening and held one polite leaf cup of toddy that he had only pretended to sip. His kurta and dhoti were an austere white, his waistcoat a lawyerly black.

He did not appear to hear the singing. But his eyes were on the dancers: wasn't that girl in the red sari the one who had come with baskets of wild hibiscus that she had flung carelessly into a corner of his factory floor? And that man who was dancing with his arm around her waist, wasn't he one of the honey-collectors? It was hard to tell, with their new saris and dhotis, the flowers in their hair, the beads flying out from necks, the firelight. The man leaned forward, trying to tell which of the sweat-gleaming faces he had encountered before in his small workforce.

The brown-suited, toadlike figure sitting on a stool next to him nudged him in the ribs. "Something about these tribal girls, eh, Amulya Babu? Makes long-married men think unholy thoughts! And do you know, they'll sleep with any number of men they like!" He emptied his cup of toddy into his mouth and licked his lips, saying, "Strong stuff! I should sell it in my shop!"

A bare-chested villager refilled the cup, saying, "Come and dance with us, Cowasjee Sahib! And Amulya Babu, you are not drinking at all! This is the first time people from outside the jungle have come as guests to our harvest festival. And because *I insisted*. I said, it's Cowasjee Sahib and Amulya Babu who give us our roti and salt! We must repay them in our humble way!"

A tall, hard-muscled man stood nearby, listening, lips curling with contempt as his relative hovered over the four or five friends Cowasjee had brought with him, radiating obeisance as he refilled their cups. Beyond the pool of firelight, cooking smells and noise, the forest darkened into shadows. Somewhere, a buffalo let out a mournful, strangled bellow. The drums gathered pace, the girls linked their arms behind each other's waists, swaying to the rhythm, and the men began to sing:

> *A young girl with a waist so slender that*
> *I can put my finger around it,*
> *Is going down to the well for water.*
> *With swaying hips she goes.*
>
> *My life yearns with desire.*
> *My bed is painted red.*
> *Red are my blankets.*
> *For these four months of rain and happiness*
> *Stay, stay with me.*
>
> *Without you I cannot eat,*
> *Without you I cannot drink.*
> *I'll find no joy in anything.*
> *So stay, stay, for the months of rain,*
> *And for happiness with me.*

One of the girls in the line of dancers separated herself from her partners. She had noticed Amulya's preoccupied expression, wondered how a man could remain unmoved by the music, not drink their wine. She came forward with a smile, her beads and bangles jingling, her bare shoulders gleaming in the firelight, orange sari wrapped tight over her young body. The toddy made her head spin a little when she bent down to Amulya. As he tried to scramble away, she stroked his cheek and said, "Poor babuji, are you too pining for someone?" She leaned closer and whispered into his ear, "Won't you come and dance? It wipes sorrows away."

Amulya looked up beyond her childish face, framed by curling hair which smelled of a strong, sweet oil, at the flamboyant purple flower pinned into her bun. It had a ring of lighter petals within the purple ones, and a pincushion of stamens. *Passiflora*, of course. Yes, certainly *Passiflora*. But what species?

Despite the haze of alcohol that made her eyes slide from thing to thing, the girl noticed that the man's gaze was not on her face, but on the flower. She unpinned it and held it out to him. A deep dimple pierced her cheek. The drums rolled again, a fresh song started, and she tripped back to her friends with a laugh, looking once over her shoulder.

"Hey, Amulya Babu, the girl likes you!" Cowasjee cried, slapping Amulya's thigh. "You can turn down food and drink, but how can you turn down a lusting woman? Go on, dance with her! That's the done thing in these parts!"

Amulya stood up from his chair and moved away from Cowasjee's hand. "I have to leave now," he said, his tone peremptory. In his left hand he clutched the purple flower. With the other he felt about for his umbrella.

Amulya understood he was an anomaly. When still new in the town adjoining the jungle, he had tried to make himself part of local society by going to a few parties. Songarh's local rich, they too had hopes of him, as a metropolitan dandy perhaps, laden with tales and gossip from the big city, conversant with its fashions, bright with repartee, a tonic for their jaded, small-town appetites. He had had many eager invitations.

After the first few parties, at which he refused offers of whisky and pink gins, and then waited, not talking very much, for dinner to be served and the evening to end, he had realised that perhaps his being there was not serving any purpose. Was he really becoming a bona fide local by attending these parties when his presence emanated obligation?

Today – these festivities at the village whose people were his work-force – he had thought it would be different. He had, for a change, wanted to come. He had only ever seen tribal people at work – what were they like at play, what were their homes like? The opportunity had seemed too good to miss; but Cowasjee, in whom the bare-shouldered village girls seemed to unleash more than his usual loutishness, had ensured that this evening was like all the others.

Amulya looked around for someone to thank, but everywhere people sat on their haunches drinking, or they danced, enclosed in worlds of private rapture. The drums had speeded up, the twanging could scarcely keep pace. Where was his umbrella? And his office bag? Was his tonga waiting for him as instructed? Was anyone sober enough to light his way to the tonga?

"Oh sit, sit, Amulya Babu," Cowasjee said, tugging Amulya's sleeve. "You can't go without eating, they'll be sure their food was too humble for you, they'll feel insulted. The night is young and we have stories to swap! Have you heard this one?" Cowasjee cackled in anticipation of his punchline.

Amulya sat again, annoyed and reluctant, barely able to summon up a strained smile to the yodelled laughs that accompanied the ensuing discussion about why a woman's two holes smelled different despite being geographically proximate. "Just like the difference between Darjeeling tea and Assam!" one of Cowasjee's friends shrieked. "Both in the hills of eastern India, but their aromas worlds apart!" The third said, "You bugger! More like the difference between the stink of a sewage nullah and a water drain!" They nudged each other and pointed at the girls dancing by the fire. "She's for you," giggled one. "How 'bout taking her home and confirming the Assam–Darjeeling hypothesis?"

The tall, muscular villager stepped out from the shadows, one fist clenched around a long bamboo pole. In two rapid strides, he and his weapon were towering over them. Cowasjee shrank back on his stool. The obsequious middleman noticed the threat and scurried out from a corner. He said something over his shoulder to the drummer, then to a woman tending a cooking pot. The drums fell suddenly quiet. Confused, the dancers stopped mid-stride. The woman called out, "We will eat now, before the chickens run out from the rice!"

The stringed instrument played on, its performer too rapt to pause. The man with the bamboo pole stepped aside, not taking his expressionless eyes off Cowasjee.

* * *

Far away, Kananbala heard the faint sound of drums, like a pulse in the night. Another night of waiting. At nine-thirty the neighbour's car. Slamming doors. Shouts to the watchman. Ten. The whir of the clock gathering its energies for the long spell of gongs to come. The creaking of trees. A single crow, confused by moonlight. The wind banging a door. Ten-thirty. The owls calling, one to the other, the foxes further away. Then the faint clop of hooves. Closer, the clop of hooves together now with the sound of wheels on tarmac, whip on hide. A tongawallah cursing. Amulya saying, "That's it, no further." His voice too loud.

Kananbala dropped her age-softened copy of the Ramayana and went to the window. She could see her husband hunching to release himself from the shelter of the tonga, too tall for its low bonnet. She turned away and returned to the bed, picking up her Ramayana again. When Amulya entered the room and looked around for his slippers, she did not tell him she had put them under the table. When he asked her, "Have you eaten?" she pretended to be immersed in her book. When he said, "Are the children asleep?" she replied, "Of course. It's so late."

"They only served dinner at ten. They wouldn't let me leave without eating, what do you expect me to do?"

"Nothing," Kananbala said, "I know . . . " Something caught her eye and she stopped.

"What is that?"

"What? That? Oh, it's a flower."

Amulya's voice was muffled beneath the kurta he was pulling off over his head. She could see his vest, striped with ribs, his stomach arcing in. She looked again at the flower, dark purple, wilted. He had placed it under the lamp near the bed. In the light of the lamp she could see one long, black strand of hair stuck to the gummy edge of its stem.

"I know it's a flower," she said. "Why have you brought it home?"

"Just wanted to identify it . . . " he said, leaving the room.

She had often asked him before: were there women at the parties he went to? The host's wife? Her friends or relatives? Why could she, Kananbala, never be taken? He always laughed with condescension or said, exasperated, "I have never met women at these parties, neither do I aspire to." And what of today, the festival at the tribal village – could she not have been taken? If she were a tribal woman herself, she would have needed no man's permission.

Amulya returned to their room with a large, hard-covered book. He sat near the lamp and opened it, then put on his black-framed spectacles. He picked up the flower in one hand, turned the pages of the book with the other, looking once at the pages and once at the flower, saying under his breath, "*Passiflora* of course, but *incarnata*? I've never seen *this* vine in Songarh."

Kananbala turned away, lay back against her pillow and shut her eyes. She could hear pages rustling, Amulya murmuring under his breath. She wished with a sudden flaming urge that she could stamp on his spectacles and smash them.

Amulya laid the flower against an illustration in the book and whispered, "*Incarnata*, yes, it is *incarnata*. Roxburgh has to be right."

* * *

In about 1907, when Amulya moved from Calcutta to Songarh, he could still see the town had been hacked out, maybe a hundred years before, from forest and stone. The town perched on a rocky plateau, at the edge of which he could see, even from the house, a dark strip of forest and the irregular, bluish shadows of the hills beyond. In the distance were broken-down walls of medieval stone – the ruined fort, the *garh* from which the town took its name. A few walls and one domed watchtower, enough to fuel Amulya's fantasies, could still be discerned in the ruins. In front there was a shallow pool with inlayed stone patterns around its edges. Beyond the fort lay an ancient, dried stream-bed that separated it from the forest and hilly mounds. It was said that an entire city would some day be found buried around the fort. Some claimed Songarh had been one of the centres of Buddhist learning in the ancient past and that the Buddha himself had rested there, under a tree, on one of his journeys. On his first visit to the fort Amulya saw that there was indeed an ancient, spreading banyan tree with its own jungle of stone-coloured aerial roots. The tree had a knot on its main trunk that in a certain light looked like the face of a meditating man.

When Amulya brought his family to Songarh, it was no longer a centre of learning, but it had acquired new importance after the discovery by the imperial geologists of ores of mica. There was even more lucrative material below the forests somewhat further away: coal. Among the patchy fields of millet and greens there grew a tiny British colony of people who supervised the coal mines and the nearer mica ores from the salubrious climate of Songarh, which was chilly enough in winter for log fires. Before long the town had a white area near the fort where the handful of miners lived, forming a compact society of their own.

Over time, Songarh acquired a main street with a few shops. One of the earliest, Finlays, was run by an enterprising Parsi who supplied the needs of the expatriates for the exotic: coffee, fruit, fish in tins, lace and lingerie, treacle and suet, cigarettes and cheese. Indians went to the shop for fabrics and buttons, medicines and cosmetics, and returned with tins of peach halves, wondering what to do with them.

The forest watched. It was well known that leopards wandered its unknown interior. There were stories of tigers and jackals drinking together from streams that ran through it over round, grey and brown pebbles. Cows and goats disappeared, and sometimes dogs. It was useless looking for their remains. Until the mines came, and with them the safety of numbers, nobody from the town was foolhardy enough to venture into the wilderness at the edge of their homes: green, dark, alien, stretching for miles, ending only where the coal mines began.

The forest was still the domain of tribal people with skin as shiny and dark as wet stone and straight, wiry bodies. Flowers with frilly petals nestled in the black hair of the women. They were poor; many looked as though they were starving. Yet they kept to the forest, venturing out only occasionally, in groups. Some were forced into the town when the mines gouged out chunks of their forest. They lived in makeshift shanties, working at whatever they could find. Amulya employed many of them.

He had heard of Songarh in Calcutta, come on a visit, walked all over the little town and its surrounding countryside, and the knowledge that he would live there came to him like a benediction. Just as some people speak to you immediately without saying a word, and you feel a kinship as real as the touch of a hand, Amulya felt a connection with Songarh. He knew that if he turned away from it then, he would never be able to stop thinking of it, that all his life would feel as though it were being spent away from its core.

In Songarh, among people whose language he did not speak, he set up his small factory to manufacture medicines and perfumes out of wild herbs, flowers and leaves. The people of the forest knew where to find wild hibiscus flowers for fragrant and red oil, flowers of the night for perfumes, and the minute herbs for smelly green pastes that could bring stubborn, hard boils to tender explosion overnight. With a persistence he was not aware he possessed, Amulya learned the language of the Santhals, as well as Hindi, and learned enough from them of their plants to be able to expand the range of his products.

His relatives in Calcutta regarded Amulya with amused puzzlement and some irritation. He had done nothing he needed to run from, why then the self-imposed exile from a great metropolis into the wilderness? Was there anything in the world Calcutta did not offer a man like him? Submerged just beneath the surface of their talk was the sense that his departure was a scorning of their lives, the redrawing of a pattern that had already been perfected.

* * *

The house Amulya built in Songarh looked out of place: a tall, many-windowed town house in the middle of scrubland and fields that were sparsely built upon at the time. He designed it with the help of an Anglo-Indian architect trained in Glasgow, whose plan seemed to provide a judicious mix of West and East. The house was to look southward, turning its face from the road. Verandahs all along the southern façade, and the north would have rows of windows. To the west there would be balconies and terraces to let in the setting sun. These balconies would overlook a courtyard next to the kitchen, on the ground floor. The south and the west would be skirted by a garden planted with trees and flowering shrubs. Where other people gave their houses grand names, Amulya gave it a number. Although there was only one other house on that road, he stuck a board into the empty plot that said 3 Dulganj Road in tall black letters. The "3" stood for him and his two sons.

A large house, "A house for a family to grow in," the architect had said, satisfied, when he had completed his drawings. Despite all the windows and balconies, however, it turned out to be a secretive house once translated to brick and plaster – nobody appeared at the front door of 3 Dulganj Road, Songarh, on impulse and said, "We thought we would call to see you." The northern side that faced the road, with its rows of shuttered windows, seemed to tell visitors that it would be nicer to stand upstairs and watch them go rather than welcome them in.

Right across the road was the only other house in the immediate vicinity. It was one of a number of bungalows the mining company had built for its administrative staff, and the name on the gate was Digby Barnum. Mr Barnum was rarely to be seen. The house had a *porte-cochère*, from the privacy of which every morning Barnum ascended the car that would deposit him where he worked. He left at precisely nine-thirty, looking neither right nor left as his car swept out of his gates and onto the road. Nobody in the neighbourhood had ever caught his eye.

Amulya first saw Barnum on one of his early days in Songarh, when he was spending most of his time out in the open getting his house built, hours in the sun watching men work. On one of those days, Barnum's car had spluttered in its smooth getaway from the portico and come to a silent standstill only a few yards from the gate. Amulya, waiting on the road for a delivery, observed a man open the door of the car at the back and emerge, muttering English curses. "Bloody hell," Barnum said, aiming a kick at the car's bonnet, and then, folding his hands and trying a different tack, "Please, you ruddy jalopy, just this once . . . " In the bright morning sun, his skin grew more vivid every minute. Strands of hair stuck to his balding head in damp stripes. His cheeks shone in the heat, and bright pink folds of flesh ringed his neck.

Amulya turned away despite the temptation to stare.

The driver disappeared under the bonnet while Barnum got behind the wheel to turn on the ignition. It would not start. The driver brought out a crank, stuck it into the front of the car and began to turn it as Barnum stamped down on the accelerator. The car cleared its hoarse throat a few times, but there was no roar that held.

Barnum got out of the car again and stared worriedly at the empty road. He had given no sign of noticing Amulya's presence. Amulya, knowing the mining office was a few miles away, on the other side of the town, allowed himself an invisible smirk.

But now there was a sound that made Barnum look up.

In the distance, unmistakeably, the clopping of hooves.

Amulya stole a look at Barnum's expectant face, relishing the predictable way it fell when the man saw where the clopping came from: not a tonga, but a ramshackle cart laden with bricks. Barnum waited as the cart emptied its bricks, the men working slowly in the heat, disguising lethargy as method. The driver had given up cranking the car and stood slouching in the shade of a bright orange bougainvillea.

Barnum rushed into his house and out again. He did not look at Amulya but cast an irritable glance at the labourers who were taking their time, and at the stringy horse snuffling inside a nosebag. Somewhere a cow-bell tinkled, the leisure of the sound at odds with Barnum's snarling face and tetchy movements. "*Juldi karo,*" he yelled at the labourers. "Hurry up, you buggers. Empty out this ruddy two-penny jam tin, *juldi karo.*"

Eventually, the cart was empty and the workmen turned away. Perched on bits of half-built house they lit their beedies with sighs of exhaustion. Amulya paid the malingerers no attention for a change, fascinated by Barnum's portly efforts to heave himself into the three-sided cart through the rear. He had to sit on the dusty floor where the bricks had been, his back to the driver, trousered legs and shiny shoes dangling from the cart, facing Amulya and the labourers but managing not to meet anyone's eye. The cart returned slowly townward.

A few days later, as Amulya watched a well being dug into what would be his garden, a servant from Barnum's house came to him and shouted above the thud of the heavy hammer and the loud, chorused chant with which the labourers timed their digging, "Sahib has forbidden this!"

"What?" Amulya said, trying to hear above the din. He shouted to the labourers, "Wait. Stop!"

"Sahib says no noisy work in the afternoon. He comes home for his sleep and lunch. No work from 1 p.m. to 4 p.m."

Strutting with borrowed British authority, the servant gave Amulya a conclusive look and was gone before he could react. Amulya seethed at the servant's departing back, filled with impotent rage, knowing that he would have to obey.

When finally they occupied their new house and Kananbala wondered aloud one day if it was rude not to call on the neighbours at least once, Amulya snapped, "No need. What an idea! Have you forgotten they're British? To them we're no more than uncouth junglees."

Amulya was the only Indian to have built his home in that area, in the wilderness near the miners' dwellings and fox-lairs, far away from the bustle of the main market, from the drums of Ram Navami, the speeches and tom-toms of patriots, the nasal calls of the maulvi, the discordant bursts of trumpet music at wedding processions, the sparklers and explosions of Diwali. He heard these noises all day at the factory. As his daily tonga clattered him towards his home each evening, he waited for that miraculous moment when the shouting town would slide behind, replaced by dark trees and an echoing stillness broken only by calls from the forest and birdsong at dusk.

Except now, these past few months, scars had appeared on the smooth surface of his contentment. He had begun to recognise that he was considered an outsider in his very own Dulganj Road, and he knew that while his yearning for isolation was cause enough for him to want to remain an outsider, for his wife it was a different story.

* * *

The silence that to Amulya meant repletion locked Kananbala within a bell jar she felt she could not prise open for air. She had disliked it from the start: the large house with echoing, empty rooms, the wild, enormous garden where leaves rustled and unfamiliar berries plopped onto the grass. The want of visitors, the absence of theatre shows and festivity. Instead, cow-bells tinkling, the occasional clopping of a horse's hooves, the ghostly throb of tribal drums far away. The croaking of a hundred frogs after rain, the inscrutable sounds from the forest at night. In Calcutta, in her rambling family home crowded with siblings and aunts and uncles, there was always the possibility of a chat, the comforting sounds of nearby laughter, gossip, clanging utensils, squabbling sisters-in-law, the tong-tong of rickshaw bells, the further-away din of the bazaar, the cries of vendors, the afternoon murmurs of a decrepit goldsmith who visited them with boxes of new trinkets and a tiny silver balance to weigh them on.

The first few months after coming to Songarh, the silence of the place – silence in which she could hear herself inhale, in which she could hear sweat trickling down her face, in which she could hear leaves fall and flowers open – the resonant quiet had startled her into an unexpected garrulity.

She had no-one to talk to, however. There were hardly any neighbours who were not British, and had there been, Kananbala, who spoke only Bengali, would not have had a language to talk to them in. There were three Bengali servants who had come with them from Calcutta, one of them a maid who massaged Kananbala's head every drowsy afternoon. Kananbala babbled without end to the maid, stopping only when one day she overheard the maid and the gardener sniggering about something she had said. After this she began to wait for Amulya to return home from work, and the instant she heard the gate unlatch she ran down the stairs to ask the servants to put on his tea, then rushed to the gate to start chattering: "What happened today? Did I get any letters from home? What do you think we are having for dinner? Do you know what Gouranga said to Anubha today when she was washing the clothes?"

And so on, until one day Amulya, exasperated, snapped at her, "Leave me alone, can't you leave me alone for a little while? Just a little while!"

He seemed that very night to have forgotten what he had said to her as he caressed her hair and drew her to himself. But she had not. She turned her face away slightly so that he could not kiss her on the lips. She had felt something twisting, writhing and changing inside her with his "Leave me alone!" She was withdrawn the next day, not herself, thinking too hard to be able to put any of her thoughts into words. Then, in the quiet afternoon, she dug out the old keys she kept still, out of both hope and attachment, the keys to her unused Calcutta rooms, and, clutching them tight, she walked to the well, paused, drew a deep breath, and threw them into the deep, black water.

The years passed more quickly after that act. Their elder son Kamal had been married off, the younger one, Nirmal, had crossed the awkward threshold that stood between boy and man, and her own small frame had acquired the uneasy bulges of late middle age. She should have been as close to contentment as was possible. But now, a long twenty years after their migration to Songarh, the garrulity had begun its siege on her afresh, threatening to break down the barricades she had erected against it.

Amulya was at the factory longer and longer. These days, he left early in the morning and did not return until after dark. He grumbled that there was too much competition now from imitators. The smallest gap in supplying the shops, and someone else would occupy it.

"Even so," she asked him as they lay in bed one night, "couldn't you come home a little earlier in the evenings?"

"Don't be silly, Kanan," Amulya said, "I don't enjoy lingering, there's work to be done. When you need to send your family their twenty-five saris next puja, where will the money come from?"

"I didn't mean that," Kananbala faltered, "I was just remembering when we first came here, how you used to come home and we'd sit by the window every evening with our tea."

"It's been about twenty years since that tea," Amulya replied as he turned on his side. "The factory was smaller then, there was less to be done."

"It feels so empty, Nirmal at college, Kamal at work with you all day: not that sons are company for mothers." She sighed, "How I wish I had a daughter."

Muffled by his pillow Amulya said, "If you had a daughter she'd be with her husband, not holding your hand. Why don't you talk to your daughter-in-law? Manjula has plenty to say."

"It's not the same."

She waited for a reply, then mustered up all the decisiveness she was capable of. "It was better living in Calcutta," she said. "My family all around, the house so lively all the time."Then she stopped, feeling the old uncertainties return with the sound of her own voice.

Amulya smiled. "If you were in charge," he said, "There'd be no America, and no Australia. No-one would take ships and boats to distant places, they would just sit cuddled up in their mothers' laps all their lives. Wait and see, in a few years there'll be people from your Calcutta crowding this place."

Amulya settled deeper into his blanket, breathing in the cold air of the night and uncurling his warmed-up toes.

"Why didn't you ever ask me before we moved to this town?" Kananbala continued, almost in a whisper. "Why didn't you ever ask me about building this house? I'd have liked being closer to my relatives. Did you never think of that?"

Kananbala had said this many times before, and she wanted to stop, but she could not.

"Are you asleep?" she whispered into the night towards Amulya, "Did you hear that owl?"

She heard a gentle snore and then a whistling sigh.

The night creaked and rustled. The cold air carried to her the urgent whine of a fox. Answering foxes echoed its call and their barks multiplied across the forests and fields, drawing circles of sound around the house. The foxes were the companions of her long, wide-awake nights now. She recalled how, when Amulya had declared his intention to live in Songarh, everyone had stared at him in disbelief and Kananbala's father had laughed: "Arre, all you will hear there are foxes, Amulya." Not just foxes, she had wanted to tell her father later. In her lonely, wakeful hours she had stared out of the window as the roar of what she thought was a lion reverberated in the forest.

The lion's roar was a secret she could not share with anybody else. The others slept on, oblivious to the throbbing wakefulness of the jungle. Sometimes she felt she was looking at the house from the outside, with the impersonal, measuring gaze of a jackal, or closer, at the windows, swooping owl-like through the night, finding her husband sprawled on the bed in their room, Kamal and his wife Manjula entwined in each other's arms in a corner of their double bed, and Nirmal, open-mouthed in sleep in his rooftop room, his cigarettes hidden at the back of a drawer where he thought nobody knew. It was only at Nirmal's window that she lingered briefly but then flew away, shaking off the house with every slicing motion of her wings.

One day she would disappear into the trees, she really would, never to be found again.

"I feel alone here," Kananbala whispered into the darkness and then, embarrassed by the sound of her voice, turned to stare out of the long window by the bed, which framed a moonlit neem tree hazy through the mesh of the mosquito net.

* * *

The year was 1927, an early summer day. As usual Amulya had woken at four-thirty and left for a walk in the half-light, almost before anyone else was awake. It was how he had always been in Songarh – though he recalled wanting never to lift head from pillow in Calcutta. This was a time when the forest, the cool air, the purple sky, all of it was his alone. He watched the low ridge in the distance beyond the ruins, a shadowy hump at first, begin to reveal the dark points of trees across its spine as the sky paled behind it, preparing for the sun. Some days the ridge looked not like a ridge but like the remains of some prehistoric animal which only he could see. As the sky paled further, he turned back for his cup of steaming, straw-coloured tea and two buttered toasts. By eight-thirty he had left home in a horse-drawn tonga. He would be at work an hour before anyone else, look over the accounts, inspect his factory in solitude.

That morning, however, he had barely stepped off the tonga when a man sprang from nowhere and flung himself headlong into the dust, clutching one of Amulya's ankles as if it were the edge of a precipice. Trying to drag his foot away, feeling one black sock lose its grip around his calf, Amulya looked down at the back of the man's head. Until the man raised himself from Amulya's polished, black-leather pumps there was no way of telling who it was.

"Let go, arre baba, kindly let go," Amulya snapped, "What's the matter? Can't you get up from there!"

"You're my father and my mother, Sa'ab, you are everything I have in this world! I have nobody else!"

Amulya thought he recognised the man at last from his voice, although it was tear-cracked and distraught: just a few days before, as he had entered the bottling room in the factory he had heard the same voice say, laughing, "The old bastard hasn't come poking his nose here today. Think he's dead?"

The man who had spoken was scratching himself under his dhoti.

"These shrivelled-up, thin ones go on for ever," his companion had said.

"Then we'll live a hundred years, won't we?" the first man had chuckled.

He had stopped as Amulya entered. Amulya had not smiled. He found it difficult to attain any kind of easy familiarity with his workers. Impossible to say, "Arre Ramcharan, and how is your son? Is your wife still away in her village? Sure you're not chasing any pretty girls now her back's turned?"

Amulya tugged his foot out of Ramcharan's grasp. "What is the matter, Ramcharan?" he said, his voice curt. "Stop all this weeping and wailing." He fitted his brass keys one by one into the three Aligarh padlocks on the factory door, entered, hung his umbrella on its customary hook, and then, turning towards Ramcharan, noticed for the first time that they were not alone.

There was a woman standing a little away from the door, her dark skin set off by the grubby yellow of her old sari, her sun-paled hair straggling out of its bun. She was slender and young, little more than a teenager, with a smile that seemed to lose its way when Amulya looked in her direction. He recognised her. He could never have forgotten the face of the girl who, at that harvest dance in her village two years before, had given him the purple passion flower from her hair. But where was the vivaciousness he remembered, the glow of her dimpled face, the teasing laughter? This woman had a famished look, the kind stray, starving bitches feeding pups often had. She held a small bundle in her arms, so languidly Amulya thought it might fall any minute. When it moved he realised it was a baby.

"My son got her pregnant, Sa'ab, she says, and she arrived this morning with the baby...it can't be true...my son is married, he's a good boy, he has children of his own, but the coward wouldn't even come out of our house to throw her out...what am I to do, Sa'ab? If I return her to the forest those jungle people will slaughter us for this with their sickles ...they'll excommunicate her for going with an outsider...she says we must take care of the baby...but what are we to do, Sa'ab, we are poor people, we already have eight mouths to feed and one salary, and what will our relatives say!"

Ramcharan's voice rose and rose until Amulya said, "Quiet! Be quiet!"

Ramcharan sat on his haunches in a corner of the room and, burying his face in his knees, began to moan, "They'll kill us...they'll kill us all if we send the baby back."

Amulya flipped through the order book and his diary. Decided there was no help for it, he would have to write off the day. He scribbled instructions for his accountant and then, with the woman and Ramcharan squeezed alongside the tongawallah in the front, he sat at the back watching the road give way to fields and then scrubland as they clattered to the Christian orphanage mission beyond the edge of Songarh.

That evening he returned home well after dusk and washed off his day-long deposit of sweat, pouring mug after mug over his thin, nut-coloured body, sighing with relief. He walked out of the bathroom in a soft, unstarched dhoti and kurta, feeling something within him unfurl at last. He knew his daughter-in-law would have left him a large cup of tea and some food. Amulya ate alone, gazing down the room that ended in a full-length, stained-glass window in the east, a window he had positioned thus; he sat at a round table with brass lion paws at the ends of its legs, a table he had bought at an auction. As he chewed, the knot inside him seemed to loosen, and the anxiety of the day's events began to recede.

After he had drained his cup, he wandered into the garden. Now, where there had been weeds and bathua, there grew a soft carpet of doob grass. The kitchen garden was dark with the enormous, olive-coloured warts of jackfruit clinging to the sides of the tall trees. Green coconut clustered far above and sometimes the afternoon quiet exploded with the noise of their falling. The saplings had seemed tiny when they were planted, impossible to imagine those twigs with four or five leaves storing the power to soar thirty feet. Their branches now jostled for space, and the sky was barely visible through the canopy the leaves had created high above.

In the shadow of these trees was a low swing-seat, and it was here that Amulya came that evening, as on all others, after he had walked all around his garden. Usually he inspected each tree in turn, noting every new bud, every yellowing sapling that had given up the attempt, every cutting that had begun to hold up its head. He would look at them tenderly, wanting to stroke and pat them as if they were pet animals. He had created a garden where there had been wilderness. He had cleared weeds, planted fruit trees, flowering shrubs and creepers. He had not been indiscriminate, however. He had disdained the flamboyance of pink kachnar, the rich orange of tecoma. Instead, he had planted his garden with flowers that would gleam white in the darkness and scent the night-time air. His only concession to colour was low bushes of the yesterday-today-tomorrow, the *Franciscea hopeana* he had found with great difficulty, which turned from purple to almost white over three days, perfuming the air around it. The rest of the garden had pure whites: a spreading *Magnolia grandiflora*, its petals creamy against shining green leaves, the snowy blooms of *Jasminum pubescens* tumbling over the well area, and a *Jasminum sambac* to provide scent and flowers for Kananbala's gods. A few gardenias. Two shefalikas, which he thought of as *Nyctanthes arbortristis*, that let fall showers of their small, scented flowers – orange-stemmed, but that brief appearance of colour beneath white petals was pardonable as a kind of poetry. Against the wall he had put *Cestrum nocturnum*, said to harbour snakes, but Amulya was willing to risk poisoning for the fragrance of its white sprays of flowers.

That evening, though, he failed to notice that the buds on the gandharaj were beginning to open and that the mango would very soon burst into flower. He could think of nothing but that tiny bastard baby swaddled in a torn, brownish sari, and of its mother, who had stopped it crying by wrapping her sari around it and putting its mouth to her breast with an ease that seemed born of weeks rather than days of practice. She had been apathetic, almost sleepy, until the time came to part with it. And then she had begun a series of gasping, high-pitched sobs that had lasted throughout the tonga ride back from the far-off orphanage into town. Now, hours later, it was still her sobs he heard, not the birdcalls of dusk. He had gazed stoically at the road as Ramcharan hissed, "Shut your weeping, you stupid woman!" while the tongawallah had spoken throughout the ride only to his horse as if oblivious, or disapproving, of his passengers and their unholy errand.

I'll have to look after that baby, Amulya said to himself, settling into the garden bench, taking out his pipe and hunting in his pocket for matches. There's no other way. The fees . . . better remember to tell the office to pay the orphanage on time. Then he wondered if he needed to add the business of the fees to his will, stipulating that it should be paid for as long as required. He made a mental note that it had best be done. No need to tell anyone at home about the child though, not even Kamal. No need to expose them to something so unsavoury.

From the upstairs verandah Kananbala could see the white of his cotton kurta, smudged in the fading colours of the evening. She never broke into his evening solitude in the garden, but that day, powered by some urge she could not have identified, she went towards him, barefoot on the grass. He did not see her come, and when she was before him, asking, "What are you thinking?" he looked up as if bewildered by her presence. It took him a moment to focus on her face, his eyes at first as startled as if he were looking at a stranger. Then he replied, "Oh, it's you. What is it?" And then, as she said nothing, he returned to mapping out the financial arrangements for the orphan, sucking on his pipe as he visualised the columns of his bank book.

Kananbala stood there a minute or two, and then turned to walk back to the house, wanting Amulya to call out to her, half expecting him to. But he did not. She looked back once at his still, angular frame, a shadow on the garden bench, lost to her. He might as well have been one of his trees, she thought, walking away. The few hundred feet separating the upstairs verandah from the garden bench became a vastness impossible to cross.

* * *

In October that year, they had their first house guests after a seven-year interval. Relatives were visiting from Calcutta for the puja holidays: there was Amulya's cousin, his wife, and three children. Kananbala, unused to visitors, had spent all of September planning for their arrival. She was more anxious than eager, she discovered, but could not admit it to anyone. Amulya would have said, "You're always complaining. You say you're lonely, then when visitors come, you say you don't want them."

So Kananbala complained to herself. More and more, she found solace in talking to herself. She found she could effortlessly become two people and have conversations that sometimes went on a whole afternoon.

There was an additional worry. The relatives had come with a marriage proposal. Nirmal was twenty-four now, and he had just got himself a job in the district college teaching history. It did not pay very much, but it was a government college, and besides, he was the son of a reasonably wealthy man, which made him an eligible groom.

"Why put off something that needs doing? He's old enough. What're you waiting for? I tell you, Amulya, gentle, shy, good girls are as hard to find as . . . " – Amulya's cousin was picking at the fish on his plate – "as good, fresh river fish in Songarh!" He laughed at his little joke, then, noticing no answering smile, explained in a conciliatory tone, "Boudi's cooking is wonderful, but what can you do about the fish you get here? It just is not the same as . . . "

"Yes, not the same as fish from the Ganga," Amulya said, trying not to sound testy. The visit was nearing its end and he had heard the fish commented upon several times.

"Nihar's niece – you remember Nihar, don't you?"

"I remember."

"Well, Nihar's niece – is her name Shanti or Malati? – Shanti, yes, Shanti – she's sixteen, and from what I hear, a pleasant, home-loving girl. I met her a few years ago, pretty girl. And what a house her father has, on a riverbank. Beautiful! It's a well-to-do, good family, same caste as us, naturally. Nirmal could not pick better . . . this tomato chutney, it's good, but I think there's nothing like chutney . . . "

"Made from Calcutta's green mangoes? Yes, I agree," Amulya said.

The cousin looked a little unsettled, but only for a minute. "If you like," he continued, "I'll go back to Calcutta and make some cautious enquiries. What do you say? I'll write to you as soon as I find out what they think. Then Nirmal can go off and see the girl. I can go with him, it is Nirmal's wedding after all!" The cousin drank a glass of water with noisy satisfaction and rose.

"But this place you live in," Kananbala's visiting sister-in-law said later that evening, picking up a shingara and biting into the warm crust, "I don't know, but I couldn't live here – in Songarh, I mean. Yes, I know, it's clean and empty and Calcutta is dirty and crowded and noisy. But the crowds and noise keep me alive! It's so soundless here, I thought for a moment I'd gone deaf!" Kananbala's sister-in-law looked in her direction and said, "And I don't think it's doing you much good either."

"What can I say?" Kananbala replied in a hurry, to deflect the threatened analysis of her health. "I know you can buy shingaras in shops everywhere in Calcutta now, but not here. In Shyambazaar I'd have had someone run down the lane and conjure up a feast from all the sweet shops. Here Manjula and I make them."

"Oh well," her sister-in-law said contentedly, "They *are* delicious, and home-made is always better, isn't it? I tell you, we can buy everything, but catch your brother agreeing to eat a shop shingara or cutlet. He can smell anything stale a mile off."

Kananbala felt confused, simultaneously put down and complimented. She got up and shook out her sari. "Manjula," she called out from the head of the stairs down towards the kitchen. "Bring some more shingara if you've finished frying."

Already, it was twelve days since the visitors had come. The Songarh ruins, they had declared, did not compare with the Victoria Memorial in Calcutta, nor the forest with the grand Botanical Gardens. The ridge was too tiring to walk to. At Finlays they chuckled over its provincial selection. "What would this Finlays say to Hogg Market, eh?" Amulya's cousin had asked his wife, and then said to the puzzled sales boy, "Never heard of bandel cheese? B-a-n-d-e-l cheese? No?"

Soon, they had run out of things to do and spent the holidays sequestered in Dulganj Road, exhausting even their fund of gossip about relatives. Confronted by her visitors' boredom and scorn, Kananbala had begun perversely to long for the solitude of her daily life.

The fortnight ended, and it was time for the visitors to go. Two tongas had been called for four o'clock. Amulya and Kamal were to go to the station along with a servant carrying a hamper of food for the overnight journey: dinner and breakfast had been packed, and an earthen pitcher of cool water. There was some confusion when one of the horses was discovered to be lame. A servant went in the other tonga to get a third.

As they waited, Amulya's cousin said to Kananbala, "Boudi, I will send you a picture of the girl as soon as I reach Calcutta. I'm sure you'll like her. I know your household, she'll make a perfect daughter-in-law. Shanti is her name, I'm sure . . . sings well, cooks well, and has lived a secluded life always. So unspoiled. Not like our Calcutta girls. And as for this rascal," he said, chuckling at Nirmal who stood looking at the empty road, willing the tonga to appear, "he needs someone to keep him in line. I will make all the arrangements!"

Kananbala retreated upstairs after the tongas had left, and stood at the window with the remnant of her smile of farewell. As she turned away, she caught sight of herself profiled in the shining teak front of the cupboard. Her head was invisible, lost in the elaborate carvings that began halfway up its doors. Headless, the body was that of a stranger, grotesque in the bumps that it was made up of: a large – no, hillocky – bump of a chest, an almost equally bulbous curve at the stomach, and then the falling away of thin legs beneath a cotton sari.

Kananbala turned to the mirror next to the cupboard. When had that double chin settled there? When had the chin sprouted those two hairs? When had her skin turned the colour of her husband's tobacco? She stared at the reflection, feeling herself grow breathless, her throat contract.

* * *

Their visitors had, in the manner of all visitors, made a detailed note of their appearances. "You're growing fat already, Kamal, that's quite a paunch you've got yourself, eh? The first sign of wealth and ease!" they had observed in one direction, and in another, "My goodness Amulya, the sun has blackened you so much you're invisible in the dark!" But it was their comments about his wife that had touched a raw nerve in Amulya. He had overheard their sister-in-law saying to Kananbala, "Didi, I had only heard from here and there that you're not well . . . but look at you! You seem a hundred rather than fifty! Of course you were always dark, never had your mother's fair colour, but look at you now! Skin like dried-up leather, and is it your scalp I can see through your hair? Songarh's water is bad, I know, I can see half my hair's fallen out in just two weeks here! Come to Calcutta with me and I'll look after you, I really will. Oil massages, cream and flour for your face, baths in rosewater . . . when I send you back Amulya Babu will think he has a new bride!"

Amulya remembered a time when Kananbala was petite and pretty, with curling hair that refused to be pinned down, and heavy-lidded, lustrous eyes she lined with kajal morning and night. She would race up the stairs at Shyambazaar – those were steep, old-fashioned stairs, dark and undulating – she would run up the stairs two at a time balancing bell-metal plates of food and once even a harmonium – always too impatient to wait for the servants to do their work. A time when she would step out to the terrace to watch him walk down the narrow lane

28

towards the house and ask as soon as he arrived, "Did you remember to get my lace?"

And now? It took no time to digest his relatives' comments. He could hear them in his head for days after they had left. He realised that over the last two months he too had noticed changes in her, and not just in her appearance. All these years – setting up the factory, building the house, planting the garden, the busy years – of course he had not forgotten about Kananbala. "How could I," he thought, "living with her every day of my life since I was nineteen and she sixteen?" But it was true, he admitted: just as your tongue obsessively returns to a painful tooth rather than a healthy one, now that Kananbala did not seem quite herself, he seemed to be thinking about her all through the day, even at work.

He began to make notes in his diary; it would help, he thought, to understand exactly what was happening, systematise it a little. He chose a page that was for a Sunday and so would not be required for work, and made observations in his angular, jerky handwriting:

> *K shuffling rather than walking. Yesterday saw her holding wall when going down stairs to kitchen. Asked what matter. Said dizzy, unstable, knees weak. Seems healthy, but complaining of being ill.*
>
> *Saris looking crumpled or stained, with turmeric etc. Unpleasant. Told her last night, and she said, Do I smell?*
>
> *Notice lips moving even when she thinks she is alone. Talking to herself? Disturbing. Also fingers move restlessly, on furniture, her own body etc. even when she is spoken to, as if writing something all the time. Try to decipher, but impossible. Complaining less, but more silent. Does anyone else notice? How to ask?*

Entries of this kind crowded the page for Sunday. The next page said: *Ordered coconut oil, 25 gallons; paid Salim; order book up to date, orphanage payment made for this month.* And so on. Wednesday had just one word scrawled across the page: *Doctor.*

Amulya called in the physician, who checked Kananbala's blood pressure and asked her about constipation and gas. He tested her knees and made her walk in a straight line across the bedroom floor. In the end he turned to Amulya and said, "Nothing wrong, sir, nothing at all. Simply in the mind. Ladies get bored in small places. Madam needs amusement!"

"Maybe you should find something to do," Amulya remarked grimly to her as the doctor's tonga clattered away. "All this comes from having too much leisure."

"But I work all day," Kananbala said. "Do you know how much I have to do to keep this house going?"

"That's not enough," Amulya said. "You should do something else. Why don't you cultivate a hobby? Sew? Knit? Draw pictures? Look at Brahmo women: they read, play the piano, talk about anything under the sun, just like men."

"Would you let me do all that Brahmo women do? You don't even let me go alone to Calcutta. Kamal has to go with me – or even Nirmal. And they never want to."

"You'd never be able to go on your own. I send them with you for your safety." Amulya pushed his feet into his slippers. "Tell me," he continued in an indulgent tone, "can you find your way *anywhere*? You may be fifty, but you'd still be a lost little girl on the roads of any big city, what with your Shyambazaar at the other end of Howrah Station. Come now, tell Manjula to bring me a cup of tea."

He put his pipe into his pocket and walked out to the garden.

* * *

A month after the relatives had left, there arrived an envelope thicker and stiffer than usual. Inside were two sheets of blue notepaper closely scrawled upon, and a photograph. Amulya handed Kananbala the picture and began to read the letter. As she looked for her spectacles, which she had still not got used to, he exclaimed, "What a coincidence, the girl's father used to be my uncle's lawyer before he retired! He helped him win that Pukurbari case."

30

Kananbala brought the picture of Nirmal's prospective bride into the wavering yellow circle of lamplight she was sitting next to. She reached out and raised the wick a little and put on her glasses.

Amulya said, "Apparently that house they have in Manoharpur by the river is like a palace, and this girl Shanti is the only child. There is no mother, and no other brothers and sisters. It's good when a girl doesn't have too many relatives." And, after a short pause and the satisfaction which comes with finding the right word, "*Uncomplicated.*"

Kananbala examined the photograph in the light of the lamp. It was an oval face that could have been a little less bony. The girl's hair was pulled back in a plait that returned in a snaky curve over her shoulder to the front of a simple, narrow-bordered sari. Not the latest fashion in either hairstyle or clothes – though, Kananbala thought, I hardly know what the latest fashions are. There was nothing remarkable about the face except its thoughtful expression and the eyes which seemed a strange, light colour, she could not tell what. The irises unusually large, filling up the eyes; the lashes overlong. The gaze was slightly unsettling because of the straight, thick brows that pressed down on the eyes. Kananbala wondered if the picture had been touched up in a studio.

Nirmal was almost eight years younger than his elder brother, an autumn flower, more precious to Kananbala for being late. She still caught herself examining his every feature in as much loving detail as she had when he was a baby. Where Kamal had turned out rather nondescript, ill-humoured, dyspeptic, and already showing signs of jowls, the sharp lines of Nirmal's face, his quick movements, his air of irresponsibility and a sudden, noisy laugh which made his eyes dance, convinced Kananbala she was not being biased when she felt he had grown into a handsome man. She knew mothers were not supposed to have favourites, but it was Nirmal who came straight up to her room first from school, then college, and now from work, to tell her stories of all that had happened during the day. He would do nothing without consulting her first, and their dependence on each other was absolute, this she believed.

She looked again at the picture in her hand, the picture of the woman to whom Nirmal would belong. She felt too tired to think about it all.

"Let's see the picture," Amulya said, reaching out. "What do you say? I think Nirmal should be sent off to see the girl. I have a good feeling about this match."

Just as you did about Songarh, Kananbala said to herself.

* * *

Nirmal married Shanti in March 1928. The wedding was in Manoharpur. The bride's father, it was said, had roused himself from years of isolation to invite all his forgotten relatives and the neighbouring villagers. He lit up the riverbank with a hundred and one oil lamps. From a week before, shehnai players sat in bamboo machans at the entrance to the house, playing their pipes. Bikash Babu disliked the shehnai's wail, but was determined to fulfil every conventional expectation the groom's family might have. The groom's party – Amulya, Nirmal, Kamal and Manjula – left Songarh on the overnight train to Calcutta. They were to join up with other relatives there and then take the train to Manoharpur in a merry, festive group.

Her prospective daughter-in-law's magnificent house, its wooden staircase, its mirrors and chandeliers, its riverside setting and splendid garden were to remain a story for Kananbala. Though some women disregarded such superstitions, she knew as a good mother that her presence at his wedding would only bring Nirmal bad luck. So, heeding tradition, she stayed back, alone in Songarh with the household's two servants and three temporary cooks, resigned to custom but anxious and feverish, preparing for the wedding party to return. For the two weeks they were away, she did nothing but order the servants around, have food cooked, and ready the house with an energy she had to dredge up from her past. She rose early and went to bed exhausted every night. The rossogullas had to be creamy enough to dissolve on the tongue, the salty snacks crunchy enough to be heard in the next room. There had to be great quantities of everything. The Oriya cooks hired from Calcutta were instructed to cook the best lobster they had ever made. The fish was to be brought from Calcutta on the overnight train, packed in ice. She made lists of things she needed to remember.

In quieter moments, after the servants had locked up for the night and left her alone with the drowsy maid, she pulled out her jewellery box and began to put aside all the ornaments from her own trousseau that she would give the bride. She lingered over her heavy gold bangles with the snakeheads that she loved, with their solid round feel and emeralds for the snakes' eyes. Nirmal's wife must wear them. She held the bangles in her hand and tried them on one last time before setting them aside.

The night before the wedding party was to arrive, an owl's call interrupted Kananbala's half-awake dreams. She was breathless and thirsty and tangled up in the bedsheet when she awoke. It was dark outside, but she felt the urge to step out of the house and go to the forest.

As if sleepwalking, Kananbala rose from her bed and sidestepped the maid who slept on the floor. She opened her bedroom door and went down the stairs. At the front door she came upon a heavy padlock on a chain. The older manservant, Gouranga, was sprawled before it, snoring. She had forgotten how securely the front door was locked each night. She tried to think where the key was kept – the servant's waist, of course. She remembered the side door and half ran to it, but that was locked too.

The stillness of the night, punctuated by the owl's hoot, cracked open with a roar: the lion! The lion no-one else could hear! She ran up the stairs, forgetting to shuffle, and went out onto the roof.

At last she was out in the open, black night, under a nail-paring of a moon, looking into the shapeless gloom of the jungle. The lion roared again. No owl or fox answered it. She stayed there, her mind crowded out with thoughts that allowed her to think nothing, till the horizon paled and the first bird sang.

* * *

Nirmal and Shanti were given the room at one end of the top-floor terrace, the only one on that side of the roof. They spent their first night together on a bed prickly and damp with the traditional flowers, the noise and ribaldry of their visiting cousins seeping into their sleep. In the cold hour just before dawn, Nirmal found, half awake, that he and his new bride had curled up against each other for warmth. He gathered courage and kissed her on the forehead. Shanti slept on.

Soon after, a thunderous knocking made Nirmal throw Shanti's arm away and run to the door. Shanti sat up, surreptitiously wiping eyes sticky with sleep. When Nirmal opened the door, his mother rushed in.

"Come on, it's late," she exclaimed, "Can't you see the sun high up in the sky? Your father will be back from his walk soon."

"Ma, it is only ... " Nirmal peered at the clock on the wall, " ... five-thirty!"

"Don't argue," Kananbala snapped. "The house is full of relatives. They will all be up soon and do you want to be caught still snoring? There is so much to be done!"

Nirmal looked in amazement at his mother, who had now begun bustling about the room, tidying up. He saw his mother picking up and beginning to fold the sari Shanti had let fall on a chair the night before. Next to it on the floor were the clothes he had worn, his silk kurta and dhoti twisted up and thrown in a corner as if he had been in a tearing hurry. His embarrassed gaze went to the bed with its crumpled sheets, the two pillows on it bunched close together, still indented where their heads had been and, all over the room, the squashed flowers that had begun to smell of rot. He could not look at Shanti who, he saw from the corner of his eye, was making futile attempts to mimic her mother-in-law's efforts to clean up.

Before he could stop himself, he said, "There's no need to do all this, Ma, you never clean my room, so just let it be! I'll do it later." He wanted to bundle his mother out and slam the door on her. He wished he lived on an island far away from his family, his parents, his cousins' sly glances waiting downstairs.

34

"My grown-up son, already telling me what to do, a day after his wedding!" Kananbala said with a mocking smile. She swung around to Shanti, who had now begun to smooth out the bedsheet and brush off the flowers. "Shanti Bouma, go, have your bath, the water is hot. The servant can't heat it again and again."

She turned to Nirmal. "You too, have your bath, go to the downstairs bathroom. And send Manjula up. Manjula will show you where everything is, Shanti. She will bring you downstairs for breakfast when you've finished."

Kananbala stood by the door sentinel-like, watching as Shanti rummaged for the keys to her new cupboard. Then, in a confused moment when she felt she was regaining consciousness, or emerging out of deep water for a lungful of air, she saw Shanti's growing desperation: at her new home, at the new people around her, the new man who was her husband, at her distance from her father and from everything she had known, at her failure to find the right key. In Shanti she glimpsed herself at sixteen, the morning she had woken up with Amulya next to her, bony, unknown, overnight her husband, a man she had only glimpsed through her veil the evening before at her wedding. Tenderness surged through her, transforming her scowling face. She went across to Shanti and took the keys, picking out the one that was needed. In the gentle voice she kept for children, she said, "You'll soon know your way about, and then things won't seem so strange any longer."

Shanti had been stoical throughout, even at the leave-taking from her father, her room overlooking her river. But at Kananbala's unforeseen sympathy she felt her lips tremble, and before she could stop herself she had buried her face in her sleep-crushed sari and burst into tears.

* * *

Two weeks later Kananbala sat waiting as usual for Nirmal with his evening tea. The house was empty of wedding guests save for one lingering relative. Things were beginning to return to normal, but not quite, Kananbala knew. Nirmal had begun to return home earlier, even though his job was a new one; what must his students think, Kananbala wondered, seeing Nirmal slip out of college half an hour or even an hour earlier some days? Surely the boys he taught, clever fellows only a little younger than him, were making fun of their teacher who was in a hurry to be home with his new bride?

As every evening, Nirmal came to his mother's room first and sat chatting with her. But she could see his heart was not in the tales he was telling her about his day. He was sitting on the edge of the chair, as if settling into it would commit him to more time. He stole glances at the clock on the wall in the corner and then, half rising, said, "I'm tired, I need a bath," before he fled to his room. From the evenings that had gone before, Kananbala could predict he would not be seen again until dinner time.

The terrace was a darker, emptier stretch that night. Kananbala walked to its end and stood at the low parapet. From here, she could almost look into the Barnum house, where lights blazed from every window and the lawn filled and emptied and filled again with people holding glasses. Beyond the house, in the memory of the day's light, the ruins of the fort were still discernible to those who knew it was there. She walked back across the terrace to the room which Nirmal and Shanti occupied. It had long French windows, four of them, giving onto the terrace. The venetian blinds were as tightly shut as sleeping eyes.

Kananbala pushed open the door. Nobody in the house knocked; besides, it was only seven-thirty, no time for locked doors.

Nirmal was on the bed, his head half in Shanti's lap. She was singing something, her fingers in Nirmal's hair, her face close to his. Her sari had slipped off her shoulder.

They looked up as Kananbala entered and, startled, moved quickly away from each other as if to say that they had not been touching at all. Shanti stopped singing mid-syllable. Wide-eyed, she sprang off the bed and then turned away flustered, busying herself with something near the dressing table.

"Ma," Nirmal said after pause, "we were about to come down."

"No need for you to come," Kananbala replied. "But Shanti, it is time you started helping us with dinner."

Kananbala woke the next morning, heavy-limbed, yet hollowed out by the dark space within her. She could scarcely lever herself from her bed, exhausted by her night-time battles. The ceiling had pressed upon her, iron rafters and all, and then the serpentine posts of the bed, fleshy and pliable, had tried to choke her. She had been jolted awake, gasping for breath, her heart pounding. Looking across the bed she realised it was not the depth of night, for Amulya's space was empty: he had left for his walk and so it must be dawn.

She thought of the relative who had stayed on after the wedding, a cousin they called Chotu-da. They were finding it difficult to get rid of him, although he was a doctor and everyone expected him to be a busy man. He was rotund and garrulous, waiting for mealtimes and sleeping in between. Kananbala decided to put aside her distaste for him and tell him some of her symptoms.

Chotu-da pressed a stethoscope to her chest, admiring afresh the soft, enveloping bulk of her bosom.

"Only palpitations, normal at your age," he pronounced, at the end of what Kananbala thought was an unusually long examination of her lungs and heart, "And maybe a touch of gas. Tell Amulya to get you fruit salts. Or maybe something from his famous factory – he has a cure for everything, doesn't he?" Chotu-da laughed. His round, jocund face gleamed with sweat, his eyes bulged behind thick glasses. He wondered why he was hungry so soon after breakfast.

"Perhaps," he enquired in a careless tone, "Manjula could make me some sherbet, and . . . such fresh air, in these parts. One never feels this way in Calcutta."

"Even the rice tastes better, doesn't it, Chotu-da? One just can't help oneself!" said Kananbala in a flash of her old impertinent self, the one she thought had dried up for good.

The doctor gave her a wary glance, but then thought he had heard wrong: the woman was looking as harmlessly preoccupied as she always did. He rose to go. He thought he would wait in the verandah for the sherbet, hoping it would come with a little something.

"I ought to leave," he said to Kananbala. "My practice must be suffering. But you have not been letting me go! And this child!" He chuckled at his young son, who was hunched outside at the table glowering over a book. "He's got so fond of you!"

He showed his topaz ring to the boy and said with the growl that usually accompanied this ritual of his, "See that's the eye of a tiger I hunted and killed in the forest last night. The other eye is still in the tiger's head. Both the eyes can still see, and they find naughty boys!" The boy, now nine and lost to make-believe, looked at his father with disdain.

* * *

The upper dining room had along its length large windows that washed it in the still-cool morning light. It was the morning after Chotu-da had left. Kananbala had finished bathing and changed into a fresh sari. She began the walk towards the stairs, holding the walls and chairs along the way and then the banisters for support. She climbed down the thirteen stairs of the first flight and the fifteen of the next. The walls seemed to tilt too close to her. On the landing, she paused and panted, staring unseeing out of the window that lit the stairs and framed the tree over the small terrace on the first floor. She could hear Shanti singing in the kitchen. The girl was petite and soft-spoken, but when she sang it was a low, rich voice that emerged, as if from a much larger body. She was singing of holidays, and clouds in the sky.

Kananbala dragged herself towards the kitchen, then paused outside in the corridor to get her breath back. She could hear Manjula, who sat chopping vegetables, saying, "Ah, I used to sing that too, long ago when I still had a voice. Sing another one. At least now there's some entertainment in this dull old house. You'll know in a while how stifling this little hole of a Hindustani town can be. How I miss all my relatives, I hardly see them once in three years."

Shanti's quiet voice said, "I'm used to small places. Whenever I went to Calcutta I always felt like running back to my village by the river."

"Oh, just wait and see. You're happy now, all newly married, Nirmal rushing home to come to you, sitting with you, talking and doing God knows what else, hm . . . ?"

"Oh, no!" Shanti seemed to giggle.

"But wait until you've been married a few years, then this place will show you its true colours."

No-one spoke for a while. Kananbala heard the grinding stone going across its slab, a soft sound, as if something wet was being crushed. It must be the mustard for the fish, she thought. She wondered, trance-like, if the fish had been cut. Her mind rehearsed the daily ritual. Gouranga would come early in the morning with the fish he had bought – in Songarh it was usually carp – and he would show it to Manjula for approval. Manjula would stand away from it, protecting her fresh, post-bath sari from fishy impurities. Her lips would curl in an impatient sneer, and she would say, "Rui again! And Gouranga, couldn't you find any smaller? Or more dead? Eh? Tell me: did they starve these fish before they sold them to you? Did they suck out the blood first? Oh, for some live fish that swim in a bucket for a while and show real blood when they're cut!"

Kananbala swayed, sickened by her memory of the daily fish-cutting ritual. She held the door to steady herself. She had delegated that work to her daughter-in-law as soon as she had one. She had always been nauseated by the raw, fishy smell, by the sliminess of cut fish. She had never been able to make herself wash or cook it, though she ate it – all parts but the head – with tolerance if not relish.

Now, with that old sensation of tossing her head out of water for air, she gasped and became aware of her daughters-in-law's voices in the kitchen.

Manjula was saying, "Go on now, sing us another."

Again, that low, husky voice snaked out from the kitchen, this time with a melancholy song. Kananbala edged closer. Shanti sang on, cutting a messy jackfruit, as if oblivious of her oily hands and of the others in the kitchen. Damp, hessian bags of vegetables lay around her, spilling out their contents. Ponytails of spring onions stuck out of one, alongside creamy heads of cauliflower. She sang as if transported to a different place and time, chin resting on her raised knee, eyes focused on the jackfruit she was cutting, but far away from it, from Songarh and from Manjula who sat slicing potatoes nearby. Shibu ground the masalas just outside in the courtyard, trying to make less noise than he usually did.

Kananbala stood by the door, massaging her knee and looking at the tranquil scene. "What a voice," she said. "You whore, why don't you get a job on the streets?"

Manjula's bonti clattered and fell to the floor. Shibu ran in from the courtyard and stood at the door, his mouth open. Shanti's song stopped and turned into a brief, horrified gasp as she leapt up and ran out of the room, her oily hands smearing her new sari.

"Is the jackfruit cut? Let me see what spices you've ground, Shibu. Why is everything such a mess today?" Kananbala went on as if she had said nothing at all out of the ordinary.

The next day, as Amulya was dressing to go to the factory, Kananbala asked him, "You dandy, who're you fucking these days? Is it a Brahmo lady in a georgette sari?" She turned away before the stunned Amulya could say anything, and went into the verandah. Amulya rushed after her. Nirmal was sitting at the dining table at the far end of the verandah, the *Statesman* crossword beside him, abandoned again without a single square filled.

"Do you know what you said?" Amulya looked at her as if at a monster who had sprouted four heads in place of two.

Nirmal got up from his chair so quickly it almost fell back. He lunged out to stop it falling. "Baba," he quavered, "I didn't say any-thing."

Amulya paid him no attention. He seized Kananbala's arm. Nirmal stared at them in disbelief. In his twenty-four years, he had never seen his parents touch except once, a lifetime ago, when he had run into their bedroom one afternoon in pursuit of a marble.

Amulya was shaking Kananbala's arm. "Do you know what you said?" he repeated, his face contorted beyond all recognition, inches from hers. Strands of his waxed hair stood up where he had clutched it.

"I just asked when you'd be back," Kananbala said, looking bewildered. "Why are you so agitated? Will you be very late?"

"That is not what you said!" Amulya shouted.

"Why are you shouting? What did I say?"

"What did you say? Don't you have any shame? How can I repeat it before other people?"

"But there's no-one here," she said, "Only Nirmal. Do we have secrets from our children?"

* * *

Shanti had stopped singing.

She had stopped singing once before, when her mother died. At that time she had thought she would never want to smile again, let alone sing.

But slowly the songs had come back. Her father had coaxed her as soon as he felt able. "I need to hear your songs," her father would say. "It's bad enough having to get used to your mother's absence, why your songs as well?" She had tried, her voice breaking every few lines at first, but then she began fiercely to school herself, walking alone by the river every afternoon, singing to the water. Unknown even to herself, she had begun to hum under her breath as she did her chores. One day, catching her father looking at her, she realised what she was doing and turned away to hide her shame at being happy again.

My mother-in-law called me a whore. Her mind churned with the thought. She saw me singing to her son, she burst into our room, not once but twice, and the next day she called me a whore. That servant boy, what must he think? Being called a whore before everyone by my mother-in-law. And Nirmal – how can I tell him this? Would he believe me? He adores his mother. And he hardly knows me. And I? I hardly know him, really. Despite all the things he says to me and all the things we do. They're all strangers. What is this household I've been married into? What am I doing here, without a single friend? If I could run back for a day and see

41

everyone and be in Manoharpur in my own room! I wonder if they've changed anything in that room. And Mala, Khuku, Bini, do they ever think of me? Has some new friend replaced me for them? Do they still walk along the river laughing about everyone in Manoharpur? Should I tell Baba about this? No, that would only worry him. Is he all alone? What is he doing with his time all alone? Does Kripa remember that he liked the lemon pickle I made? And his mango saplings? Does he still measure them every week with that foot ruler?

She sat down with a thump on her bed and rested her head in the crook of her arm, exhausted.

* * *

The next ten days passed with no further outbursts from his wife, and Amulya began to think he had dreamed what Kananbala had said to him that unbelievable morning. Had she actually said "fucking"? Was that possible?

Was it possible he had imagined it all, a waking dream perhaps? It was true that his memory was wobbling these days. Sometimes, things he needed to remember would slip past him like the morning mist: he saw it, knew it – that fact, that phrase, that word, that name he needed – but when he tried to grasp it, utter it, it was no longer there. Wasn't it a fortnight ago that he had said to Shrikant, his accountant, "I made the monthly payment to that orphanage. Where's the receipt?"

Amulya had been meticulous about paying the orphanage the sum he had settled on, to ensure the child was properly looked after.

"You didn't make the payment," Shrikant replied, not looking up as he continued to tot up his columns of figures.

"What nonsense, I wrote out the cheque here at this table. I remember doing it along with all the salary cheques."

"Sir," Shrikant hesitated, "you said you would, but it was late and you left it . . . "

"Bring me the cheque book, I'll show you," Amulya said.

Shrikant was right. Amulya had not written out the cheque.

In his garden that evening Amulya's anxiety over his wavering memory prevented him noticing anything, even the baby mangoes that had begun to replace the flowers on the mango trees. He was so troubled by the incident that he remained cocooned in himself all through dinner as each member of his family tried separately to recall if they had done anything to ignite his wrath.

It was the day after his argument with Shrikant over the cheque, he now calculated, that Kananbala had uttered those unspeakable words. She had said nothing unusual since. Amulya found it harder and harder to believe she had indeed said what he thought she had said; perhaps, like the unwritten cheque, it was his imagination alone. Chaos seemed to retreat to the cloudy, cobwebbed corners of the ceiling. Like all the secrets it seemed able to wrap into itself, the house had soaked up Kananbala's singular outbursts, hiding everything from the world outside its walls.

That was not the end of it, of course, thought Amulya, memory proves all too accurate just when you wished it had failed.

It was two weeks later that Shanti watched as her mother-in-law told Kamal he was a donkey with syphilis.

The very next day she said to Manjula, "Milk-white skin, hm, just like a marble cow. Nobody vainer than this simpering slut in all of Songarh!"

The week after, at dinnertime, Kananbala spoke pleasantly enough to Amulya, but her words were, "If I chopped your head in half with a cleaver, I'm sure I would find nothing but cowdung inside."

By now it was no longer a secret. Amulya was sure that the two young women, his daughters-in-law, were comparing notes. More than Manjula, he was concerned about Shanti. Picturing her certain disillusionment and bewilderment, he felt especially culpable: a new bride he had brought into the house ... to be insulted the way she had been! And then the servants. It was unlikely that they valued discretion and loyalty over the human urge to tell a juicy story – and even less so in Songarh, hungry for happenings, where the illness of some neighbouring cow or a squabble between relatives provided conversation for days.

"Do you know what she said today?" Manjula sighed to Shanti one afternoon soon after as she sat on her bed, folding betel leaves into neat thirds and chewing on a paan.

The fragrance of the tobacco in the paan wafted towards Shanti. She picked up a bolster and put it on her lap, getting comfortable. "What?" she enquired as the paan reduced Manjula to mumbles for a moment.

"I heard her telling Kamal's father he has the testicles of a goat! And then downstairs, in the courtyard, she stroked Shibu's head. Imagine! Stroked the servant boy's head! And said . . . "

"Oh yes, I heard that as well," Shanti said, not wanting to hear it again.

" . . . that he is her only true child, the only boy who cares! Her other sons are bastards born of the tongawallah!"

Troubled, Shanti looked up at Manjula's merry face. "Don't you think it's worrying?" she said, "What will happen now?"

"Oh nonsense, what'll happen? Nothing will happen. The old woman is losing her marbles. They all do," Manjula said. "We'll have to do a lot of looking after, just wait and see, she'll get her pound of flesh. Apparently she had to slave for her mother-in-law – and that one was completely senile by the time she was fifty-five. She used to smear her shit on the wall and our ma-in-law had to clean up. No wonder she's gone mad now – she's getting herself a five-year head-start, she's only fifty."

Manjula stuffed another paan into her mouth and with her mouth full, said, "You know that saying, don't you?"

Shanti never knew any of Manjula's sayings and could seldom make sense of them; she thought Manjula made them all up.

"What saying is that?"

"When the silent begin to speak, the mango will fruit in winter."

* * *

44

She is not mad, she cannot be, Amulya said furiously to himself that afternoon as he strode along the rutted fields to the edge of the forest, even as Shanti and Manjula sat gossiping on Manjula's bed. He had not been able to calm himself to do any work at the factory and, to Shrikant's astonishment, had got up, collected his umbrella, summoned a tonga, and left.

He was on his way to the ruined fort. It comforted him to sit soundless among the fallen stones, thinking of nothing in particular, waiting for his sense of calm to return. The fort was his ivory tower; he went to it whenever he needed to think anything through in solitude. Perhaps it was the suggestion of evanescent empires, the grittiness of centuries-old stone, or perhaps the memory of people who, in those ruined rooms and dark passages, had lived lives as real as his own. It might have been the twisted grey-brown bark of that tree with its suggestion of the Buddha's face.

He reached the rim of the fort and sat on a block of fallen stone, a tall, greying, angular figure watching the blue and brown flash of a kingfisher swooping into a large shallow pool at the edge, which at this time of year had some water still. The folds of his dhoti spilled wavelike on his stone, lifting a little at times in the breeze, picking up dust. Amulya did not notice. In an hour or so the sun would begin to set. The birds would know and begin to call out to each other.

He willed himself to listen to the birds and think of nothing else, yet wave upon wave of yearning churned his insides as he longed for the Kanan he had known to return. How had he let her slip away? To him she was still the teenager he had married, her collarbones jutting out, dimples piercing her cheeks, her spine ridging her back when she bent, her eyes doubtful when he joked about something, with that second's delay as she understood, and then laughed. I've watched her grow into a woman, a mother. She's always been so sensible, so full of common sense, so gentle. She's hardly ever argued with me, never said anything cruel even when scolding the children.

Am I forgetting? Were there signs all along . . . ?

He tried puzzling out what had happened to her, blamed himself, forgave himself, blamed it on her age, her difficult time of life, thought he should have spent more time with her, thought he should not have taken her such a long distance from her family in Calcutta.

At last he stood up and straightened his stiffening back. He began to walk home. She would not be allowed to wander the house any longer, he had decided. He would not let her become the local joke.

TWO

Nirmal was writing a letter of application to the Archaeological Survey of India. "Dear Sir ..." he began, and then paused, fingers poised over his typewriter. "I beg your indulgence with regard to my application for the post of ..." He crossed that out, and tapped the keys again, "Dear Sir, I have the honour to ..." He stopped, restarted, "I am a lecturer in History at Songarh Degree Coll ..."

It was five years since John Marshall had written in the press about the discovery of ancient civilisations at Mohenjodaro and Harappa, and at that time Nirmal had cut out and kept Marshall's article from the *Statesman*. He had then collected clippings from whatever he could lay his hands on, though few newspapers came to Songarh. The particular edition of the *Illustrated London News* in which Marshall had first published the discovery in 1924 had been the hardest to find. Eventually, by asking a friend of Amulya's who knew a man in the Indian Civil Service, Nirmal had obtained a copy of the paper with its lavish pictures of all the Indus seals and the enormous mounds.

Inside the packet for Nirmal, the man from the Civil Service had also enclosed a letter that a British official had written some years earlier. The letter described hillock-like mounds all over northern India that people took to be natural formations when, in truth, they were the accretions of ancient civilisations. "When wolves still howled where Notre Dame and St Paul's now stand," the letter went, "and the very names of Athens and Rome were unheard of, there lived and toiled on these sites the remote ancestors of the villagers who tenant them today. It is with some feeling of reverence, then, that the Western *parvenu* should view these populous ruins and know himself to be but a creature of yesterday."

In later years Nirmal wondered at the disproportion between the brevity of the note and the conceptual apocalypse it had caused inside him. He had read it once, looked at the pictures in the *Illustrated London News* of seals and pots and bricks glimmering against a dark background, then gone back to the note and read it again and again. It was as if he had simultaneously been robbed of all individual will – for his future had been decided for him at that moment – and charged with an energy he had never known. For the next three years he went on private expeditions, modelling his techniques on whatever he had been able to glean from reading articles here and there. He went to the Songarh ruins and looked at the hillocks behind it afresh, as if a layer of fog had been peeled away from his eyes. He began to call them mounds instead of hills and yearned for the day when he could start digging to find what they concealed. He went to the outskirts of Songarh, where there were old temples and scattered ruins, and scrabbled around with a garden khurpi and measuring tape until knots of village children gathered and chattered to each other and laughed at him.

He had recently read that with the discovery of Mohenjodaro and Harappa, the Archaeological Survey had received more funds for its work in the valley of the Indus. If they had the money, Nirmal reasoned, they might take on apprentices. He had no experience, but he did have a degree in history. But why would they employ him, a small-town college teacher, when there must be Sanskrit scholars, experts in numismatics, and scholars of other kinds struggling to be a part of the Indus Valley's three-thousand-year-old past?

"They could start me off *somewhere*, even if not at the Indus," he reasoned. "Then by degrees . . . " The thought of his probable rejection by the Survey filled him with gloom in an instant. He lit a cigarette and fiddled with the cigarette tin. He yawned and looked at Shanti's hair, a dark storm across pillows and sheet. She was almost asleep. He took a deep drag, blowing smoke out through his nose, and gave his typewriter an irritable glance. Then he pushed it away and went towards her.

"Don't you think," he murmured, caressing her hair, "it's possible to make a habit of almost anything?"

"What do you mean?" she said, her voice sleep-thickened.

"Here we are, you and I," he said. "We didn't know each other a year and a half ago and now I can't write a letter for looking at you . . ."

"Go back and finish your letter," Shanti said, raising her head. "Go on, archaeologists need persistence. How will you ever dig out ruins from the earth if you don't persist?"

"I'm persistent about things I want," Nirmal said. He felt under her sari in the region of her stomach. "Now imagine if this were the mound at Harappa, how would I go about finding a route to . . ."

Shanti slapped his hand away. "If you can get used to anything, you can get used to doing without *that!*" she giggled, hiding her face in the pillow. Then she looked up, her face still half hidden, and said, "And I'm not sure it's even safe any more, with the baby coming."

"Imagine," Nirmal said, lying back against the headrest and taking his cigarette from the ashtray. "A year and a half ago, I wasn't even married. Now I'm going to be a father in some months. A year and a half ago, I didn't know you. A year and a half ago, my mother was normal. Now for a year and a half she hasn't left her room . . . and it all seems routine. I even feel happy. I forget about her, that she's imprisoned. I feel trapped if I'm stuck in the house for a day and I forget she can never go out and meet other people or see other things."

Shanti felt fingers of annoyance twist her insides at Nirmal's sudden change of attention from her to his mother. She tried to smile and touched his hand. "Quiet, let's change the subject," she said. "Don't you know that babies can hear in the womb? Do you want ours to grow up with unhappy thoughts? I want the baby to overhear only music and laughter. Come here to me."

* * *

49

One floor below, Kananbala paced her room waiting for the Barnums. Every weekend Digby Barnum went out with his wife. Kananbala, awake most nights, had made a habit of sitting on the windowsill and watching their car leave, mysterious, full of promise, heading for destinations beyond her imagination. They would return very late and honk outside until the watchman woke and unlocked the gate to let them in.

That night, the watchman did not come to the gate despite all the honking. Barnum stumbled out of the car and his driver lunged after him from the other side. It was the first time Kananbala had seen him. She was wide-eyed with disbelief, never having seen a drunk man before.

"Bugger off!" Barnum yelled at the driver, "Bugger off, you black bastards, sleeping on the job!"

He shoved aside the driver, who stepped back, looking uncertain as his boss untangled his legs enough to reach the gate, a gate like a wall of wood, and then began to bang on it with his fists, shouting curses.

Kananbala, not understanding a word, was spellbound. Amulya stirred in his sleep and pulled his pillow over his head. Kananbala willed him to carry on sleeping, leaving her alone to spend the night as she always did, suspended in a world nobody else knew.

Then Kananbala saw Digby Barnum's wife for the first time, a woman as elongated as a eucalyptus leaf and as pale. She was in a gown that her curves formed into something smooth and flowing, its silk gleaming in the lights of the car. Her shoes had heels that she tottered on as she hurried to her husband, saying something Kananbala could not hear.

Mrs Barnum reached her husband and tugged his sleeve to make him stop banging on the gate.

His arm shot out and hit her across the face.

Kananbala touched her own cheek as if she had been hurt.

The woman stepped back, holding her chin. The driver, frightened, cowered by the car.

"The real man, as always," Mrs Barnum said, in a voice as clear as the sound of spoon against glass.

Barnum paid her no further attention. He returned to the closed gate. "Ramlal, you sister-fucker, open up! Can you hear me? You're sacked!"

Mrs Barnum strolled up and down the road as if none of it mattered to her. Her husband continued to shout. Amulya mumbled, "Bloody Sahibs, think they own the whole country."

Kananbala wanted to say, "They do." But she had almost stopped breathing so he would go back to sleep. Amulya turned on his side, and in a minute Kananbala heard his snore again.

The gate creaked open. Barnum pushed the spindly watchman aside so that he fell, and he and his wife went in. The car followed. The watchman got up, yawned and dusted himself off.

"Bastard," the watchman spat in Hindi towards the house. "Drunkard," he said, closing the gate again.

* * *

The windows were Kananbala's only view of the world. If she traversed the length of the room and looked through all three windows, tilting as far as she could, she could see to the end of the road's curve on both sides. Kananbala was at the windows all day, and often most of the night.

Almost at dawn, when the air still retained a memory of the cool of the night, she waited for the brinjal colour of the sky to grow lighter and brighter. When the sky turned properly blue there came the man who promised that his papayas were from Ranchi, and then the bhuttawala, fine wisps from corn sprouting like golden hair out of the basket on his head. In the early days, when they had first lived in Songarh, vendors never came that far. Now, she had heard, there was a new cluster of houses further down, with Indian people, clerks and teachers, those who would buy from carts.

Kananbala could tell the time from the calls of the vendors, the flower-seller just after dawn, the fruit-sellers in the morning, the vegetable man in between. Bread from a bakery in the market came in a tin box welded to a creaking bicycle. A bangle-seller, handcart

51

glinting red and gold, stood at the gate sometimes and called out for a long five minutes, seeing a woman at the window and scenting a sale.

She could not go to the gate to buy bangles, she knew.

She had not left the house since Nirmal's wedding, nor even her room very often. She knew she had said things she should not have. She could not think where the words had come from, nor could she precisely recall what they were. But from people's faces she could always tell when something wrong slipped out. They did not look so appalled any longer, but all the same they did not let her meet outsiders. The roof was out of bounds too. They were afraid she would jump, as she had once threatened to.

Amulya came back from the factory every day at noon, and sat with her as she ate her lunch, returning to work in the afternoon heat after settling her in for her nap. Each evening, after the gardener had left, he led her down the stairs and out into the garden to walk forty-three steps this way and forty-three that, for a long half-hour. She got tired and breathless, her knees felt weak, so he had often to hold her through the latter part of the walk. He would encourage her, saying, "You must do this, make yourself do this, or else your muscles will rot."

"Why?" she would beg. "Why do I have to walk in this heat? I don't go anywhere. Why must I walk?"

"One day you will find you can't even get up from your bed," he would say.

At times, enraged by her fatigue, she stood still and hissed at him, "You carbuncle on a cow! You stinking hyena!" He would grimace, but continue to direct her forward.

After the half-hour was over, he would sit her down on the swing and light his pipe. Then he would tell her all that had happened during the day, and about the two new houses in their immediate neighbourhood. One of the houses was indeed occupied by Indian rather than English people, he said once, a retired couple from somewhere, no children. "See, I told you it was the right decision to build here." He had exhaled a cloud. "Just watch how this area changes now."

She listened, sometimes responding with a comment, sometimes spitting out "son of a donkey" or "tail of a sewer rat" or "frog with warts" – words her mind concocted unbidden. If she did that, Amulya would clench her hand to make her stop. When she felt the pressure of his hand on hers, she knew she had said something she should not have, and tried to be quiet. She wondered about the irony of his belated tenderness, but she did not question it aloud.

Manjula, observing them every day on the garden bench, said to Shanti, "Look, now the old woman's got it made. She has us to serve her night and day, and her husband's discovered romance in his old age. Oh Ma, what wouldn't I give to be her? Don't you know what they say? Ripe fruits get cotton-lined baskets."

Shanti now thought hard of other things when Manjula spoke with her customary venom about her mother-in-law. In two months, Nirmal would take her back to Manoharpur and she would walk by her river again, waiting for her child. Until then, she would close her ears, hum the old songs, and shield her stomach with her hands as if to shut the ears of her unborn baby. Inside, just under the tight-stretched skin of her belly, she felt she could hear a minute heart gallop like a horse, an unformed mouth trying to form words to say to its mother.

* * *

Some weekends there were parties in the Barnum house, and on those evenings first the van from Finlays would come, then the electrician for the lights, and then the smells of alien food. In the evening there were fairy lights in the lawn and the indistinct, shiny forms of the Barnums' friends who came and went in cars that never let them down outside the gate, but always under the covered porch you could not see into. Kananbala waited, and watched, and waited, hoping to see someone, something.

Only Mrs Barnum was now regularly visible. She had taken to swaying out of the car when they returned from their parties and stopping at the gate for the watchman; then she would walk the length of the drive, making a detour across the lawn before she agreed to enter the house, her long silk gowns trailing in the grass, her white shoulders gleaming in the darkness. Kananbala would watch her with eyes full of greed.

Every few months Digby Barnum went away for a week or two, maybe to the mines in the interior. Those weeks, in the afternoons, Mrs Barnum would leave the house alone and return in a different, long car, driven by a young man who could have been Tibetan. On one such night Kananbala watched as Mrs Barnum leaned through the car window and talked to the strange man before she began to walk towards her house. She happened to look across and saw an Indian woman's face drinking hers in at a window on the other side of the silent black road.

"How extraordinary," she muttered, and yet, perhaps because she was only half English – the other half unknown – she turned again, and waved at Kananbala's dark, immobile shadow.

Kananbala had never in her whole life waved at anyone. She was confused about what to do. Her hand would scarcely rise. But in a rush she stuck an arm out through the bars of the window and awkwardly, like a child in a bus, waved as well.

The day after, when Mrs Barnum returned with the strange man, she pointed Kananbala out to him and he looked up and waved too, a wide smile crinkling his eyes. He and Mrs Barnum looked at each other and, laughing, Mrs Barnum said something to him in English. The night was still and quiet and Kananbala could hear each word, but she understood no English.

Mrs Barnum said, "Poor old thing, Ramlal says she's completely mental, babbles dirty words at people; fun, don't you think, darling? Would you like it if I did that to you?"

They laughed together and the man said, "Go on, say something, that'll be delicious."

Mrs Barnum waved at Kananbala every night, whenever she returned from anywhere. Kananbala waited for her at the window. Barnum thought his wife very odd to get out of the car outside the gate, whatever for? Once, when he saw her waving upward after they had returned from a shopping expedition, he decided it was time to be stern. Larissa had no sense of propriety, really. What must the servants think, their mistress waving at the local mad woman? There was something in all those things people said about mixed blood. The longer he was married, the more he felt sure of this.

* * *

The following week Barnum left on one of his long trips. Kananbala had got used to watching Mrs Barnum go out every afternoon and return every night, later and later, with her young man. It had been playful, all that waiting to see what new, subtly shimmering gown Mrs Barnum would be in each night, when she would arrive, and when she would notice her at the window and wave.

But tonight was different. Tonight Kananbala's throat contracted, her heart thudded and her fingers went cold as she watched Mrs Barnum and the young man returning in his car.

It was perhaps one in the morning. The night was luminous, with a great, wobbly, yellow egg yolk of a moon bobbing behind trees that swayed in the breeze. Kananbala leaned outside as far as her bulbous body would allow and waved with both arms when the car stopped and she saw them out on the road, a few yards from the gate of the Barnum house. She knew she had to stop them.

Kananbala had seen Mr Barnum that afternoon. He had come back before time and found Mrs Barnum absent. Kananbala had seen him drive off soon after he arrived, perhaps in search of his wife, and return without her. From a little after twelve at night, Barnum had been waiting outside the gate, concealed in a cascade of bougainvillea. Kananbala could see from the way he stood hidden that he intended to catch Mrs Barnum and her lover together and then . . . what? Kananbala stared mesmerised at the spot in the bougainvillea into which he had disappeared.

Mrs Barnum wondered why the Indian woman was waving with both arms. Then, with a happy laugh, she raised both her own in imitation. Her lover bounded out of the car and ran behind her. Kananbala saw his teeth gleam as he smiled. The road was bright with the moonlight, in which they had grown sharp shadows that followed them. Mrs Barnum was giggling and making as if to push the clinging young man away. Her high heels clattered on the tarmac.

They reached the gate. He kissed Mrs Barnum's fingertips and murmured something that Kananbala thought the breeze floated towards her. She looked away in panic at the distant, dark outline of the fort and the shadowy bulk of the forest, wishing something would stop what she knew was going to happen.

Barnum stepped out of the leaves and orange flowers.

Mrs Barnum swivelled towards him. In a quick rattle, she exclaimed, "Darling . . . is everything alright? The Munby party . . . went on so long . . ."

Mr Barnum pulled his hand out of his pocket, thwacked the side of his revolver into her cheek and snarled, "Shut up." His wife stumbled back with a gasp of pain. Before Barnum could turn the gun the other way, Kananbala saw the lover leap on him. Mrs Barnum followed with a scream. Kananbala shut her eyes in terror and opened them a second later to see the lover diving back into his car, driving off. Barnum lay on the ground bleeding from his throat. Beside him, Kananbala could see the moon return the curved glint of a knife.

Mrs Barnum looked around, her moonlit face spectral. She tore off one of her long earrings and looked down at her hand as if surprised by it. Clutching the earring, she knelt by Barnum's side for a moment. Then she rushed to the gate and ran in.

Fortunate, Kananbala thought, that she does not let the watchman lock the gate the nights she is out.

The murdered man lay on the road, a dark, shining puddle forming beside his stomach as the owls resumed their soft night-time exchanges.

Kananbala lay down beside Amulya on the far edge of their wide bed and, trying to breathe as quietly as her panting would allow, in her head she began to make up a story.

* * *

The next morning Amulya was sitting at a table in the bedroom, drinking his first cup of tea and unfolding his newspaper, when Nirmal raced in.

Amulya looked over his newspaper with a frown.

"What is the matter, Nirmal, can't you walk? Must you always run? Who'd believe you're going to be a father?"

Amulya took a sip of his tea with a grimace, "This tea is overdone, it's bitter. Who made it?"

"Do you know, Baba," Nirmal said, breathless, "there's been a murder in the house opposite. They think the woman killed her husband. He was left dead on the road last night, and she was sitting upstairs brushing her hair, as cool as you please."

"What? Barnum?" Amulya exclaimed. "That can't be!"

"No really, Baba," Nirmal said, "It's true. Haven't you looked out of the window at all this morning? There's mayhem. I saw some police high-up go in and there are three more policemen in the house, searching for the weapon."

"Weapon? How was he killed?" Amulya asked, standing up to go to a window, curious despite himself.

"Knife," Nirmal said with satisfaction. "In the stomach and ribs, apparently. The police are taking the lady away for questioning. She keeps saying she was out for the evening and when she came back she went straight upstairs, didn't know anything about this, hadn't expected her husband back for another week."

Nirmal stood at another of the windows and looked out, his tall body in its thin, night-crumpled kurta outlined by the sun. Kananbala went and stood beside him. She noticed that her head did not reach his shoulders and looked up at Nirmal with a surge of pride and indulgence.

"Isn't it good riddance that man died? He was a real son of a pig," she said to him, tender, confiding.

Amulya snorted. "He certainly looked like one! One bad Shaheb less! Maybe the woman will go away from this big house now and . . . "

"Most likely they'll put her in jail. Or send her to the Andaman Islands," Nirmal said. "The British have jails even for their own female killers . . . and Mrs Barnum is only an Anglo . . . they really hate Anglo-Indians, don't they?"

"They do have special jails," Amulya said. "I think they have special jails for British criminals . . . in the hill stations."

"So their murderers are not troubled by the heat?" Nirmal laughed.

Amulya gave his son a disapproving frown and continued to look out of the window at the house opposite. A minute later, he put his glasses back on and returned to his newspaper.

Nirmal stepped back from the window. "The police are coming towards our house!" he said.

"I want to meet the police," Kananbala announced.

Amulya put his glasses down with a clatter and abandoned the newspaper in a heap on the table. It fluttered across the room in the breeze. He returned to the window which framed the house opposite. It looked much the same except that the gate was open, and there were people going in and out of it. There seemed to be a dark patch on the road near the gate. It had been encircled with white. A lacklustre havaldar stood in the shade of the bougainvillea's orange bloom, drawing on a beedi. Something about the way the blossoms poked incongruously out from behind the havaldar's head, as if he were sporting a flower here and there, reminded him of another flower in a tribal girl's hair, the girl who had tried to make him dance in a forest clearing. He smiled to himself at the idiosyncrasies of memory, its insensitivity to the passage of time.

He returned to the present with a jolt: their own gate was opening and the person pushing it open was a policeman.

"Nobody is to bother your mother," Amulya said to Nirmal. He turned to his wife. "You're not to talk to anyone, have you understood? Now, is my bath water ready or not? What has happened today? Is everyone stuck at a window?"

Not getting a response from either Nirmal or Kananbala, he went outside to the head of the stairs and yelled, "Shibu! Is anyone around? Bring my bath water. What a bunch of fools, something happens to a stranger and they forget everything else."

Kananbala was peering so hard at an upper window in the opposite house that Nirmal said, "Are you feeling alright?"

"Babu, the police are here," Shibu called out in a high quaver from downstairs a little later. Amulya gave up all thought of his bath. He smoothed his clothes and went downstairs to the drawing room.

* * *

The policeman had finished asking everyone questions, even Gouranga, who stammered that he was always asleep by nine-thirty and had seen nothing. The policeman tapped an impatient finger on the arm of his chair and with a preoccupied air refused another offer of tea, then called the servant back and said, "Alright, tea, bring me a cup, my throat's dry with all the talking." He turned to Amulya, running his fingers through his sweat-damp hair. "Is that all? Is there anyone else in this house?"

"Only my wife, but there's no need to bother my wife, is there, Inspector Sahib?" Amulya said. "She is ill and never goes out. In fact none of us in this house have anything to do with those people."

"Precisely, Amulya Babu, precisely!" the policeman said with new energy. "She never goes out and you said your room is right opposite that house. What does that make her?"

"What?" Amulya said.

"Makes her a witness. Bird's eye view. Ideal witness. We have to ask her if she saw anything."

"But she is not well," Amulya repeated, full of trepidation.

"No need for worry, Amulya Babu," the policeman said, soothing. "We are human too. Give us a chance, we are servants of the state, doing our jobs."

* * *

Kananbala looked at the drawing room with wondering eyes. It was perhaps a year since she had been in that room. It seemed dark, a little musty. It seemed to have many more cushioned chairs, heavy carved arms poking out from the sheets that shrouded them. Why were they covered? she wondered. Were there no visitors at all? Did they never use the room? "Why the sheets?" she asked in a whisper, and Amulya said tersely, "Dust."

She saw that the polished table-tops were dull with dust. What were her daughters-in-law doing?

Kamal steered her by an elbow into a chair. Kananbala's face was hooded by the aanchal of her sari. She took a quick look past its awning at the policeman.

"So Mataji," said the inspector, "Did you see anything? Tell me everything. Even what you do not think important. *Especially* what you don't think important." He turned to Amulya and Kamal: "One's work has over the years taught one that witnesses often leave out the most crucial detail. They cannot know what is useful for a police investigation."

"Of course, of course," Kamal said, crooking his thumbs through the striped braces of his trousers. "Witnesses have no sense of the value of certain clues."

Kananbala tried to slow her thundering heart. After all her isolation, to have to speak before a stranger, and on something so important, something that might save her friend's life. She would surely get it wrong. Taking a deep breath, she said, "What would an old woman do lying? Yes, I did see something."

"Go on, Mataji," the policeman said with a warning look at Amulya.

"The poor man had just come back. He must have been tired, these British people work so hard. He had been away for several days."

"How many?" the policeman asked, and turning to his deputy rapped out, "Noting everything, aren't you?"

"I think three or four days."

"Carry on."

"There were some tribals waiting at his gate. The guard was not there. It was already quite late, and the road was dark. They surrounded him and they were arguing and fighting. One of them was very tall, with long hair, very dark."

"Did you hear what they said, Mataji?" the policeman asked. "Did anyone have a knife? Could you see their faces? Would you recognise them?"

Kananbala seemed to flail under the flurry of questions, making a few incoherent noises in response. Amulya, alarmed, half rose to take her away. The policeman gestured him down and returned to her.

"Did you see any weapon?"

"The tall man had something at his waist. But I can't say. It was dark, I could not see so clearly. My eyesight . . . the doctor has said I need new glasses, but for that my eyes need to be tested and . . . And they were fighting: something about the mine in the forest, and money. They are poor people after all and they have homes in the forest . . . "

"What happened then, Mataji?" The policeman tried patiently. Old ladies had to be handled with care.

"Then there was a scuffle, some confusion, what happened inside the crowd I couldn't see. But the group left quickly, ran away. And the man was on the ground."

"Where was Mrs Barnum? The guard says she had gone out and given him the evening off as she always did when her husband was away." He turned to Amulya and said, "Strange thing to do, isn't it? You would think she needed the guard with her husband away."

"Oh, she was at home all night after she came back. I saw her coming back. It must have been quite early still – I had not yet had dinner. Then she was upstairs," Kananbala said, pausing as if trying to remember. "I can see her quite clearly from my bedroom window when her light is on. She often forgets to draw her curtain. She was sitting at her window and yes, of course! For a little while she played her piano. Didn't you hear it?" Kananbala asked Amulya.

Amulya looked at her and said, "Piano?" He wanted to tell her not to talk so much. Could it be long before one of her vulgarities slipped out? What if she called the policeman a cuckolded jackass as she had the gardener just before he left?

"Well, she plays something every night and Nirmal told me it's a piano. What do I know of such things?"

"Did you see Mrs Barnum come down?"

61

"She didn't know he was back, I think. Poor girl! Maybe she never heard the car with her piano playing!" Kananbala said, "To think she stayed up all night in her room not knowing her husband was bleeding to death downstairs. She might have been able to save him. How she must torment herself with the thought." Kananbala sighed.

The policeman scribbled in his notebook and then turned to Amulya: "She will have to be a witness."

"Out of the question," Amulya said.

THREE

A month passed, and half of another. The Barnum murder began to fade from memory. In the absence of reliable witnesses, the investigation lost its top priority status and files went from desk to desk, losing a page here, getting dog-eared and tea-ringed there. It was a messy affair into which the mining company did not press for much poking about. Digby Barnum's short temper and foul mouth had not earned him many friends at his workplace, and besides, other cans of worms lay buried that might inadvertently be unearthed. The man reputed to be Mrs Barnum's lover left town. The police lost his trail in Calcutta – from where he had fled to Sydney, people said. The house opposite 3 Dulganj Road seemed to have stepped away from the town. There were no parties, and Mrs Barnum hardly ever left the house. People stopped talking about the killing.

Life resumed. Amulya signed a lucrative deal with a leading Lucknow shop. Nirmal went to Manoharpur and left Shanti with her father for the birth of their child. The first child would be born, as tradition demanded, in her childhood home, even though Nirmal disapproved of the tradition, saying Manoharpur was no place to have a baby; it didn't have a hospital nearer than the next town, which was far away.

Kananbala, oblivious of the coming baby, wondered if Mrs Barnum knew what she had told the police. Perhaps she had got her into trouble. Maybe their versions did not match. For a while Kananbala's curses dried up with anxiety. When Amulya walked her in the evenings, he found her distracted and inattentive. If he stopped speaking and merely smoked his pipe, she did not seem to notice.

* * *

That year, the monsoon was tardy coming to Songarh and the heat incandescent. Yet, though the afternoon light was still blinding, the evenings, with a whiff of a breeze that seemed to come from somewhere else, brought hope of rain and yearnings for impossible things.

At 3 Dulganj Road the air seemed especially charged as the house waited for its first baby – ever. Manjula had never conceived. After three years of being married, she had come to regard her childlessness as evidence that she had, unknown to herself, displeased God. She had sought to make amends. She had made Kamal take her across the country, tying strings around trees in Sufi shrines and brass bells in devi temples in the hills; she had fasted and prayed, and collected blessings from all kinds of godmen. But nothing had worked.

Now that there would be a baby, something made Manjula sigh and take longer over things; something, she found, made her absent-minded, made her stop on the terrace between chores and gaze up for longer than she knew at clouds inching into the sky. And then she would tell herself, old cloth will be needed to cut up into small sheets. A pillow would have to be made, filled with black mustard seeds to mould the baby's soft skull into a perfect shape. She would retire for her afternoon snooze exhausted, thinking she must hunt out old saris to stitch into kanthas. Can one woman manage a household this size? she would mumble. A fine grandmother my ma-in-law will make, lifting not a little finger for the baby.

* * *

Nirmal squinted at the mirror as he shaved, wondering if he looked different, more fatherly. Perhaps it would seem real once he saw the child. Would it be a boy? It wouldn't matter, boy or girl. But if it was a boy! He would take him travelling, they would climb mountains together, rummage in ruins. Nirmal began to feel a tiny pulse of excitement somewhere inside him at the thought. He combed his hair back from the high forehead he had got from his father and went to the terrace for his second cigarette of the morning. Peering into the horizon, he noticed there were grey clouds over the ruins and the ridge, and the rest of the sky, though blue, seemed to have darkened a little with clouds scattered about it, curdled milk clouds. The light was more mellow and the early morning breeze seemed to have a feathery touch.

Nirmal sighed with pleasure and sat down on the parapet, lighting his cigarette. Shanti was not there to screw up her nose and say, "What a horrible smell, how can you smoke that?" She had tried it once herself, and then again, and to her surprise quite liked it. Nirmal had been both shocked and entertained by her attempt to smoke. He had chuckled once he had got over his horror. "I'll take a photograph," he had said, teasing, "and show it to Baba. He'll send you off to Star Theatre to be an actress."

"Well, your mother already calls me a whore . . . " Shanti had shot back.

"You know she has no idea what she's saying."

"It's not pleasant to be called such things anyway," Shanti had said. "Never heard such words all my years in Manoharpur."

"We can't always get what we want," Nirmal had said, looking away annoyed. "It's also painful for *me* to see my mother not in control of herself."

"She never calls *you* any names."

It had become a quarrel. They had never quarrelled except as a joke, and it had taken them both by surprise. Now, smoking on the terrace, Nirmal found himself longing violently for Shanti, even to quarrel with. He was to go to Manoharpur in three weeks, when the baby was to be born. He wondered how to keep himself occupied until then. Perhaps he would go earlier. Perhaps his father would agree to his going earlier, and his head of department at the college would let him. Anything was permitted a father-to-be. He began to plot the best way of putting it across to his father.

The first drops of a small rain fell on his face. He looked up at the sky, letting it rain on his face and dampen the cigarette between his fingers.

FOUR

The rain pattering down on Songarh had still not arrived in far-away Manoharpur. The air lay over the town thick and still. The heat coloured the mangoes in hues of fire, cooking hard, green, young fruit into plump yellow-reds that scented the heavy air. There had never been such a year for mangoes. They were hanging in twos and threes, weighing down the trees, such multitudes that their custodians could not be bothered to guard them, and boys perched on branches eating them and aiming the hard centres at unwary passers-by.

Shanti was looking speculatively at the garden and the river. Tossing aside sage opinion about her condition, she walked, with the precision of someone unsure, down to the edge of the water. How close the river seemed, she thought, this river of her childhood. Every year it seemed to come a little closer and, with a fatalism for which she ridiculed herself, Shanti felt her destiny tied to that wide liquid ribbon. The steps on which she remembered idling with her friends had disappeared under water. If she peered from the verandah into the brown-grey water, she thought she saw her three friends floating immaterially below, trussed in mossy ferns. Staring down she saw her own face a few feet below the water's surface, hair trailing like smoke, skin furry with slime, snakes slithering in and out of her dead ears. She ran to the puja room as quickly as she could with her distended stomach and prayed for the image to be cleaned away from her memory, for the baby to be born, for Nirmal to be there in time for the baby's birth.

Downstairs, in one of the mansion's wide verandahs, sat Bikash

Babu, Shanti's father, with Ashwin Mullick, the other man of property in the village. Potol Babu, schoolteacher, the third member of that afternoon's club – only by virtue of being educated, upper caste, and from Calcutta – wished some old acquaintance could chance upon them so that they would know at home in Baghbazar what elevated company he kept.

Bikash Babu felt a little defensive before Ashwin Mullick. The money in his own family, the money that had built the pillars and the Roman arch, the money that had built the stately ghat, down the years there was less and less of it. Ashwin Mullick, on the other hand, had been the topic of some ridicule when he began his coconut oil enterprise: oil was the right business for that greasy man, people said. But now, it was undeniable, he had reason to be smug. Not only was he giving his friends loans, waving away interest with a patronising shrug, his house was on high ground and he watched the progress of the river with amused complacence. Bikash Babu's house, arcadian, picturesque in its seclusion as it faced the river alone, surrounded by fields of tender green rice-stalks, was the most vulnerable.

"What a pity about those mango trees of yours," Ashwin Mullick was saying. "Wasn't it an experiment you were interested in?"

"Well," Bikash Babu said, "I just wanted to grow the U.P. Dusseri in my little Bengali garden. The trees looked healthy enough until the river drowned the far end of the garden."

Potol Babu sighed. "What a sad irony," he intoned in English, "that the water that is our Saviour is so easily turned into Destroyer. Truly, like Lord Shiva . . . "

"What happened to that project you had, Bikash," Ashwin Mullick interrupted, "of building a dam, or was it a dyke?" He sucked his pipe. The tobacco was fragrant, imported.

"Can anyone hope to stop the mighty Ganga?" Potol Babu attempted in a mournful tone. "I do believe that . . . "

"That engineer came, from Braithwaite & Sons," Bikash Babu replied. "He said . . . "

"Did they send a Sahib or a local?" Ashwin Mullick enquired, knowing the answer.

67

"They sent Dr Mitra, a very bright engineer," Bikash Babu said quickly, aware that Braithwaite had not given the problem its due, had not seen fit to send its Scottish Chief Engineer. Bikash Babu's sense of being ridiculed was still fresh. People had turned up to look at the engineer after word got around that Bikash Babu had hired an English firm for his problem. But the man looked much like them. He was short and bulged in both directions. His bald head gleamed in the hot sun. He was not even in a suit, just a dhoti like everyone else.

"He got his degree in Scotland," Bikash Babu told his sceptical listeners. "They think very highly of him. He was here for several days and examined the problem – oh, he was at the riverbank at all sorts of odd hours, with complicated instruments. He thought such a massive river changing course cannot be stopped. But he said that at its current rate of movement, the river –"

"These engineers," Ashwin Mullick sniggered. "Do they know geology as well these days?"

" – will not endanger the house for the next two generations."

"A fine house it is," Potol Babu said, noticing Bikash Babu's face grow darker. "A fine house that future generations will see and admire. That Burma teak central staircase, those great Roman columns, the Belgian mirrors, that billiards room! There is no equal in Manoharpur – except Ashwin Babu's wonderful home, of course."

They fell silent, each irritable for a separate reason they found hard to identify. Ashwin Babu suspecting a slight, knowing his house was newer and had a staircase of mere brick and marble, not Burma teak, because of one fatal moment's economising; Bikash Babu knowing people saw him as an old eccentric who needed to be placated; and Potol Babu wondering if he had sounded craven when truly he admired the architecture of both houses.

The afternoon sky dropped lower over the three, the warm air clasped them closer, damp and unbreathable, like a sweaty embrace. A fat, turquoise-coloured fly killed itself in the dregs of the tea.

* * *

As the smell of roasting corn scented the afternoon air, the women who were bent in their rice fields, the children squabbling in the hard-earth courtyard of their small school, their teacher brandishing his cane, the egrets poking about for food, all paused and looked up at the sky. Every day it came down a little closer. Today, its high, flat blue had swelled and darkened. It had become warmer, the air more palpable, more inert. It smelled of moisture.

Shanti lay looking out of her window, unthinkingly caressing her stomach, picking at jamun that multiplied into more purple berry shapes against the sides of her silver bowl. From her window she could see sociable tufted bulbuls trilling to each other from different branches of the bakul tree. The tree had now reached the first-floor window. What a little tree it had been, Shanti thought, when she used to water it, a young girl wandering the unruly garden looking for pretty weeds. She rolled the jamun around the bowl with her fingers and picked a fat, gleaming one to suck on, anticipating its acid hold on her throat.

Bikash Babu sat in his room downstairs, a book on his lap. He was not looking at the lines in the book but at the thin, white ones on the polished red floor of the study. They looked innocuous, like chalk outlines drawn by an untidy child and left unwiped. But he knew it was the water. It had soaked through the earth, crept up the roots of the house that burrowed deep in the soil, and was now leaving a damp trail on the red floor. At the edges of the rooms the water was spreading dark, irregular shadows, which made their way up the walls, puffing the plaster up as if there was something behind trying to get out. Bikash Babu did not need to touch the patches again to know they felt clammy, like a sick forehead, and cool like a dead one.

Some time early in the evening, the trees began to bend and sway, and a fresh breeze that smelled of sea and weeds, earth and distant places, rummaged through the papers on Bikash Babu's bureau, moved like a spirit through the still curtains, disarranged strands of hair on the sleeping Shanti's head, and banged the verandah door shut.

Kripa the maid, chewing a paan on the verandah and looking with a vacant post-meal gaze at the expanse of leaden sky over the river, saw a distant cloud that grew dark and bulbous, gathering speed and force as it rushed across towards the house. Before the tobacco in the paan had even begun its work, the cloud covered the sky. The surface of the placid river shimmered and then shattered as water hit water. The wind gathered strength. The coconut palms at the house's side bent like mad women with wild hair trying to touch the earth. Somewhere nearby something crashed and fell.

The servant boy went up the stairs two at a time, trying to restrain the rebellious saris drying on the roof on clotheslines strung from end to end. He yanked them off and bundled them onto his shoulders, stopping only to lean over the parapet and call down to Kripa, "Look, the rain!" It got heavier as he ran down, each drop big enough to make a flower shudder and droop with the force. Sky and river had merged.

By the time it had been raining for three days, people were commenting on how heavy and relentless it was, unnaturally so. The thatched roofs of mud huts had flown far away in the wind and the lightning streaking across the fields had scorched a whole clump of supari trees.

Bikash Babu called the servant boy and the gardener to the verandah. His mild face was distorted by a scowl. "Don't any of you notice anything?" he roared. "Can't you see the armchairs are standing in water?"

They looked at their toes.

"What are you looking at the floor for now? Remove them! Put them inside! Their legs will rot. Here," he said, starting to lift one of the heavy chairs, not making much headway.

"No, no, Babu, what are you doing?" the gardener exclaimed, rushing to the chairs, shouting in turn at the servant, "Come along, boy, they won't go in on their own!"

The chairs were large and heavy. They reclined back, far enough for a comfortable siesta. The servants struggled under the weight.

By the end of the week, the carpets had to be rolled up and put away. Bikash Babu began to wear his dhoti a little higher, exposing a length of thin, smooth calf. Shanti tried not to stare when her father

70

came upstairs and sat down on the edge of a chair beside her, distracted by his thoughts.

They looked out of the window and then, as people do, spoke together.

Bikash Babu was saying, "How are you feeling? If only your mother were alive, I would not be worried."

Shanti was saying, "Baba, do you think the house is in danger?"

"Why should it be? Is it built of clay?" Bikash Babu sounded sharper than he intended. "Haven't you seen with your own eyes how strong the walls are? Don't you remember how the workers' solid iron tools broke when they were trying to take down the old kitchen wall?"

"I was just thinking," Shanti began, "maybe we should move to . . ."

"There is nothing to think about," Bikash Babu cut in. "Every monsoon we go through this nonsense. As did my father and grandfather. In a week or two the rain will lessen and then the water will go down. Just a few dry days in between the rains will be enough."

Bikash Babu scraped back his chair and left the room for his lunch. Shanti turned her face into her pillow. The first six months of her pregnancy she had been on her feet almost all day. Now she had migraines that split her face in half and made her want to wrench her head off. Her skin was stretched taut, shiny and thin, like tissue holding back a tide. If she pricked herself with a needle, she thought, her insides would drain away. At night she had dreams that made her afraid to go back to sleep. Some nights the snake-headed bangles her mother-in-law had given her tightened noose-like around her neck and she woke up, heart racing, still hearing her mother-in-law's voice in her ears, saw her mouth curled with contempt as she repeated that word again and again. "Whore," she spat out, her dark face twisted, "whore, go sing in the streets." Another night Shanti saw Nirmal sinking into the river, bit by bit, calling out to her in desperation. "Pull me out," he shouted. "Give me a hand, call someone." He looked up at her beseechingly but, unable to move, she stood and watched the water wash over the top of his head, flow over it, flow past the house, carrying in it a red hibiscus.

71

Shanti made herself open her eyes and look at the alert-eyed bulbuls on the bakul tree to empty her mind of the images that crowded it.

Kripa was serving fish to Bikash Babu in the dining room. She was older than him by a few years, and so thought she had the right to say what she pleased. "A few days more and you won't have to buy the fish, they'll just swim onto your plate."

Getting no answer, she continued, "I've had to put so many bricks under the stove to raise it above the water. I'm cutting and chopping on a table, can't squat on the floor any more. At my age, is it possible to work standing so long?"

Bikash Babu was grim. "What's the point of grumbling?" he said, "What am I to do? I'm not causing the rain, am I? And where are we to go, abandoning our house? It's just a matter of a few weeks."

"In a few weeks," Kripa said, "I'll grow scales and fins. I tell you, I'm here because of that poor girl, frail as a flower, motherless. If her mother were here . . . "

She returned to the kitchen, feet making eddies in the water on the floor. Turning to look at Bikash Babu, she muttered, "Lord knows how he can eat like a stork, picking at the food with water up to his ankles."

* * *

It rained on.

Over the sound of drumming water, Kripa heard a scream, her name in the scream. She ran up the stairs, hearing the twisted calls of "Kripa-di, Kripa-di!" come closer. Upstairs she found Shanti clutching a table for support, mesmerised by a puddle between her feet, her sari damp. "What is happening to me, Kripa-di?" Shanti moaned. "What's coming out of me?"

Kripa shouted down to a servant, "Run, boy, where are you? Go and get Jonaki's mother!" The servant boy hitched up his dhoti. Jonaki's mother, the village midwife, lived beyond the paddy fields and the village pond, a difficult distance to cover in driving rain. He ran to get an umbrella. Not much use against the sheets of water cascading from the sky. Even so.

Kripa hurried to the study where she thought she would find Bikash Babu. There was nobody in the room, yet she stood transfixed. The lowest shelves of books were only half visible through the muddy water which seemed to be gaining height before her eyes. A sheet of paper glided by, the writing on it shivering before the ink streamed out, spreading a swirl of blue. A leaf floated past the legs of the armchair. Upon the table were two pictures, one of Shanti and one of her mother. They smiled down at the water, serene. Kripa picked up the pictures and waded out in despair.

She came face to face with the servant by the stairs and looked at him in horror.

"Still here, you fool? How do you think the baby will come if you just stand here? Go and get Jonaki's mother!"

"But the river," the boy croaked. "It's broken its banks. If I step out, the water is up to my neck. Our ground floor will be completely flooded now."

Kripa ran up the stairs again, gasping. Her knees ached. Midway her right knee caught so agonisingly she had to stop and clench her teeth till it unlocked. She came across Bikash Babu leaning against one of the pillars of the upper verandah, staring at the swollen river. His eyes had retreated deeper into his head. The skin around them looked warty. Kripa did not see any of it. For the moment she forgot a lifetime of trying to cultivate deference towards her employer. "*Now look where you've got us!*" She was not speaking but screaming. "Obstinate as a stuck cow in the middle of the road! What'll we do now? Didn't I say we should have gone away! Now look at that flood, and the baby on the way!"

"The baby," Bikash Babu repeated.

"Don't you even know poor Shanti's started her pains? A month too soon! Do you notice nothing? And nobody can get out for the midwife. Did you expect me to remember how to deliver a baby?"

Bikash Babu had turned away and was looking out again. His thin cotton kurta was transparent with rainwater, skin shining through it in patches where it stuck. "The river will drown the house today, it's broken its banks, it's finding a new path," he said in a murmur. She could hardly hear him over the drumming of the rain. "Can you hear its roar? Can you feel its power?"

Kripa tried to interrupt, then gave him up and began to hobble back to Shanti.

"The river will make this house its own. What are these grand houses but arrogance? My grandfather would boast of the Italian marble. That marble will be the river's bed now. Fish will swim in and out of our finest teak shelves and nibble our ivory figurines. Frogs will lay eggs in our English porcelain, water snakes will twine our pillars. The windows will fall off and flow down to the sea. My grandfather's bust will stare into weeds, the ink from our papers will colour the water black, moss will ooze out of burst bedding, beds and chairs will float out like boats, the rooms will lie empty for fish to breed in them."

Sharp lines of rain shot into the verandah. The breeze soaked his clothes and his spellbound face. His lips moved unheard. "The arrogance," he whispered, "the arrogance."

FIVE

The clouds that had collected and exploded over Manoharpur two weeks before had hardly paused over Songarh. There had been just enough rain to fill the shallow pond at the fort, to wash dust off the trees and to make the earth breathe a warm, moist breath. After the brief rain stopped, Nirmal went to his college and Kamal and Amulya to the factory.

The house quietened as always after the men left for work. The flurry of hot water for baths, breakfast, the last-minute ironing of clothes over, the house seemed to sigh with relief at emptying, and there was a lull before the sounds of grinding and frying and other kitchen work began. The gardener could be heard drawing water from the well for the plants that were shrivelling in the late summer heat. The rope squeaked and screeched one set of notes as it went down and with a different monotony as it came up. The maid quarrelled with one of the servants in a corner of the courtyard. Manjula finished her daily argument with Gouranga about how long the fish had been dead before he had bought it. Then she went to the kitchen, cursing, "Not a soul to help me cut the vegetables any longer, Shanti gone, and other people ill . . . you numbskull, grind the mustard with the green chilli, *with green chilli*!" In a little while the oil hissed and sputtered with vegetables and fish. Time passed. A bael fell with a thud into the garden. Gouranga tottered out and picked it up to make sherbet out of its orange, aromatic pulp.

At last Manjula finished anointing her face with cream and flour and went for a second bath.

The doorbell rang.

Gouranga opened the door and leapt away from it. It was Larissa Barnum, followed by her khansama, in grey uniform, complete with tarnished brass buttons and grey cap.

"Ask them!" she ordered.

The khansama said to Gouranga, "Where is your Mataji? Memsahib has to see her."

The servant stammered, "Upstairs, but . . ."

"What is he saying?" Mrs Barnum demanded.

" . . . she does not see anyone."

The khansama translated.

"What nonsense," Mrs Barnum exclaimed. "I need to see her. If she is upstairs, I will go to her."

And that was how 3 Dulganj Road had its first British visitor, a visitor who reached the bedrooms upstairs. Mrs Barnum darted curious glances around the first Indian home she had ever been in as she went up the dark stairwell that opened into Amulya's stained-glass verandah and led to his bedroom. Her heels clattered on the cool, hard floor. Manjula, hearing the unfamiliar sound in the bathroom through a cascade of water, wondered what it was, then returned to her iron bucket and mug.

Mrs Barnum swept into Kananbala's room and trilled cheerfully, "Well, here you are, we meet at last!"

Kananbala, startled, leapt up and exclaimed, "Oh Ma, what's this?"

"Tell her," Mrs Barnum ordered the khansama, who was hovering at the door.

"My memsahib would like you to come with her for a while, please," the khansama said in Hindi. "It will not take long."

Kananbala understood Hindi, though she did not speak anything but Bengali. She looked at the khansama and Mrs Barnum in speechless surprise. She had not left the house for what seemed like forever, let alone with strangers. It was impossible. She said so.

"That is absurd, quite absurd," Mrs Barnum said, and walked up to Kananbala. Firmly, she took her arm, trying to lead her out of the room.

"Don't worry," she said in a reassuring voice. "It's only across the road, there's nothing to worry about. You'll be back before anyone knows. D'you realise we've known each other for ages and never met?"

Kananbala looked up at Mrs Barnum's smiling, confident face bobbing considerably above hers. What strangeness! Her clothes, the colour of her skin, the way she walked, shoulders thrown back. She noticed Mrs Barnum's earlobes were long and pierced with green stones, that her front teeth were stained yellowish, that she smelt of roses and smoke. Kananbala had looked at Mrs Barnum so many nights and evenings separated by road, window grill, and distance that to have her so close seemed a revelation. Impelled by some irrational force, Kananbala felt she could not stay in her room any longer. She felt as if she could do anything at all, *anything* to get out of the house. She looked down at her sari, not one of her going-out ones, and smoothed it, saying, "I should change . . ." But nobody heard her anxious murmur.

Mrs Barnum, dropping Kananbala's arm, was standing at her window, the same window at which she had seen Kananbala every night looking out, waving to her. She examined the view from that window towards her own house across the road, the bougainvillea at the gate, the window upstairs, curtained against the world, the *porte-cochère*. How much had Kananbala seen that night, Larissa Barnum wondered. How different it all looked from this side of the road! Then she heard a muttering of voices behind her and called out to the servant, "Shoes, get her shoes, *joota, joota*!"

Kananbala divined what was required and went and slipped her feet into the good, wine-coloured velvet pair that Amulya had got her once from Whiteways in Calcutta, a pair she had never worn. She walked through the verandah, down the stairs, out of the gate and onto the road, suffused with an unreality that made her stagger. The light was too bright, the trees too tall, the road too long and smooth. She had not been outside the house before dusk for months. For months, she had seen the world outside from her window, or by evening light when Amulya took her to the garden to make her walk. She stumbled again. Mrs Barnum held her elbow and said, "There, it'll be alright, it's just strange at first. What bastards, to lock you up." The khansama thought it best not to translate everything.

The car was parked outside the gate. The khansama got into the driver's seat, while the two women sat at the back. Kananbala began to panic and looked wide-eyed with questions at Mrs Barnum. "Where are we going?" she quavered.

Mrs Barnum understood the question despite not knowing the language. Gaily, she laughed, "A surprise, it's a surprise!" The khansama dutifully translated this as he started the car.

The car rumbled down the road. It began to move faster, too fast for Kananbala who stared bewildered out of its window, her heart thumping with the novelty of it, with the speed. She had barely focused on one tree or building or clump of bushes when, already, it was part of the past. The wind rushed into her hair and made strands escape from her tight bun. Her aanchal slid off her head; there was nothing she could do to keep it on. Bare-headed, hair flying, she put her face to the rushing air that made her eyes water. A feeling of exhilaration swept over her, something overpowering, something she could not remember feeling after she was newly married.

* * *

Amulya returned home at midday, as he usually did. Sitting on the bench by the front door, he took his shoes off, calling out, "Arre o Gouranga, where are you? Bring me some water!"

He rose and in slippered feet walked up the stairs towards his bedroom. In the long verandah-room, the light streaming in through his stained-glass window was a mellow monsoon colour. Amulya paused to admire it, relishing the thought of at least a month of rain, and reached out for the glass of water Gouranga had brought. "Where is everyone?" he enquired. "The house is very quiet, what's happening?"

"N . . . nn . . . nothing, Babu," Gouranga said, and, almost grabbing Amulya's empty glass, scampered out of the verandah as if pursued. Amulya watched him disappearing and muttered, "Dolt . . . fifteen years and still he isn't trained . . . just can't make a horse out of this donkey."

He turned into his bedroom saying, "Are you there? I'm back."

He stepped in. "Are you there?" he said again, peering into the curtained-off dressing area.

Amulya stood puzzled, brows knit, wondering where Kananbala could be. Then, thinking she might be – uncharacteristically, he admitted – with Manjula in her quarters, he sat down with the newspaper to wait for Manjula to call him for lunch. He flipped it open to the editorials and began to read. The silence was broken only by the rustle of the paper and the monotonous tinkle of cow-bells.

Much time had passed, his hungry stomach told him. He pushed the paper aside as if everything in it was nonsensical and got up.

Looking into the corridor, he bellowed "Bouma!" towards his absent older daughter-in-law.

Manjula appeared, wiping her hands on her sari, looking drawn with worry. Like the rest of the household, she was terrified of Amulya's temper.

"Ma has gone out," she stammered when he asked. "I was having a bath . . . Mrs Barnum . . ."

Amulya stood stock still for a moment, then turned away from her without a word. The thought that his wife had left the house, defying him – even in her disturbed state she knew the rules – that she was making a fool of herself with a stranger, that the stranger in question was an Anglo-Indian murderess! He could not stretch his mind far enough to accommodate all these facts together. He summoned Gouranga and sent him across the road to call her back. Gouranga returned after ten minutes, not daring to speak.

They could not say at Mrs Barnum's where Kananbala was. She had been taken away in a car by Mrs Barnum and her khansama.

Amulya sat in his armchair by the window and stared at the wall opposite, frozen into inaction by fury and astonishment. He could not think of returning to the factory. Where would he begin to hunt for his wife? What did the Barnum woman intend to do to her? Perhaps there had been some development in the police investigation and she was going to silence Kananbala? Maybe the police had lied to Mrs Barnum and told her Kananbala was about to depose against her? Could one put anything past a woman who had killed her husband for the sake of a lover?

He sat straight-backed, saying nothing to anyone, unable to still his mind. Manjula peeped in through the door at his preoccupied face, his rigid body, and stole away. She sat in her room eating a hurried, stolen snack to make up for their forgotten lunch. Her afternoon nap was out of the question. What if her father-in-law summoned her? "What a lot of trouble the woman is," Manjula spluttered under her breath with exasperation. "What the hell is the old bag up to?"

* * *

The car sped over the smooth road and then turned into a narrower one that was bumpy. Around them were fields of stubble, the earth damp, exhaling, grass shooting out almost before their eyes with the new rain. They had left the houses behind, and now, apart from a villager's hut or crop-guard's shack, there were no buildings. The car bumped and lurched more and more until they passed first the rustling shade of a eucalyptus stand, then a stretch of open field, and then Kananbala knew where she was, though she could hardly believe it.

There, across the horizon, was the spine of the ridge, its body visible too, closer than she had ever seen it. This close, she could see the slopes had trees and scrub poking out of them, and the trees continued right down to the flat ground where they became the forest and met a dry stream-bed. The same forest she could see from her window, the forest where her lion was.

The car twisted round the dirt track and turned the corner, and Mrs Barnum said, "There! Now, have you seen that before?"

They were before the ruins of the fort. The car had stopped. Kananbala took no notice of Mrs Barnum helping her out of the car as she stepped across, hesitant at first, then with strong strides, to the old stone walls. She touched the stone with a wondering hand and looked around. She saw the enormous, aged, banyan tree that had sent out hundreds of aerial roots, now joined with the ground. Kananbala stood among the roots, looking up at them towering past her, a forest made by just one giant tree. She noticed the bark on the tree's main trunk had knotted up into an odd shape, and looked closer.

"That's meant to be the face of the Buddha." The khansama translated what Mrs Barnum was saying. "He is said to have meditated here. This tree is supposed to bring people peace. It certainly does me!" She laughed. Then she said, "Shall we go further or stop here?"

"Stop!" Kananbala said.

"Right! Bring out the hamper, khansama, and the carpet, will you?" Mrs Barnum tripped ahead calling out, "Come, there's more!"

She reached for Kananbala's hand again and almost pulled her along. Kananbala watched the wine-coloured velvet of shoes that had lain perfect in their tissue wrapping for years grow beige with mud. She smiled a sudden, radiant smile of uncomplicated happiness, and then she saw a shallow pool of water, faded arabesques on the floor around it. She almost ran towards the water, ungainly, wobbly, sari entangling her legs. Mrs Barnum let go, watching her. The pool was cool with water from the new rain, not much deeper than a big puddle, but Kananbala, forgetting she was a woman in her fifties, threw off her shoes as children do and sat dipping her toes, then let her feet slide in, shivering at the touch of water.

Mrs Barnum was busy with the hamper. The khansama laid out a bright, striped duree, and on it a tablecloth that covered a portion of the middle. He took a few boxes out of the hamper, and a bottle. He laid out forks and napkins. Then he stepped back and said in English, "I will wait in the car?"

"Yes, I suppose . . ." Mrs Barnum was irresolute for a moment and then said, "Yes, go to the car. If I need you, I will call, thank you."

Kananbala saw Mrs Barnum crouching next to her, her peacock-blue dress trailing in the dust. Mrs Barnum had a bottle in her hand, and string.

"Ah," she was muttering to herself, "Now let's see . . . um, yes." She tied the neck of the bottle with string and slid it into the water of the pool. She took the other end and tied it to a tree root. Then she rubbed her palms together in glee, exclaiming, "Now our picnic begins!"

* * *

When the afternoon was at its most silent, they heard someone at the door of 3 Dulganj Road. A servant came upstairs to Amulya's room, followed by a stranger. It was a thin, balding man in a crumpled dhoti and a grey, sweat-stained shirt. Under his arm was a rolled-up, long, black umbrella with a wooden handle. In his other hand he held a very small, worn cloth bag of the kind people used when buying vegetables from the market. He came into the room and stood silently for a few minutes, opening his mouth as if to say something, then shutting it again. After this happened a few times, Amulya said, "Sit down. Where have you come from?"

The man remained standing.

"Kindly sit!" Amulya repeated, sounding a little impatient. "What's the matter?"

Amulya did not think the man was from Songarh. His clothes marked him out as being from rural Bengal. Amulya was filled with foreboding.

Then the man began to speak.

After many minutes, he finished what he had to say and left the room. Amulya's normally rigid back drooped semi-circular, and his skeletal face caved in further. He put his hands over his eyes as if he could not bear the daylight any more.

Gouranga, who was hovering just outside the door, heard a sound of anguish, something between a groan and a cry, from inside the room and fell back a few steps, startled. What could Kananbala have done, he wondered, to make Amulya Babu feel like this, where could she be?

* * *

82

They sat on the duree in the shade of an old spreading tree. Kananbala did not recognise most of the things Mrs Barnum laid out. There were sandwiches, cut fine and thin, wrapped in damp cheesecloth. Lunch boxes revealed cream biscuits and chocolate eclairs. One box was deep with small cakes studded with ruby red raisins. Mrs Barnum brought out cheese and a knife. She opened a tin of condensed milk and dipped a finger into it saying, "Try it, scrumptious!" She dipped her finger in again.

Kananbala shuddered at that. How could she eat anything contaminated by someone else's saliva? She tried to smile and picked up a biscuit. But what if the bread slices had meat in them? What if the cake had egg in it? Yet if she did not eat, wouldn't Mrs Barnum be displeased?

She started to babble, worried. "Slut, whore, daughter of the devil, syphilitic hen."

"Pity we can't understand each other!" Mrs Barnum said, "We'd have such a jolly time."

Kananbala bit into the biscuit mumbling fresh expressions of horror through the crumbs.

Mrs Barnum said, "The wine must have cooled a little by now, let me see." She drew the bottle out of the water and tested it. "Yes, it'll have to do." She produced a corkscrew from the hamper and opened the bottle as Kananbala watched intrigued. Mrs Barnum poured the deep red liquid into two crystal wine glasses and then, ceremoniously, held one out to Kananbala.

"Cheers." she said. "Go on, there's no-one looking, try it!"

Kananbala knew about wine glasses. Magazines had woodcuts showing degenerate men drinking out of those glasses. Voluptuous, loose-moralled theatre actresses in Calcutta were said to drink out of such glasses. She shook her head.

"It's alright," Mrs Barnum said smiling, gentle. "It's just wine. Not liquor. Theek hai!" she said, hoping that would reassure Kananbala.

Kananbala, uncomprehending, shook her head again and turned away to the pool. "I should have packed lemonade." Mrs Barnum said, downcast. "I'm such a nitwit sometimes. Digby was right, I have no sense, I don't think things through. You're a fool, an imbecile, he'd keep saying, all the time, at the drop of a hat, my mixed blood, my bad blood, my stupidity."

Mrs Barnum was talking almost to herself, drinking rapid sips of the wine, not touching the food.

Kananbala looked up at the woman next to her. She looks young, must be only in her thirties, she thought, or maybe a little older – maybe the colour on her cheeks is rouge.

Mrs Barnum had a fine-boned face on a long neck that emerged stem-like from her dress. As she spoke, a knobble in her throat bobbed a little under the thin surface of her skin. Her fingers clutched her glass too hard and she jerked her head as she talked and paused and talked again. Kananbala watched her, fascinated. That she understood nothing did not seem to matter. She knew Mrs Barnum was saying something she needed to say, something she could say only to her, Kananbala.

A kingfisher sliced into the pool having sat immobile in a tree for several minutes. The blue of its wings was the blue of Mrs Barnum's dress and Kananbala, excited, tugged at the frock and pointed to the bird. The young woman looked down at the older one with a start as if she had only just realised she was not alone. Then, thinking she understood what Kananbala was saying, she chuckled, "Yes, Digby did think I was a vain strutting little bird – I suppose I am."

She took another sip of her wine and sighed. "What a soup I'm in, what a godawful soup." She was contemplative for a while, listening to the birds. Then she began to talk – and talk – beginning to feel a curious sense of lightness pervade her. Perhaps because of Kananbala's incomprehension, she felt entirely understood. She spoke into the ruins and to Kananbala, without stopping except for wine to wet her throat. She spoke about her childhood, about Digby courting her, about Digby beating her with his belt and, once, slamming her face into a door. She talked about her lover, the things he did that Digby had not done. She spoke words she had never thought she would. She spoke of the ease with which the knife had slid into her husband, first his stomach, then somewhere else, she did not know where. She spoke of the blood, of the resistance of skin, the obstruction of bones, the sick ache in her heart and between her legs and in the pit of her stomach for her lover who had to run away.

Kananbala listened.

At last, exhausted, Mrs Barnum stretched her arms out over her knees and buried her head in them.

Looking at the bent head, Kananbala seemed to decide something. She picked up her crystal glass gingerly by the stem and took a long gulp, screwing up her mouth at the taste. She gasped as she felt an unfamiliar warmth inside her. Mrs Barnum looked up at the sound. Kananbala made a wry face and Mrs Barnum smiled back at her, incredulous. Kananbala took another long sip, giving Mrs Barnum a look of mingled fear and triumph.

Mrs Barnum smiled wider, her eyes glazed with wine and the clouded sun. Bending, she brought her wine-stained mouth to Kananbala's cheek and gave it a soft kiss.

* * *

Even as Kananbala was taking her first sip of wine, Amulya emerged from his room, his face composed, his back straight again.

"Come here," he said to Gouranga, still by the door. "Send someone to Dadababu's college. He must run, and if he finds a tonga, tell him to take a tonga, and bring Nirmal back here. If Nirmal is teaching in a class, tell him to interrupt and go in. Get him back home immediately. Have you understood?"

Gouranga nodded and hobbled down the stairs as fast as his arthritic knees would let him. He knew the visiting stranger must be downstairs somewhere, and he would find out what had happened from him.

It was in the kitchen, as he had thought, that the stranger sat, holding a glass of something. Around him in a spellbound semi-circle were Shibu, the gardener, and the maid. Gouranga barged into the room and yelled, "Arre o, tear yourself away, there is a job to be done, boy!" Then, having sent Shibu off to Nirmal's college and established who was boss in the kitchen, he sat down with a grunt next to the stranger

85

and said, "So tell me, what's this news you've brought? Nothing good, I can see that, nothing good." He lit a beedi.

Now, with many tellings, the stranger had got into his stride. The event, real enough five days ago, too real almost to grasp, seemed to have become a story, something that had happened to storybook people. He put his head in his hands afresh, simulating the despair he had truly felt the first few days, and with a heavy sigh that was an unconscious emulation of the lead actor in a jatra he had seen, he began again to speak.

* * *

When Nirmal at last returned home and rushed up to his father, Amulya, unlike the stranger, was still unable to put what he had heard into words. Being able to articulate what had happened meant being able to understand it, grasp it, digest it, even to a degree accept it. He cleared his throat, told his son to sit down, walked to the window and walked back again. Eventually, for the first time in his life, Nirmal snapped at his father. "What is it? Can you tell me what's happened? What's the matter?"

There had been a great flood in Manoharpur, Nirmal's father's voice said. It had come into the house, marooned it. Shanti had gone into labour too early, a whole month too early. Nobody could get out of the house to get a doctor in time. The maid, who had some midwifing experience, had done her best but . . . only the baby could be saved. Not Shanti. A healthy baby, but at what cost? Shanti had died giving birth. Nirmal needed to go to Manoharpur right away, although it was too late for him even to see Shanti's dead body . . . the countryside had been too flooded for anyone to reach the next town, where there were three telephones . . . a telegram or letter . . . nothing had been possible.

But there was his baby. He needed to go and bring the baby back, a baby girl named Bakul, as Shanti had always wanted.

* * *

Perhaps an hour later, at four in the afternoon, there were sounds of car doors slamming. Then, after a long pause, Kananbala was to be heard shuffling up the stairs. She stumbled into her room, somewhat unstable, cheeks warm, velvet slippers unrecognisable, hair straggling out of its pins, sari askew.

The silence brimmed with unspoken words. She knew she was in trouble. She ought never to have gone out of the house at all. Had she forgotten how furious Amulya could be? His fury was more potent and more frightening than Durvasa Muni's, especially when he said nothing at all. She glanced in his direction. She had thought only of his face all the way back from the picnic. She had wanted to drink in the last of the wind through the fast-moving car's window, imprint the landscape on her mind before being locked away in her room again, but despite trying to feel the joy she had on her way out to the fort, she had been filled with dread at the idea that Amulya would have come home for lunch in the meantime and not found her where she ought to be.

Amulya was not looking at her. He sat with his head in his hands, eyes shut. Nobody took any notice of her. Her act of what had looked like desperate rebellion, her drunkenness, her ruined velvet slippers, all went unremarked.

* * *

Nirmal left for Manoharpur that night. The household began a vigil for its motherless infant.

They waited a fortnight, then it became a month. Nobody came.

On the thirty-first day, Amulya wrote to Bikash Babu with a polite enquiry: "If you could find out from Nirmal what his plans are, it would be a great relief to us," he wrote. "He was in a state of shock when he left Songarh, and we, his mother and I, have been anxious. Of course we know that as long as he is with you, he is in the best possible care, but still, parents worry. We wish we could also be with you through this grief that has devastated both our families . . . "

They counted the days for a reply. Five or six days for their letter to reach Manoharpur . . . or maybe seven or eight since it was going from one mofussil to another, and then the same time for a reply to arrive. In two weeks it would be reasonable to expect news.

Every day, when the postman passed along Dulganj Road jingling his bell, Kananbala waited at the window, willing him to stop at their gate. Amulya searched through his mail every morning when he reached the factory before he even hung his umbrella on its hook. Every morning he began with hope but was ready for disappointment.

At the end of twenty days, there was a reply.

"This is very puzzling, and extremely worrying," Bikash Babu's blue ink said, foregoing the standard greetings and enquiries about health.

> *Nirmal was almost unable to look at his baby. He was disturbed when he was here, and did not speak much. He was incoherent when he did speak. He refused to come away from the room where Shanti had spent her last day. We could not intrude. Nirmal was here for that night, but the next morning when we woke up, he had already left. He said nothing to us. All this time, through this month, I have assumed that he returned to you — to calm down — and that he would come back to us for his baby when able . . . I understand his grief, I feel it myself, I have lost my daughter, my only child. But it is greater for him, losing the mother of his child, and we are broken-hearted for the little one who will never know her mother.*
>
> *Shanti's old maid, Kripa, is taking care of the baby. Please have no worries on that count. For the rest, what is there to say? God's ways are inexplicable, we think of Him as merciful, but in these times when the darkness seems unending, we wonder.*

Nobody knew where Nirmal was, neither in Manoharpur, nor in Songarh. He had not been seen for a month.

Should they inform the police? Enquire in hospitals? In morgues? In which city? Ask their relatives in Calcutta? Search out his college friends? Where could they begin to look?

Kananbala and Amulya spent the next three weeks staring down at the empty road, as if Nirmal would materialise on it. They looked up every time someone was at the door. Amulya attempted to mimic normality: he went to his factory every day as usual but sat at his desk forgetting what he had meant to do. He took out his old Roxburgh and Hooker volumes and looked up illustrations of plants, but the page stayed open on the same spot for hours. It was as if a cold, dead hand was squeezing him inside, making it difficult for him to breathe. He began to dread leaving the house, and eventually stopped going to the factory.

The house echoed silence. Everyone crept about. The maid and the gardener stopped fighting, feeling the silence devour everything.

One afternoon, the stillness was broken by a guttural groan that came from deep within Amulya. He gasped that a lion was clawing his chest apart. His pulse faded, came back, and faded again, this time for too long.

The doctor came, thumped Amulya's chest, and placed a shining glass before his nose. He lifted Amulya's limp wrist and pressed his finger into it, searching for a pulse. He tried once more palpitating the chest, then shook his head, passed a hand over Amulya's staring eyes, and turned away to pack his stethoscope into his hinged case.

Kananbala looked out of the window and exclaimed with a happy laugh, "Isn't that Nirmal coming down the road?"

But Nirmal did not return.

PART II

THE RUINED FORT

ONE

A mop-haired boy in a thin pullover and flappy shorts entered the puja room, swabcloth in hand. Small statues and pictures of gods and goddesses were arranged on a platform along one arm of the L-shaped room and at the other sat a priest, rummaging in his cloth bag, taking out and making a pile of dog-eared little books of mantras. Prominent ribs striped his bony chest which was bisected by a dirty-grey sacred thread. He had an elastic mouth with long fleshy lips, shaped as if it could accommodate a banana across its width. When he saw the boy enter, the mouth stretched in an expression of revulsion and he rose and stepped with alacrity onto the terrace outside the puja room.

The boy heard the priest muttering "Hari, Hari", and from a corner of his eye he could see the priest sprinkle Gangajal over himself. He grinned and stuck his head out of the room, calling out, "I'm sure I touched you, purohitmoshai, you'll need a bath now, won't you? And there's no hot water left!" The priest gave him a malevolent look and snapped, "You can stop your gob, you rascal! I'll teach you to be cheeky!"

The boy laughed and returned to the puja room, wiping the floor with his stale, fish-smelling swab cloth. He retreated to the terrace to wait. The morning still felt new; the outline of the building opposite was smudged, the distant line of hill and forest whited out by mist. A moonlike sun had struggled out, too weak still to dry the dew-wet grass. He blew out to see if his warm breath would make a cloud. It did.

A woman's voice behind him made him stop. She was frowning at his thin sweater and scolding. "Can't you see it's cold? Go, put on something more!" She pulled her brown shawl tighter and entered the puja room. She sat down at a distance from the priest and said, "Yes, purohitmoshai, we can start now."

The priest felt around in his orange cloth shoulder bag and produced one more of his dog-eared books. From the slot between his hairy ears and bald head he took a pencil stub and poised it over the notebook. "First things first," he said. "Tell me your names so I don't have to keep asking at every puja I do. I know the caste and gotra, of course, so you needn't bother about those." He was new to the house, taking over the family's duties that morning.

"The head of the house is Kamal Babu," the woman began, "and . . . "

"Slowly," the priest said, droning out the name at the slow speed he wrote it, tip of tongue edging out between his lips, "Kamal Kumar Mukho . . . "

"Then there's Nirmal Babu, his younger brother, but he won't be here today."

"Won't be here today?" the priest looked up. "Won't be here at Saraswati puja? Too modern for God, is he?"

She said, "No. He just works in a different city."

"Oh, alright, who's next?" the priest said, disappointed by the bland explanation.

"Then there are the women," she said. She rattled off the list: Manjula, wife of Kamal; Kananbala, mother of Kamal; Bakul, Nirmal's daughter, still a child, only eleven."

"Bakul has no mother? And what about Kamal Babu? No children, hm? Barren wife?" The priest looked up from his notebook.

She stiffened and said, "I think that is all."

"All? What about you? You don't count yourself among the women? What's your name?" He looked her up and down, her off-white sari, her lack of bangles and sindoor, and said, "You're a widow, I see. And childless too? Ah, but whatever God wills has some purpose."

"My name is Meera and I am not part of this family," she said, sounding short. "You don't need to include me." She began to get up, then stopped and said, "But yes, there's also Mukunda."

"Mukunda?"

"The boy who swabbed the floor just now. He lives here too. He has exams coming so he needs Saraswati's blessings!" She looked out towards Mukunda's silhouette on the terrace with a smile.

"Caste?"

"I'm not sure."

"Not sure?"

"He's just a child! Does it matter? He's an orphan whom we . . . "

"Someone you shelter?" The priest clapped his book shut and reached out for his bag. "Why should he be allowed in the puja room? Charity is all very well, but can it change his caste?"

Mukunda, the baby Amulya had placed in the missionary orphanage, was now thirteen. But with Amulya had died all knowledge of Mukunda's parentage. His place in the family was an ambiguous one. He ate their food, but on a demarcated plate; he lived in their home now, but in a room out in the courtyard; they gave him clothes, but hand-me-downs; he had homework, but he also had household chores. He was awkward, lanky, easy to upset. Sometimes he felt all edges, each edge sore. He knew he was from nearby, perhaps born of a Santhal mother. Certainly, his high cheekbones and tea-dark skin made him compare himself to the tribal people he saw, but he had no way of being sure. Would someone appear out of the forest one day and claim him as her own?

Meera looked anxiously at the terrace. She was sure Mukunda could overhear them, felt something throbbing at the base of her neck, the familiar anger, and knew she should say nothing or else . . .

"Please," she snapped, despite herself. "I don't need advice on Mukunda."

"Oho, what do we have here? A real red-hot chilli!" The priest's banana mouth twisted in annoyance and he said, "If you don't keep these people in their place, soon they'll be in yours! But that's your business, just keep him away from me and from this puja room." He lowered his voice and hissed, "He almost touched me once already."

Before their argument could go any further, the rest of the family trooped into the puja room to the picture of the goddess Saraswati, who gazed out large-eyed and tranquil from her seat of pink lotus in a sea of turquoise waves, unaware of the weight of hope and yearning in the oddments of paint tubes, books, ink bottles and pens piled before her for her blessings. Bakul's books and pencils, of course, but also Kamal's account books just in case the goddess of learning had blessings to spare. Meera had added a few of her own books to the pile.

The priest stretched his twisting mouth again and enquired of Manjula – large-hipped, loud-voiced, neck noosed by a thick gold chain, clearly the matriarch – "Are you sure that boy's books are not here?"

"Ah, purohitmoshai, of course not," Manjula said. "Why would they be?"

The priest murmured some mantras in his nasal voice and returned to shredding marigold flowers and bael leaves for the puja. From somewhere downstairs a high-pitched voice shrieked, "Warty toad, miserable scum!" The priest looked up in alarm, but the voice subsided as suddenly as it had erupted.

From the terrace, Mukunda heard them begin to chant the hymn to Saraswati with the priest leading. "*Jaya jayo devi, chara chara shaarey, kucho jugo shobhita mukta haare, veena, ranjita, pustaka haste . . .*" He felt a fireball of rage somewhere inside his thirteen-year-old body, felt it spinning, growing, gathering heat. He walked away to the furthest point of the terrace, where he could no longer hear them, and looked out towards Songarh's fort, imagining he could spot from that distance the ancient banyan tree that stood near it. He climbed onto the roof's parapet and stood at its very edge, holding his arms out like wings. He felt dangerously weightless, between falling and flying. There, outside the goddess's line of vision, the sun still struggling behind him in the damp sky, he screwed his eyes tight and chanted too.

"You're not my god, you haven't done anything for me," Mukunda was saying. "But despite you, I'm going to be better than all of them. One day I won't need them any more. One day it'll be me giving them shelter."

That afternoon Mukunda crept out of the gate, willing its latch not to squeak, and then ran across the road and let himself into the other house where nobody but Bakul knew he went at that time of day. He knew that afternoons – when schools, offices and factories emptied much of the house – were for secrets. When Manjula sculpted on a face pack and Meera daydreamt about escape. When birds quarrelled and berries plopped unnoticed from tree to dusty ground. When cats rummaged unwatched in the lunchtime rubbish pails for fishbones.

Mrs Barnum's house stood bare in the unsparing afternoon sun. The two-storeyed house had once been yellow, but in the eleven years since Mr Barnum's death it had not been painted and was now scabby with black mould. The wooden gate had sections missing that had not been replaced, and the gaps gave passers-by a clear view of the *porte-cochère* that had been Mr Barnum's refuge from the street. From cracks and crevices in the walls, sturdy little peepal trees had begun to send out leaf and stalk. It was only a matter of time before the trees cracked open the house and brought it down.

Mukunda did not notice any of it. He let himself in through Mrs Barnum's tall, open front door and ran up the stairs two at a time, as always. He pushed open the door of the empty living room and went straight to a shelf in the dark corner by the old fireplace. He took out a book, the third from the left-hand side, with a blue, gilt-embossed spine, sat at the dining table, and, opening it to a page he had marked, bent over it. His finger began to follow a line of print and his lips began to form the words in a whisper.

Some time later Mrs Barnum entered the room and peered over his shoulder to see what he was reading. "Getting along with Nelson?" she said in her smoke-deepened voice. She placed a hand on Mukunda's shoulder. Her long fingernails played with strands of hair at the nape of his neck. "Look up what 'mizzen' means, won't you? And 'masthead'."

"His backbone is shot through," Mukunda said. "He's going to die."

"Of course he's going to die," Mrs Barnum laughed, lighting

a cigarette, "If he didn't, how'd he have had a square with him in London?"

Nelson had been Mukunda's hero ever since he had reached the Battle of Trafalgar in *The Book of Adventure Stories*, yet Mrs Barnum always seemed to be laughing at him. Mukunda returned to his book, trying to overlook her mocking presence. He had to finish the chapter that afternoon and also memorise the poem for that week before stealing home in time to make the tea. There was not a moment to waste.

Two years earlier, Mrs Barnum had caught Mukunda in the act – he had taken down a book from her shelf when he thought she was not looking, and was trying to read it, with no success. Don't you go to school, she had asked him. Why can't you read this book? It's not so difficult.

He had mumbled something, tried to slip away. She had caught his arm and stopped him. Tell me about your school, she had said, I asked you a question and you will not be rude, boy.

His school was a shed, he had said, and his classroom a blackboard shared by boys from four years old to fifteen. There was just one teacher who caned them when he felt inclined to, and then went off to drink tea at the shop round the corner.

What about Bakul, Mrs Barnum had wanted to know. Couldn't she read either? Bakul went to a different school with many teachers, all nuns, he said. She also had a tutor who taught her every other evening. Mukunda had tried to learn by eavesdropping, but it hadn't worked. He had not dared to ask Manjula and Kamal for tuition too.

Mrs Barnum had said nothing, but her neck felt taut with anger. You will study with me, she had said, from tomorrow. I'll make you as good as anyone else, better.

Mukunda had stolen away since then, afraid of being forbidden, to Mrs Barnum's house each afternoon. Mrs Barnum's method was simple. She told him to search her shelves and read anything that pleased him, and to ask her if something was difficult to understand. She showed him how to use the big dictionary that her husband had got many years before as a free gift with something. She chuckled with him over things he found funny and wiped away fake tears when they read bits of Dickens where children died. Sometimes she pulled out big picture books and showed him ships and kangaroos and cities in Europe.

Mrs Barnum's shelves had an assortment of books: Barnum's old books on coal-mining, romances and mysteries, anthologies of great literature, yellowed issues of women's weeklies with knitting supplements and pot roast recipes. Mukunda made his way through all of these with indiscriminate diligence while Mrs Barnum looked on, a speculative smile curling her rose-tinted lips. At times she rang a bell that stood on a tray by her table and summoned the khansama for lemon sherbet, hers with a splash of gin, Mukunda's without.

* * *

The year was 1940. It had been eleven years since the Barnum murder. Amulya's house in Songarh was now one of the older ones in that part of town. The '20s and '30s had passed, the prosperous years when Dulganj Road acquired large houses inhabited by the white men in the mining companies and their memsahibs, those who occupied the empyrean heights, never having to step down into the coal pits that kept them in Scotch whisky and soft, white shirts. Then, in 1935, one of the coal mines a few miles away caved in. Forty-eight miners were trapped under the ground for five days, until all efforts to rescue them were exhausted. There was a scandal. It was thought that since the labourers in the mines were poor Indians and the managers of the mines were expatriate British people who came and went, safety had not been a priority. One manager, who considered himself different, felt himself filling with compassion after the disaster and went to visit a dead miner's family with compensation money. He was almost lynched. The police swiftly disciplined the labourers.

The overtapped mines were close to drying up anyway and were shut down in the next few years; the British managers left. A dark fungus of desolation and poverty inched over the town. Where people had earlier come to it looking for work, now they started to leave.

Dulganj Road, always isolated, was to have become a rich suburb. Now, after the expatriates had gone, leaving empty houses, Finlays stopped stocking treacle and suet, gardens went back to wilderness, the road was pitted for lack of repair and after dark it was difficult to get a tongawallah to agree to come that way. At 3 Dulganj Road, after Amulya's death, the garden was tended for a time, but by an itinerant gardener who had to be sacked after it was found he was nurturing a flourishing field of cannabis in a sunny corner. Soon the grass was knee-high again, and wild bushes of berries at the edges were attracting birds and noisy monkeys.

Mrs Barnum's house, opposite Amulya's, was regarded as the house of Sahib Bahu, mad, bad, alone. Only Amulya's family still referred to her by her real name; any others who had known her as Larissa Barnum had left Songarh for other places. She lived alone, the khansama her only servant. There were two houses beyond hers, which, after the passing of the British, had acquired a multitude of Indian tenants. One of these, Afsal Mian, was a young, melancholic musician who taught singing. He went about town with the air of being a man whose talents were wasted upon Songarh's philistine air. He had reason to feel as he did; while he tried to impress upon his students the necessity of riyaaz, and of perfecting one note by practising it day after day, his wards' parents asked, when giving him his salary: "How many new songs this month Ustad? How many will she know before her marriage proposals start coming in?" In the evenings, sitting on the wide, old verandah in his lungi, he sang out his frustration in a rich, sad-sounding voice that carried all the way to Amulya's house.

People said nothing ever happened in Songarh; if there were no clocks you wouldn't know that time had passed. They said if you wanted to make something of your life, you had to leave. Leave, Mukunda, Mrs Barnum always said after a few of her special lemon sherbets, leave before the rot sets in, leave before you're no good for anywhere else.

Mukunda could not imagine anywhere else yet. Songarh was all he and Bakul knew, the town that defined all others for them. Their world was circumscribed by Arunagar on the left, with its knot of shops and small houses, Mrs Barnum's opposite, with the fort and ridge beyond it, and Finlays and Apsara Cinema further away, where they were not allowed to go on their own. Narrow streets meandered over the town's undulating terrain, passing through little leftover villages. Town and country were impossible to separate; shops and houses made a straggly line hemming mustard fields.

Bakul and Mukunda had populated Songarh with their own secret places and people. To them it throbbed with magic and meanings which only the two of them could share. They had been together always, ever since Mukunda had joined the household when he was six and Bakul four. They had agreed they were *both* orphans: after all, Bakul had reasoned, she was an orphan too because her mother was dead and her father, an archaeologist, was away on digs in other parts of the country for such long years at a stretch that she forgot his face in between.

TWO

"It's a dark night. You're a one-eyed tomb robber creeping up to rob a pyramid in the desert, I'm following, I'll catch you." Mukunda's gaze slid past Bakul.

"It's not night, it's afternoon, and why should I have one eye?" Bakul sounded suspicious.

Mukunda had not heard her. He pointed to a mango tree in the centre of the garden. It stood innocuous in the afternoon sun, sheltering a family of birds that flew in and out of it, chiding each other as he approached. "That's the pyramid," he said, excited, "All around there is just sand. And look, I brought something – this is all we have to eat for the days we are in the desert." He held out two onions and a handful of dried-up peanuts.

It was a Sunday afternoon. The rest of the family, heavy with eating, floated in the half-awake realm of afternoon sleep as the two of them wandered their garden of old trees and tall grass. Tangles of wildflowers nodded under the weight of pausing butterflies.

"Peanuts?" Bakul said scornfully. "Did robbers eat peanuts in ancient times?"

"I don't know." Mukunda sounded troubled. "We can pretend they are whatever the robbers ate."

"You don't know? But I thought you knew *everything*!"

"I have work to do. Do you want to play or not?"

Mukunda was offended. He tossed an onion at Bakul and strode towards the well. It was a large stone-walled well that went deep. In the thirty or so years since Amulya had dug it, it had never gone dry, though in the summer months the water became a distant circle of light far below and the thick rope played out and played out until it felt as if the iron bucket would never find the bottom; and when the splash of water meeting bucket at last sounded, it came from very far away. In the monsoon, the water in the well rose every day, a little and then more, until it was so close it felt as if only the rim held the water in and anyone could reach in and bail out water, as if from a pond. The well was overhung by a creeper of white jasmine that dropped its fragrant flowers into the water all day.

It was one of Mukunda's chores to see that the bathrooms and kitchen were always stocked with full buckets of water from the well. It was he who wheeled water out of the well several times a day, iron bucket clanging down as the wheel screeched and squeaked. Now, annoyed with Bakul, he flung in the bucket and played out the rope faster and faster so that the squeak drowned out her voice.

Neither of them heard the gate open.

Neither of them saw a man pay off a tongawallah and step in, looking around as if unsure where he was.

He was thin, his half-sleeved shirt too large, as if he had shrunk within it. His eyes cast shadows of grey underneath and his hair stood out dry and irregular. His height made him slouch a little, or perhaps it was fatigue. He looked too tired to move beyond the gate down the long, overgrown path towards the house. He stood there flanked by two large trunks and a bedroll, as if trying to decide what to do, as if he did not know the direction he needed to go. He saw the pair by the well and began walking towards them across the garden, stopping every now and then as if he had seen something that called out to him.

Bakul was shouting above the squeak of the wheel and the clang of the bucket, "Why can't we play the crocodile game? You never want to play that."

"That's a boring game," Mukunda said scathingly. "That's for babies."

Bakul looked at him, unsmiling, and turned away.

As she turned she came face to face with the man. She had seen him before. She knew she had. The man bent down and sat before her on his haunches. When he smiled, the grey shadows seemed to darken as his eyes almost disappeared, and a long deep line appeared on each cheek.

"Don't you remember who I am?" he asked her almost in a whisper.

Bakul regarded him with a wordless stare. A strand of her hair was in her eyes, it tickled, but she did not remove it. A fly buzzed about her face. The man flicked it away.

"Nirmal Babu," Mukunda said.

Nirmal had not seen his daughter for five years – since she was six – and then it had been for a few weeks, and he had not known what to say or do. He had carried that image with him on his postings and travels, of Bakul at six, following him around, not amused by anything he had to say to her, but near him, and watchful all the time. Confronted then with her childish roundness of limb and her silences, he had been as nonplussed as he felt now. Now he saw she had become a girl, a thin, long-limbed girl in a frock that slid off her shoulders, with a nose that had a little bump at its tip, a head full of straggly curls, a solemn mouth, and thick, straight eyebrows that now frowned, focusing her strange-coloured bright eyes at him. He had remembered what colour her eyes were: Shanti's colour. He had carried that colour inside him on his travels and now he drew something out of his pocket and, holding Bakul's hand, placed a small object in it. She looked down at it. It was a stone.

"It's a rare colour of quartz," Nirmal said. "I remembered your eyes when I found it so I had it cut and polished for you."

Bakul closed her fist over it.

"Did you get me the weapon?" Mukunda said. "You said you'd get me a Stone Age weapon!"

"I think I have something for you," Nirmal said with a smile. "But it may not be a prehistoric weapon. Call someone to help with my trunks, and then we'll see what there is."

"Alright, Nirmal Babu," Bakul heard Mukunda shouting. And then, "How long will you be here?"

"Forever," Nirmal said. "This time I have come back for good."

Bakul turned away from their fading voices and looked at the shiny stone in her hand. It was a colour between brown and cream, and its chiselled sides reflected the afternoon sun. In places it was translucent enough to show its depths, which seemed to be made of shards of the same brown. If you held the stone up at the sun and looked into it, there was a city of tall buildings inside, glinting, living a secret stone life.

It made a small, distant splash as Bakul held her hand high above her head and flung it into the well.

* * *

More than most children, Bakul had reason to believe she was a foundling, motherless, effectively fatherless. It was part of family lore that her father had disappeared after her birth and been given up for dead. He had returned briefly after seven months and sixteen days, then gone again, this time for a new job, and ever since, he had only returned for short holidays. Every month, from a money-order he sent home, they knew where his latest archaeological wanderings had taken him, but that was all.

Nirmal had introduced two new people to the house: Meera, a distant relative who was a widow in need of a home, and Mukunda, who, until he was six, had lived in an orphanage unaware of Nirmal's existence. Kamal's favourite joke was that having provided Bakul with a mother who was not a mother and a brother who was not a brother, Nirmal had thought his duty done and made good his escape.

Bakul clung to herself, her solitude seeming to her both romantic and inescapable. Yet she was not altogether solitary. She had Mukunda. And she had her grandmother. From babyhood Bakul had known that though other people came and went, her grandmother was there, always in the same place, alone in a little room carved out of a verandah, which she did not leave except to bathe. Bakul had never known her grandfather, never known how, by dying, he had changed her grandmother even more than he had by living. To her, Kananbala had been this way forever – her collarbones jutting out at her neck, her eyes invisible behind her glasses, a network of veins snaking green under skin as thin as that on milk, her borderless white saris catching the light from the window.

Her grandmother had not fulfilled the conventional grandmotherly duties – like telling her folktales or teaching her rhymes. Instead, Bakul had picked up a rich store of curses from her, words which she still rolled round her mouth, though she no longer blurted them out innocently at school. When Bakul was little, her grandmother's knee had still been strong enough for her. Seated there, the lisping toddler traded curses with the old woman and giggled with delight. If Kananbala called her a pat of cowshit, Bakul would call her an old donkey; if Kananbala replied with, "And you're an ugly owl," Bakul, suddenly unsure it was a game, would suspect she was being laughed at and shout, "You too!" And so it would go, until Manjula heard them and swept Bakul out of the room wailing in protest.

When Bakul came to her room, Kananbala would reach out for one of four dented tins in which she kept things Mrs Barnum sent her every month: bull's eyes, nougat, biscuits, even chocolate. Although the two women had met just once, each month the household knew Mrs Barnum's shopping trip to Finlays had taken place when a brown paper packet, borne by Mrs Barnum's khansama, arrived filled with exotic goodies. Behind the first row of tins on Kananbala's shelf were others that had come from across the road – Milkmaid condensed milk, Hartley's marmalade with orange rind suspended as if in limbo – containers Kananbala never dared open.

Bakul had her own tin too, which she kept under a layer of old saris in her grandmother's trunk. She opened it on days she needed reassurance, and the afternoon Nirmal returned was one such. The box had some oddments Bakul had to push aside to reach underneath. There was a large, frayed envelope in it, from which she took out a picture.

It showed a house. Her mother's house. The picture had been taken from across the river, or from a boat mid-stream, Bakul thought, because between her and the house in the picture there was a stretch of river water. The house looked like the ones she had read of in stories: there were tall pillars, a deep verandah, long windows, columns of trees at its sides.

Bakul's black-rimmed forefinger, the nail bitten into a ragged edge, traced a way to the upper floor. When she was younger and able to believe fairy tales, Kananbala had told her it was a magic picture, even convinced Bakul that her mother *actually* lived in the picture and could see them, could hear everything they said; only Bakul could not see her or hear her voice.

"There," Kananbala had told her, "behind that bakul tree – the tree after which you are named – can you see a window, my little grasshopper?"

The window was not visible in the picture, but Kananbala made her believe it was there.

"Your mother's there in the room behind that window you can't see. But *she* can see *you*."

It was out of that window, Bakul knew now, that her mother had looked all those last weeks as the water rose, higher and higher, until there was no escape. She longed to push aside the tree, open the window, and enter the picture, enter that room. It would have a large bed on which her mother lay and she would lie in the bed nestling against her mother and listening to her breathe.

"Your mother had curly hair," Kananbala had told her, lifting a strand of Bakul's hair. "Just like yours. Her hair was untidy too. Do you know what her teachers called her in her school?"

"What?"

"Pagli, that's what the teachers called your mother," Kananbala had said, "and that's what they'll call you if you go around looking as wild as you do."

Her mother had curly hair which spread out in a black cloud on the pillow. She smelt of Jabakusum hair oil and Pears soap and paan with scented tobacco. And her voice? What did she sound like? She would hear her telling her things, stories, things her father never did, even when he was in Songarh. Bakul had tried when she was younger, asking Nirmal about her mother and about Manoharpur, but he had always changed the subject or become more remote than usual.

It was something Mrs Barnum said to her that had in the end explained her mother's absence to Bakul, and reassured her that it was only a matter of time before she and her mother were reunited. At Mrs Barnum's, on the wall above the fireplace in the drawing room, were two clocks. The clocks showed two different times. Mrs Barnum had explained that time was different in different places in the world. Her clocks told her what time it was in Britain, and what time it was in Songarh. She liked to know what the English were up to, she said, through the day – when she was eating lunch they were stumbling out of bed, when she was at her dinner they had barely begun their tea. "Our past is their future," she liked to say. To Bakul this meant only one thing: that in Manoharpur it was still time past, in which her mother lived waiting, waiting for it to become the future in which Bakul would come to her.

* * *

"You don't dress the same way any more. What happened?" Nirmal asked his brother. All his adult life Nirmal had seen Kamal in trousers held up by braces, shirts with ties that matched.

Kamal looked down at his white kurta and dhoti. He chuckled and said, "Gandhi and all that, you know. What with so much nationalism in the air, I thought that as a manufacturer of traditional remedies I'd better look the part." But he had drawn the line at rough, handspun khadi. His kurtas and dhotis were the finest mulmul in summer and tussar in winter – both traditionally woven too, he reasoned. Today his dhoti had a narrow wine-red border and a matching burst of red poked out from the pocket of his kurta, which rose in a hillock over his stomach and then subsided. He would leave for the factory in a little while, he thought – it was almost eleven but, as on every other day, he did not feel up to going. It bored him, all those pills and potions in poor-looking packaging.

"And your suits?" Nirmal said. "Did you throw them into a patriotic bonfire?"

"Oh no," Kamal said, widening his dead-fish eyes. "Are you crazy?

They're expensive suits, I might need them again. All this swadeshi high talk will evaporate soon – and then? I can't afford to look like you."

Nirmal looked at his own bush shirt and loose trousers in puzzlement.

"For that matter, I don't think *you* can afford to look like you any more either. Your attire certainly doesn't go with your new position."

"I still have to spend my time supervising in the trenches," Nirmal said. "I could hardly go down on my knees in the dust wearing a pinstriped suit."

"Strange," Kamal said after a pause. "If the Archaeological Survey was going to look for lost civilisations in Songarh, why wait so long? After all, the ruin's been around for some centuries, hasn't it? There's a war in Europe and the way Hitler's going we'll all soon be part of your lost civilisations!"

"Well, it's only been budgeted now because I wrote a proposal to dig, and it was accepted."

"Proposal accepted, eh?" Kamal said, "And by the British Burra Sahibs no less, I suppose! So why didn't you write the proposal earlier then? At least you could have lived here and looked after your daughter instead of spending half your life gadding about the wilds of India."

Kamal got up, satisfied with his barb, and walked away from the table before Nirmal could think of a reply, a reply both for himself and for Kamal, a reply perhaps for Bakul too.

In his ten years in the Survey, which he had joined after resigning from his college job, he had avoided Songarh. Instead, imitating his disappearance immediately after Shanti's death, he had volunteered for longer-than-required postings in Rajasthan, in Madhya Pradesh, in Punjab, scrabbling the earth for past lives. Whatever leave he got from work he spent wandering around the Himalaya, walking and on mule back, in flowering meadows, in dense forests and on bare, icy slopes, collecting leaves, stones, fossils and bird feathers. He had two trunks full of things he had collected, carefully catalogued. The trunks travelled with him and stood in his tent even when he went on his digs.

Something, however, had led him the year before to put forward that proposal about Songarh, arguing that the visible remains of the fort and the mounds behind hid perhaps an entire ancient township, and that the Archaeological Survey needed to set up at least a camp office to investigate. Nirmal had known the danger: if the proposal was accepted, he would be posted to Songarh. He would have to go home.

The proposal had been described as "brilliant" and "persuasive". Nirmal should have been delighted, but he felt only a sense of inevitability. He had for long years wanted to dig in the earth around the ruined fort of Songarh to find his lost city, but it was not professional ardour that finally had made him write the proposal. It was something unconnected with archaeology, some powerful impulse untranslatable into words. Could he say that on one of his trips to Rajasthan, among the craggy ancient rocks of the Aravalli range where the ochre landscape flamed into the green-yellow of mustard fields against which shocks of magenta bougainvillea cascaded like bloodspills, he had at last felt free of Shanti? Could he admit to himself the sense of wholeness that, uncalled, slid into him then? At last the restfulness – of the first broken ramparts of Rajput forts, the smiling camels, the hapless cries of the peacock in the failing light – of looking and listening without wanting to gouge his heart out and fling it away.

He had submitted the proposal in the weeks after that. He had felt he was ready to face his home, and his daughter.

* * *

Nirmal walked to the fort for a private site survey of his own. He had already asked for two or three workers from the Public Works Department to help with the dig. He would have two junior archaeologists too, both historians who had never been on a dig before. Not much, but a start, Nirmal thought as he walked. He would have to start requisitioning equipment soon, whatever he could get within his budget.

The first glimpse of the fort's low, broken-down walls and the hillocks beyond it quickened his steps as always. Posted to Bikaner and Sindh, he had not seen it the past six years. Now, once more, excitement surged through him at the thought that he was about to live out a fantasy. For years in his youth he had dreamed of this; now he would find out if the hillocks hid cities and cultures, if the dry stream-bed was the leftover of some ancient river that had changed course, forcing the people on its banks to abandon their settlement.

He walked rapidly around, then, trying to calm himself, sat by the shallow pool and lit a cigarette. It didn't seem that long, Nirmal thought, inhaling, since he had sat at that pool with Shanti, looking out at the dimming light, the broken lines of the ruin slowly erased by dusk. Yet the edges of the memories he had of that time were blurring, little details he had thought indelible had tipped over the edge into oblivion.

Annoyed at letting his thoughts stray from the work in hand, Nirmal took out a pencil and began to scribble into a notebook he had brought with him. He listed equipment, material, manpower required, he listed books and articles he needed to look up. After a while, accepting him as part of the landscape, plump grey pigeons pecked the ground around him. He saw flashes of green as parakeets swooped and chattered overhead, squabbling for food.

But now he felt distracted by an odd sound nearby, something between a squeal and a whine. He looked up, startled.

There was a woman's voice now, saying, "That's all, leave me alone."

There was a silence, then the woman exclaimed again, "I said that's enough, will you stop?"

Nirmal got up, brushing his trousers. Could there be someone in trouble? The voice had come from inside a domed room in the ruin, one of the few structures left with its ceiling unbroken. He walked into its darkness, strong with the smell of pigeon droppings and dust. For a moment inside, he could not see anything in the sudden blackness. He could hear a woman's voice in the shadows of the dome, amplified by its emptiness.

"Nirmal Babu," the voice said, "please don't come any closer."

"Meera?" Nirmal said. "Is that you?" His eyes got used to the lack of light and he saw that it was indeed Meera. He felt aggrieved at being told to stay away and said, "I wasn't going to ... come any closer. I only heard something and thought there may be someone in trouble. I should leave you alone." He turned to go back to the pool.

"Oh no, that's not what I meant," she exclaimed, following him with a laugh. "Please don't misunderstand ... It's just this ... "

Limping behind her was an emaciated dog, brown and black, fur eaten away in patches, swollen dugs hanging to the ground. It pushed its eager muzzle into Meera's hand, whining.

Meera still had the fragment of a roti in her hand. She dropped it to the ground for the dog and said, "She's had her puppies inside there and she can be quite ferocious about them. That's why I had to ask you to stay away."

Nirmal looked at the dog, wondering what Meera saw in it. It looked mangy and had a strong, unpleasant smell. Politeness made him enquire: "And do you come to feed her every day?"

"Almost ... but sometimes it's difficult to get away. I feel bothered the days I can't come." She stopped and gave a sheepish smile. "It's silly, I know. They'd survive with or without me."

"And you walk all that way to feed this dog? You must like dogs very much."

"Not just to feed the dogs," Meera said, "I like to walk – otherwise I feel cooped up – and also I sometimes sit here and draw. It's a break from housework."

Nirmal noticed a cloth bag hanging from her shoulders and was curious. "What have you been drawing?" he asked her. "Would you show me?"

"Oh no," Meera said. "There's nothing much. Just some sketches." She clutched the bag closer and laughed self-consciously. "Lots of schoolgirls draw like me. It's only for amusement." Then she said, to change the subject, "Were you here to survey the site? I suppose it's a site now, isn't it, not just the old Songarh ruin?"

"Well, not quite survey ... " Nirmal began to explain. Twenty minutes later he realised they were sitting under the banyan tree, and he was still talking: about how he had wandered over the ruins as a boy; how he had found some shiny piece of metal there once and thought it an ancient weapon; how he had tried digging there with a garden khurpi after reading of Marshall and Mohenjodaro; how he had applied for a job to the Archaeological Survey, never thinking they would give him one. He stopped, embarrassed by his garrulity, and said, "I'm not used to talking. Either I can think of nothing to say or I talk non-stop. Really uncouth."

"No, no," she protested, "I'd have stopped you if I was bored. I'm not. But it's late. I do have to go. It's time for Bakul to come home from school. I'll leave you to your work, I've disturbed you enough."

Before he could protest or offer to accompany her, she had got up and started on her way back. "I did bore her," he thought. "She couldn't wait to get away."

His eyes followed her as she walked away swiftly. He wondered if that was the first real conversation he had had with her. He sat down again by the pool and tried to return to his notes, but despite himself his thoughts returned to Meera. She had been taking care of Bakul for the past six – or was it seven? – years, but he hardly knew her. He knew she had been widowed young – even now she was probably no older than twenty-five or -six. A mutual relative by marriage had told Nirmal about her. He had then written to Meera, asking if she would live at Dulganj Road and look after Bakul. He recalled the brief postcard that came in reply, written in a hand that made the letters look like brushstrokes. Now when he thought back to that handwriting, he thought it logical that Meera should like to draw. Her handwriting was a set of beautiful lines you could look at and admire even if you didn't understand the meaning. But he had understood the meaning, and what her letter had said, beyond its words, was that she would gladly come to Songarh, to look after a house and a child in exchange for a home.

* * *

113

It was a year after her husband's death that a letter had arrived from Nirmal asking if Meera would live in Songarh, as part of their family, and look after Bakul. His wife had died in childbirth, he wrote, and his work took him away from home for long stretches. The woman who had looked after Bakul for the past four years was too old now, and besides, Bakul needed someone who could give her more than basic care – she would soon need help with homework, someone to talk to, confide in. Meera noticed he did not write that the child needed someone to give her affection, though that was surely what his letter was ultimately saying.

Meera's own mother, a widow herself who was dependent on her son, had urged Meera to accept Nirmal's offer: "The girl will be like a daughter to you. You will never have children of your own, make this motherless one your child! Maybe this is what God meant for you all along."

Meera did not want a child. She wanted escape from her husband's parents, to whom the mere fact that their son was dead and she was alive was an outrage. It had not taken Meera long to decide; she had packed a small trunk and taken the two trains to Songarh within the fortnight.

It was now eight years since her husband's death. She knew she was supposed to mourn him for ever, but he was already slipping her guilty grasp. She recalled him only piecemeal – the way his stomach – he had a gentle paunch at twenty-three – sloped into his trousers. Or the way he couldn't eat without crunching through a pile of green chillies alongside. But his voice – she could no longer hear it in her ears as she did before, if ever she put her mind to it. How had it felt when he touched her? How did he smell when he woke up from sleep and curled up again next to her? Her store of memories, rummaged through too often, had staled now, lost their incantatory power to bring his presence back.

In the early days at Dulganj Road, she had begun to feel that Nirmal, who was not *really* related to her except by marriage, was a kindred soul. Nirmal did not speak very much to anyone, yet they always seemed to have things to say to each other when they met by chance on the stairs or in the garden. But who had heard of widows marrying again? Who had heard of a widow marrying a relative? She had overheard people commending Nirmal's compassion in taking her in.

And then, to put an end to her thoughts, Nirmal had left Songarh on his new posting, as if never to return.

Over the years Meera's attacks of discontent and anger had dwindled until she felt herself ensconced in a comfortable if rather dull routine. But in the past week, since Nirmal's return, she had felt a return of the turmoil, sensed a tiny flame flicker somewhere inside her, a flame she knew would scorch everything in its vicinity if not stamped out.

Meera stretched to get rid of the tingling that was starting between her shoulders. Bustling to the garden, she spotted Bakul swinging her ankles from the second branch of the mango tree.

"Why do you have to be told every day it's time for your tuition? Don't you know Chaubey Sir has been waiting?" she said, more harshly than she intended, when Bakul pretended not to notice her. She could not understand the anger that was rising in her, hot and heavy in her shoulders and neck. She looked at Bakul, exasperated. Meera had tried and tried to be friends with her, but there was a hard, recalcitrant centre in the child which made it difficult for other people to approach. Far from confiding in Meera, Bakul hardly spoke to her unless necessary.

Now she stayed on her perch in the mango tree just long enough to make it clear that she was not coming down because she had been snapped at, but because she had chosen to.

* * *

Bakul disliked tuitions, disliked the way Chaubey Sir's thick moustache dipped into his tea, the way biscuit crumbs clung to it, the way he droned, "If you don't memorise your tables you'll never be able to finish your Maths paper." The moment her tutor let her go, she scraped her chair back, jammed her feet into her slippers and ran across the road to Mrs Barnum's: she knew Mukunda had already gulped his lemon sherbet and read picture books while she was at work on multiplication and mixed metaphors. Besides, it was Mrs Barnum's birthday again, and if she was late, she would not get any of the cake.

"You're early," Mrs Barnum said as soon as she saw Bakul. "It isn't until five." She shook the brass bell in her hand imperiously and said, "Since you're here, make yourself useful, girl – run down to the kitchen and get the sandwiches."

The room they were in was a large one with mullioned windows that looked out on to the garden and beyond it to Bakul's house across the road. The windows had green curtains, always firmly drawn, and this gave the room the sense of being an over-decorated, dim aquarium. On one side was a fireplace, with a few chairs around it. Over the fireplace a mantelpiece, at the centre of which stood a glass globe tilting on its tarnished gold stand, continents and oceans and mountain ranges rippling on its surface. Beside it were two other smaller balls of glass, one enclosing a tiny Leaning Tower of Pisa, the other a little cottage with a red roof. If you shook these glass balls, frail, minute snowflakes floated down, clouding the tiny buildings in their private storms.

Over the mantelpiece, on the grey-white wall, gleamed the curved blade of an ornamental golden kukri. Bakul and Mukunda had been fascinated by it. Soon after they had begun coming to Mrs Barnum's to play, the khansama had told them in his sandpapered voice, "This was the kukri with which Sahib was killed. His ghost wanders Dulganj still, seeking justice. The earth where his blood was spilled never dries, not in the hottest summer. I will show you one day."

On the other side of the room was a round wooden table with six chairs. The table had lost one of its legs to termite and had a lighter-coloured replacement which had shrunk after being fixed on, so the table tilted to one side. Bakul saw it was already set with napkins and silver for six people, and a cake on a tiered cake-plate about six times too big for it occupied its centre. Ranged around the cake were empty plates with patterns of roses and vines.

Mrs Barnum rang her bell again and Mukunda entered from a dark alcove at the end of the room. "Happy birthday, Mrs Barnum," he sang.

The khansama, who was waiting just outside the room, came in clearing his throat and said, "Happy birthday, Madam."

"Happy Birthday, Mrs Barnum," Bakul repeated after him, "and many happy returns of the day."

"Thank you, m'dear, thank you," Mrs Barnum said as she rose, smoothing out her buttery frock. "So sweet of you to remember! So sweet of all of you to come!"

The khansama advanced towards the cake, which had a single tall candle stuck on it, like a pine tree on a cowpat.

"Shall I light it, Madam?"

Mrs Barnum seemed querulous. "Why aren't the others on time? Can't make people wait, can we?" She sat down and flapped a hand at Bakul. "Sit down, sit down! Don't make people wait!"

Bakul and Mukunda knew the routine, and sat down. Mrs Barnum liked celebrating her birthday every month, on an unpredictable day. All the plates, regardless of guests, were served cake and slightly dry, boiled-egg sandwiches. There was lemon sherbet in wine glasses, sweet and murky. The first few weeks, Bakul and Mukunda had been hesitant, looking at each other for guidance, not knowing what to do with napkins in rings, forks and knives. Now they waited each month for the day they would get cake and sandwiches to eat, things never given to them at home. Mrs Barnum looked around the table, smiled graciously at the empty chairs and at Bakul, and said, "How nice of all of you to remember. I can't think of a better birthday!" She adjusted her emeralds, patted her hair, and nibbled the corner of a sandwich.

When they had finished eating, the khansama had to go round the table saying "May I?" before removing their plates. Once the table was clear, Mrs Barnum moved the cake candle to the centre of the table while Mukunda went to the shelves in the shadowed alcove and pulled out a board with numbers and letters, and a heavy silver coin dating from Mughal times. A bumpy coin with uneven edges, a coin that felt like money. Mrs Barnum arranged the board and paused as if embarking on something important. She looked around at Bakul and Mukunda's candlelit faces.

"Silence now, and think!"

Bakul shut her eyes tight, frowning with the effort of thinking only about the board and its numbers. Mrs Barnum's head was bent over steepled fingers. Mukunda could hear her breathing. He stole a look at Bakul, then guiltily he shut his eyes. After a while he heard a scraping and shifting and looked. The coin was moving across the table from number to letter, number to letter. Mrs Barnum followed each movement and muttered under her breath, "No, you can't say that! That is not what happened. Really? Is that so? I'll go there tomorrow. Rat poison? Rat poison? Could be. Stars falling down, on the field, falling down. It's time for the train, Tuesday's the day, take the train on Tuesday."

As Mrs Barnum muttered and the movements of the coin grew more frantic, her eyes darted from place to place on the board, strands of hair coming loose from her net. The candle cast tall shadows. Bakul did not like to say she was scared, but she always looked away during this part. What if the spirit decided not to leave the room? Sometimes Mrs Barnum stayed in her trances for half an hour or more. And if they were late, Bakul had observed the last few months, Manjula scolded them and muttered right through dinner that it was time Bakul's freedom was curbed and she was taught to be a young lady. She thought it was best to leave, all things considered.

She tugged Mukunda's wrist under the table. They got up and crept out. Once out of earshot, Bakul said, "I know you don't like it, so I made you leave. You looked scared."

"Me?" Mukunda retorted. "Me scared? Hah! You're the coward!"

Some time after they had left, Larissa Barnum pulled off her silk frock and sat at her dressing table in her old lace-edged satin slip. She began to remove her hairpins, regarding her reflection with a quizzical air. A long face, with sharp, narrowed, hazel eyes divided by a prominent bony nose, and thick, arched, greying eyebrows. The skin on her thin neck looked a little as if someone was pulling it down into her collar. She fingered her neck, pinching up loose skin, then pulled her hair out from its net and squinted in the mirror at the grey strands at her temples. She removed the emeralds from her ears and played with them as if she would not have them for long. Her household had for a while been financed by the jewellery she got the khansama to pawn for her.

The house felt larger and emptier in the late evenings, when the khansama retired to his quarters. Mrs Barnum wrapped a dressing gown over her satin slip, went to her chest of drawers, and took out a crystal tumbler, chipped at the bottom. She half filled it with whisky from a squat-looking bottle and then went to the living room to sit at the piano. She thought she would play something with big, crashing notes, crowd the house with noise, imagined people, a party. She began flipping through her music books.

Leaning on the parapet of the roof, Nirmal tore open his third packet of cigarettes. He listened to Mrs Barnum's piano crossing the road with its clamorous dissonances, and in a tentative, reluctant, uncertain way, he began to feel as if he had come home.

* * *

Bakul moved a piece of fish from side to side on her plate as if that would make it disappear. Mukunda, who was always hungry nowadays, wondered if he could have some more rice.

"The boy will eat us out of house and home!" Manjula exclaimed.

It was a Sunday some weeks after Nirmal's return to Songarh. Nirmal sat opposite his brother, lingering after lunch, amused by Bakul's surreptitious efforts to hide her fish under a spinach leaf on her plate.

"So, Nirmal," Kamal said, with a chuckle. "Quite a comfortable job you've got yourself. You don't have to do anything but stroll down to that office! I wish I had such an easy time. The factory is full of problems. Cheaper versions of our things all over, made with artificial stuff, but who cares? Then this war cutting government budgets and to top it all we're asked to fight the British . . . and if that weren't enough, Salim is now too ill to work." He drank in a loud gulp of water and put the glass down with a thud.

"We're starting the dig in a few weeks," Nirmal said. "Not all work is visible, there is a lot of material to be bought, a lot of organising to do." Things were going slower than he wanted – too slow, he knew. They did not treat his requests with enough urgency at headquarters; everyone was preoccupied with the war in Europe – he was in a small town, and perhaps nobody else set much store by his dig. Besides, every item he requested had, it seemed, to be cleared by five different desks.

"Oh come, don't take me seriously, Nirmal, why are you getting annoyed?" Kamal said in a soothing voice. "So is the end of our local tourist attraction imminent? No more ruined castle?"

"You're digging up the ruins?" Bakul said to her father, accusing. "How can you do something like that?"

"Don't talk about things you know nothing of, Bakul," Nirmal said, sharp-voiced, impatient. "And don't butt into grown-up conversations. I've noticed this tendency in you."

"I'm not butting in, I'm just asking," she mumbled.

"I'll explain later," Nirmal said. "Just eat up now."

Bakul pushed her plate aside and scraped back her chair, then stopped as she saw Meera's frown and gesture. She waited for her uncle to get up first, drawing circles on her plate.

"Don't play with your food, Bakul," Manjula said. "Crocodiles that play with prey soon get eaten themselves, don't you know?"

"Don't you know?" Kamal said, imitating Manjula's tone as she looked at him angrily, "Don't you know, Bakul, your father is here to dig up that ruin and see if there's another ruin underneath. The things the government will spend money on when so many people have nothing to eat in this country!"

"We're not digging up the ruin," Nirmal sounded weary. He had had to explain this to countless people. "It's not done like that."

"Then how *is* it done?" said Kamal, plaintive. "If you want to see if something is under something else, don't you have to dig up the first thing? I may not be an *archaeologist* in His Imperial Majesty's A.S.I., but I'm not so stupid, am I? And what do you hope to find anyway?"

"There could be a much more ancient civilisation we don't know of. The lower hillocks in front of the ridge may be mounds hiding ancient cities, who knows?"

"And who needs to know?"

"If archaeologists had not dug anywhere, we'd have had no idea of India's antiquity," Nirmal said, pompously he realised.

"Beheeyoo," Manjula burped deeply, and then she sighed. "Will you people finish so that Meera and I can eat?"

Nirmal pushed his chair back and started to get up. He looked at Meera who was sitting there, ladle in hand, waiting to serve more food if someone asked. She was thin, he noticed for the first time, her collarbones jutting out, her eyes too large and dark-circled in a small face. She looked fragile next to Manjula's stout self-assurance. The widow's diet, he thought, all fasts and hardly any proteins. When would things ever change?

* * *

Nirmal unpacked his collection trunks that same day, after lunch. He was impressed, as he put his things away in rows, by his own tidiness. His shelves used to look so different when he was younger. He had only to open his cupboard in those days for a jumble of clothes and books and digging implements to tumble out pell-mell. But his profession and his travels had made Nirmal methodical. His father had always thought him a scamp beyond reform, even after he was a married man. What would he have thought to see him now?

Nirmal paused and sat down with a cigarette. He thought of the work that lay ahead: he had never been in charge of a dig before. He remembered the times he had spent in the ruins, first as a boy, then as a young man, stealing a smoke, walking all over the crumbling walls pretending to be an ancient king, then scraping in the dust, imagining that he could see the glint of an ancient coin. Once, he had found a curved piece of metal that looked like a weapon. Possibly bronze. It was only after he had excitedly brought it home and washed it that he realised it was ordinary tin, a part of a can. Yet he had kept it for years.

He got up, stubbing out his cigarette. The trunk had rocks and fossils, bits of flint and potsherds, things he had collected during his digs. He unwrapped them from their cotton wool and placed them on the windowsill where he could see them. Something struck him, interrupting his orderly movements. He thrust his head into the stairwell that descended from the roof to the first floor and called out, "Bakul? Are you there?"

After a minute, annoyed now, he called again, louder, "Bakul!"

He saw his daughter's upturned face emerge at the foot of the stairwell.

"What?" she said.

"Come up here," he said.

"Why?"

"Don't ask so many questions, Bakul."

"Why not?" she said, but he could see she was coming up the stairs.

"I need some help unpacking," Nirmal said to her as she emerged onto the roof.

"I have to finish my homework. Chaubey Sir will come soon."

"It won't take long, Bakul, we'll just put some things into the cupboard in the landing. I'll have to make a dozen trips down the stairs if I don't get help."

"Can't you wait for Shibu?"

"Can't you be less sulky for a change? Why can't I get a straight answer out of you?"

Immediately, he tried to placate her. "Look," he said, "I know . . ."

But Bakul had rushed down the stairs again. Nirmal felt heat surge through his face, his forehead began to hurt. He followed her to the stairs. Must be firm. He called out to her again, heard a barked "Bakul, come *here*." Bakul came back up the stairs, frowning at her own hand on the banister.

"When I ask you to do something, you are not to rush away. It's time you started to behave yourself. Is that clear?"

Bakul was said nothing.

"What did I say?" Nirmal demanded, "Can't you hear me?"

"Alright, *alright*, tell me what to do, I have to go."

Nirmal had lost interest in unpacking his trunk and showing Bakul the things in it. It's all a mistake, he began to think: he had imagined he would be a different father, different from the father he had himself had. He would not be stern and distant and fearsome, he would instead do interesting things with Bakul, they would be friends, especially as she didn't have a mother to be friends with. Had he left it too late?

Bakul looked resentfully at the red tin trunk, its paint more chipped than before. She had seen it many times. It came and went with Nirmal on each of his trips. She was still filled with rage by Nirmal's ticking off at lunch. How dare he, how dare he do that to me in front of everyone else, and all of them sniggering at me, how dare he! She wanted to spit on the trunk. She would not speak, she had decided, she would not speak to anyone.

"Do you know, Bakul," Nirmal persisted, kneeling by the trunk to open it, "we would go to such faraway places on our digs. The dust, the heat, the tents flapping in the wind. And then some days eating just roti and onions and a little daal. That's how I got sunstroke once. But it's all worth it, when you find a small piece of pottery, even a broken bit. One day I'll take you on a dig, the one here."

He was waiting to be interrupted by eager questions. Bakul continued to pile up the books that emerged from the trunk, stopping only to scratch a scab on her knee now and then. She would not meet his eye. It made Nirmal want to scoop up his daughter and hold her close. Instead, seeing her lift a worn-out, hardbound volume from the trunk, he said, "That's not just an exercise book, you know. Open it."

Bakul looked at him with studied boredom.

"Here, let me show you. I have seven of these."

He opened one and began to turn the pages. Each turn of the page revealed the fragile shape of a dry leaf. On some pages you could still just about discern the colour of the leaf when fresh and alive on a Himalayan tree. Even in their desiccation, some had flecks of red, some were pale ochre spotted with black, in some the veins stood out like skeletons, the body bleached of all colour. On every page Nirmal had recorded the species and the place where he had found the leaf. There was chestnut and oak first, then treasures harder won: the remains of a blue poppy, bits of birch bark, a leaf from the Brahma Kamal, all from the high Himalaya. His notes seemed a superfluity: he recalled to the last detail where he had plucked each leaf and pressed it, the colour of the light that day, how icy the wind had been, how lonely the steep slope.

Nirmal turned the pages, forgetting Bakul. Sometimes his forefinger touched one of the dried leaves with infinite gentleness. He stroked one that was still somewhat red and green and smiled to himself. He did not notice her leaving the room.

* * *

That evening, Nirmal sat in his newly settled rooftop room and began to look through his music. He had not touched his box of records since Shanti's death. He did not know if the record player still worked: it had wheezed and scraped even then as they lay on their bed listening to the sarangi, watching the luminous night sky sliced up by the window grill. Now that he had opened the box of records again, he thought he would look at the record player next, and maybe get a new needle for it, clean it and oil it, then try winding it up again. He used to be good at that kind of work.

Nirmal poured himself a drink, and with his cigarette smoke curling towards the open door of the verandah, rummaged through his old records, discovering treasures he had forgotten. He settled into a chair with four of them, to read the sleeve notes.

Time passed. Dinner was being laid and Nirmal had not come downstairs.

Mukunda was despatched to call him. He went to the roof, peeped into Nirmal's room and then ran down the stairs to the ground floor where Manjula was sitting behind the dekchis, looking for the ladles. The room smelled of roasted moong and ghee, bayleaf and fried fish. Manjula felt hungry just being there and hoped the men would eat quickly so that she could start. Steathily, she popped a piece of potato into her mouth.

Mukunda announced, "Nirmal Babu will eat later. He is drinking."

"What?" Manjula gasped. "Drinking? Hari, Hari! In the house?"

Dropping her ladle with a clatter, she pushed back her chair, gathered her sari and lumbered up the stairs. Meera followed, pleading, "Didi, Didi, let it be, he can eat later, I will heat it up . . . "

"Quiet!" Manjula hissed. She had reached the room on the roof and she strode to the door and swung it open. She wanted to see for herself.

Nirmal, she saw, was not just drinking. He was smoking too. The incriminating bottle of rum stood on the table with no attempt at concealment. The room smelled to her like a house of vice. She had only imagined what such places were like.

"My god!" Manjula yelped, shutting her eyes in alarm. Then she took another determined breath and tucked her sari firmly around her. "Nirmal," she called out, opening the door again, but not stepping into the room. Nirmal had stubbed out the cigarette and was standing up, taken aback by the invasion.

"Don't you remember there are children in the house? Growing children! How can you bring yourself to do something like this?"

Meera flapped about behind Manjula saying, "Please calm down, let's go downstairs."

Mukunda had followed them to the terrace. He took a quick look into the room again on the pretext of announcing, "Kamal Babu is waiting for dinner."

"Run down and start the rice," Manjula ordered him. "We're coming."

Turning to go, she sent a parting shot in Nirmal's direction. "What would your father have said, Nirmal? This is a decent house. If you must do . . . all this . . . do it somewhere else!" She gathered her sari again and flounced away, throwing one last righteous glance in the direction of the rum bottle.

Nirmal leaned on the parapet looking out, his shoulders hunched with annoyance. It was an unusually clear night, stars piercing the black shadows of the trees, the moon hanging in the sky, a fat yellow melon.

"Don't mind her," Meera's voice said in the darkness. "She doesn't mean badly."

Nirmal turned and saw her moon-washed face, startled she had not left. He chuckled and then sighed. "We must seem like such junglees to you. How can you bear to live with us?"

For a moment they listened to the foxes beginning their exchanges in the forest.

"Do you like it here? In Songarh, I mean," Nirmal said, to fill the silence.

"Yes," Meera said. "Yes, of course. As long as I can go for walks, I'd like anywhere."

"You came here . . . when? . . . the same year as Mukunda, wasn't it?" Nirmal said. "Yes, it was the same year. I was here in Songarh, waiting – waiting in fact for you to write and let me know if you'd be able to come. I went and brought Mukunda then. I'd been a few weeks at home. I was very restless. And then one day, nothing else to do, I went to the orphanage to see who our family had been supporting so long. I saw him, we liked each other and I came back with him. And you arrived soon after, isn't it?"

"It's a good thing he was taken out of there," Meera said.

"Yes, of course, that is when you arrived," Nirmal said. "You met him before you saw Bakul and you said, 'I thought it was a girl I was to look after.'"

"You remember that?" Meera laughed. "I was really taken aback."

"I left for Rajasthan so relieved," Nirmal said. "It . . ."

Mukunda's voice floated out to them in the darkness, hesitant: "Dinner is getting cold . . . Manjula Didi is very angry, she says she'll put the food away . . ."

* * *

That night as the house slept, Meera awoke. She could not be sure, but she felt that Bakul was not in her bed across the room. Maybe in the bathroom, she told herself, and drifted back to sleep. But woke again the next instant. She got up and stumbled to Bakul's bed to check. Had she fallen off the bed as once she had? The sheet was creased, the pillow flung to one side, the bed empty.

Is she ill? Meera wondered in panic. Why didn't she wake me?

The room was ominous in the darkness. Meera had never liked the house. It had seemed gloomy and full of foreboding from the start. She was reluctant to open the door that shut their bedroom off from the corridor, but she went to it, and pushed it open a crack. Manjula and Kamal had the next room. She did not want to wake them and made herself navigate in the dark.

The corridor outside was eerie, the high ceiling disappearing into the darkness, the floor bathed in the light of the moon. She could not help glancing backwards, tense at every creak. She could hear something from the direction of the stairs and stole towards it. Could it be true the house had a ghost? Don't think of all that, don't be a fool, just find her. She felt her way up the stairs until her eyes got used to the different clarity of moonlight, and she found she was beginning see quite clearly. She walked up a flight of stairs and came to the landing.

The cupboard on the landing was open and Bakul was on her knees at its base. She sat in the centre of a pile of torn paper and fragments of leaves. Savagely, panting, she was tearing up Nirmal's books. When she noticed Meera and looked up, her eyes were glittering, unseeing.

* * *

Before school the next morning, as on every morning, Bakul peeped into Kananbala's room. Her grandmother was babbling in her sleep, drool spilling from the side of her mouth, darkening her pillow. "Take the lion away," she was muttering. "There it is again, so large, its fangs are red . . . with blood, look it's clawing his chest, it'll kill him like this. Is anyone there, is anyone listening to me? Nobody listens to me . . ." Kananbala struggled to open her eyes; she knew she was awake, yet she could not wake up. She could see the sunlight streaming through the window, she was cold and wanted to pull her blanket closer to her chest. She sensed Bakul in the room, but there was the lion to be chased away.

Bakul went up to her and stroked her head. "O Thakuma," she said. "Wake up, you're dreaming."

Kananbala mumbled and groaned and Bakul shook her a little harder.

"Wake up, there's no lion, it's me, Bakul! Get up, I have to go to school soon!"

A little later, Bakul stood behind Kananbala, combing out her white hair. It had thinned in patches, enough to show bits of scalp.

"You're going bald, Thakuma."

"I'm not a young beauty, am I?" Kananbala replied, closing her eyes with pleasure at the comb going over her scalp. How good it felt when . . . the comb went hard over her skull. Kananbala winced and exclaimed, "Unhhh!"

"Did that hurt?"

"What do you think?" Kananbala sounded irritable. "Not so hard!"

"Your mother had such a head of curly hair," she said. "You've inherited it. Poor child. Didn't live to enjoy anything. Never saw you."

Bakul, who had heard this before, felt impatient with her grandmother for repeating things. Sometimes she ticked Kananbala off and said, "Yes, yes, you told me."

"Your father was so different before," Kananbala continued, her eyes still closed, feeling the light touch of Bakul's fingers in her hair and on her shoulders. "Such a light-hearted, playful boy. He never walked, only ever ran. He never spoke without eyes full of laughter. Who would know him now?"

Bakul scowled behind her and made a face.

"I didn't tell anyone then," Kananbala continued. "But I'll tell you one day. I know who killed that man in the house opposite."

"You!" Bakul laughed. "That's what you always say. You don't know anything."

"And then I went on a picnic," Kananbala went on in her nostalgic voice. "You would never know one like it. It was . . . "

Through her semi-somnolent stupor, Kananbala heard someone come into the room and scrabble around somewhere close behind her. She opened her eyes as she felt her bed jerk and wobble. "Oh Bakul," she called out, quavering. "It's an earthquake, help me!" She looked around in alarm, clutching the sides of her shifting bed.

She saw Nirmal's hunched form straightening out from under the bed. He had dragged her trunk out. As she watched in horror, he opened it and began to toss out her saris. He seemed not to notice his mother at all.

"What? Nirmal? What are you . . . "

From beneath Kananbala's saris, Nirmal dug out Bakul's precious box.

"What are you doing, Nirmal?" Kananbala said, frantic. "What're you doing under the bed with my trunk?"

"I'll show you what it means to lose something precious," Nirmal said in clipped accents towards Bakul as he picked her aluminium box out of Kananbala's trunk. "You'll know how to be responsible with other people's things now."

"Don't take that," Bakul screamed and lunged out. "It's my box, don't touch my box."

She dived across the bed to Nirmal and tried to grab the box from him. "Nirmal!" Kananbala exclaimed. "What are you doing, have you lost your mind?"

"Lost my mind, Ma?" he said as he left the room. "Is there anyone in this house still sane?"

* * *

Nirmal's new office was at the edge of Songarh, a small building that, besides him, contained two other officers, a junior assistant, a clerk, and a man who doubled as peon and tea boy. Nirmal's desk was empty but for a small pile of papers on one side, and a few books. The other officers, Sharma and Negi, were chatting by the window. Office politics, Nirmal could tell from the odd snatch that drifted towards him. "Mr Bullock is very partial to Banerji," one of them was saying. "Arre bhai, don't you know Banerji was his student. That's why he gets the good postings, always."

Nirmal took another sip of water, trying to calm the fury that still raged inside him. How many years of collecting had it been? Twelve? Fifteen? When had he started it? That oak he had sat under when walking through the western Himalaya. That maple, the rhododendrons, all of different colours. Most of them were leaves from high altitudes, times when he had left his digs on getaways to walk through the hills, even if the hills were a train- and bus- and then cart-ride away.

Bakul had destroyed it all.

He scraped his chair back. It fell. "I have to go," Nirmal said to the room.

They watched him leaving. "The man is peculiar," Negi said. "Doesn't talk, doesn't like company."

Nirmal strode out. He took out his flat silver cigarette case, one of his brother's rare birthday gifts. He lit a cigarette and breathed out with a deep sigh. The band around his forehead seemed to loosen its grip. He noticed that the verges of the red-earth road were piled here and there with slabs of mica, bright mirrors for the morning sun.

Why had Bakul chosen to destroy the collection he valued so much? She knew what it meant to him, he had told her just the day before! He could not imagine such malevolence in a child of eleven . . . or was it twelve? That morning, when Meera had told him what had happened – what had she said? "Dada, I think Bakul has ruined one or two of your books" – he had felt as if he would explode. One or two of my books!

* * *

Not far away, Mukunda sat at Mrs Barnum's table trying to read. Mrs Barnum had not emerged that afternoon, and he felt the page float away from him again and again. The words were hard and unfamiliar, and the bit he had reached in the Library of Literature Volume One did not interest him. All he could think of was the turmoil in the house that morning. He had seen Nirmal on his knees before his torn books, particles of crumbling, old, dry leaves and bits of paper tossing around him in the light morning breeze. Mukunda dreaded the anger that would certainly stifle the house. Why had Bakul done this?

He slapped the book shut and wandered to the back window overlooking Mrs Barnum's garden, a garden like no other. More a wild forest of tall trees with a large pond at one end, filled with fleshy water lilies. A hidden pond, right at the back of the house, difficult to spot except from one of the upper windows. Today, looking down, Mukunda saw something move in the pond. He ran down the stairs and out into the garden as fast as he could. He was sure Bakul was in it and he knew she could not swim. He was irrationally certain she was trying to drown herself because of the morning's troubles.

He tore off his shirt and as he tried to wade in he realised the water went quite deep, too deep for paddling. He let himself float, sheathed by the sudden silence of the water. Weeds waved around him shadowy, weightless. Something, a fish he thought, brushed past. He could see Bakul struggling a few feet away and struck out towards her. The stalks of the lilies swayed, dark and fat. He reached her and took hold of her hand, trying to force her out of the water. She came out spluttering and spitting, pushing him away.

"What are you doing?" she yelled. "Leave me alone! I was just starting to float!"

She dived back into the water, flailed about, emerged spitting water and retching, "I think I swallowed something."

Bakul's hair was plastered to her skull in strands. She had a water weed over her ear that she flung at Mukunda. Her thin summer frock clung to her new peach-sized breasts. Mukunda stared at them, the darkness of the nipples, the swelling they topped. As if independent of him, his hand reached out to touch them.

"Don't do that," Bakul said, slapping his hand away. "It tickles."

Mukunda gently squeezed her breasts. "It's not soft," he whispered, "I thought it would be."

* * *

When they reached home they tried to slide in unnoticed, knowing their wet clothes would earn them a scolding. But Manjula was waiting outside and so was Meera. "Do you know how late it is?" Manjula asked. "And how disgraceful you both look? Why are your clothes wet? What were you doing?"

"You'll catch a cold, Bakul, go and dry your hair at once," Meera said, wanting to smooth over Manjula's acrid disapproval.

"I fell into the pond," Bakul said, scowling at Meera, "and he had to come in and get me." She slipped past her aunt, who had a swift and stinging slap when she had a mind to use it. Manjula's voice followed her from the garden: "This time I've had enough. I've told Nirmal once and I've told him again, they need some discipline, they're not babies any more, but does anyone listen to me in this house? Do I count for nothing?"

Bitterly she muttered, "God's ways are strange, that He should give children to those who don't care for them and leave me childless."

* * *

In his room on the roof the next day, Nirmal lay in his bed trying to read a translation of a story by Chekhov, "The Steppe", but its vast open spaces and the characters' wanderings under the enormous Russian skies made him feel even more stifled than usual in Songarh. He longed for the desert sky in Rajasthan again, where eyes could not look far enough to reach the horizon. He flung the book aside and got up, wondering what to do.

An office holiday. The two other men in the office loved holidays though their working days were indolent enough. They went home to wives, the demands of children, the muddle of large families. So much seemed to happen in the lives of Negi and Sharma that they revelled in: relatives' visits, weddings in the neighbourhood, trips to the bazaar; even illnesses seemed to be the cause of drama and gossip. By contrast, Nirmal thought, he had been a bystander for years. People thought him aloof, he knew, arrogant perhaps. He was content with that. And yet, sometimes, he yearned for the populous cacophony of other people's lives despite the knowledge that it would certainly make him unhappy.

He walked around the room hunting for his box of matches, an unlit cigarette between his fingers, and his eyes fell on the aluminium box. Bakul's box! It was on the windowsill. He had forgotten all about it.

He picked it up. It rattled. He took the box to his bed and looked at it: dented in one corner, the aluminium surface scratched, its latch askew.

Bakul's box contained many things she had herself forgotten the provenance of. Nirmal picked out, one by one, a pink plastic necklace, some flat, brown seeds he recognized as tamarind, a sad-faced rag doll in a red sari, a small tram car – beneath its windows a smiling girl with starry eyes and yellow hair said "Perkins Nougat" in a speech bubble.

At the bottom of the box he found three envelopes. On one, to his astonishment, he recognised his own handwriting. The postmark said Bikaner. He opened the envelope and saw he had written in large block letters: "Dear Bakul, I am in a place that has animals called camels, and trees called palm." Something like a camel was drawn next to the words, standing under a palm tree.

There was another envelope, and when he shook it three photographs slid out. The smallest one, curled at the edges, showed Shanti's house in Manoharpur. He had not looked at it, or at a picture of it, for twelve years. He had almost forgotten – wanted never to remember – that house. But it all came back, every last detail, the moment he saw the picture. There was the tree next to Shanti's window, the one she had named Bakul after. There was the verandah he and his father-in-law used to sit in to chat over tea, and then those neighbours of Bikash Babu would drop in and begin their interminable conversations about the same things every day: the impending flood; the Scottish engineering firm; the mango and coconut trees; how the neighbour's court case was progressing and whether it had reached the district judge.

Nirmal gazed at the picture for longer than he knew. Then, putting it aside, he turned to the other two. One was of Shanti: the one that had arrived with the marriage proposal. Nirmal paused, smiling at the recalcitrant look on Shanti's face. What was it like, having your picture sent to a stranger for his approval? He wondered if other men, other prospective husbands of Shanti, had seen that picture of her. Did some of them still have it lying around in their homes? Or had their eventual wives thrown it away or torn it up?

The third picture had the two of them staring at their wedding photographer. Nirmal glanced at it and put it aside. That thin, young face, the mop of hair, was that me? He went to the wardrobe mirror and studied the shadowed face that looked back at him. The hair was combed straight back like his father's. There were deep lines on his cheeks, bracketing his nose. His face was still thin, but not thin as in the picture. Gaunt. Old. An old face. At just thirty-seven, he was an old man. And yet, not a patriarch as his father had been, not even an authoritarian like his brother.

His thoughts slid back two days. He had heard a knock on his door and prepared himself for another invasion from Manjula, but it was Meera. He was self-conscious about his dishevelment and did not want to call her into his untidy room with its rumpled bed, although he knew it was she who would have it cleaned later in the day, get the maid to make the bed and pull out filled ashtrays from under chairs and bed. He had stepped out onto the roof, shivering slightly in the early morning chill, and said, "Is anything wrong?"

"I ... "

In the soft light of the morning, her skin seemed luminous. He saw she had already bathed, and her hair loose, wet, had painted a ring of damp over her shoulders. Little specks of water hung diamond-like to it. She usually had a direct gaze, but today she would not look at him.

"Actually I came up to put the clothes out to dry ... "

Nirmal noticed a small iron bucket with wet, wrung-out clothes next to her. He waited, still wondering why she had called him out. " ... and I thought I should tell you ... please don't be angry with her, she's young, and doesn't know ... Bakul, she has damaged some of your books ... "

"Books? Which books?"

"The staircase cupboard, books there, I ... "

Before she could finish what she was saying, he had rushed down the stairwell to the landing. Someone had begun to move the shredded books to one side, making piles of the scraps. Nirmal had knelt on the floor, tossing the scraps this way and that until the small space of the landing was covered with torn paper, in the middle of which he sat, inchoate with rage.

He felt sheepish about it now, about Meera watching him, trying to calm him, trying to salvage whatever little seemed retrievable. That evening when he came home from work he had seen that three of the books, painstakingly stuck back together, had been left on a windowsill in his room. Nobody but Meera would have done it.

What did she think of him? he wondered. A middle-aged man, sentimental about pressed leaves? A stupid man who had tried to punish his daughter by descending to the level of the child? Sticking back those pages must have taken Meera all day. Why had she done it? And Bakul, did she hate him so much that she had lashed out the only way she thought would hurt?

He looked at the photographs in his hand again, and for the first time weighed his own culpability. That little aluminium box contained all of Bakul's memories of her mother, her most precious belongings. What had he done to add to them? Could he possibly make up for his neglect? Nirmal sat alternately smoking, looking at the pictures, and smoking again. Then, all at once, he seemed to reach a decision and got up from the bed.

I must show Shanti's house to Bakul, he thought. That's the only way I can give her some real connection with her mother. I ought to have taken her there long ago. She still has a grandfather; she must meet him.

He felt as if something had loosened inside him, given him space to breathe again. A surge of excitement made him push the box away and go out to the verandah. He would book railway tickets, it would be their first journey together. He would take Mukunda too, open up the boy's world. They would stop in Calcutta on the way, he would show them the Victoria Memorial, he would show Bakul a real tram, not a tin box.

And since he couldn't possibly manage the two children alone, he would take Meera too. He could barely wait to tell her, to see her eyes widen and her face light up.

Charged up by the thought of travel, yearning already for the familiar clacking of a train, Nirmal put his shoes on and went down the stairs. Why spend the entire holiday at home? he thought, and began to walk rapidly towards Finlays, looking for a tonga he might hail on the way.

* * *

Meera was running her fingers through a sari that was draped over a mannequin at Finlays. The mannequin was on a pedestal by the door, two feet taller than Meera, a pasty white with apple-red lips. An orange sari with a gold border rode its buxom body. Meera looked down at her own sari, her usual off-white, this one with a narrow brown border. Some day, she fantasised, I'll again wear sunset orange, green the colour of a young mango, and rich semul red. Maybe just in secret, for myself, when nobody's looking, but I will.

Unknown to her, Nirmal was watching from outside. It had brought him to a standstill, to see her doing something so ordinary, looking at a sari, the kind of sari that a widow could never wear. Beside the outsized orange and gold mannequin, Meera looked shrunken and drab, clutching her cloth shoulder bag as people milled around looking at things, buying things. Shop assistants and customers brushed past, indifferent to her. It was clear to them, as to Nirmal, that she was not there to buy anything. He was overcome by an unexpected twist of tenderness at her awkward presence, at her solitude in that crowded shop.

He went in and said, "What a surprise!"

Meera sprang away from the mannequin as if tainted by association.

"I . . . um . . . I had to bring the children out . . . it's a holiday . . ." she stammered. "They're just over there, in the bookshop."

Nirmal hesitated, wondering if he should, then sidestepping his misgivings he said, "There's a tea stall outside. Will you have some?"

There were two sets of folding tin tables and chairs under an awning. Looking around, feeling self-conscious, Meera sat in one of the chairs, hoping it would not tear her sari or leave a stain, rust-brown on white. How odd it would seem to people who knew her, Meera, drinking tea in public with Bakul's father. What conclusions would they jump to?

She said, "I brought the children for a treat. They don't get out much . . ."

"Didn't you want to go to the bookshop too? I remember you used to read my father's books. Surely you've finished them all in these six years."

That he should have remembered how he had come upon her once raiding Amulya's old glass-fronted book cupboards made Meera smile into her tea.

"Well, I'm reading some of them for the third or fourth time. I don't buy too many new ones." She looked away.

"Were Baba's books good enough to re-read? What did he have? I've hardly looked really. I remember he read a lot of . . . botany."

"Oh, you'd be surprised," Meera giggled. "Many solemn books. But also romances! Really. *Jane Eyre, Wuthering Heights* – those English novels. One called *The Satin Roses of Cairo*. They all have his name on them." She stopped, thinking she was being improper. "I wonder where the children are," she said. "I should go to the bookshop and fetch them." She started to gather her things.

"Do you want a cream bun?" he said on impulse. "Did you know Finlays makes very good cream buns? Well, at least as good as any you can get in Songarh."

She put her bag down but kept her hand on it as if she would rise any minute.

"Cream buns?" she said. "At our age?"

But she ate one, wiping the spilling cream surreptitiously with a white handkerchief embroidered with pink roses. She wondered if the hanky was clean. Nirmal noted it was the only bit of colour in her wardrobe and watched it touch her lips.

By the end of the cream rolls, the lemony sunlight of the March afternoon had melted without warning into dusk. Meera wondered what she would say at home about the time she had been gone. Who would make the tea before Kamal came home? What would Manjula say about this long absence? And what would they say when they saw all of them return *together*?

What was it about darkness, Meera thought, that altered things? Always those injunctions from parents, from husband, from relatives, *Come back before dark!* What exactly, she had wondered, would happen in the dark that could not happen in the day? But sunset and rising panic had been with her since she could remember. Someone brushed past her. Meera suppressed a shriek. It was a figure hooded in a no-colour shawl.

"Tonga, Mataji?" the man enquired in a reedy voice.

At last they were in a tonga. It had two long hard seats back to back, facing opposite directions but united by a common backrest. Meera listened to the quiet creak of the wheels, the brisk clopping of hooves, the happy ringing of the bells. The sharp smell of the horse, its particular mix of dung, sweat and open air, drifted back to her in the breeze and she breathed it in, relaxed by the rocking carriage. She sat with Bakul at the back, listening to Mukunda chattering with Nirmal in front about horses and whips. They reached the swell of the slope that would turn into the homeward road. The thin, shrouded tongawallah whipped his horse, veins snaking down his wrists, river-like. The horse glistened with sweat despite the chill in the evening air. The tonga hurtled, gathering speed as the slope charged steeper and steeper down before rising again. Meera took a deep breath of the rushing air and tried to tuck her hair into its pins.

Divided from her only by a sheet of thin, hard wood sat Nirmal. If she leaned her head just a fraction, she would be able to rest it on his shoulder.

She shut her eyes for a moment and held tight to the armrest.

THREE

E ver since that tea with Meera, Nirmal found he was unable to focus on the paperwork before him by the time the tea boy came in at four each day with his steaming brown cups. What kind of theodolite? How many? Tents or no tents? Were there enough labourers available locally? He had requisition forms to fill out, letters to write, but his mind kept returning to the ruin, or if he was honest with himself, to his knowledge that Meera was perhaps at the ruin at that moment, alone, feeding the dogs, making her drawings.

On the fourth afternoon he gave up the struggle and left the office early, saying he was going for a site survey. He walked right round the ruin, but found no evidence of Meera. He walked into the dome but heard only mewling sounds and a low snarl. Thinking she had gone further afield he wandered towards the dry stream-bed, but he did not find her there either. Disconsolate, and now edgily aware from his feeling of disappointment that his trip had had no professional basis at all, he began to walk back towards the entrance to the fort.

This time there she was, walking rapidly towards the dome as if she were late, shredding rotis as she went. Her cloth bag swung and bounced off her hip with each quick step she took.

He stopped and crept back behind a broken-down wall, sweat beading his forehead. What was he thinking? Why had he come? It was ridiculous. She was a distant relative, a widow; if she sniffed a trace of longing in him she would be offended and shut him out. If anyone in his family or neighbourhood got to know, there would be turmoil; Meera would certainly be ostracised, and perhaps he would be too.

He peeped around his wall, realising the absurdity of his situation: how could he leave without her seeing him? If he did not walk out now, he would have to skulk around for as long as she decided to stay there drawing. He could see she had settled down, leaning against the banyan tree. The dog sat next to her, alternately scratching its ears and sniffing its rear.

He took a deep breath and tried to emerge as if taken by surprise. She saw him and put down her sketchbook.

"I'm sorry," she said. "I should have realised this has become a workplace now – I really shouldn't idle here."

Her words triggered an idea in Nirmal's head and he blurted it out before he had even thought it through.

"You're not idling, actually. What you're doing could be work!"

"What do you mean?" By now he was next to her, bending down to the dog in an effort at friendship, to which the dog was responding with the most imperceptible of tail-wags.

"I mean that we need site sketches before we start, detailed ones. Do you think you could do them for me?"

"Wouldn't you need a professional?" Meera said. "I only sketch, I'm not a draughtsman."

Nirmal sat beside her and said, "If you'd agree to show me some of your drawings I'd know."

With some trepidation, she opened her sketchbook and began to turn the pages. There were drawings of trees and flowers, a few of the dog. The lines were sharp and fluid. She had also drawn the ruin from various angles. Nirmal saw that the drawings were more atmospheric than accurate. How, for instance, did the dome look *exactly*? How large was it in relation to the pillars? Meera had smudged away some lines, softening the drawings in the style of charcoal sketches, hidden away architectural details behind pastelly trees and clouds. He wondered how to tell her she needed to change her style for the drawings he required. Of course he would also get a professional to draw it, and photographs would be taken every day.

She was looking at his face as he turned the pages. When he turned the tenth page, Meera almost snatched her book away.

"Did I see something I shouldn't have?" Nirmal sounded offended.

She laughed nervously and said, "I think that's all, there are blank pages after that."

"These are wonderful sketches, they really convey the feeling of this place."

Meera looked away, unable to hide a smile. She had been drawing ever since she had come to Songarh, but she had not thought anyone would be interested.

"Could you try to do this a little more systematically?" Nirmal said. "Do the front first, then one side, then another, keep the lines clean as if it's a diagram, give as exact a sense of proportion as possible. Just draw the building as if you were drawing a map." He would not ask for more, he thought, or she might be frightened off.

"I'll try," she said, "but I only have a little time every day, so it won't be quick enough for you."

Nirmal got up and dusted his trousers.

"A little time every day is enough," he said. "For a start."

* * *

Over the next few days Nirmal turned to his papers at the office with something like his old single-mindedness, rejoicing in long hours of work as he planned the Songarh dig. He was suffused with contentment of a kind he had not felt since his return. It was a rare feeling, one that usually came to him, if it did, high on a mountain ridge, the immense folds and humps of hills and valleys falling away before him, edges muted in the evening air. At such times, he saw himself as if from the sky, an infinitesimal speck on a gigantic fold of earth, and yet as significant, as inseparable a part of the mountains, pink sorrel and trees as were the flying squirrels that scampered up the deodars beside him.

Nirmal felt now that the house was getting used to having him back, and Bakul was less truculent. In the evenings, she sometimes followed Mukunda to Nirmal's rooftop and stood by while Nirmal showed Mukunda how to identify constellations. Sometimes when he sat with the boy, showing him picture books with photographs of the Acropolis and the tomb of Tutankhamen, he noticed Bakul looking over his shoulder. He said nothing to her. If he did, she would leave, he knew. He had returned her box to its place under Kananbala's bed but had not forgotten his plan to take her to Manoharpur. One evening he said, "When do your summer holidays begin?"

"Oh, a long long way off," Mukunda said. "I don't know the date."

"I know," Bakul said. "We get a calendar of events right at the start of the year. It's from May the tenth. Right up to the end of June!"

Nirmal got up and went to a calendar on his wall. He put a big red circle around 12 May and smiled at the two of them. They looked at him with questions in their eyes.

"How would you both like to go to Calcutta? And then to Manoharpur? We'll have a first-class compartment all to ourselves, with four bunks, with a bathroom and a mirror. We'll go to the zoo and the Indian Museum. We'll ride a tram and clop on horses in the Maidan, what do you think? We'll visit Bakul's grandfather and take a boat down the river at Manoharpur."

* * *

That night, Mukunda lay awake in his tiny room out in the courtyard. Mosquitoes sang around his ears in their high-pitched whine. He swatted them against his skin almost without noticing. He heard in his mind the train's far-off whistle, urgent, destined for more important places than anywhere he had ever gone. The sound had been a refrain in his orphanage, which was not far from the railway line. All day they could hear trains going up and down. They would rise to the sound of the Sealdah Goods and stumble out, chewing on neem twigs to clean their teeth. At midday it was the Danapur Down, and if that train was late, lunch was late. At night, tossing and turning, fists clamping down hungry, hollow stomachs, they would listen to the sound of the train whose name they did not know; it went so late at night, it could have been a spectre in their dreams, and so they called it Bhoot Rail, imagining it transported ghosts across the country.

It was he, Mukunda, who had hatched the plan to run away on a train. He had convinced three older boys they could do it: he knew he could not do it alone. He and the others – Birsa, Subhas, and Michael – stole out of the orphanage one mid-morning and raced down the path behind their building. A small distance away was the jungle that separated them from the railway track. They were not allowed there, but today they ran, tearing through scrub and grass, butterflies rising ahead of them like petals, insects buzzing angrily. Ran through patches of damp, stabs of nettle, dense shade broken by pools of brilliant sunlight, thrust out at clumps of bright flowers as they passed, tugging them off and waving them as they sprinted, shouting and laughing. At last they reached the edge of the forest and saw a narrow road across which the railway track went. It was quiet but for the alarmed chatter of a family of monkeys and their own hoarse breathing. Even as they wondered if the train would come, they heard the tracks hum and sing, heard the far-off agitation of its whistle. Before they knew it, it was upon them, a blur of chugging metal and smoke, and they were jumping up and down, waving frantically at the train to stop, slow down, so they could get on, make their plan work, run away, reach another city. But at the windows of the train people were leading their separate train-lives, peeling a banana, looking out unseeing, or reading as they tunnelled through towns and waving boys, hardly aware how they had been waited for, watched with yearning; indifferent people close enough for the four boys to see but evanescent, vanishing with each clack of wheel and belch of black soot. A child in the last coach waved back at the boys, and after that there was emptiness where the train had been, and the quiet, filled once more with the chatter of monkeys.

Mukunda remembered the caning they got when they returned, and the ache in his stomach from hunger. The warden had made them stand in the corner and watch the others eat: they were to get no food that day or the next. That would teach them.

A journey on a train! Mukunda had known that day that he would travel, go far away, very far.

Despite the lateness of the hour, Bakul was announcing to Kananbala, "Do you know, we're going to see my mother's house, on a train!"

"A train, eh? You little tadpole, who'll take you on a train? Don't you know nobody leaves this house? Look at *me*."

"Oh, you're just jealous! You don't know what a train is! Just because you've never even left this house!"

"A train! I went on a train, I went on many trains, but that was long ago."

* * *

In another room, Manjula was saying to Kamal, "When did we last have a holiday? I tell you! What a rotten day it was when my father decided to marry me into this family, so far from any city, any excitement. Why don't we ever go anywhere?"

"Why, we went to Varanasi just three years ago. Have you forgotten already? And that trip to Puri and Dakhshineshwar? Who took you on that?"

"Those trips were all to pray for offspring, they weren't holidays, just days of fasts and mantras. And the prayers didn't work. Nothing's worked in my life!"

"Stop grumbling," Kamal said. "Stop sounding as if I'm responsible for everything."

"Who is, if you aren't?"

* * *

In her bed next to Bakul, Meera lay restless in the driftland between sleep and waking. She and Nirmal were together in a tonga, returning from town. Her head bobbed near the collar of his crumpled blue shirt, his eyes laughed down at her and she could see the shadow of stubble growing away from his chin, darkening the lines of laughter that went down his cheeks. Like all tongas, this one was cramped and their hips and shoulders jolted together with each rut in the road. The horse panted on the uphill stretches. There was no sound but the hunh hunh of the horse's breath. Overhead, the fleshy ears of semul swayed bloodshot against the blue, breezy, springtime sky.

She opened her eyes and stared at the ceiling, now properly awake. It had been about twenty days. She had finished three drawings of the ruin. They were becoming more useful, more accurate. Every afternoon she left the house furtively after lunch and went to the ruin. Manjula had grown accustomed over the years to her ill-timed, eccentric walks and asked no more questions. The children were either at school or playing. This time had always been her time alone.

But now, Meera knew, at some point every afternoon, the time was no longer entirely hers. She no longer sat contented with her dogs. She waited. Nirmal would appear sooner or later. He would look at her drawings and comment on them and tell her which part of the ruin to draw next, which detail to emphasise. He would sit back, light a cigarette, and tell her about his work that day, about his travels years earlier. He would ask her about the life she had left behind, a life so long ago now it seemed to be someone else's.

Meera knew that their conversations would lead nowhere – they *could* lead nowhere, and if anywhere only to disappointment. But for the brief time they sat there among the ruins, with the dog and its tubby puppies gambolling around them, she did not want to look into the future. It was enough to be happy in the present, to inhale the smell of his smoke, the smoky smell of him.

* * *

The trip Nirmal had planned was still far off, but Bakul had a calendar in one corner of the tuition room on which she had ringed a date two sheets below. She had begun to cross out the large printed numbers on the sheets on top, one by one, every day. At mealtimes she talked about the food they would carry on the train, and at other times she informed Mukunda of the delights of Manoharpur and Calcutta. That she had only a dim, imagined notion of both did not cramp her style.

At Mrs Barnum's, on the mantelpiece over the fireplace, stood the globe made of glass. Mrs Barnum never let them touch it, but today, when Bakul begged, "I must see where Manoharpur is, please Mrs Barnum, let me look at the globe," Mrs Barnum smiled, her thin face creasing.

The globe was hollow, filled with a liquid within which floated green ferns and weightless rocks. If spun hard, the blues ran into the greens and the yellows became browns, seas tumbled into the mountain ranges, and the Americas merged with Asia. Bakul sat hunched over it at the dining table, now spinning it, now turning it more slowly until she located India, distracted in between by the tiny giraffes and zebras that were painted into parts of Africa. Mukunda said, "Silly, your Manoharpur won't be on the globe, the globe is for big places."

"It will!" Bakul was passionate, "Thakuma said it's near Calcutta, just some distance away, through rice fields and lotus ponds. First we have to find Calcutta." She spun it again.

Mrs Barnum came over to the table and with a long, amber fingernail tapped a point on the globe next to the turquoise of the sea: "There," she said, "there's your Calcutta."

She sat back in her chair and closed her eyes. She could see herself whirling, spinning, her dress swinging out. "Dancing the night away," she whispered. "I was always dancing the night away in Calcutta, and going to the cinema in my sea-green gown, the men in their bow ties and the champagne afterwards, my feet not touching the ground for dancing, always the prettiest girl at the ball, all the men waiting for Larissa to dance with."

Mukunda picked up the Leaning Tower in its glass bowl and watched the snow fall. It could mesmerise him, the snow falling, it made him dream of places he had never seen, places waiting for him to reach them. He imagined himself inside the globe, feeling the snow on his face, walking into the tilted tower and looking out from its minute windows, watching the whiteness drift about him.

He was too shy to tell Bakul of his daydreams, but he wanted to sometimes. He wanted to tell her that his dreams took him far beyond

Songarh, beyond Calcutta, across oceans, towards icebergs. What would she say? She would certainly say, "Take me with you! I want to come too!" Would he? Perhaps. But what would he do with a girl on a ship? In the stories he was reading, none of the tall, rough men ever took girls with them on their ships.

* * *

That evening, meeting Nirmal alone at the foot of the stairs, Manjula stated: "I think taking the children on this trip is a bad idea."

"A bad idea?" Nirmal was nonplussed. He was unwilling to start a conversation that would ruffle his new-found calm. "Don't worry," he said climbing up the stairs away from Manjula. "It may never happen."

"Those two shouldn't be taken on holidays together. They disappear for hours, we don't know where, and half the time they're with that Anglo woman who drinks and smokes. Nirmal, I think . . . "

"It's alright," Nirmal said from the landing towards her upturned face. "They're only children playing, Didi, don't worry. I'd better rush. Work to do. Now the dig's approaching there's so much to do."

He turned away. It was only since announcing the trip that he had sensed a real dilution in Bakul's hostility towards him. Leave me alone, he wanted to tell Manjula, do not interfere.

"Work to do," Manjula mimicked in an undertone. "They're all the same, men, think they have important work and we're just stupid idlers."

* * *

Late the next afternoon, Nirmal sat with Meera at the ruin somewhat distracted, not really looking at her new drawings. He knew his colleagues at the office were scenting scandal. Someone had seen him with Meera at the ruin one afternoon, and they were beginning to talk about his daily disappearance. But for the moment he pushed the thought aside. This time alone supplied the missing words to the story of his day and completed it for him.

147

He turned the pages, looking for drawings of the dome's left side, finding only birds and dogs.

Meera was busy with the dogs some distance away. He continued to turn the pages. She jumped, startled by his sudden, loud laughter.

"Oh no," she said, running to him, "you've got the wrong book!"

He snatched it away from her flailing hands and continued to chuckle. "It's very good," he said. "It's very, very good." He was looking at a caricature of Manjula, her nostrils flaring over a bull neck and folds of skin, eyes bulbous with rage, ears hung with enormous gold studs, hands on rolling hips.

"You should be a cartoonist too," he said, turning the page and looking at Kamal, whose paunch flowed pillow-like below his kurta, while his small hands stuck out from his body like stalks from fat brinjals.

"Please, Nirmal Babu," Meera said, urging. "Please give me . . . "

Nirmal turned the page and came upon a picture of himself. Not a cartoon. A sketch. His forehead and cheeks had been carefully shaded in. His hair was drawn in separate strands. His eyes were thoughtful. On the next page another picture of him, from a different angle, this time with a book, glasses on, long legs looped over a chair-arm in the way he knew he always sat while reading. On the page after that yet another picture of him sitting under the banyan tree at the ruin, this one unfinished. They were not sketches. They were a declaration of love.

Meera looked away, aghast.

The earth felt as if it had begun to roll under her feet. She thought she would fall. She felt dizzy and held a tree for support.

From far away she heard Nirmal's voice. "It's an earthquake, I think it's an earthquake." He looked around, wildly shouting, "Bakul! Ma! We have to go home. Get away, get away from the building, it may fall, it's already crumbling! I must get Bakul." He began to run down the path, away from the ruin, but was forced to stop. It was like walking on water. The beaten earth around the fountain moved like an animal shaking itself awake. It rose and fell as if the animal had become a wave in the sea. They heard a deep, distant rumble from somewhere far beneath.

Manjula and Kamal, who had run out into the garden when the house began to shake, could see Mrs Barnum across the road in a long, blue nightie, hair in curlers, shouting for her khansama. She flung open the gate and ran across the road to them. She had never come to their house since her picnic with Kananbala.

"It's an earthquake isn't it? Eh, girl?" She was smiling at Bakul, "Your first?" She reached the others, hair coming loose, nightdress falling off her shoulder. Turning to Kamal she remarked – speaking as if they were outside for a garden party – "D'you think it'll be as bad as the last one? Now *that* was an earthquake, but I was in Calcutta that day and dancing enough to shake the floor without any help from quakes."

"If only we had a conch!" Manjula exclaimed, almost tearful. She was too terrified to take notice of Mrs Barnum's exposed shoulder and dishevelled hair.

"I know you're supposed to blow a conch to stop the earth shaking," Mrs Barnum said. "But not even Triton blowing his wreathed horn would stop this!"

"Where's Mukunda?" Bakul exclaimed. "And what about Thakuma?" She ran towards the house for her grandmother while Mrs Barnum shouted, "I wouldn't go inside the house if I were you – it might fall on you!"

"Radha Krishna, Radha Krishna, Radha Krishna, save us, keep us from harm, Radha Krishna," Manjula muttered.

"It's over," Kamal said to Manjula. "Can't you see? The house is still standing, and nothing's moving any more."

"Over?" Mrs Barnum said. "What a pity! So short!"

"Where's Meera?" Kamal said. "And Nirmal? Why didn't they come out? It's a holiday and he's at work? How very odd!"

* * *

Meera stood clinging to the banyan tree for support, heart thudding, the salty taste of nausea in her mouth. The ground beneath her was still, but she was filled with terror that it would begin to roll again. She looked around for Nirmal, saw him emerging from behind the ruin, laughing like a boy. The minute he had realised it was not a major earthquake he had forgotten all about Bakul and his mother and hurried to examine the ruin instead.

"It's so broken down already there's nothing left to break," he shouted. "Can you believe it, not even the dome has fallen in. No damage seems to have been done at all."

He reached her and said, out of breath, "Magnificent, don't you think it was magnificent? The plates of the earth shifting, continents changing shape, mountain ranges rising, oceans migrating. Amazing it's all hot liquid deep inside! Fire below the oceans."

Meera looked at Nirmal and wondered if the quake had perhaps dislodged some bit of his brain.

"Millions of years, it's taken millions of years for these continents to separate from each other, drift away," Nirmal was saying. "Then anchor themselves in the places where we find them now. Us humans? Even the ancients I study? We're as new as the butterfly, born today, gone tomorrow."

"Yes, I suppose so," Meera said. "Do you really think it's safe now?"

"What if it weren't?" Nirmal said, his eyes sparkling. "What if it all began again and we were all to die? What would you like to do before you die?" He laughed at her bewildered face and said, "Come now, tell me."

"Onion, garlic, fish," Meera said, surprised by the words that came out of her mouth, the clarity of her enunciation. "I'd like to eat everything I'm forbidden. I'd like to eat *everything* once before I die."

* * *

Mukunda sat on the floor in Mrs Barnum's bedroom. He had rushed in when the earthquake began, thinking he would find her and take her away from the moving floor and shaking walls. The room smelled of whisky. An opened bottle had tumbled and darkened the carpet. All around him were things that had fallen out of shelves and off walls and tables: a broken picture, a cracked vase, books. Surrounded by the debris, Mukunda was reading. In his hand was a sheet of thin, translucent onion-skin paper which began, "My darling, it truly seems the Antipodes without you. I'm surrounded by strange people, my body is here and my mind with you always, beneath our banyan tree. I'm working my hands raw, will make enough one day to get you away and we'll be together again."

Mukunda's heart thudded louder than it had when the earth had begun to shake. He could see a long white feather and two more letters inside the box, but the handwriting was hurried, and even though he did not pause over words like Antipodes which he could not understand, it took him too long to read the long, looped scrawl. He knew everything would end if he were caught. He thought he heard someone, pushed the box aside and ran out, the letter ringing in his ears.

"My darling, it truly seems the Antipodes . . . " A letter to Mrs Barnum, he thought, it could only have been from her lover. It must be true then that the two of them had murdered Mr Barnum and planned to run away together.

It could not be true – she was too kind to kill anyone.

What was he to do? Where was Bakul?

FOUR

Beyond the Songarh ruin, thickets of acacia and ber stretched to the hilltop on which a small, white temple shone in the afternoon sun. The temple was not old, but it had acquired a reputation for benign power.

Meera looked around, noticed bees skimming the air over mauve wildflowers that grew close to the ground, thought of Nirmal's extraordinary question after the earthquake the day before and her own ridiculous answer. What must he think? He had not questioned her further, merely looked at her as if for the first time. But she felt a spasm of shame whenever she recalled her gluttonous words.

The afternoon sun was too hot for comfort. Overhead, the sky stretched empty and high, no hint of clouds. Summer had come upon them as suddenly as it did each year, the heat an oppressive presence to get used to all over again. She stumbled over stones and clods of earth up the path to the hill, wiping her perspiring face with a corner of her sari. Her usual path, but why did it feel harder today? Under the trees, where patches of green shade alternated with bright bursts of sun, it was a little cooler and she paused. She could see empty bottles and matchboxes thrown aside here and there, two crumpled cigarette packets, not Nirmal's brand. She knew this was a favoured place for trysts and shook her head. She was not here for a tryst, there was no reason to feel guilty. She had come to draw the fort.

She reached the edge of the ruins and paused. Nirmal was already there. The dog sat beside him and the puppies tumbled over each other and around him as if they were old friends.

Nirmal tried not to stare at Meera, at the perspiration on her upper lip, her blouse translucent on her back with sweat, at the bits of hair that stuck to her cheek, the sari with which she was wiping her face.

"It's become hot, hasn't it?" she said, self-conscious all of a sudden. She looked the other way, spotted a steel tiffin-carrier beside Nirmal, and recognised it as the one she had packed for him that morning. She gave him a puzzled look. He held it out to her and she took it. She opened its clasp and saw in the top container two pieces of fried fish, and below it rice. In the third bowl she knew there was a vegetable: she did not need to look further.

She looked up at him, filled afresh with disgust at the greed that had made her say what she had to him the day before.

"Go on," Nirmal said, "nobody's looking."

"I can't."

"It's very good fish," Nirmal said gently. "Wonderfully cooked. A good way to break a long and pointless fast." He looked away from her and began to play with the puppies while she stared at the container of fish in her hand, wondering if she felt like eating any after so many years of abstinence. What was it like, the texture of it, the smell of it, the feel of those tiny, translucent, thorn-like bones in the mouth?

She broke off a fragment with her fingers. She turned her head away from Nirmal, almost afraid that he should see her in the act. Though he seemed absorbed in the puppies, she knew he was looking at her out of a corner of his eye. In her confusion she swallowed the fragment whole, without tasting it.

She gave a nervous giggle and said, "There! I've done it! Tasted the forbidden fruit!"

A light breeze was collecting dry leaves. Parakeets chattered overhead as Nirmal looked at Meera and smiled in congratulation.

* * *

Ever since the earthquake, when he had found the letter to Mrs Barnum, she had been transformed in Mukunda's eyes. Her silences began to seem sinister. Her gin and cigarettes seemed to mark her out as a fallen woman, as in the thrillers Mukunda had read. He would find himself looking at her long fingernails and wondering if she had had to wash blood out of them. *Could* she have killed a man? Or helped someone kill? He felt the hairs on the back of his neck tingle when she came and stood behind him, caressing his shoulders as he read. He thought of her plunging a knife in through skin and bone and heart. But then, when she sat by him and explained passages from *Lamb's Tales from Shakespeare*, he did not know what to think. He would have to read the other two letters, he thought, to find out the truth. Maybe they were not letters to her – after all, she was not named in the one he had read.

Ten days after the earthquake, Mukunda got his chance. He did not know how much time he had. He had been trying to read the difficult beginning of *Lord Jim* at Mrs Barnum's dining table when she said, "Carry on, I'm going to Finlays, back soon," and was driven off by the khansama. His hands began to tremble, his knees shook, but as soon as he saw the car departing round the corner he ran to her room.

What a lot of things Mrs Barnum had in her bedroom, he saw in panic. He had not noticed them during the earthquake. He tried to guess where the box had dropped from. In the corner he could see the vase that had fallen that day. A picture on the wall of a green-faced, drunken-looking woman, cracked right across. Two carved, teak almirahs at the far wall, both locked, so that ruled them out. The bed was a large one, with a dark-purple, velvety cover smoothed over it. The foot of the bed was draped with a tiger skin, its glassy-eyed, open-mouthed, spear-toothed head snarling straight at the pillow. On the wall beside the bed there was a high shelf piled with oddments.

It was this shelf Mukunda decided to search. He stood on a chair, pushing aside dusty old ornaments, books, a box – but this wasn't the one. He tried to be careful about replacing things in the same order. He remembered the box with the letters was greenish and made of wood. Finally, in the far corner, he saw the box he wanted. He pulled it towards himself and opened it. There was the white feather.

But the letters? There was nothing else in the box. He shook it in disbelief.

"Satisfied, Mukunda?"

Mukunda froze on the chair, feeling as if his knees had turned to water. The box fell from his hands with a thud. The feather lay half out of it. Slowly, he turned around.

Mrs Barnum looked taller than him, even though he was standing on a chair. He wanted to get down, but couldn't. He wanted to say something, but his tongue felt like paper.

She sat down on the bed and began to stroke the head of the tiger. She wore a silk dress the tawny colour of the tiger's skin.

"Is this what you give me for my trust?" she said, her voice hoarser than usual.

I wanted to prove you're innocent, Mukunda wished he could say. I only wanted to prove everyone is wrong. I wanted to know the truth. He felt he would start to cry if he opened his mouth.

"Come down from that chair," she ordered.

He climbed down, legs shaking. He could not take his eyes away from the hand stroking the tiger. It had a large, green-stoned ring on one long-nailed finger.

She got up and lit a cigarette. She inhaled and coughed. Maybe it was not so bad after all. She could not be furious if she was smoking, she always said it relaxed her. He opened his mouth to explain and took a deep breath of the smoke around him.

She whirled back towards him. "Don't say a thing," she hissed. "Don't try. Go away, leave. Never come back. *Get out of here, get out!*"

Her voice rose as she spoke. She coughed violently and wiped her eyes. Mukunda edged away, out of the room. As he left he heard her yell into the passage.

"And as you leave, look up 'betrayal' in the dictionary, will you? Look up 'treacherous', look up 'cheat'!"

* * *

Nirmal was announcing over tea that at last everything was in place – the officers, the theodolites and cameras, the labourers, the tents, the permissions and paperwork – and in two days they would begin to set up the dig at the ruin.

"What will happen now?" Manjula said. "Maybe a castle will be found under the ruin! I don't mind if this old ruin is destroyed if a grand stupa is found. Something will happen at last in this boring old town, and people will come to see it."

"Nothing will be destroyed, even if anything is found," Nirmal repeated. He felt too elated by the thought of the work ahead to let anything else occupy his mind. "We'll start with the mounds at the back. It's delicate work, it'll take months maybe. We'll put up some tents there. The labour especially cannot keep coming and going all that distance."

He looked sidelong at Meera for a response, but she seemed distracted by thoughts of her own. Since the afternoon she had eaten the fish he had brought, Nirmal noticed that she seemed to be going through the polite motions of conversation and interest, but was far-eyed. She had stopped coming to the fort, or to the roof to dry clothes in the morning. He never found her alone to ask for an explanation. Not that she owes me one, he thought, but even so – there are drawings she needs to finish.

"That's the end of the romantic couples, isn't it?" Kamal chortled. "The pigeons weren't the only things billing and cooing there."

"The ruins will be crowded for a while, yes," Nirmal said, filling an awkward pause. "No room for the ghosts of kings and queens either."

"Especially canoodling kings and queens," Kamal said, looking at a brown spot on the scratched wooden surface of the table.

"Quiet," Manjula said. "Can't you see there's a child here?"

Bakul, who had been reading a book in the slanting early evening light by the window, all of a sudden pushed it aside and sprang up. "Mukunda? Mukunda!" she called, leaving the room.

Meera got up and began to clear away the cups and teapots, clattering them onto a brass tray.

Kamal said, "Ah, what's the hurry? I still want another, can't I have a cup? Please make me one."

Meera stopped. She found an unused cup on the table, began to pour tea into it, spilling a puddle on the saucer. She added a quick dash of milk.

"Oho," Kamal said sadly. "All these years, and you can't remember I don't like milk in my tea."

"I'll get a fresh cup." Meera turned on her heel and left the room.

"Why are you being difficult?" Manjula said. "Just drink it."

Nirmal got up to follow Meera into the kitchen, somehow he'd get a minute with her alone. But Kamal said, "Oh Nirmal, don't go away while I'm having my tea, tell me about the excavation, what happens next exactly?"

* * *

Mukunda was running from Mrs Barnum's bedroom, down the stairs, into the garden, not noticing the dark, jackfruit part of it that they avoided in the evenings, not noticing the vivid orange of the large setting sun cut up by branches of trees. The khansama was in the garden, shooing his hens into their coop. "Hutt, hutt, hutt," the khansama called out. "Hey Mukunda," he said. "Help me with the hens!"

Mukunda wiped his tear-blocked nose and eyes and tried to say something, then ran towards the gate.

"Come tonight, I'm slaughtering a chicken." The khansama chuckled. "When its head is chopped off and it rushes about dripping blood, that's really funny, you'll like it."

Mukunda ran through the gate that hung loose on its hinges. One of its wooden panels had rotted away, the other was nailed on somehow, and a piece fell down with an exhausted clunk as he banged the gate behind him. He ran down the road in the twilight, faster and faster, panting, seeming directionless and desperate. His breath came in sobs. He left the main road and ran down a dirt path that went through fields mellow in the setting sun. The last birds quarrelled and chattered over their choice of evening perches as he jumped over ditches, his flapping slippers leaving a cloud of dust over his hair and face.

At last he could see the ruins and the ridge behind it. He went into the inner courtyard with its large pool of red stone, dim arabesques still struggling out of the dusty earth around it. The banyan tree nearby was beginning to grow larger with deep evening shadows.

He flung himself down at the base of the banyan tree.

Bakul was already sitting there. She said: "You heard too? From tomorrow they're digging up the ruin. We won't have a ruin to come to any more." She looked around at the mosses and ferns creeping out of the walls, the broken walls they had clambered over so many times, imagining rooms where now there were none.

Mukunda looked at her uncomprehendingly. He had not noticed she was there at all.

"My father *had* to do it," Bakul said. "He *had* to come back and spoil everything."

Mukunda wished he could put his head between his knees and cry. He wished he could explain things to Mrs Barnum, or at least to Bakul. But he could never speak about what he had done, not to anyone. He knew he would never forgive himself for losing Mrs Barnum's trust, never stop feeling the sense of shame that made him want to be sick. He sank his head into his knees and felt the salt of tears in his mouth.

"No room for the ghosts of kings and queens any more," Bakul mimicked. "He thinks that's so funny."

A swoop of green parakeets above made them look up. In the early evening sky there was one bright star. The banyan tree to which the birds were heading was now a shadow.

"Hey," Bakul said to Mukunda's buried head when he did not reply. "Come on, it's bad, but not *so* bad. He says they won't spoil it all." She felt alarmed by his stifled sobs and got up saying, "Let's go, it's late." She was frightened of the darkness and the black shapes in the trees but could not admit it to Mukunda. Out of the night-time forests came foxes and leopards, she knew. She had seen pairs of foxes, curiously dog-like, sometimes even in broad daylight in the fields.

They started to run down the tree-filled path back towards the fields. It was still easy to see the ruts in the pathway and leap over them in the soft purple light. The darkness seemed to gather and snuff out the shapes around them, making everything look bulky. They could smell crushed eucalyptus, sharp and fragrant, over one part of the track shadowed by the lean trees. Soon it became difficult to see exactly where they were stepping. They held each other's hands as they scampered on as swiftly as they could. When Mukunda stumbled, Bakul clutched his sleeve harder and said, "Careful, there's a big stone there!"

Mukunda looked back. Was someone following them, someone from whom they had to run? He could see nothing but the snarling tiger on Mrs Barnum's bed. Over the sound of their panting and their flapping slippers, he could hear it – something behind them. He held Bakul's hand tighter and whispered, "Don't be scared!"

"I'm not," she whispered.

They reached the fields. There was more light in the open, away from the trees. Bakul tugged at Mukunda's sleeve as they ran down the humps that separated one field from the other.

"Look," she exclaimed. "Look! Up there!"

He stopped running and looked up. Above them, as far as they could see, the blue-black sky was sequinned with stars, so many stars that the sky did not seem to have the space for them, and yet it seemed endless, a vast, sparkling dome arched over the star-washed field, so many stars that if you stood looking up for a while you felt dizzy. Through the stars streaked a white, flaming trail of light, light of a kind they had never seen, arcing downward until it disappeared into the horizon.

Hand in hand, they stood in the middle of the empty fields under the star-filled sky, their troubles, fear, and the long way they still had to go before reaching home, all forgotten.

* * *

Meera sat in the kitchen, not noticing that she had not switched on a light, that her midriff and arms and feet were aflame with mosquito bites, that in fact if she had tried switching on the light it would not have worked because there was a power cut.

She could think of nothing but the terrace at dusk, ten days ago, when Kamal had come up to her with an unobtrusiveness she wouldn't have thought him capable of, and said, "You really work too hard."

She had smiled a polite smile. "Not at all, I'm just taking in the pickle bottles. I didn't want to risk the servants breaking any."

"I was just thinking how difficult it must be for you, how lonely."

She had laughed, bemused more than disconcerted, and said, "I'm used to it."

"Oh, but it's a great pity, the dreadful rules our society makes, and the blindness with which we impose them on ourselves. I think we need to rebel a little." He was absorbed in brushing off a bit of blackness his white kurta had picked up from the terrace wall.

"I should collect the bottles." She edged away from him to the corner of the terrace where bottles of mango pickle stood ranged in a row, still warm from the daytime sun they were storing.

As she bent to pick up the bottles, she felt a hand on her back where her blouse dipped, scooping out bare skin. She leapt away, startled.

"Don't be alarmed," Kamal said, "I just wanted to . . . say that if you need anything, tell me. Don't think twice." She saw his gaze travel over her as if he were mentally unfurling her sari and unbuttoning her blouse.

He paused. Then looked skyward and said, "We should have some rain soon, shouldn't we?"

Ten days had passed since that evening. He had said nothing more, made no move to touch her, but if he looked at her, she knew he was looking beneath her clothes. When his eyes travelled over her body she shuddered as if a lizard had slithered over her skin. Why had he done this, she asked herself again and again. She had lived in the house so many years and he had never attempted anything of the kind before. What had unleashed this sudden lechery? She thought back to the past fortnight and could recall nothing out of the ordinary. Their conversations, if they could be termed that, always took place at the dining table, when he asked for a second helping of something and she served him.

It struck her like a blow. Of course! He must have caught wind of her friendship with his brother! And decided he too would try his luck. She stood up in agitation. Of course! That was it, it was how men thought: friendliness with a man could be nothing but flirtation, and if you flirted with one you were easy, a slut, game for more.

What was she to do? The only woman she had to talk to was the man's wife. Making accusations to Nirmal about his brother was impossible. What if he said she was overreacting to friendship and sympathy? What if he did not, and confronted Kamal instead?

Meera lit a lamp when she realised there was no electricity, then pulled out the rice canister and poured three cups onto a plate. Methodically, she began to sift through it for stones, trying to quiet her mind and decide what to do.

* * *

A little while later, when Mukunda and Bakul stole back into the house that evening from the fort, they saw Meera hunched over a plate in a pool of yellow lamplight, her shadow tall on the opposite wall. Her rigid back and bent head discouraged questions. They crept past her, knowing they were in for a scolding. Even in the wide verandah on the first floor that ended in Amulya's stained-glass window – one of the panes had cracked and been replaced by one in plain blue that was thought to match – there was nobody. This was where Kamal sat drinking tea every evening. A lamp had been left there, darkening the sooty cobwebs high up in the ceiling. Bakul and Mukunda edged closer to each other. They padded out onto the small terrace that led to Manjula's quarters, hearing an indefinable murmur of voices emerging from there.

"I think she's right," they heard Kamal's voice saying, "it's been a mistake all along."

"It's not a mistake because they're late one evening." This was Nirmal.

"Come, come, Nirmal, all of us make errors of judgment. Don't you remember Kundu Babu? First he got his daughter married off to that man who turned out to be impotent, to top that they say he had just one eye, then she came back to her parents and they couldn't look at anyone for the shame."

"What has Kundu Babu got to do with this?" Nirmal sounded irritable.

"What I mean is that elders make mistakes, don't you see?" Kamal's voice sounded placatory. "If you ask me, the first error was our father's. We were not that rich anyway, what was the need to act the godfather?"

A match struck. Kamal said something more, too low to hear. A faint cigarette smell floated out towards Bakul and Mukunda. In the far distance, they could hear the lonely cry of a fox calling to its mate. They sank to the floor of the terrace, still warm with memory of the daytime sun, and leaned side by side against the wall. Sweat made their clothes stick to their backs.

"We need to be practical, Nirmal."

"Practicality's not everything."

There was a brief silence. Above Bakul and Mukunda, a pimpled half-moon had struggled up into a sky fragmented by the canopy of leaves that hooded the terrace. Cold, white, distant stars stabbed the trees. The fox called again, closer, this time answered by an echoing cry. In the distance, they could hear the faint tuning of Afsal Mian's tanpura.

"Think of the expense!" they heard Kamal say. "He's growing, but the money in Baba's will is not, is it? All these years he's been eating us out of house and home. I tell you, Nirmal, there are good institutions for boys like him. They'll take over and our headache will – I mean, he was Baba's responsibility, maybe in some way, but how are we –"

"I'll look after him, whatever is extra. We don't need to send him away for the money." Nirmal sounded shorter and more abrupt than he had before. "You won't have to worry. You haven't had to worry so far."

"My dear boy, money is not the only expense, you know," Kamal said.

"I tell you, having to be here, managing the boy and Bakul, it's not easy, Nirmal. The girl's growing up, so is he! Just the other day I was in a real fright when . . . "This was Manjula. She lowered her voice, so Bakul and Mukunda could not tell how they had frightened her.

Then her voice again, louder. "That's all very well, Nirmal, and you might think they are children, but they aren't. Look at today. Not back yet, it's so late, we don't have any idea where they are or what they're doing! And they do this all the time. You may not worry, but I do!"

"There's nothing to worry about," Nirmal's voice was stubborn. "They've been friends since they were four and six. I trust them. They're like brother and sister."

"But they are *not* brother and sister, Nirmal," Kamal said in a patient voice. "And they are both of the age when . . . "

Manjula snorted. "They won't even know what they are doing before it's done. And then some terrible disaster. How will we ever show our faces?"

Someone put a glass down with a clatter. Mukunda and Bakul drew closer; she could feel Mukunda's breath on her face, warm, smelling of malted sweets. They were talking of sending Mukunda away. Their voices contained a terrifying darkness.

"Still," Nirmal was saying, "I don't think they're up to anything. It's true they're late tonight. They just need a good scolding."

"A scolding?" Kamal snorted. "That boy needs a hiding! Ideas above his station. But then we've spoiled him, so what do you expect?"

Manjula interrupted, "I tell you, Nirmal, you've stayed in the mountains too long, you have no idea. Is it only in darkness that people get up to trouble?"

"Mukunda is part of this house, he's Bakul's only friend, we cannot just send him away." Nirmal's voice was implacable.

"If you don't do anything now, you will regret it at leisure, is what I say," Kamal pronounced. "But she's your daughter."

Bakul and Mukunda heard a chair scrape across the floor and shrank further into the dark niche of the terrace, their hands in a tight, sweaty clasp, a sick tide of fear churning their stomachs. "I'd better see what Meera's doing about the rice," they heard Manjula say. And then the first notes of Afsal Mian's melancholic voice joined the strings of his tanpura.

Nirmal went out to the garden for an amble. It had been a trying evening: first that long argument with his brother and sister-in-law, then having to take the lead in disciplining Bakul and Mukunda for disappearing. Kamal had been of the opinion that the boy needed six strokes of a cane. Finding the tact and patience to dissuade him had been exhausting.

Breathing in the gardenia and raat ki rani his father had planted, he took out his cigarettes. No harm competing with their fragrance, he said to himself. He wished Meera would come out to the garden. It had been so many days since they had had a real conversation, despite seeing each other at every meal.

Nirmal strolled around the house to the back. Dull, yellow light striped a square patch of the darkness and he walked closer to look, curious. It came from the room at the corner of the courtyard, Mukunda's. Through the window he saw Mukunda hunched over a book beside his candle, tracing a line, lips moving without a sound. He had stripped down to his shorts. Sweat made his skin shine in the candlelight which contoured his young, thin body with dark shadows. Nirmal noticed the taut muscles of Mukunda's upper arm as he fanned himself with an exercise book. His chest, which had also developed muscles – all that work with the water buckets, Nirmal thought – tapered down to a waist that showed a faint line of hair. His face had lost most of its childish curves. Now the cheekbones were sharper than before, the cleft in the chin deeper, the lines stronger. Only his eyes still seemed long-lashed, almost girlish.

He frowned to himself and, forehead puckered with thought, trudged back to the house. He had never looked at Mukunda so closely before. But tonight . . . He could hardly bring himself to admit that his fatigue that night came from arguing the whole evening not only with Kamal and Manjula, but with a part of himself as well.

He padded up the deserted stairs on his way to the roof, to his room. He thought he deserved another smoke, and an after-dinner rum. And perhaps Meera would be on the terrace.

When he reached the first floor, however, something struck him, and he turned towards the room where Bakul slept. He peered in through the open door and saw her shadowy form sprawled across the bed like a prone Jesus, her bare legs pale in the moonlight from the verandah. She had flung her sheet aside in the heat. Her night frock was bunched up near the swell of her newly acquired hip curve. Her wildly tousled hair covered her pillow.

Nirmal crept away.

* * *

The next day Meera was sitting in Kananbala's room, head bent over a sketch, when Kalpana the maid came in and, unhampered by any perception of Meera's absorption in her work, said, "Give me the soap, and bring out the clothes to be washed. You've left nothing out in the courtyard."

Kalpana, lanky and slouching, had a penetrating voice, a tight bun, straight thick eyebrows, and a dark moustache. She leaned a sloping shoulder on the door as she waited for Meera and said to Kananbala, "How're you, Thak'ma, thought up any juicy swear words recently? How about dung-faced donkey? Or grease-nosed sister-fucker?"

Meera breathed in deep, said nothing, and continued with the tricky bulge of the dome, erasing a line that had come out wrong.

"Arre baap." Kalpana turned a wide-eyed look of make-believe astonishment towards Meera. "Everyone's too busy today," she observed, "drawing things that have been around for hundreds of years. What with people spending all their time wandering here and there at ruins and temples, I suppose I don't need to wash clothes and keep house either!" She wiped her face with an ostentatious swipe of her sari and sat down on the floor, staring at Meera, whose pencil wobbled under her sarcastic gaze.

Mukunda appeared and fidgeted by the door. "Manjuladi wants you in the kitchen," he said.

Meera scowled at him. "Tell her I can't come just now," she said. "I'm doing something. Is it possible in this house to get any of my own work done?"

165

"Oooh, your own work!" Kalpana's voice was mocking. "You have a lot of your own work these days!"

Meera's forehead began to throb. She saw the maid looking her up and down, saying but not saying what everyone thought: that Meera was a glorified maid too, one with an education, a maid who was aspiring to the master, a widow who had begun to dream up an impossible future.

She pushed her chair back so hard as she stood up that it fell. Her sketchbook and pencil dropped to the floor unregarded. Mukunda looked at her face and edged away. Meera went up to Kalpana, who stood in a hurry.

"If you can't speak with some decency," Meera said, "don't speak to me at all. Do you understand?"

Before the maid could reply, a quaver came from Kananbala's direction: "And who is it you're fucking these days, Meera?" she was saying. "Who is it you're fucking? Who – is – it – you're – fucking?"

Meera whirled towards Kananbala, horrified. Kananbala's eyes were invisible behind glasses on which the morning sun shone. Her smile was sweet and denture-less. She repeated the words in a sing-song, absent-minded tone, rattling one of Mrs Barnum's tins to keep time. Kalpana guffawed. Meera rushed out of the room, tears stinging her eyes. She could not, *could not*, continue living in Songarh. She must leave. Anywhere would be better than here. She would go to her brother and beg for shelter, she would look for a job in a city, anything but this nightmare.

She ran to the middle room and sat on the edge of her bed, shoulders tingling again with that familiar pain. Her life had boiled over when she wasn't looking. What did I expect, she thought, remembering one of Manjula's sayings, that I'd sprinkle cold water onto hot oil and not get burned by the sputter?

She became aware after a while that her breath was a noisy wheeze. Where's my trunk? she panicked. Where's the trunk in which I brought my clothes when I came here? The thought began to grow and cloud her mind. She got up and looked under the bed. She tried the attic in the long room. She could not make out its familiar mustard colour among the shapes huddled there. Frantic, she rushed up the staircase to the loft, but it wasn't there either. As she came down the stairs, she encountered Kamal going into his rooms. He smiled at her with the new smile he had manufactured just for her.

Meera ran down the stairs, hand sliding on the banisters. Nirmal was coming up and paused at the landing to let her pass. "Where are you rushing to?" he said, sounding eager, but she did not pause.

She stopped by the door to slip her feet into her chappals and let herself out. There was a heaviness in the air, the stillness that comes before a downpour. She began to walk with rapid steps. As her distance from the house grew, she stopped and looked up at the louring sky.

There was a sudden sharp slap on her face, of wind. It gathered force and buffeted her sari. The tall trees at the edges of the fields bent double, surprised by the squall. Dust gathered into ochre clouds and rushed towards her. She covered her face with the corner of her sari and screwed up her eyes. Above her, the tin-coloured sky cracked and warped with lightning. The gulmohars glowed an intense orange, gathering the half-light. She felt the first drops of rain on her arms and the sweet, brown smell of water meeting dry earth. It came down faster. She removed her aanchal from her face and looked up at the sky, holding her face up to the rain, shutting her eyes against what was already a torrent. Under the trees sheltered a few straggly clumps of people who looked at her in amazement.

Something unlocked deep inside her as the rain fell on her face, and into the earth next to her, muddied her sari and gritted her slippers with dirt. In some other place, where nobody knew her, she would start all over again. She would leave as soon as she could. She would get away to a big city where nobody knew her. She would make room for herself.

Already the rain was tapering off, leaving only the damp earth smell which wiped out all memory of the smouldering days that had gone before.

* * *

It had been only about six months since Nirmal's return to Songarh, and the serenity he had thought was his to keep had scattered over the past fortnight, leaving in its place a profound disquiet. Smoking his fourteenth cigarette of the day, he rested his elbows on the parapet of his roof, listening to Mrs Barnum's piano which even from this distance was violent and lonely and sad. The crashing notes were reassuring, a sound from long ago, unchanged since his childhood. He wished he was a fossil responding to geological time, creaking, calcifying, hardening, going deeper and deeper into a rock-face or river-bed, metamorphosing over thousands of years from flesh and blood and marrow into stone; better to be a fossil than human, on the cusp of some painful new development almost every day.

In the years since Shanti's death he had grown so accustomed to solitude that he had lost the ability, perhaps even the need, for friendship. And now, all of a sudden, Meera had told him she was going away to her brother.

"Going away," Nirmal had repeated.

"Yes."

"When will you be back?"

"I . . . he wants me to stay, he says there's a school near his house, I could teach drawing . . . or something else. His wife is lonely too and my mother wants me as well."

She had wrapped her sari a little tighter around her, taken a last look at the ruined fort and turned away from the dogs still tangled up in her sari, pawing her for more food, rolling over in delight at seeing her again. "I just came to see the pups one last time, I have to leave tomorrow."

"They've been waiting for you every evening," Nirmal had said. "They couldn't tell why you'd stopped coming, they kept looking towards the path thinking you'd appear."

"I know," Meera had said. "How could I have made them understand? I was thinking of them too, but it wasn't possible to come."

"I can't understand!" Nirmal had burst out. "Why this sudden decision to go? Couldn't you stay a little longer so that —"

Meera had stopped him mid-sentence. "I have to go," she had said. "It's all settled." She had started to walk away, then stopped to say, "If you

168

could carry on feeding the dogs, just until the puppies are older . . . "

Sleeping or awake, Nirmal thought the same thoughts. What had changed? Had he done something to make Meera leave? Had he suggested anything inappropriate? Was she offended that he had brought fish for her to eat? Surely not! Was she afraid of the new-found ease of their proximity?

He was not just bewildered about Meera. His mind swung between her and Mukunda; he felt unable to free himself from them. Again and again he remembered the time he had first gone to Mukunda's orphanage because he had nothing to do, the whim of a pleasant winter morning – he had thought he would go and see the boy his father had left money for in his will – and he had returned with Mukunda, all of six years old.

Manjula had opened the door to Nirmal that distant afternoon; behind him was the boy. He had a thin face with a dimpled chin, greasy hair, large eyes bright with curiosity, and curly, long lashes, like a girl's. He was in a blue shirt that looked as if it belonged to someone much older than him, his shorts came down to well below his knees.

"This is Mukunda," Nirmal had explained. "I have brought him home."

The argument over whether or not to keep Mukunda had continued for two or three days. Nirmal had refused to give in. The boy was too good for the orphanage; they taught them very little, fed them even less and beat them if they disobeyed. After all, our father wanted him looked after. He must be given a place, a life.

"What, in our bedrooms?" Manjula's voice trembled with rage. "Do we know what caste he is? He could be any caste, he might even be a Muslim. I will not stand it. Hari, Hari!"

"I'm not sending him back," Nirmal had insisted. "He can stay in my room."

"Your room! That's in the middle of the house. I will not allow any such thing. I will *not*."

There was a compromise. The boy would stay, but in the outhouse. Would he be scared? Nirmal had asked him, and Mukunda had flashed a brilliant smile. "Me scared? I'm not scared of anything!"

And now Mukunda had to go. Kamal and Manjula had won the long battle.

In bringing Mukunda to the house, he had been whimsical, Nirmal thought. Now he was going to turn him out with equal arbitrariness. He would disguise it, of course. Do it on the pretext of sending him to a good school in Calcutta. He would take care of his needs and comforts. He would tell Mukunda it was for his future, to broaden his world, give him new opportunities.

But Nirmal could not disguise it from himself. He had brought in the child when it was convenient for him, and now that Bakul was growing up it was no longer convenient.

Nirmal chain-smoked and paced on the terrace and longed for the time before he had returned to Songarh, when he had slept in his low-slung camp cot, separated from the open sky only by the canvas of his tent, too tired by day-long work in the sun to think or worry or feel.

He had only wanted to study earthquakes, he thought, not be their cause.

* * *

Meera was ready to go. All her things had fitted into the trunk with which she had arrived. Her train was to leave in an hour. Mukunda had gone to fetch a tonga to take her to the station. She walked from room to room, checking if she was leaving anything vital behind.

Someone touched her arm. She turned around, suppressing a scream.

"What's the matter?" Manjula said, "I just wanted to . . ."

"Oh, Manjuladi." Meera sat down on the nearest bed with a thump. "You startled me." The touch of Kamal's hand on her back was never far.

Manjula looked over her shoulder to make sure nobody was eavesdropping and took a small bundle from her waist. She opened it and held it out to Meera.

"What's this?"

"Just keep it," Manjula said. "You never know when you might need help, a woman always needs something to fall back on."

170

Meera opened the bundle. In it was a thick gold chain and six bangles. They felt heavy in her hand and glinted in the darkened room.

"I cannot," she said. "I can't take this."

"Don't fuss," Manjula said in an urgent whisper. "And don't say a thing, I haven't told anyone about this. Just pack it away quickly. Gold is a woman's parent and husband when she has neither. Look, here's Mukunda coming up the stairs." She gave Meera's hand a quick squeeze.

Meera watched her go and was stabbed with the certainty that Manjula knew. She must. She must know what her husband had done.

But there was no time for thought. Mukunda had arrived with a tonga. As Meera got into it, she looked back at the house. It seemed a little smaller, or perhaps the trees had grown since the first time she had seen it all those years ago. The paint had begun to blacken in patches, and she could see a little peepal begin to send out its leaves from a crack in the upper floor, near the parapet she had leaned over so many times to look out at the ruins. She wondered if she would ever see it again. She wondered if she felt sad or afraid or relieved.

Opposite, a window at Mrs Barnum's creaked open and they heard a voice call out, "Bye bye Meera, and see that you come back now and then!" Then the window slammed again and only the clucking of a hen broke the afternoon quiet.

* * *

Meera sat in the train and watched Mukunda shuffling about on the platform outside, nothing to say, yet unable to leave until the train did. She wondered what errand she could give him to ride over the waiting time, but there was nothing; the station was not metropolitan enough for a magazine stand, and she had food. Each time she said, "Don't wait Mukunda, go home," he smiled and replied, "What's there to do, Meeradi? I'll watch your train leaving." Around him people jostled and pushed. He seemed thinner outside the house, or perhaps,

Meera thought, I haven't looked at him properly for ages. He was in a shabby, blue, oversized shirt darned roughly near one shoulder. Meera felt something inside her wrench at the sight of the darn. He must have darned it himself, this old hand-me-down shirt. She wished she had bought him some clothes before leaving. He had been withdrawn, his ebullience smothered the last few days. Ever since he had heard of his own impending departure for a new school in Calcutta, he had even stopped playing with Bakul.

Now he would not look at her, standing there in his patched-up shirt, tracing the dirt on the platform with his slipper. She wanted to reach out and hold him.

"You and I came here, to the house, the same year, and now we're leaving for new things the same year too," she said. "You'll go to a good, big school, see a big city, become a real scholar! We'll meet again, won't we?" She put her hand out through the train's window to touch his cheek, but the train had begun to move. "Look after yourself, Mukunda," she cried out, feeling a sob in her throat, not knowing what she was crying about, her eyes wet. "Come and see me sometime, come and see me sometime soon."

Nirmal rushed into the station a minute too late, just in time to see Meera's face, striped by the bars of the train's window, recede from view.

* * *

A fortnight later, another tonga came to the door, a different set of luggage was piled into it, and Nirmal and Mukunda left for the railway station in a cloud of dust. Bakul trailed back into the house after they had gone. She paused by the well, and by the mango tree. She kicked a pebble all the way to Mukunda's old room, could not enter it for the pain of seeing it empty, then wandered back inside, going from room to room, almost breathless with the terror of knowing she would not find Mukunda. When people died, you did not see them again. She had never seen her mother – it was so, it didn't hurt. But to know Mukunda was not dead, that he was alive, and going further and further away with every turn of the tonga's wheel. To know he was alive but far away in a different world, doing things she could not visualise, making friends she would not know. Forgetting her by and by, stopping even to think of her. To know that he would begin to forget what she looked like. To think that she would not hear his voice every day, close to her ears. To know that today could have been just a normal day, like any other, when they'd have wandered the garden, and played and talked. To think that yelling "Mukunda!" in the general direction of the well or his room would no longer bring her an answering shout.

Bakul went from room to room, trying to subdue the scream that was building up inside her. She would not cry, she would not give the grown-ups that satisfaction. She would never speak to her father again. Couldn't he at least have waited for the promised Manoharpur holiday before sending Mukunda away? "No," her father had said in that impersonal way he had. "The dig's just started, I can't go on holidays now. I have to go to Calcutta on work next week, and I'll take just Mukunda this time. We can go to Manoharpur later. We'll go together, this isn't the last time you'll see him, Bakul, be sensible."

Wasn't it? She knew it was the last time, she knew she would never see him again, and if she did, it could not be the same. Mukunda knew that too, though neither of them had said anything that morning as they lay on the grass in the garden. Bakul's frock had picked up reeds and thorns, stubborn burrs which Mukunda had tried to loosen, squinting at them in frustration. She decided she would not wash the frock in which she had spent that last morning with Mukunda. She would keep it as it was, in a corner of her cupboard, and the thorns would remind her of him.

On the windowsill in the tuition room she noticed something. She picked it up. It was a thin, long, bamboo flute. Mukunda's flute; he had bought it at the Songarh mela a few years before. He had learned to play strange little tunes on it. How could he have forgotten to pack it in his brand-new trunk with his brand-new clothes?

Bakul sat on the windowsill and stroked the flute, running her fingers over its ridges and holes. She put it to her lips as if to play it.

Then she raised the flute and hit herself with it on her open palm. She looked at her palm, then hit it again. She hit it again and then on and on, as if in a trance, until her palm went red and blistered and her skin split.

PART III

THE WATER'S EDGE

ONE

"Look, a skeleton!" one of my workmen exclaimed.

However busy I was, and however many buildings I was building, I always supervised each one's first day of digging. That day I sat on a tin folding chair on the building site, shaded by my usual large, black umbrella by then so worn out that the sun came in through its many minute holes as if through a salt cellar. The week before we had cleared out the last of the debris from the crumbling mansion we had demolished, and work on the foundations of a new building had just begun. I had been arguing with my manager about some detail in his accounts when I heard the workman's voice: "Look, a skeleton!" After a pause I heard another labourer snort with disappointment, "Hah, just a dog or cat, Nandu, carry on."

I looked into the tumbled earth and, within a tangle of bleached weed roots, I saw an almost perfectly preserved brownish skeleton of what must have been a dog, with the mouldy remains of a blanket and an aluminium dish from which it must have eaten all its life. I sat on a stone next to the grave filled with disproportionate grief for this dog I had not known, for the family that buried its dish and blanket with it because they could not bear to part the dog from its possessions. I thought without reason of the children that may have pranced around with the dog in that vanished mansion's garden.

There was a house once whose garden I knew, every last tree, and where the stairs had chipped away and which of the windows would not shut. The ophthalmologist asked me once, "Do foreign bodies ever interfere with your vision? Floating black specks?" And I thought, not bodies, houses, and not foreign, ground into my blood.

"Shall we carry on, Babu?" the labourer had enquired after a bemused pause. The sight of me sitting practically in the dirt next to the dog's grave had startled him.

I could not imagine shovelling the dog out with its things like the rest of the rubbish we were daily heaping into trucks and sending away.

Eight families now live in slabs, one on top of the other, over those bones and the dish, which I planted deep in the foundations. They know nothing of it, naturally; skeletons have no place in new apartments.

People are afraid of ghosts in old houses. I know it's the new ones that are haunted, by the crumbling homes they replace. Old houses don't go away. They lurk crumbling and musty, their cobweb-hung rooms still brooding over the angled corners of shining new kitchens and marbled bathrooms, their gardens and stairwells still somewhere there in the elevator shafts.

Left to myself – despite my profession – I would let old houses remain exactly as my memory told me they always had been. Termites would write their stories across ceilings and walls, their wavering lines mapping out eventual destruction. Once the termites had dissolved the houses, returned them to the earth, a natural cycle would be complete.

I know all about houses and homes, I who never had one.

I am Mukunda. This is my story.

* * *

Other people have fables about their naming. My grandfather called me Nachiketa, they may say, and then my father changed it to Arjun. I have none. Who named me? Why did they give me a Hindu name? I have no answers to these questions. Perhaps Amulya Babu, who I have been told placed me in the orphanage that supplies my earliest memories of the world, gave me this name on an impulse when asked to fill out the official form. Perhaps my mother, whoever she was, had always thought that if she had a boy she would name him Mukunda.

People have stories too about their physical features: well into old age, they debate if they have their father's nose or mother's chin. Are they tall because their grandfather was? And will their children inherit their family propensity to insanity or baldness? Of all this, I am free. I admit I spent some years of my childhood scanning strangers around me, wondering if the map of their faces would show me a way to my lost parents. But not for long. Among parent-owning boys, I began to feel a sense of freedom as I grew up: they had a hundred things forbidden them, I had none. I could make myself as I pleased. I was free of caste or religion, that was for the rest of the world to worry about. I felt released from the burden of origins, from the burden of belonging anywhere, to anyone.

* * *

In college, my friend Arif and I did pull-ups from the branch of a mango tree, I to get broad shoulders, Arif to become taller. Arif's hair had thinned, but he was so muscular he looked menacingly strong, like a short, bald boxer. In truth he was too gentle, sweet-tempered and squeamish to smash a cockroach with his slippers. We were friends because we were both outsiders: I, provincial, casteless, wealthless; he a Muslim. I was taller than Arif so I liked walking next to him, my thatch of hair combed back in a puff, my new belt with a rearing unicorn buckle gleaming at my waist. I had two loose, white cotton shirts which I wore with the sleeves rolled up, and we would saunter along Chowringhee together, stealing looks at Anglo-Indian girls in skirts, wondering how to begin a conversation. Despite our city-boy airs, we were too shy and nervous to begin speaking and the Roxannes and Lisas slid past, animated, not noticing us. We lit cigarettes, feeling looked at as we exhaled. We tried to appear jaded, but we gaped at Calcutta as if it were a foreign city.

In this way we both reached our eighteenth birthdays, his date and month certain, mine whatever I wanted it to be. It was 1945 and we had both finished our Inter. I had no precise notions about the future, but the world of work and earning my own money began to beckon me like a spell. All my life I had lived on charity. I had not been aware of it my first few years in an orphanage, but the next few, in Nirmal Babu's family, I had felt it as keenly as a blister that the rough edge of a slipper keeps rubbing. At eighteen I determined that I would never depend on anyone again. I knew that Nirmal Babu wanted me to study further, but I knew equally that I would not. As soon as I got a job, though just a poorly paid clerkship at a tannery, I stopped collecting the interest on Nirmal Babu's fixed deposit. I wrote Nirmal Babu a brief letter saying I had passed and he did not have to send me extra money any longer. I gave up my room in the college hostel and left no forwarding address.

I cut my ties with Songarh as once it had with me. I was now alone in the world. No solitary pilot in the clouds, no climber on the point of a peak, could have felt my combination of vertigo and euphoria.

* * *

Now that I had finished college, I began to look for lodgings and meals. Get a wife, the boys at the hostel chuckled, a rich one, aren't you an eligible groom, you casteless bastard. Arif was about to leave Calcutta, having landed a job as an accountant for a rich relative, a textile manufacturer in Lahore. Two days before he was due to leave, we went for a long walk through the streets of Calcutta, heading in a pleasantly aimless fashion towards the house in which he was a lodger. It was a still sort of day, and heavy clouds were beginning to collect. A thread of light streaked through the sky now and then, and the low rumble of distant thunder reached us after a minute's pause. We had idled in the green of the Maidan, eaten a plate of kababs and rotis on the street in Dharamtolla and then meandered towards College Street. Arif was looking into the window of a bookshop while I stood facing the street, saying to him, "Hurry up, I think it's going to rain."

It was then that I saw them standing on the pavement across the street, Nirmal Babu holding a cloth bag in one hand, his face thinner than I remembered, his hair higher up his forehead than before. Beside him, a girl who must have been Bakul. She looked like Bakul but for the sari, I had never seen her in a sari – if she had turned a little to the left I would have seen her face. I stared across the rush of traffic and people. I willed her to turn towards me. I had only to cross that wide road crowded with moving cars and stumbling people and I would be next to them, saying, "After all these years!" But how could it be that I had seen them and they had not seen me? They looked away instead, towards the other end of the street. Sometimes they spoke to each other and Nirmal Babu looked at his watch.

I turned to Arif. "You go on to Suleiman Chacha's, I have to . . ." I could still see Nirmal Babu's tall head bobbing across the street. Just above him hung a sign for Cuticura Vanishing Cream, rusted and askew, the pink-faced model peeling paint. Behind him a line of bookshops, books tumbling out of them onto the pavement. I started to cross the street, pausing in the middle to let a tram pass. It stopped before me like a wall. I cursed it for stopping just there, just then. But it had, for passengers, I thought stupidly. That's it – Nirmal Babu and Bakul were looking the other way waiting for their tram, and now it had come. I ran as it began to move. From the outside I could make out Nirmal Babu shuffling around in the men's section, looking for a seat, and Bakul's face in the women's section, just a few feet from mine. I opened my mouth to call her, maybe I even did, for it seemed to me that for a moment she peered out, as if looking for someone, but then the tram began to move, she turned away and I fell back.

"A 23!" Arif said, looking at the receding tram. "Why didn't you call me, it would've gone direct to Suleiman Chacha's . . . Hey Mukunda, are you listening? You look as if you've seen a ghost."

"It's nothing," I mumbled. "We're on the wrong side of the road, couldn't have reached it in time even if we'd run." Instinct had made me rush towards them, but that moment outside the tram, seeing them not seeing me, wondering if they wanted not to see me, stirred my old bitterness about the way I had been cast out of their lives.

* * *

Suleiman Khan was Arif's landlord – Arif was a lodger in his house, and we both called him Suleiman Chacha, deferring to his age. When we reached his house after our day-long stroll, he was reading his newspaper, his parrot nibbling his shoulder. Chacha's face was hidden behind the *Statesman*, but I sensed his eyes upon me now and then. When I was about to leave, he spoke. It would be lonely for them without Arif, he said. They had always had a lodger, before Arif there had been others. Would I like to live in Arif's room?

He was hesitant. The words came stumbling out and stood there between us, growing in the silence. It was almost presumptuous of him. I was perhaps the only boy in the college who visited Arif at home and ate there with him. Visiting was bad enough, but *living* there! It was unheard of for a Hindu to live in a Muslim's household, especially in those times, when people could talk of nothing but whether the country would be fenced into Hindu and Muslim pens, India and Pakistan. If it were, which would I choose? I did not feel much of a Hindu, or anything at all in particular, with my origins such a matter of speculation and hearsay. Instead I had the offer of a roof over my head. I must have begun to smile, for I saw Chacha smiling at me, and then at Arif, who slapped my shoulder and said, "It's not the hostel, Mukunda, you'll have to civilise yourself!"

Suleiman Chacha had offered me a home when I was about to become homeless. Did he perceive my need because he sensed he too would be homeless soon? Did he know then that by the next year mobs would roam the streets looking for kills, that he would have to come home before dark every day? There must have been some hint of prescience in his spontaneity with me, or else why did he offer his home to me, a near stranger?

I brought my trunk and moved into Arif's room. They would take no rent and gave me two meals a day. They had no children, they said, and they had a big house. They had never taken rent from Arif either. I was astonished by their generosity and knew that I could never match it.

* * *

Suleiman Chacha was a teacher of history. He had for many years taught at a run-down school in Baghbazar, and although the school had the reputation of being a rowdy one in which the boys seldom came to class, they trooped into Suleiman Chacha's. Chacha knew not only about the emperors, but also about their concubines, slaves, wives and generals. His classes often went beyond the set forty minutes as he chatted about the households, bazaars, roads, doctors, schools and peasants of times past. Most of the other teachers were only too happy to have a class after Suleiman Chacha's because they had about twenty minutes less to teach and could blame it on him, although some, jealous of his popularity among the boys, had complained to the headmaster that he did not teach by the syllabus and left students unready for examinations. But the headmaster was perhaps under Suleiman Chacha's spell as well, and did nothing to rein him in.

On many sultry, dark evenings at his house, as we sat out in the verandah waving mosquitoes away with our handfans, I too listened spellbound to Chacha talking of Jahangir's library, or of Bahadur Shah's last melancholic journey to Burma. For Suleiman Chacha the past was always in the present. In this he reminded me of Nirmal Babu, who used to measure time in centuries rather than minutes and seconds. Music reminded Suleiman Chacha of what Tansen sang for Akbar, kababs provoked a story about Lord Clive's khansama, a painful boil he had on his knee made him chuckle about slanging matches between the vaids and hakims of medieval times. As he spoke, clearing his throat often, I not only saw the past before my eyes, I could even smell and hear it. Yet when I tried to repeat his stories to anyone, they never sounded the same.

In appearance he was not imposing. He was a short man, barely reaching my shoulder. His hair had fallen out early, leaving him with a bald scalp that shone with the perspiration that is Calcutta's gift to its citizens most of the year. His beard was neat, though sparse, and his bony, longish face was sheltered on either side by overlarge ears whose lobes almost reached his jawline. His only striking feature was his eyes, which were a luminous grey, shadowed by eyebrows that with their very luxuriance compensated for the paucity of hair on his head and chin.

Chachi and he had been married very young, and by the time I came to know them, her habitual manner with him was a kind of exasperation. She berated him, sometimes loudly, sometimes in mutters, for everything: for letting his bathwater go cold on winter mornings; for forgetting to give the milkman her instructions; for filling up the house to such a point with his books; for his visitors coming too early and leaving too late. Chacha listened to her with a twinkle in his eye, and when she paused he said, "Come, Farhana Begum, it has been so long since I had a scolding, have I strayed into the wrong house?"

Their house, though situated in a shop-crowded gulli, was an airy one, with two floors and a small patch of dusty ground that had a mango and a lemon tree. Chacha had inherited it from an uncle who had died childless. The house had little furniture, and it was very clean, but you could see that the coverings were threadbare and the curtains had an infinity of darns that showed against the light when the sun shone through the windows. They could afford just one fan, and it was run only in the afternoons and at night in the large middle room.

There were reasons for their ascetic existence. Chacha's pay was meagre – when were schoolteachers ever rich? – but also, if ever there was spare money, he could not resist spending it on books and music. Each time he came home with a new or secondhand book or record, he would creep upstairs trying to hide it in his clothes, while Chachi, detecting it by his demeanour, would cry out, "Again! You've done it again! Wasn't this the month for a new kurta? Do you know that the children make fun of you at school for your clothes?"

"Aha, Farhana Bibi, but I had been looking for this book for months, and just as I was about to board the bus, I saw it on the stack and then bargained . . . I had money left and bought some nice bangles for you, but in all this, do you know I missed my bus and . . . "

"Don't tell me all this rubbish, I don't want to know!"

He would turn to me for support, "This is a brilliant book, bhai, read it and tell me, tell your Chachi . . . " He would hand me the book to look at, then snatch it back in a few seconds to open it and smell the pages. If it had a beautiful engraving on the title page he would show it to me. He would remove the dust jacket and finger the gilt embossing on the spine, and by then, having forgotten all about Chachi's scolding, would go to her saying, "See, Farhana, see what beautiful lettering there is!"

Chachi would leave the room, but we could hear her muttering in the kitchen and each time she passed us. By dinner time, though, I would find the hot roti going first to Chacha, and at night there was peace as he read his new book and she darned clothes, humming old tunes under her breath, and I paced up and down wondering what to do until Chacha looked up with a frown and said, "Can't you sit still? Read that book I gave you last week."

* * *

I was nineteen and had lived at Suleiman Chacha's for a year, though I cannot remember the month or day or season, only irrelevant details about that day. For example, I recall I had eaten bread with tea that evening. I rarely had bread to eat as it was more expensive than rotis, but that day I happened to walk past my old school, the one Nirmal Babu had put me in after Songarh. The bakery next to the school was still there, and the smell of fresh baking which had tormented me through my school years still filled the lane. I could not stop myself; I spent all the change in my pocket on a cylindrical loaf of fresh bread. When I returned home with the bread in my hand, Suleiman Chacha said, "Now we have a rich lodger! Time we took some rent."

Chachi said, "If you wanted bread so much, why didn't you say so? I thought you liked my rotis."

I took out the yellow Polson's butter I had bought as well – even more flamboyant an expense – and toasted the bread on their electric ring. To this day the smell of fresh toasting bread makes me feel faintly nauseous. I handed them the thick, crisp, brown-edged slices soaking in salty yellow butter. Chacha dipped his into hot tea.

Chacha's feet were in soft old chappals indented with toe circles.

His kurta–pyjama was worn out, with several stitches loose. We were sitting as usual in the wide verandah in the last of the daylight. There was some noise from far away, a few explosions of firecrackers, and Chacha said, "Someone celebrating something." He lit a cigarette and exhaled with a sigh. I could smell the smoke, pleasantly pungent. Despite the noise, a quiet contentment spread over the verandah, as if we were nestling in a translucent globe that fended off the world. The cups, the saucers, the faded purple flowers on them, the faint aroma of tea, even the chips in the old gilt edging on the saucers, all seemed to have a perfection that made me unwilling to touch anything and mar it. In the west, the last fragments of orange in the sky deepened to a luminous pink.

After we had finished the loaf and drunk all our tea, Chachi wrapped the remains of the butter in its paper while I went up to the roof to smoke.

My match remained unlit. In the distance, ringing the horizon, was an incandescent necklace of terrifying beauty: the city had been set on fire. Orange flames leapt, subsided, started somewhere new. The sky had turned an eerie red. I could hear a distant, monotonous roar broken by the odd high-pitched scream. Another of those explosions and I realised they were not firecrackers at all, they were probably bombs. An oily pall of smoke hung over the sky, smelling of hair and flesh and burning rubber. Although I knew I was too far away to be in danger, I felt a fog of fear rising within me and obliterating everything else. I knew something larger than I could comprehend was pacing out there in the darknesses between the firelight, something my instinct told me would change things forever.

I was too riveted by the flames and cries of people to notice that Suleiman Chacha had joined me. He reached into his pocket and pulled out a packet of translucent cigarette papers. I jumped at the sound of foil. He began the fussy business of layering his paper with tobacco. He did not look up at the flames until his own roll of tobacco was glowing in the darkness.

"I think we'll have to go away for a while," he said, as if discussing a summer holiday.

"Go away? What do you mean? Where to?"

"My relatives in Rajshahi," he replied. "They have been asking me to visit for years anyway. This is a good time."

"There's no need for you to go anywhere," I exclaimed. "None of this will affect you. It's the slums they're burning."

"Oh come, nothing to do with anything burning, I just think your Chachi needs a change. She's getting a bit depressed."

"If she needs a change, go to Darjeeling. Why don't you?"

"Those relatives need visiting," Suleiman Chacha said, half laughing. "What if they forget us? And you do know I have a room or two in an ancestral house there. Shouldn't I lay claim?"

I knew as well as he did that he could not discuss the real reason for going away. I had sensed from the time I began living with Chacha that the political upheavals and violence all around, the news of rioting in Punjab and in the Muslim pockets of the north worried him deeply, as they did everyone else. We used to discuss it now and then, but as troubles that simmered at a distance from us, that might scorch us at the edges but not burn; we had never thought the flames would come close enough to threaten us.

Now they had.

When I walked into a room where Chacha was sitting with his friends, or even just with Chachi, there was an instant lull in the conversation and then they would begin to talk of something innocuous. And where Chacha had earlier routinely gone out and met his Hindu friends, now he seemed to meet only his Muslim friends, and at home. When they did not think I was in the vicinity they argued with each other about leaving the country. One afternoon I left the house when I heard quiet sounds of sobbing at the doorway as I was about to enter. More and more, I had begun to feel like an outsider in the place that had become my home.

"You don't need to leave," I repeated, but I was drained of conviction. These days people I had thought of as ordinary and level-headed talked of storing bottles of acid as weapons. If the mob came for Suleiman Chacha and Chachi, where would I hide them? How would I save them?

Suleiman Chacha took another deep drag, but his cigarette, as these rolled ones do, had gone out. He fumbled in his pocket for matches and lit the damp-looking blackened roll again.

"You can carry on living in the house," he said again. "In fact it would be a good thing not to put a lock on it – who knows what may happen. Look after it until we are back."

"How long will you go for?" I asked.

"I hope it won't be for long," he said. "Let these troubles subside and I'll be back before you know it."

"What about the school?" I said.

"I'll tell them nothing," he said. "I'll just say that I'm going on leave for two months."

"Surely they will guess?"

"The headmaster's a good man. He has not asked me to leave. Somehow," he chuckled, "I think he will be relieved if I go."

* * *

I knew about the ancestral house in Rajshahi: Chacha was reticent about his past, but Chachi was not. That house was a source of acrimony between them, more so when money ran short. Chacha was the second of four sons of a government official in Rajshahi, and his father had left behind land and a large family home. It was meant to have been divided equally between the brothers, but Suleiman Chacha, who did not live in Rajshahi – nor altogether in the material world – had been cheated out of his share. It existed, theoretically, but he could not lay claim to it any longer. As the end of each month drew near and Chachi's housekeeping money dwindled, she felt a keener sense of deprivation than she ever did at the beginning of the month. At such times she would say to me, "If we got an eighth share even, and could sell that rice land, we would have enough not to worry. Then I would cook you phirni and biryani every day, and we could have ceiling fans in every room and not sweat through the summer. But will your Chacha do anything about it? People like him should never marry, just sit under a tree and be the Buddha."

188

Chacha ticked her off briskly, saying, "Pipe dreams, more pipe dreams. When will you stop?" But it was this faint wisp of a possible windfall from their land that kept them both going as they dug into the backs of cupboards for small change in the last week of every month.

And now all of a sudden Chacha and Chachi were being forced to set off for Rajshahi, to claim their share of the home and land they had lost long before.

* * *

The most perplexing question about Chacha and Chachi leaving turned out to be not the job or the house or relatives and friends, but their parrot, which they would have to leave in my care. I do not like birds at close quarters. They belong in an element different from ours and that is where they should remain. I felt as much affection for the lizard that crept behind my table lamp as for the bird in the cage. Both, I hoped, would keep their distance from me.

Suleiman Chacha's parrot was called Noorie. She looked as all parrots do, bright green, with a scarlet-purple band around a neck which seemed to be able to swivel a full circle as she watched people from her cage. Every night, Suleiman Chacha would cover the cage with a cloth, all the while muttering to the bird in a coaxing tone he used only with her. During the day, Chacha and Chachi would take turns to tempt the bird with curly green chillies and grain. The cage was large, with a swing in it. It was kept in the wide upstairs verandah overlooking the trees, so that Noorie, I thought, could envy her free compatriots at leisure.

I am being unjust, for the bird flew free in the house much of the day. As soon as Suleiman Chacha had finished his morning prayers he went to the cage and lifted the cloth with a flourish, making chucking noises at the bird, which responded with a series of clicks of its beak and a soft word or two. Chacha had taught her to say his name and half a dozen other words, a repertoire he was inordinately doting about. As parents do with young children, he would coax the bird into speech for his visitors.

189

Murmuring to each other, they would be thus united every morning, after which Noorie would perch on a door or, when it was available, Chacha's shoulder as he went about his chores. Sometimes it alighted on me too, its claws poking through my thin kurta, its feathers tickling my ears. I am sure it knew I did not want it there.

"Won't you take Noorie with you?" I asked Chachi, anxious not to be left looking after the bird.

I had followed her into the kitchen where she now sat on the floor, leaning against the door, picking rice over for stones. She peered into the rice, pushing bits of it away with her forefinger so that there were two heaps on the big plate, separated by a golden river of bell metal. She did not look up. Her voice had a tremor, as it often did these days.

"We've no idea where we'll stay, how can we carry a bird with us?"

"But you do have a house, you will live there, and it's only for a month or two."

"I have never seen this house. It has so many of his relatives already living in it. I would be happy if they gave us a corner to sleep in."

I felt sure she was exaggerating, being upset at leaving Calcutta so unexpectedly. I looked up with trepidation at Noorie who was perched upon the kitchen door clucking and muttering to herself, unaware of her destiny.

* * *

They left two days later. Chachi had made some parathas for the journey and packed some other dry stuff: biscuits and muri. They were taking no more than a trunkful of clothes and a bedroll. The night before they were to leave, Chacha took me around the house, showing me the electric meter, telling me about the bills that had to be paid each month. He even showed me where he kept the papers for property tax, and gave me a post-dated cheque for a payment due four months later.

"But you'll be back by then," I insisted.

"Of course, we will," Chacha said, his voice tender, as if I were a child he needed to console. "This is just in case we get delayed . . . "

Chachi had bought a week's supply of crisp, green chillies and half a kilo of the grain the bird liked to eat.

"You know the sound Noorie makes when she wants a chilli, don't you?" she said. "And remember, her bowl must have water at all times."

"I know it is a bit troublesome," Chacha said, "but you will need to clean out the cage every so often."

"It's no trouble," I mumbled, feeling the weight of a stone in my heart.

"Talk to her every morning," he said, "before you leave for work. She'll be lonely with nobody in the house. She's not used to it."

"You will be back in no time," I said again.

"Of course," Chacha said. "Why would I want to stay away from my own home?"

Noorie seemed to have understood that something was afoot and had been flapping about inside the cage, making harsh noises. Before they left, I covered the cage with her cloth.

They did not want me to go to the station with them. "I don't want Noorie to be alone when we leave," Chacha said. "We can manage this little bit of luggage on our own."

I watched them trudge down to the end of the lane, bent sideways by their bundles and trunk. The corners of my eyes were damp with tears and I brushed them away, feeling both impatient and nonplussed by my despondency. They vanished from sight without turning. I shut the gate and went back to remove the cloth from Noorie's cage.

"Now it's just you and me," I whispered, wanting to be consoled. She stayed in the corner of her cage and would not come out.

* * *

My maudlin temper had left me by the next morning. It is strangely comforting how much distance sleep can create between events. I looked around my empire. Silence had replaced the usual morning sounds: Chacha's gargling and loud throat-clearing as he brushed his teeth, Chachi's series of sneezes early each day. For the first time in my life there was no-one for whom I felt obliged to vacate a chair. I could put my feet up on the table. I could be whoever I wanted to be, I was in a house all to myself in a city where virtually nobody knew me. I was filled with a sudden sense of elation and space. I flung the cover off the parrot and opened the door of her cage.

"I'm free!" I announced to Noorie. "And you are too!"

Noorie would not leave the cage.

I did not care. I threw in some chillies and her grain. When I reached inside her cage for her water bowl she flapped her wings and pecked me, drawing blood.

"You'd better not do that," I snarled. "It's just you and me now!"

I am ashamed to say that I hardly thought about Chacha and Chachi rumbling their way across to Rajshahi, backs aching against the hard seats of a crowded train, weary and worried, not knowing what awaited them at their destination.

* * *

I lived in Suleiman Chacha's house for a long period without any real change in routine. I took no liberties. I did not, for example, shift from my small room to one of the larger ones. I fed the parrot every day, as I had seen Suleiman Chacha do, but she often left her grain untouched and would refuse to come out of her cage. I had not imagined birds mourned, but this one certainly seemed to. Once or twice she pecked me hard on my wrist when I was putting in or taking out her food and water. "Bastard," I would spit at her then. "Just come out and I'll wring your stupid green neck!" I would lock her in her cage and leave for work at the tannery, returning late in the evening, stripping my sweaty shirt as I leapt up the stairs two at a time. I would find her crouched in the corner as I had left her, as if she hadn't moved at all in the nine hours I had been away. If I reached out to check her water bowl, she'd peck at me again and I would yell, "Haraami! If they weren't coming back, I'd make parrot stew out of you!"

But Chacha and Chachi had not returned a year later. They did not return to see the country cut in two in 1947 or to watch the British leave, they did not return for the speeches and the new flags. They were away during the worst of the killings and of course, since they were Muslim, I did not expect them among the refugees who staggered into Calcutta. They must have found something for themselves in East Pakistan – that was the explanation I gave myself – they must have put down roots, and perhaps they would write and send for Noorie one day. I did not want to let in the thought that they might never have reached Rajshahi at all, that they might have been slaughtered on the way.

For months after Chacha and Chachi left, I locked the doors and windows every evening, fearing the house would be invaded as a Muslim's. Just as I began to think I was safe, a mob came one night with torches and yelled for Suleiman Khan to come out, or else. I heard their shouts and slipped out of the back, hiding behind a low water tank. But for the certainty that I would be dead within minutes, there was no place for thoughts in my mind. I heard footsteps approaching the tank, a voice calling out, "I think the mullah's hiding here." I saw feet crush the grass next to me. When the man shone his torch into my face, he exclaimed, "*You*? You here?" Luckily for me he was from my neighbourhood and I had often chatted with him at the local shop when I was buying eggs and cigarettes.

I crept out from behind the tank. I had lost my voice. In some sort of whisper I managed to say that Suleiman Khan had fled and left me the house. "Left you the house?" he exclaimed. "You lucky runt!" I managed to smile, and the house got a reprieve.

But I did not. The tannery at which I worked as a clerk was owned by a Muslim. He decided to close it down and leave.

I had few friends. Most of the boys at my Intermediate college had scattered and I had not kept in touch. The only man who seemed to have any sympathy for me was the head clerk at the tannery, who took me to a roadside stall for lunch the day we were to part. We sat facing each other, legs across a wooden bench, aluminium plates of steaming rice and fish curry before us. Barababu washed his hands in water from his glass and shut his eyes, muttering a prayer. Then he plunged his fingers into his rice.

"Look," Barababu said. "Think about me. I have a wife, three daughters. It's not half as bad for you. You just need to look out for yourself. I envy you, my friend."

"Envy? I'm an unlucky bastard," I said. "The moment things seem to settle down, I'm back on the street."

"The street?" Barababu exclaimed. "You have a roof over your head, gifted from the heavens. How much more luck do you want?"

"That's not mine," I replied. "They'll be back any day. And the money they left is all gone. I need to find money to pay bills and taxes."

"My dear boy," Barababu said, focused on picking a bone out of his fish. "Nobody who has gone is coming back. Have you seen anyone return yet? Your houseowners must have taken over a Hindu house in Pakistan by now, and you have been left with theirs. It's enemy property, my son, enemy property! You're the lucky bugger who was in the right place when he needed to be."

He put a ball of rice and fish into his mouth and, looking beyond me, chewed with great absorption. His mouth empty at last, he chuckled softly and said as if to himself, "Such luck, and such naivety." His mouth twisted and again he returned to his fish. A tiny speck of gravy clung to his moustache.

I could see Barababu did not think it possible, but despite what I had said to the mob, I truly had never considered Suleiman Chacha's house as my own, to do with as I pleased. His words flung wide a half-open door in my mind.

"I suppose I could do something with the house," I said. "Or else how will I pay the bills?"

"Look, son," Barababu said – I noticed that he had taken to calling me "son" more and more – "there are scores of people who have come across the border, not scores, hundreds, thousands, millions!" He gesticulated at the crowded streets around us. "They all need places to stay! Rent out those rooms! You'll never need to work again. And if you still want work, I'll introduce you to a relative of mine. He's a builder, and he's been saying he needs a young man like you."

Barababu insisted on coming home with me that afternoon, to better advise me, he said. He cast an appreciative look at the garden as I was opening the gate and as soon as we entered, he darted to the corner and, hitching up his dhoti, shimmied up the mango tree.

"You don't know how much my soul longs for this," he said in rapture, looking down at me through a fringe of leaves on a high branch. "The village, our trees, the fruits I plucked as a boy. In Calcutta's shanties where does one find trees? I've decided, my boy, I'm going to return to my village and tend whatever land I have."

"Won't you come down?" I said. "I'm not sure the branches are strong, it's a young tree."

"Oh, I know all about trees," he said, clambering down with more agility than I would have thought possible for a man his age. He followed me to the front door muttering, "Two storeys, eh, and it must be on, what, two hundred square yards of land?" As I put my key into the lock, he thrust his hand into the dirty cloth bag that hung from his shoulder and produced a small glass bottle of clouded water.

"Muslim house, ehm, you know, one can't be too careful . . . " he said. Unscrewing the bottle, he sprinkled a few drops of water on the doorstep and, as if by accident, a few drops on me, mumbling an unintelligible mantra. Then, purification rites over, he walked in and examined each room in turn, murmuring approval, saying only, "This parrot, you must get rid of this parrot. Look how it's shitting everywhere."

I spent the next few days ruminating over Barababu's advice. For hours I leaned over Kalighat Bridge, watching the murky waters below. At low tide there was hardly any water and the banks revealed years of filth. But at high tide it was brimming, a quiet, liquid brown. A mud hut perched halfway down its right bank, and coconut trees peered into the water. It was a world away from the city's clanging trams, jostling crowds, rotted odours and streets crowded with emaciated beggars who all said they had not eaten for many days. As I leaned over the bridge I thought of the unthinkable, of betraying Suleiman Chacha's trust. I could sell the house, or rent it out and make it a tenement. I could live like a zamindar, I could work for pleasure. I could write books, compose music, travel. I could be a real gentleman.

The next morning when I uncovered Noorie's cage, she was speaking. Something — it would be too pat to say it was some change in me — but something had provoked her to speech again, and she was repeating the imprecations I had hurled at her all those weeks. "Bastard," she was squawking. 'Sister-fucker, bastard, sister-fucker." Spoken in that nasal, unmodulated parrot voice the words sounded grotesque, even though they were part of my normal, daily conversation. In a distant corner of my mind, it rang bells I did not want to hear. I remembered an old, half-mad woman in a tiny room in Songarh, Kananbala, whose swear words I used to parrot for fun. I did not want to be reminded of that world.

I took care when speaking to Noorie after this, but she had already mastered my obscenities, and to my discomfort, uttered them almost to the exclusion of anything else.

TWO

When I think of the man I worked for next it is his hands that I visualise first of all. They were pale and long-fingered, with a slight tremor. Each finger had at least one ring on it, and each ring had a different, potent stone – I could identify a topaz, a cat's eye, a ruby, even a diamond. In all he wore twelve. A year into my employment, when I was able to enter his room without prior permission, I found him at his polished desk, twisting one of the rings round and round. He looked up as I came in and said, "Do you know what these rings are? They are my destiny." He fisted his hand and held it to his chest. "With these rings I keep my destiny imprisoned in my own hands."

I had got this job only because of Barababu, after long months of searching when the city had seemed filled with Inter pass boys like myself, all unemployed. I had been tempted then, by the seduction of ease, of living a landlord's life off Suleiman Chacha's house. Aangti Babu's job had come just in time to stop my zamindari fantasies. I was afraid now and said, eager to please, "The rings are your destiny, and you are ours, Sir."

In private we called him Aangti Babu and joked that ten fingers were too few for him. The word always went around the little office very quickly when Aangti Babu left for a mysterious errand in the afternoon. Nobody suspected a woman, save possibly a woman astrologer. He never let on which astrologer he had just discovered, but we found out all the same. There was a man in Bhowanipore, not far from where I lived, and I went to him as well after I discovered he was Aangti Babu's latest find. I had never believed in future-telling, I was simply curious about Aangti Babu's passion.

The astrologer sat at a bare desk in a small room. He was an old man in thick glasses which shone. I could not see his eyes behind the lenses. The glasses covered most of his small, pouchy face. He did not smile a welcome. He hardly even looked up as he said, "Birth chart?"

I was uncomfortable, for the curtained-off door behind him was open and I felt sure someone was eavesdropping. Despite my scepticism, I began to feel the astrologer knew everything about me and it was important that nobody else find out.

"I have no birth chart," I mumbled.

He reached into a drawer with a sigh and took out pen and paper.

"Time of birth?" he asked me, like a government clerk.

I told him I did not know.

"Date of birth?" he continued in tones laden with the same weariness.

"I'm not sure."

"Not sure." The man let out a high, startling sigh that ended in a laugh, and picked up a glass of water from the windowsill near him. "Moshai, I am an astrologer, not a magician. I need some details." He sipped his water as if he was already done with me. I half expected him to look over my shoulder and say, "Next!" although there was nobody else waiting to see him.

"I thought you could read my palm," I said, now not wanting to leave without some knowledge. "Or maybe my face," I said. "There are those who read faces." What had I come for? I was no longer sure. I had forgotten my curiosity about Aangti Babu by then. Perhaps, like others who go to such people, all I wanted was attention. I felt disappointed, as if I had been denied a gift.

The shining lenses turned upward towards me. He regarded me for a second without comment. I looked away from his unspoken ridicule.

He held out his hand. I put mine forward, saying, "I don't know if it should be the right one or the left . . ."

He scrutinised my palm for long minutes, and I looked with him, as if I had never seen it before. It was creased, untidy, crowded with crosses and wild strokes slashing it in two. I have seen palms that have scarcely any lines. Mine was not one of them, far from it. I waited as if for a verdict.

"A veritable atlas," he said, his fingers tracing the longer lines on my palm. "What rivers of desire, what mountains of ambition!"

"I wanted to . . . I mean I was hoping . . ."

"Want, want, hope, hope," the astrologer parroted, "this is what your palm says too, moshai, your palm is nothing but an atlas of impossible longings." He poked my lifeline and said, "Nothing but longing."

For a while after that he said nothing. My arm was cramped from holding it over the desk. The ornate wooden clock on the wall counted out the hour. My hard chair had no armrest. His bent head, his opaque glasses, gave nothing away. I began to wonder if he was asleep. Or dead. I coughed as if I needed water and moved my chair to make a scraping sound. The astrologer jumped up and exclaimed, "Tuesday's train! Tuesday's train!" Then he shook himself a little, and as if he was continuing a conversation, he said, "Life is made of brick and stone, brick by brick."

"I am a builder's assistant," I informed him. "I have been working there for almost a year. Now my boss has started sending me to negotiate with people." I was proud of this. Just a few days before, Aangti Babu had sent me to talk to some prospective buyers.

"Hm." He mumbled something and then said, "Have you come to talk about yourself or to listen?"

I shut up, ashamed.

"What d'you want to know, eh?" he said. "Let me tell you. Your past is cloudy, but your future clear. Your past shows homelessness, your future shows homes, this is most visible. Yes, you will be married. Yes, you will do very well in your job. You will have money. You will go far beyond your beginnings. You will not have a child. No, you will not travel very much. Anything else?"

I felt a mixture of annoyance and disappointment. But suppressing my impulse to be rude I asked him in a humble tone, "Anything else you could tell me about how my life will be . . ."

"No more. But wait." He squinted at my palm again and bringing out a magnifying glass, examined one part of it. The top of his head was near my nose. Strands of copper-grey hair poked upward out of his balding scalp like new saplings in a brown flowerbed.

"I see you standing on some steps, there is water before you, but will you step into it and swim? Or will you keep standing on the bank?"

He dismissed my palm and pushing his chair back he said, "It's late, that's all."

Before I could ask him what he meant, he had disappeared behind the faded curtains that hung limp at the inner door. The newspaper on the desk came suddenly loose in the air from the fan and scattered all over the room as I rushed about trying to gather it in my arms.

* * *

Aangti Babu was indeed noticing me more. For the first year or so in the office I had been hardly more than a tea boy who recorded Letters Received and Letters Sent, Affidavits and Powers of Attorney Drawn Up in a large red ledger. I would watch Aangti Babu enter the office self-absorbed, apparently unaware of the flurry of sycophantic gestures made for his benefit by the head clerk, the supervisor, visiting contractors. Sometimes, I later noticed, he would deliberately drop something at his feet so that whoever was near him had to bend to pick it up. So great was our desire to oblige him that we would all dive together, knocking each other about in the attempt to reach the elusive pen or paper clip. I observed during one of these dives that although his hands were white and long-nailed, the little finger's nail even painted red, his soles were cracked and dirty. Even so, that Durga puja, I went to his house to touch his feet and get his blessings.

He looked at me as I rose from his feet and said to a man sitting next to him, "This is the boy I told you about."

I touched that gentleman's feet as well, my heart racing. Aangti Babu had been telling someone about me!

Aangti Babu said, "So, do you feel like a change? Can you abandon the ledger and come with me to a site tomorrow?"

I looked up from their feet in gratitude and disbelief.

We were to meet the next day at a site in Ballygunj, which was too

200

prosperous an area to be part of my daily life. I went early and waited for Aangti Babu to arrive. A half-demolished old building stood in a large overgrown garden. The labourers had not yet arrived. I could see they had not progressed beyond knocking out the front windows, which made the building look as if its eyes had been gouged out. Through the gaping holes, you could see darkness and corners, dusty red floors. At the back of the building was a shabby outhouse, two rooms at most, with a broken tap next to it, dribbling water.

I walked past the outhouse, thinking myself alone, but I was startled by a man who emerged, shaking. His head shook and his body shook, his hands which held the door shook. He had dirty white hair and yellow eyes. His shoulders sloped into a shabby shirt without buttons. The open neck showed bones beneath wood-coloured flesh covered with grey straggly hair. Behind him, a thin young woman appeared, and tried to make him go back in. She was young, but her face had a tired, youthless look. He would not obey. In a reedy voice, looking all the while at me, he protested, "Leave me alone, I will not go. I will not go."

I turned away and walked out to the gate, bemused. I forgot him the next instant for Aangti Babu had just appeared, his starched white dhoti and crinkled kurta looking dazzling in the bright, early light. It was already hot. His armpits were circles of translucent cloth. I hurried to him and held an umbrella over his head to shade him from the sun. I was fumbling with nervousness. It was the first time I had been alone with him at a real building site, and Aangti Babu could have a filthy temper. I did not want to put a foot wrong. The overseer had joined us. He was a tall, hawk-faced, monosyllabic man, who did not scurry around Aangti Babu as the rest of us did. He listened to the instructions directed at him without any apparent anxiety that he would forget something.

"Those mango trees must go, we'll get space for the water reservoir," Aangti Babu was saying as we reached a grove at the back. "Tell me what we get for the wood, and don't sell it to the man who takes the windows, he gives a bad price for wood."

Aangti Babu took rapid strides, assessing the work to be done.

"Level that earth," he said, pointing one way; "pile the bricks there," he ordered, pointing another. "Stack up the windows, count them first! And what about the stair grills? Have to get a better rate than we did last time. There was a carved banister on the upper staircase, I want that fitted in my house. See to it, will you?" I took note of everything on a scrap of paper, uncertain which of the instructions were for me and which for the overseer.

We rounded the corner and arrived at the outhouse, now with its door shut, the tap outside dribbling as before. "Still here?" Aangti Babu said, sounding tetchy. "See to it, will you?" He wiped the back of his neck with a damp, grimy handkerchief as I struggled to keep the umbrella over his bobbing head. As we were leaving the site, he said his first words to me. "See what we do? Will you be able to?"

The next time I went to the site, the land around the house looked clean and spacious. There was suddenly a lot of light where a dark tree- and grass-filled garden had been. The trees were gone, the outhouse was gone as well. The tap still ran, wetting the earth around it.

* * *

Aangti Babu's method was to buy old houses, some abandoned in a hurry by those who had gone away because of Partition, some that were owned by too many warring relatives, some occupied by tenants the landlord no longer wanted. As a result he got them cheap. He knew how to get rid of unhappy relatives and lingering tenants. Then, if the neighbourhood was a good one, he might build a mansion and sell it at a profit to a rich man. Sometimes he let it lie fallow for years, saying, "A gold mine, you will see, one day it will be a gold mine." He would stick his little finger into his ear and with one eye closed prise around until the fingernail emerged with wax rimming the end. As he looked at the wax he would repeat, "You will see, my boy."

My workplace, in a building in Bowbazar, consisted of two rooms, one occupied by Aangti Babu and the other by everyone else and a tea kettle and stove that hissed all day. Outside was a street market where slimy vegetable peel rotted underfoot and vendors shouted far into the evening. The building was a dilapidated one, and the rooms were small, painted a mauve that had greased into grey, no advertisement for a builder. There was a narrow, dark patch of corridor outside Aangti Babu's own room. It was here that I now sat proudly at a table, inkpot before me, register and ruler and house plans ranged by my side, a bulb in a cheap saucer-shaped tin lampshade hanging over my head, conferring on me a yellow halo.

Apart from me there was a tea boy, assorted contractors, plumbers, electricians and labourers who passed through, and two men Aangti Babu had on hire who were, I suppose, small-time thugs fallen on hard days. He used them when he had to deal with neighbourhood roughnecks and so on. There was a flabby scowling one called Bhim, who was quick to swear and pick fights, and a cadaverous, tall Anglo-Indian called Harold, with a hollow-cheeked face and an overlarge, pockmarked, boozer's nose. He had been a rugby player and a boxer, his physique exhaled scrimmages and uppercuts. Temperamentally, though, he was a melancholic who in fallow times recited the Lord's Prayer and a poem he had learned in school that went, "Look up at the stars, look, look up at the stars ..." He would intone this every day as evening fell, and sometimes even when the sky had clouded over and the day had dimmed before time.

I could not imagine what use he was to Aangti Babu until one day a small mouse was caught in the office trap and I saw Harold take it out. He cradled the mouse in his hand and looking at its terrified little face said in a sad, gentle voice, "Wee, sleeket, cowrin', tim'rous beestie, O, what a panic's in thy breastie!" As he spoke he squeezed the mouse's neck, he squeezed it until the mouse's eyes popped.

I had thought of myself as sentimental: I remember brooding over things for days at certain times of life, even crying in secret, though boys do not. When tenants had to be ejected by stealth or force, when bribes had to be paid, when I looked at the ravaged faces of people watching their homes being demolished, I would tell myself this was the real world, the one all grown men lived in. When Harold and Bhim were deployed, I would look away, escape in my mind to the Buddha's gnarled face in the tree at Songarh's ruin, still a refuge though I had shut out everything else related to that town. I knew we were doing nothing illegal; the tenants being ejected had no legal right to the place, the teary-eyed sister who came for one last look at her parental home had not inherited a share. Compassion had no place in the world of finance, Aangti Babu was fond of saying. There had to be someone who lost, or else how would there be anyone who gained? This was how money circulated. If ever I hesitated he would say, "Who has the legal right? All I ask of you is to do what is legally right." At times I wondered at the bitter, poetic justice of my work: driving people out of their homes when I had once been shunted out myself.

I learned the work quickly. There were certain things I enjoyed: seeing a building rise from drawings on a page, finding swift, decisive solutions to problems on building sites, having the labourers look up to me, walking past a building I had put up when lights shone in the windows and curtains rode across them, yellow and red. I found in myself an unexpected capacity for being *practical* about things, despite my occasional unease. This is why Aangti Babu began to rely on me more and more. I looked on him as a benefactor who was teaching me a trade; he treated me differently from the others. The tea boy now had to bring tea to my table; I no longer sat outside the kitchen on the bench with the peons and Harold and Bhim, waiting my turn. People began to fear and respect my closeness to the boss. After a lifetime of deferring to other people, now there were those who deferred to me. I saw in their faces my old face.

I returned home only for Noorie. On the way back from work, I bought her chillies fresh each day and fed them to her one by one, telling her about what had happened at work that day. "Aangti Babu sent me on a site visit and I found the local goondas had surrounded the building site," I would say. "Sister-fucker," Noorie would say, "bastard." Her claws digging through my kurta to my shoulder had begun to feel familiar and companionable. "I can call in Harold and Bhim, and you know how menacing they can be together, they don't have to lift a finger to get results," I'd say, holding a chilli out to her. "What d'you think Suleiman Chacha would say about my work, eh?"

I wondered what he would have made of me now, he who could not get himself a share in his own property. I could have solved that problem for him. And Nirmal Babu? I did not like to think of him – Nirmal Babu, who could not let ruins dissolve without combing them with paintbrush and toothpick. What would Nirmal Babu have made of my trade, when he wanted me to bury myself in books and emerge after twenty years, a scholar with a dusty library and a receding hairline?

"Haraami," Noorie would screech, breaking into my thoughts and dropping the chilli in her beak. "Gaandu."

"Not for long, Noorie," I would say on days that were harder than the others. "I'll save some money and then I'll look for a different kind of job. I wasn't made for this." She would make quiet clucking sounds, matching my tone, nuzzling my hair with her beak.

Noorie's swear-words had begun to sound like endearments. In my friendless world, she was all I conversed with, and swearing was to us a kind of communication. Once, on an idle evening, especially amused by her squawked vulgarities, I wondered if Kananbala had died and been reborn as a parrot. Noorie's wizened face did in some ways resemble the old woman's. What would Bakul have said to my outlandish notions?

But I could not allow thoughts of Bakul. That was something I never permitted myself. I picked up a chilli and returned to Noorie. It was she, not Bakul, who was my constant companion. It was only to her that I could confide how my success made me afraid that perhaps I was changing into someone my old self would have despised.

* * *

Some time after I had settled in at Aangti Babu's and was looking after quite a lot of his affairs, Barababu, the head clerk from the old tannery, dropped in at the office to see me. When we had finished sharing our disbelief over the day's heat, he began to fumble inside his old cloth bag and eventually fished out a white envelope stained ochre at one corner with turmeric.

"Daughter's wedding, Mukunda, no easy matter. It'll be a load off my mind when it's done," he chuckled as he handed over the invitation.

"You will come, won't you? It's a village wedding and we are village people, but it would give me great pleasure if you took the trouble."

I reached their village a day before the wedding. I had only just put down my bags and was asking Barababu how he was when a young girl came in with an elaborately arranged plate of food which she placed on the table before me. Her other hand held a covered bell-metal tumbler of water. I caught only a glimpse of her face, for she had her sari aanchal demurely over her head. She was accompanied by her mother, who said to Barababu in a loud voice, "Your daughter, my goodness what a stubborn child she is! A busy day and yet she cooked all these things! Wouldn't listen to me when I said, let's send for some mishti and shingara! No, Ma, she said, Baba's friend probably always eats shop food, living alone, he must have good home food!"

I sent a polite smile in the direction of the young girl's sari-covered face. "Come, Malini," her mother commanded, and turned to leave the room. Obedience itself, the girl followed, but then at the door, seeing her father's back was turned, she gave me a deliberate, long, almost cheeky stare, her sari falling off her head to her shoulders. If I had not thought it inconceivable, I would have said she stuck her tongue out at me.

The following evening, after the wedding and a big feast, I sat with Barababu and his relatives, sharing their post-wedding euphoria and a hookah that was going around. Barababu said, "Everything in life has an apposite time, my boy, everything has an apposite time. Now you, for you it is time for grihaprastha – do you know?"

"Grihaprastha," I repeated, drowsy from too much food.

"Yes, grihaprastha. How old are you now? Twenty-one?"

"Twenty-one! That was another life," I said. "I'm twenty-three, I was born in '27."

"Proves what I'm saying," Barababu said, crowing. "You should become a householder now. It's time for you to have a wife, children. Are you going to wait till you have dentures?"

"Children," I said. "I don't even have a bride in mind. And I don't have parents to find a bride for me."

"I admit it will be difficult getting a bride for you – you have a good upbringing, and yet nobody knows your caste," Barababu said. "But I don't believe in such things." He looked around at his somnolent audience. "I say, judge a man by his actions. And by your actions I would say . . . " He looked around again. "You are fit to be the husband of my own daughter, yes, my own daughter, though I am a Brahmin as ever a Brahmin lived and breathed."

* * *

I had never been conscious of needing a wife, yet I had never felt as contented as I did after I married Barababu's middle daughter, the girl who, when she became my wife, told me she had indeed stuck her tongue out at me that morning in the village. After our son was born, I felt there was nothing left for me to want or need. My wife laughed when I marvelled at his ten tiny toes, his pudding-soft bottom.

"I'll go back to that rascally astrologer," I said to her. "'You'll have no children,' he said. I'll show him my son!"

My wife smiled and said, "Perhaps he is not a child. You worship him like a little god, after all."

She was right. I was fascinated by my son, by the fact of having a child. We had named him Goutam, after the Buddha I remembered in Songarh's banyan tree. But I never called him that, using instead a range of sweetly ridiculous endearments. He was a year old now, and for eleven months I had celebrated his birthday every month, just as I remembered Mrs Barnum doing. On the twelfth of every month I made my wife cook payesh and light a ghee-lamp before my son and I brought home something special – fish fry, or cutlets – for our evening meal and a slice of sweet pastry for him. "More celebration is better than less," I told my wife when she protested at my extravagance. "We'll spend our entire lives celebrating, the three of us."

From the floor where I was sitting, I looked up at my wife as she lay on the bed with her face at its edge, her long, untied hair trailing my knee, her rounded face dimpled with laughter. My son lay by me on the cool floor trying to suckle his toe. I twisted a strand of her hair around my forefinger. It was two years since we had been married, two strangers who had only her father in common. She had been brought up in a little village and had not read beyond folktales and children's stories, while I was now a city man who had over the years read everything in Suleiman Chacha's collection. In many ways she was still a child, spontaneous, playful, and as eager to please me as it was difficult to please her. Our early days had not been easy: strained silences, sulks and misunderstandings, followed by long nights of lust-filled apology. Gradually, we had grown accustomed to each other, companions in a lonely big city. There were still many things we could not share with each other, but there were others I knew I could share with nobody else.

I let go of her hair and stroked her cheek. She held my finger in her hand and put it in her mouth, caressing it with her tongue.

Sitting on the door, Noorie clucked down at us like a wise, worried old hermit. The only scar on our smooth existence was my wife's dislike of Noorie and her fear that the bird would peck the baby. But I was sure this would change.

My childish fantasies of adventure and romance were now so absurd I never recalled them at all. This room, with my wife, my baby and my bird, seemed everything I could have wanted. I looked around then and thought that if I could catch life and imprison a little bit of it to have again and again, this was the bit I would trap in a glass jar, to shake like those foreign cottages with falling snow, and to enter at will.

* * *

By this time, Aangti Babu had begun to look for opportunities further afield. He talked of towns near Calcutta that were changing: some were becoming district headquarters; some, it was rumoured, would become capitals as newly independent India was organised into different states. Aangti Babu seemed to be collecting information on a variety of such places.

One afternoon, he summoned me to his room.

"Bring your things tomorrow, we will travel out from the office. One night, maybe two."

I had gone on trips with him before, but this is the one I recall most clearly. We took a train on a metre-gauge line, I in the third-class compartment with Aangti Babu's luggage, and he in the first. I did not resent this. I enjoyed the solitude of the third-class crowds where village women sat on the floor, baskets of produce by their sides, full or empty depending on the time of day, their windswept faces watching the speed-blurred world outside with an exhausted, absent look. I liked the sense of having nothing to do but watch the green, pond-filled, banana-leafed countryside pass by, sipping tea scented with the damp earth of its terracotta cup.

I was soothed and refreshed by the time we got off the train at a kutcha platform made of beaten earth and shielded from the world outside by one metal railing on which hung a sign with the name of the station in Bengali and English: MANOHARPUR. I rolled the name round on my tongue, sure I had tasted it before. Manoharpur. Had Suleiman Chacha mentioned it? Or maybe . . . had I heard of it from someone in college? I only knew that I knew the name.

We were not able to get a tonga or a rickshaw; there seemed to be none at the station. We began to walk, Aangti Babu cursing the lack of transport while I mouthed Manoharpur, Manoharpur with every step I took, trying to remember. We had to walk through the small town, through its little bazaar, out into the countryside, down a beaten-earth road past mud huts and rice fields with white egrets meditating among the rushes, before we reached a grand iron gate that was out of place in its surroundings. We walked up a long drive shaded with trees of jackfruit, coconut, bael, and mango. The boxes and bedrolls that I was carrying had grown so heavy by this time that my shoulders were on fire. Once we reached the deep verandah that fronted the house, I set down our luggage with a sigh and wiped my sweat-streaming face.

Aangti Babu sat in one of the cane chairs and said, "Go, see to things, call someone."

I walked around the garden to the back of the house and, without warning, came upon a river. It went right past the house, a wide, pale-brown expanse. I walked down to the riverbank, astonished by the nearness of it. The edge of the bank was only a few feet away from the steps that led up to the back verandah, which was deeper and grander than the one in front. It was empty – no chairs, no tray of tea left over from the morning. You would have expected such a verandah to be the chosen spot, whether for conversation or solitude, but it appeared to be abandoned. On the opposite bank I could see the tops of small huts and the occasional brick building. But they were far away. I forgot my errand as a low flat boat passed me, pushed along with a pole that the boatman flourished with ease. A breeze came up from the river, cooling my heat-flushed face. For some reason the whole scene made me feel inexpressibly sad and filled me with a sense of having been there before, in a past life, a feeling so powerful that I felt almost afraid of its force. Had I been a river frog or mouse in that house in my last birth? Why had Aangti Babu come here, I wondered in a sudden surge of sick panic. Was he planning to take it over and knock it down as well?

Before I could earn Aangti Babu's ire for my absentminded – and, I must remark, uncharacteristic – delay, someone came up to me and said, "Aah, the people from Calcutta?"

I thought we would walk in through the house to the front where Aangti Babu waited, but the man led me out the same way I had come. So, I thought, the house is not yet empty. I studied the back of the man I was following. His grey-white hair was cut in a circle as if the barber had set a bowl on his head and then wielded his scissors. Beneath the circle of hair was bristly scalp where shaved hair was rapidly growing back. He was not tall – the top of his head was well below my shoulders – but he had that self-important, bustling air with which many short people try to make up for their stature. He looked back every so often to see if, like an errant puppy, I had strayed somewhere. At these times I took the opportunity to study his face, which was pockmarked and dull, with one eye oozing a purulent infection. I decided I would not look at him any more, for fear of catching his disease.

Aangti Babu said to him, "Well, will you not invite us in after this long journey?"

"I would, I would," said the self-important man, turning obsequious now. "But it is such a ruin inside, I am ashamed! Ashamed, huzoor!"

"Nonsense," Aangti Babu said, heaving his portly body out of the cane chair. "I insist."

"Please, huzoor, it is more private to talk here!"

"The old man is in the bedroom, isn't he? He is sick, isn't he? I insist! I must see!"

Where Aangti Babu insisted, few could resist. I knew this from experience, and had already begun to move towards the closed main door.

The room inside was truly in ruinous shape. I had seen many old, ill-maintained houses by then, but this one was the worst. Its curtains had rotted and smelled of mould; its floor had worn away in patches to reveal the brick beneath; the furniture, like fallen soldiers, was maimed, some missing legs, some arms, some thrown aside as if just so much wood. An enormous framed mirror hung askew, so dusty that it was impossible for us even to discern a shadow of our faces in it. Moth-eaten blankets covered some of the furniture. Portraits, I supposed of family elders, hung in ornate frames. Both frames and portraits were grey with fungus. Even the staircase that went up one side of the room, a sweeping arc of a staircase, looked as if the step of a mouse would cause it to sigh and collapse in a heap of dust. The only thing that was relatively intact was hanging from the ceiling: a chandelier of enormous size, festooned with gigantic cobwebs.

Aangti Babu sneezed and growled, "This is the house you want me to buy?"

"Ssh, speak softly, huzoor." The man showing us around looked over his shoulder towards a half-open door, and begged, "As I said, it is dusty here, we will be more comfortable outside . . ."

It turned out that the house belonged to a very old gentleman, apparently heirless, and now very ill. We were speaking to a local man who had made himself indispensable to the ailing owner as a kind of nurse and manager rolled into one during the past year or so. Now that the old man was so unwell, his nurse wanted to sell the house before some inconvenient heir appeared. It was rumoured there was a possible candidate.

"We have to verify all this, of course," Aangti Babu said. "My lawyers will look into the papers."

"Huzoor, there is nothing amiss," the man said. In a fit of bravado, he continued, "Others too have seen these house papers."

"Oho," said Aangti Babu. "Are you trying to tell me there are other takers? Hah." He took a paan out of his silver travelling paan-box and stuffed it into his mouth with contempt. "In that case," he said with his mouth full, "why don't you sell to these others?"

He chewed a little, then shot out a red stream of betel juice that spattered the white wall of the verandah and coloured the arm of the cane chair standing near it.

As I deduced, Aangti Babu knew that the man had got his master to sign away his property in some illness-induced haze, either by force or guile, I did not like to think which.

"And what about the furniture? You said it's included? I'll have to think of disposal, so we may as well get it clear," Aangti Babu said, making it sound like a casual afterthought.

The man was sullen, having been beaten in the negotiations so far.

"I said nothing about the furniture," he grumbled.

"Oh well, that is your concern, not mine," Aangti Babu said, and made as if to leave. "We'll take the house, but we want it empty. Please get rid of the furniture – and the old man, of course. Let me know when he goes. I can't wait long. Don't want money locked up."

I could see the man making rapid calculations. What would he do with crystal chandeliers and carved Victorian whatnots there, in that little town? The man's wife had arrived and was standing at the edge of the room. She gave him an exasperated look.

"Oh well, if you want the furniture so badly," the man said, "you can have it, but for a price."

We left the house after some more haggling. As we made our way down to the station, having decided to return to Calcutta that same day, Aangti Babu chuckled and extracted another paan from his box. "Thinks he's very clever, that fool," he said to me with glee. "Gave me all that furniture for a song. I'll get three hundred from the auction houses for just one of those chandeliers. Did you see it?"

"What?" I said. The chandelier had looked like nothing much to me, a dusty assemblage of glass, its only virtue being that it was intact in a room full of disabled furniture.

"My boy, you have a long way to go and lots to learn, just stay by my side." He giggled a little and made a dipping motion with his ringed fingers. "Dip one of those chandeliers into the river and pull it out and you'll see the crystal. Genuine Belgian, nothing less, nothing less." He laughed again. His mirth caused a spasm of coughing, red betel juice spewing out groundwards from him like lava from an upturned volcano. "You have a lot to learn," he said.

We reached the station. Despite his good humour, he did not ask me to travel in his compartment, but as I retreated to the end of the train with our luggage he said in jocular tones, "Now all we need is for the old stick to die."

When I returned home that night I was feeling unusually melancholy and hardly noticed my wife's hands straying over me.

"What is it?" she complained at last.

I told her about the house and the river. "The old man," I said, "dying, so alone, cheated out of his home. Why should anyone spend his last days so alone? It was a place called Manoharpur – have you ever seen it? An idyllic place! And to die in such misery surrounded by such beauty!"

My wife was fed up. "You and your gloomy fits! I tell you! It's many years yet before you'll grow old, and you sound ancient already." She turned on her side, disgusted by my sombre mood and want of ardour.

I stared at the dark ceiling. That feeling I had had, of having seen the house before, was too secret for me to share with my wife. From her lack of interest I knew it had no connection with her, to my life with her. I said no more, though I was awake for a long time.

To end this story: this was the only instance, to my knowledge, when Aangti Babu made a loss. The old retainer to whom we had spoken turned out to be playing a double game. He had apparently taken earnest money from five parties before Aangti Babu, showing all of them forged documents. By the time anyone found out, he had disappeared. Nobody could report him to the police because they had broken the law by trying to buy the property from him. Aangti Babu seethed and cursed, but there was little he could do. Neither he nor anyone else knew where the original deed was, without which nothing could be bought or sold.

I was for once delighted that a deal had been a hoax, and not in the least discomfited by my disloyalty. I felt happy to think the house was to remain as it was, serene by the river, untouched.

In a few days the house became just one among many others, and I forgot all about it as I immersed myself in preparations for another demolition.

* * *

A few months later, Aangti Babu called me early into his office. He had told me the previous day that he would need to see me first thing in the morning, so I was ready, my heart uncomfortably loud, my forehead damp with fear. I tried to reconstruct the week that had gone before, the days immediately preceding, and could think of no mistakes I had made in my work.

It was business he wanted to discuss. He asked me to sit down. I had always stood in his room, and continued to stand, my head a little bent, deferential and attentive. He looked up at me, irritable, and said, "Can't you sit when I tell you to? I'll get a crick in my neck looking up and talking."

I lowered myself into a chair as Aangti Babu stuffed a paan through his betel-red, flaky lips.

"Listen carefully," he said. "You have to handle this on your own, so take some notes and remember what I say."

I looked around for paper and a pencil, furtively so that Aangti Babu would not comment on my lack of readiness. But he did not bother, having shut his eyes, joined his fingers to make a pyramid, and begun to talk.

"This is another big house, a little bit like the riverside one we went to some months ago," he said. "It has a lot of land, and it's in a locality we think will prosper. The town is a small one now, but I've been told there is a good chance of it becoming district headquarters in a year or two." He opened his eyes and startled me with a question. "Do you speak Hindi?" he enquired.

"Yes, yes, I grew up outside . . ."

"Alright," he replied, shutting his eyes again. He had never been interested in knowing anything personal about me. I was used to it and expected nothing different.

"The house is owned by two brothers. There is a dispute." Aangti Babu smiled to himself, his eyes still shut. "There always is. Or how would we make a living, eh? One of the brothers has sold this house to me," he continued. "He needed money – failing business, large family, all the usual things. Now the problem is this." He opened his eyes. "Are you listening?"

"Yes, of course," I said.

"Then say something now and then," Aangti Babu said, eyes narrowed, before shutting them again. I began to mumble a response at the end of each sentence. The fan whirred and creaked above us, paddling the still air. The morning had turned oppressive. Sweat pasted back to shirt and shirt to chair. I looked with longing at the covered glass of water on the desk, but did not dare. My pencil was slithery with the sweat on my hand.

"The house was owned by *both* brothers. The one who has sold it claims he tried to persuade the other to sell and has even given the other his share of the money. Hah! The old story!"

"Huh," I agreed.

"Anyway, that's none of our business. The older one had power of attorney over the younger because . . . oh, I forget the details. The older one has sold it using the power of attorney. So *legally* we are absolutely alright."

"Then . . ." I said in a murmur.

"The younger brother is refusing to move out. Oh, it's fine, we've dealt with this kind of situation before. I got a better price from the older brother because there is this problem. And this one is easy . . . the younger brother, I mean. He's not a tenant. He's signed his rights away. All you need to do is to tell him to go, remove himself, leave the house . . . persuade him."

"Persuade?" I said, nonplussed. "Hasn't the older brother tried to do that already?"

Aangti Babu opened his eyes in sudden fury. I saw the bags under them were grey and red blood vessels snaked their way through the whites.

"If I were your age, I'd jump at this and not ask stupid questions," he snarled. "It's just that I am too busy to go and attend to this business. Do you understand?"

"No, no, I mean, yes, of course," I stammered.

"*Persuade* him to leave. Understand? I've got Bhim and Harold there doing the normal things: banging on doors at night, ringing their bell and vanishing, breaking a window or two. It hasn't worked. I want you to go there. I want an empty house. If you have to cut his water and electricity . . . if you need to frighten him ... But no police. Don't get into trouble with the police. Just get him out."

Aangti Babu found a notepad and wrote a few lines on it. He wrote laboriously, hissing under his breath the words he was inscribing. I heard what he was writing before I saw it. When he was done, my hand, which did not seem to belong to me any longer, reached for the slip of paper. Aangti Babu's handwriting was neat and rounded, like a child's. The note confirmed what I had heard, but still the stubborn recesses of my brain refused to let in the information staring at me.

* * *

I walked out of Aangti Babu's room feeling unconnected with my limbs. I was in the office, yet not in it at all. My ears had begun to whistle as if I were all at once weak with fatigue. When the tea boy clattered a cup on my table and said, "What, have you gone deaf? Here's your tea," I looked at it for long minutes, as if I did not know what a cup with hot brown liquid meant. Throughout the day I did the things I had to, but almost without knowing what I was doing.

At home, my wife startled me when she touched me on the elbow as I stood in the jasmine-scented darkness of the verandah, my mind racing ahead of my body. At dinner, seeing my untouched food, she exclaimed, "If this is what landing some responsibility does to you, just stay an assistant all your life, that would be better for all of us."

At last the day of my departure arrived. I did not know what I had packed or how I got there, but some time in the afternoon, long before the train time, I found myself in the milling chaos of Howrah Bridge, staring at the barges that creaked along the flat, muddy river. People collided into me and cursed as they passed, ant-like beneath the towering metal arcs of the bridge. Trams clanged by, reduced by the crowd and the bridge to mechanical toys. I walked along looking at the river and one barge that had an orange and green tattered flag fluttering from its prow. Beside me the superstitious were bowing and whispering prayers to the Ganga.

I felt speechless and prayerless, my mind in turmoil.

Twelve years after Nirmal Babu had sent me away from Songarh to Calcutta, I was going back to Songarh. Aangti Babu had bought my old home from Kamal. I was to evict Nirmal Babu from the house I had grown up in.

And Bakul. I was to evict Bakul.

THREE

I sat by the window, my hair tossing in the wind. Outside, shadows rushed backward into the moon-pearled night. The breeze that came through the open window was warm, but still it dissipated the stuffiness of the overheated, third-class, metal compartment. Beside me, on the next bunk, a hunched form lay asleep, snoring in a rumble, then exhaling with a whistle. From above, the arm of another man drooped down almost into my nose. The train seemed to be chugging along with my thoughts. "Bakul, Bakul," each turn of its wheels said as it rushed over the plains of Bengal towards the hilly plateau of Songarh.

For all these years I had not allowed myself to think of her because it would open gates to misery that I knew I didn't have the power to shut. I never let my mind draw her picture: her turned-up nose, her always-wild hair, the down on her thin cheeks, and her eyes, like pools of river water, which stared rather than looked. From the time I was six and she about four, we had been together. On cold winter mornings we would watch our breath mist and mingle, in the heat of summer afternoons we would throw buckets of chilled well-water at each other and squeal with delight. When Bakul first menstruated, it was to me she came running, alarmed, excited, voluble – I was sickened and horrified at the blood stains, thinking she had somehow hurt herself. We were each other's secret-sharers, we were two orphans who had found refuge.

We had no sense of our lack of other friends. Perhaps it was unnatural. A boy and a girl, so intimate, not even related. It must have bothered people, although we were joyously oblivious of their concerns.

That is why I was sent away of course – I understood that now, as a father myself. But at that time, when Nirmal Babu told me he was putting me in a school in Calcutta and that I would have to leave Songarh, my mind had no room for reasons. Poets talk metaphorically about broken hearts, but I know that mine was broken then. I felt it cracking, a physical pain, a knife in my ribs, when Nirmal Babu told me I was to leave and repeated it when I did not believe him. When I asked why, on the way to the station – just once, I never asked again – he smiled in a way I knew to be false and said it was for a better education and to take me away from being ordered around by others in the house. That night when I was thirteen, and the world was ending as the train bumped and jogged me away from Bakul and Songarh, I had to bite the blanket so that Nirmal Babu would not hear me cry. I made up my mind: I would never go back to Songarh, never speak to him again for tossing me around from orphanage to Songarh to Calcutta – a game of badminton and I the shuttlecock.

Once he had put me in the school, Nirmal Babu paid the fees on time, wrote me letters a few times a year and twice came to see me. I especially remember the first of those visits, seeing him in the corridor, Motilal the peon saying to Nirmal Babu, here is your boy, and I looking but not looking at his shapeless bush shirt, his big toe poking out from a clumsy sandal, his loose trousers, his gaunt face oddly eager to please. We walked out across the heat-deadened playing field and through the school gates in an awkward silence punctuated only by polite questions from him. He realised, as I did, that plucked out of Songarh's spaces for casual companionship, where there was no need for conversation, we were both at a loss. We tramped through the Indian Museum and walked past the Geological Survey, heat curling out of cement footpaths, driving ticklish trickles of sweat down our backs, Nirmal Babu asking if I'd like ice cream between holding forth on the Gandhara and Kushana periods as I trailed a few feet behind, keeping back the question I wanted to hurl at him: "Why did you give me a home and then throw me out of it?"

I lay back on my hard wooden bunk now, staring into the darkness. I was being sent back again to Songarh, a lifetime after being sent away. Except that I was a shuttlecock no more, rather an arrow tearing through the night to do harm.

* * *

The man in the next bunk began to let out phlegmy snores. I was far too agitated to sleep. I could think of nothing in particular, yet my head was crowded with so many thoughts that there was no place for them.

Mrs Barnum. I had not thought of her for years. Was she still alive? She had decided to sketch me the minute she saw me. "Sit still," she had exclaimed, pointing to a big blue-cushioned chair and scrabbling around for her pad and pencil. "What bones! Boy, what is your name?" When she showed me what she had drawn, it was a boy with an angular face, large eyes, dimpled chin and a nose that was a little too long for the face. "That's not like me at all," I had thought, though I did not dare to say so. Bakul had begun to laugh when she saw the sketch and said, "Yes, that's just how he looks. Funnyface!"

Would I see Mrs Barnum too, I wondered. How would it be, even if years and years had passed since she caught me prying in her bedroom? How could I have snooped around as I did then, especially after the way she had educated me with whatever books she had in the house, her encyclopedias, her *Women's Weekly* magazines and romances? I remembered the first of her monthly birthdays, spooky affairs to which she summoned spirits and told our futures. She was festive in a full-length lace gown and tiara, darting from place to place, stroking my cheek in passing. She had clapped her hands. "Music!" she had exclaimed. "You children must have gaiety and music!" She had picked up the bell by her side and shaken it until the sound pealed out. After five minutes, we heard the khansama come up the stairs wheezing.

"Yes, Madam?" he said, his obsequiousness ostentatious.

"We must have music, khansama, put on the record, that record!" She settled back into her chair, eyes closed.

The khansama shuffled up to the dusky alcove at the far end of the room, where a brass-horned gramophone stood. There was a record in place already, a black disk we could see from our chairs. He dusted it with a corner of his shirt, wound up the gramophone and put a heavy needle on it as it began to rotate.

We sat rigid in our chairs as sound snaked out from the player. I could recognise none of it as music. It began with a tremendous noise that sounded like a tree falling or a ship crashing into ice. Then it became almost silent. If I didn't have sharp ears I would have thought the music had ended. But then it became once more loud and menacing, a huge mix of discordant sounds rising and falling. I kept expecting some singing to start, but there was no human voice. I imagined in the music the dramatic, solitary snow peaks Nirmal Babu talked about, gigantic open spaces and tiny rivulets. The music would swell, then melt down and once or twice I half rose from my chair thinking it had ended, but it started again. I looked at Bakul for help. Mrs Barnum's eyes were closed and a smile touched the edges of her lips. All of a sudden the music dwindled. For a few seconds I thought with relief that it had actually, at last, ended.

This time the silence was broken by the thin sound of a flute. I recognised flutes. In the orphanage we had played them too, and I had a flute of my own that I had bought at a fair. But this one sounded like no other. It was only after I met Suleiman Chacha and whistled him the tune that I came to know what it was – the "Finlandia" by Sibelius, he told me, music from very far away.

Whenever I thought of Bakul later in the Calcutta school dormitory, creaking in my charpoy, swatting mosquitoes, I thought of her with that music, in that house, by the lily pond where I had swum with her, where I had felt her lips crushed against mine, felt her peach-sized breasts through the wet cloth of her thin, summertime frock, her mouth pressed on mine and then away, her hands inside my shirt, and then fumbling in my shorts that seemed to have come alive. In moments of fantasy I used to dream of setting sail with her, charging through black seas and sparkling icebergs to the end of the world. I felt I could almost hear the flute that stilled the icy waves and wondered if Bakul heard it too.

The train to Songarh sped on. I had not thought of my wife or son since leaving home. But this did not occur to me at the time. When the real reason for the journey nibbled at my mind, I pushed it away.

* * *

So much had changed in Songarh in the years I had been away that I could find no familiar landmarks and grew more and more confused on my way from the hotel to Dulganj Road. Everything looked meaner, smaller. I was used to Howrah, which I thought the most enormous, grandest, busiest station possible; Songarh's two-platform station reminded me of the mofussil towns I visited with Aangti Babu. Finlays had peeling paint, a signboard hanging askew, and stiff, pointy-breasted mannequins. I could see that the small shops that lined the single major road sold cheap, tawdry things. There were some new streets and buildings, however, and I misdirected the tonga many times until we had a quarrel over the fare and it was past five when I finally stood before the door of 3 Dulganj Road. Once my home.

I had fantasised in the train that I would stumble upon her, surprise her alone, but Bakul was not in the garden, nor was she by the well. I walked through the empty garden to the front door. I took a deep breath, ran my fingers through my combed hair, reached out for the familiar brass knocker, then realised it was no longer there. On the wall by the door, I found instead a switch for an electric bell. When I pressed it, somewhere far inside I heard an answering tinkle and the bark of a dog.

My heart had begun to beat uncomfortably. I tried to slow down my breathing, wanting to be calm and coherent. I looked back at the garden to distract myself. A madhabilata was in full flower on one of the walls. It had not been there before – a pink flowering intruder in a garden of whites. The mango trees had grown and small, green fruit were visible even at a distance. The sun was still hot and high in a stark-blue sky.

The door had not opened. Enough time had passed for me to ring the bell again. I pressed the switch harder this time.

As soon as the bell rang, I heard an agitated voice above the frantic barking of the dog; it came from just behind the door.

"Who is it?" It was a young boy's voice.

I almost replied, "It's me," as I had always done years before, but then remembered and said, "I . . . my name is Mukunda."

"I can't open the door. I don't know who you are."

"Listen, I have to see . . . "

"I told you, I can't."

I could feel sweat tickle my scalp and bead my forehead. My fresh blue shirt had started to stick to my back. Annoyance at talking to a door and having the dog bark on at me made me shout:

"Look, whoever you are, I have to see Nirmal Babu and I am not going until I do. Where is he? If you don't let me in I'll just climb over the courtyard wall."

There was a brief lull in the barking. Then the voice, which had a slight tremor, now said, "You can't scare me. You can't climb over anything. I won't open the door. And the dog bites."

I looked at the door with exasperation – a block of wood I had seen countless times before. I stepped back and looked it up and down, wondering what to do. To the right, by the well, was the outer door that led into the courtyard and to my room. I could see that it had a lock on it. Although I had threatened to scale the courtyard wall and it would have been possible to do so, I felt foolish thinking about it. I returned to the door and shouted, "Are you still there?"

No answer.

"I just want to see Nirmal Babu," I said, "I am . . . an old friend of his. Tell him it is Mukunda. Or tell Bakul it is Mukunda."

I waited. After a moment the voice, sounding less belligerent, said, "You'll have to wait outside, I can't open the door. They'll be back soon."

I walked back into the garden. I plucked a leaf in passing and began to tear it into tiny, mango-smelling shreds. I wandered towards the well and stood leaning over its wall, which seemed much lower than I remembered. The white jasmine next to it was still there, still scattering the water with its flowers. I could discern the dark reflection of my head in the distant circle of light that was the base of the well. I dropped in a stone. The splash sounded far away, the circle of light wavered and broke and then stilled itself again. All the water I had drawn here! All the buckets I had filled!

I began to walk around the garden, bored by my thoughts, tired of waiting. I did not know much about plants and trees, but could see that it was now a beautiful garden, filled with the old fruit trees I recognised, fragrant bushes and creepers and many new saplings tied with stakes. Despite the greenery and the well, there was a not a drop of water to be had and the heat had parched my throat until I could think of nothing else, not even the boy's odd behaviour. Finally I sat down in the old garden swing-chair, too downcast and tired to care about my clothes crumpling into a sweaty mess. I closed my eyes and began to rock.

* * *

I must have dozed off. They were standing over me looking down, frowning and curious. Like the bears finding Goldilocks, Bakul said later. It was almost dusk. Their bodies were silhouetted against the soft light. I blinked away my sleep and tried to stand up. The swing jolted forward hitting my legs and I fell back into it.

Bakul giggled, then covered her mouth with her palm. I managed to heave myself out of the swing.

"Have you been waiting long?" Nirmal Babu said. "I am not sure we have met." He sounded wary.

"Oh, Baba," Bakul squealed. "Can't you see? It's Mukunda!"

I was not surprised that she recognised me. I had expected no different. I would have known her too, anywhere. Her face had changed, but only a little: her cheeks curved now where they had been thin and flat, and her hair reached her waist. It was tied back but around her face it scorned the hairpins and oil, or whatever it was she had used to neaten it; strands that had broken free curled at her neck and forehead. Her eyes were the same odd colour, only her gaze was different, amused and enquiring where it had been watchful and sullen before. In the light of dusk her sari, the yellow of mustard flowers, glowed against her ill-fitting white blouse which drooped on one side to reveal a thin gold chain. The sari fell away in curves I should have expected, but still I was astonished.

I looked away.

"Is it really you, Mukunda?" Nirmal Babu enquired. He adjusted his glasses – I had never seen him wearing glasses before – to look at me closer.

"Of course!" he said. "I thought you looked familiar. How stupid of me. How could I . . . What a shame, the boy made you wait outside. But he was not to know."

* * *

I climbed the stairs, sliding my hands on the banister as I used to when I lived in that house, running up and down many times every day, on errands repeated again and again. I could almost hear Manjula and Meera calling, "Mukunda! Where is that boy! Hiding again!"

The corridor at the head of the stairs looked the same, but the plaster on the ceiling had begun to flake. My professional self noted its sandy gaps, the exposed bricks, the patches of mould near the bathrooms, the rusted iron beams that held up the roof, the walls that needed painting, the cloudy glass panes that had cracked in places. The almost derelict interior was at odds with the garden, in which every plant and tree seemed cared for.

Nirmal Babu and I sat at the table, a smaller one than there used to be near those windows. A grizzled brown and black pi dog sat at his feet, painstakingly cleaning her paws with her tongue, and then rubbing her eyes with her paws. Next she scratched her ears and furiously nibbled the base of her tail. Then, placing her head between her front paws, she shut her eyes and heaved a loud sigh. Nirmal Babu smiled down at her and said, "You remember Meera, of course."

"Of course," I said.

"She used to feed stray dogs at the old fort. After she left I began to feed them and I brought one of the puppies home – and here she is – twelve years old now."

"Exactly as many years as Meera Didi and I have been away," I said, not meaning to sound reproachful. "How is Meera Didi?" I asked him, to break the awkwardness between us. "Do you have any news?"

"Oh yes," he said, looking uncertain. "I . . . see her now and then, she teaches art at a school in Darjeeling – there are beautiful walks up the hills there – you know how she liked walking – and she paints and sketches. In fact . . . " He got up and walked to a corner and took down a framed landscape showing cottages and trees tumbling headlong into a valley. "This is one of hers."

I held it and admired it. The feeling of verticality it induced, the sense of energy in the trees and hills did make it an unusual picture. Nirmal Babu took it back and returned it to its place on the wall after a smiling look at it. "Yes," he said, "the walk down that slope is very steep, you need a stick and sturdy shoes. But it has beautiful orchids and ferns and unusual rhododendron." Then he remembered me and said, "She asks about you, she was always fond of you."

Was there any truth, after all, in the gossip we used to hear that last year in Songarh? Another silence began to twang the air between us.

Nirmal Babu looked towards the stairs, saying, "What is Bakul doing . . . cooking up a feast for you?"

I pictured Bakul in the kitchen telling the servant to make tea, trying to find things to serve me. She had never been one for cooking anything. Eventually, though, she came up the stairs, followed by a boy of about twelve who carried a tray with food, water and tea. He wore shorts that flapped below his knee, and a grey kurta drooped at his shoulders. His ears looked like handles to hold his head by. His hair, cut very close to his scalp, emphasised his outsize ears. He gave me a sidelong look, then put the tray down on the table. It was the same brass tray and I could have sworn that the china was the same I had washed sometimes.

"This is Ajay," Bakul said. "You must forgive him for not letting you in, but we tell him to keep the doors locked. Baba and I rarely go out together, but when we do . . . "

"Really, it was nothing," I said.

Holding his cup of hot tea and lighting a cigarette seemed to settle Nirmal Babu's diffidence and he said, "What a pleasure it is to see you, Mukunda, really. I wondered all these years if you had finished college, would I ever see you again. Tell me, what do you do? Have you married? Do you have children?"

He listened patiently to my answers and when I said things that I thought were funny, mainly about my child, he smiled, but he did not laugh his rich, strange-sounding laugh that always ended in a smoker's cough. He looked changed. Those glasses had altered his face. Grey hair, not unexpectedly, though if I think about it now, he could only have been about fifty then. It was more than age. His face had darkened and his eyes were circled with shadows. He looked like a man who did not sleep very much, or well. He was fidgety in a way I did not remember from before. He had grown thinner, which made him stoop.

I felt remorseful. Why had I cut myself off from him? Why had I not come to visit? Why was it he I had blamed all those years for the way Manjula used to serve me smaller portions than everyone else, her spoon a safe five inches away from my untouchable plate? For the way Kamal made me run errands; for the rat-infested quarters I slept in; for the far end of the table reserved for me? What had I felt so embittered about? And why had he become the core of my simmering bitterness? Now, face to face, I felt nothing of the old anger – or perhaps I was looking at him with the triumphant magnanimity of the strong for the weak.

When Nirmal Babu left the room briefly, Bakul said, "Baba took premature retirement because he had a heart attack. He has diabetes too. But he's so stubborn. I know he eats all kinds of forbidden things when I am not there to stop him."

"You – a guardian angel!" I said. "It's hard to imagine you watching over your father with a diet book and prescription."

She had a sly smile as she looked up from tickling the dog behind its ear. "As hard as to imagine you married and a father."

She stopped, seeing Nirmal Babu return. "What do you do, Mukunda?" he said. "Didn't you want to go to college? I remember you wanted to climb mountains and cross seas, you wanted to be an explorer. Wasn't that so?"

"Yes," I said. "What romantic notions we have as children. And look how it's turned out. I'm just a clerk at an architect's, most days chained to a desk!"

I did not elaborate. Aangti Babu was no architect and I was no longer an innocent clerk. I slid over the true nature of my work. I should have told him the reason for my trip at once, but of course I could not.

"Can I walk around the house?" I said to change the subject. "Just to see . . ."

"You don't need to ask," Nirmal Babu said. "It's always been your house. I hope you will stay here as long as you're in Songarh."

Bakul followed a few steps behind as I walked into the middle room that led off from the wide corridor. There was only one bed there in place of the two that had been occupied by Meera and Bakul. When I looked enquiringly at Bakul, she said, "I've moved to the front room so that I can look out of the window." The little room that led off her old one was empty but for a jumble of boxes and oddments. The narrow bed, and Kananbala's white-shrouded form curled up in it, were gone.

"She died," Bakul said before I could ask. "Just a couple of years after you went away. One morning we found her – by her bed – on the floor. She must have called in the night but nobody . . . . I slept in the next room and I didn't hear anything. If I had, maybe . . ." She banged the door shut and said, "Let's go outside."

I opened my mouth to tell Bakul about Noorie, the way her cursing always reminded me of Kananbala, but then, not knowing where to begin, I did not.

Nirmal Babu was waiting for us in the garden. The custard apple and grapefruit trees would soon be full of fruit, he said proudly. Near the gate, he showed me fifteen young guava and lemon plants that he said would all grow to flower and fruit in a few years.

"Baba sits there every evening and talks to his trees," Bakul said. "He says he has no time for beds of annuals, it's trees, vegetables and fragrant creepers he wants. I think he wants me to start digging too, but I'm not in the least interested."

I smiled in recognition. It is only to gardeners that their gardens seem places of wonderment and drama. Even today I can identify no more than a few common trees; if I wanted pleasant surroundings, I would get a gardener.

Nirmal Babu lit a cigarette. "When I was young," he said, "I wasn't interested in gardens either. My father was so disappointed that nobody in the family was interested in the garden. We just pretended we were, to make him happy."

"But we aren't pretending, are we Mukunda?" Bakul smiled.

I looked at her, unnerved. I wondered if she sensed something, as she had always done with me, and the real reason for my return to Songarh came back to me with a heart-stopping jolt.

* * *

The stunted trees that grew out of the walls of Mrs Barnum's house had acquired a wild, strong life; it was almost impossible to tell that the house had once been yellow, so deep was the layer of black soot and fungus on the outer walls. The front door was open, letting out the same smell – old books, carpeting, caramel and woodsmoke – that the house had always manufactured. We climbed the wooden stairs and turned into the familiar drawing room. I had not wanted to pay a visit. Mrs Barnum's "*Get out! Never come back! And look up 'treacherous', look up 'betrayal'!*" still rang in my ears, but I could not have explained this to Bakul. It was the only secret I had not shared with her.

Bakul whispered, "She's kept it exactly the same, I don't think you'll see anything changed. But the khansama went away to his village – he became too decrepit to work."

Watching her skip up the stairs, I began to feel trapped in a quicksand of sadness. The more I struggled to be light-hearted and happy, the worse I felt. There was still nothing Bakul and I seemed to need to explain to each other. If she glanced in my direction, I felt I knew what she was thinking. I could tell without looking which of her teeth was crooked from when she had fallen and hit it against a stone. I knew at the end of the day her calves would probably ache as they used to before, when she would say, "Mukunda, please, please, press my legs for a bit and I'll do your English homework before tuitions tomorrow."

How could I have forgotten all of this and never come back to see her? I did not allow myself to think how different our lives might have been if I had.

Mrs Barnum looked up from a book as we came in and said, "Ah, Bakul, on time as usual." Then she noticed me and took her reading glasses off and screwed her eyes up in my direction. I wanted to run out and away. It was a lifetime ago, but I could still see her hand stroking her tiger skin, then lighting a cigarette, looking at me up on a chair, riffling through her letters.

After a minute she said, "It's the boy, isn't it? The boy I drew? Mukunda! Why haven't you come for so long? Did you go away somewhere?"

"Oh, Mrs Barnum," Bakul said, "I told you, he went off to study in Calcutta. Then he forgot all about us and never wrote or came," she said.

I walked across the room and knelt by Mrs Barnum's side. She looked at me as if I could never do any wrong. She caressed my face and traced my cheekbones with her fingers. "Oh, those bones," she said mischievously. "If I were younger, my boy!" She pointed to a space behind her head, and there it was: her sketch of me at thirteen, hanging on the wall in a wooden frame.

She beamed. "This is like old times! We must celebrate! What was it you children liked to eat? Sandwiches and lemon sherbet? We must have some!" She reached out for her bell on the side table and rang it loud and long. Then she turned to me and said, "Young man, sit down, don't make me crane my neck so!"

I sat, feeling as if the part of me that had rotted that long-ago afternoon in her bedroom, when she had found me searching through her letters, had just been amputated – leaving me miraculously healthy once more.

I saw Bakul slipping out of the room. Mrs Barnum tapped me on my arm and leaned forward. "Now tell me, how do I look?" she asked me and pursed her lips, which were shakily painted with a dark-pink lipstick. Her papery cheeks had two circles of rouge the colour of the lipstick, and thin, greasy hair twined about her ears. She seemed tiny where once she had been tall.

"Beautiful," I said fervently. "You haven't changed a bit."

She leaned towards me and whispered with an impish smile, "Don't you want to raid my bedroom, search it for clues, turn it inside out?"

She had not forgotten, and she had not forgiven. I should never have come. I almost got up to leave.

She laughed out loud, ending in a wheezy cough, slapping her thin, chiffon-covered thigh, saying something I could not understand for her coughing. "Your face!" I thought she was saying. "Your face, child!" Then she leaned closer to me, her lips flaky, her breath like old river mud, and I thought she said, but it was not clear through all her coughing and laughing, "Here's a secret for you: I did kill him. Slid a kukri into his stomach and turned it round a few times, good riddance." She spat some phlegm into a handkerchief and leaned her lips towards me again, but by then Bakul had returned to the room carrying a tray with glasses and a plate of sandwiches. Mrs Barnum shifted and lit herself a cigarette as if she had confessed nothing at all. To Bakul she said, "You've been too long! And who's that with you? Is it . . . "

For behind Bakul there was someone else.

A man. A young man. A man with a lazy, elegant slouch and a mop of hair over his high forehead. He held the curtain aside for Bakul's tray, his height reducing hers to a child's, and came into the room as if it belonged to him. He was in a dark suit and blue-grey tie loosened as if he could no longer stand to be constrained. A French beard, combed and waxed, stuck out at a strange right angle, making his otherwise handsome face look faintly comical. Touching Mrs Barnum on the shoulder as he passed her, he flopped into an armchair and said, "What a day! I need all the sandwiches I can get! And some swawbewwies and cweam wouldn't be too bad either." He spoke English like an Englishman, but with a lisp.

"There are no strawberries in Songarh," Bakul said.

"There are, if you have the imagination," Mrs Barnum said swiftly. "That's the trouble, nobody has imagination!" Then she said, "Mukunda, this is my nephew Tommy. Tommy, do you know, Mukunda was Bakul's childhood playmate. We had such a grand time those days, the three of us."

"Thwee, Aunty, were you the third? You've always been such a baby. Did you play house-house? Or was it hide and seek?"

Tommy spoke to Mrs Barnum with an indulgent smile as though she were a child he needed to pamper. He reached out and picked up a sandwich, raising an eyebrow at me. "Do have some, old fellow," he said.

I spoke English, but when I was confronted with anyone fluent in that language my mouth filled with wool and I could hardly get a word out straight. I began to chew a sandwich to avoid speaking.

"And are you Bakul's welative?" Tommy enquired. He looked at Bakul with a smile. "She doesn't say much, never told me she had long-lost bwothers."

"Oh, no, darling," Mrs Barnum exclaimed, "Mukunda was an orphan boy they took in. And then he went to Calcutta to study. Now you must be a big man, aren't you, Mukunda?"

Bakul held the tray towards me and spoke so that only I could hear. "Won't you have your lemon sherbet? It's getting warm."

Tommy raised an eyebrow. Then, as if he had lost all interest in me, he turned to a pile of magazines on a corner table. Settling his long frame into his armchair and putting his feet up on the chair facing it, he said, "Don't let me keep you from chatting. It'll be nice to hear all your stowies." He began flipping through the pages of the magazine.

"Oh, but you should hear the stories Tommy has to tell," Mrs Barnum said. "Such tall tales about the clubs in Bombay and the races and dances. I don't believe a word of it, Tommy, I tell you I don't!"

"You just need imagination, Aunty," Tommy smiled playfully at her again, and reached out for her wrinkled hand, "That's what you said, didn't you? Can't you imagine yourself dancing at the Yacht Club? I'm shwo you'd be the toast of the town even now."

"Oh yes," Bakul said enthusiastically, "Mrs Barnum can still foxtrot – she taught me."

"We must have a dance then, Bakul," Tommy said in a teasing tone. "Now, this minute!"

I felt the conversation twisting and eddying around me, the characters and incidents in it unknown to me. I laughed when they laughed, but I could not understand their jokes. When one of them, usually the nephew, stopped and said with ostentatious politeness, "No, we're weally talking too much. Mukunda Babu hasn't had a chance to tell us anything about himself," I could not fill the minute's pause that followed. The sandwiches tasted nothing like they used to when the khansama made them. The bread was dry and there was so little butter the two slices separated and curled at the edges. I was no longer hungry, but I ate one nevertheless. It was worrying me in an obscure way that Mrs Barnum rang her bell for a servant who did not exist. I did not want to look at Bakul smiling at Tommy, laughing at his jokes, glancing at me as if to say, "Isn't he wonderful?" Our recently excavated closeness was buried, it appeared, for good.

Then Tommy got up and played a few notes on the piano, still standing, his tall, lean frame like a question mark over the black- and bone-coloured stripes of the instrument. He sighed, looking theatrically around the room, "Stwauss! Ah, how I miss swirling awound the woom to a waltz! Can you play, Mukunda Babu, or would you like to dance? I'm happy to pwovide the music!"

I got up from my chair. "I was never a dancer, and I really must be going."

Tommy whinnied and said, "Oh, Mukunda Babu, I didn't mean to scare you away. Do please sit down."

"I have to go," I said, and turned to Mrs Barnum to say goodbye.

Tommy perched on the stool and began to play, eyes closed as if there was nothing in the room but his music. Mrs Barnum sat before him, her face lit by the evening light that shone in from the single window in the room, her expression rapt – as if she were looking upon divinity.

It was the three of them now.

Dinner was over. Nirmal Babu had refused to let me return to the hotel to eat. The power had gone off so we were sitting in the garden to get away from the stuffy heat of the house. It was very still outside but for the passing breath of air that ruffled the creepers, releasing the scent of white flowers gleaming in the dark. I am sure I had never noticed the fragrance twelve years earlier, but now it was a key that unlocked all my memories. And if that were not enough, there was Bakul next to me, perfuming the night herself with a heady mix of soap, talcum powder, and something else I could not identify.

All around us loomed the black shadows of watching trees. The only point of light was Nirmal Babu's cigarette and, further away, a dim yellow flickering from Mrs Barnum's upstairs window. The houses down the road, new and old, were bulky shadows. A chair had been brought out for Nirmal Babu, while Bakul and I occupied the stair before the front door. Bakul swivelled a semi-circular palm handfan, wiping her sweat with her sari when it trickled down her neck. Because she wanted to fan both of us with single strokes, she had settled down close enough for me to feel her brush against me. In the shadows I could not tell what Nirmal Babu made of Bakul sitting there next to me. He said nothing.

I wondered if Bakul's closeness was indeed necessitated by the fan. All through dinner I had felt her brushing against me, by accident I had supposed, as she leaned across to serve me. Her arm would stretch out right near my ear, touching it, or her hip would nudge me as she turned with the ladle towards her father.

Now in the darkness, as she fanned us both, each individual particle of my body seemed separately alive. I was conscious of every tiny move she made, every accidental touch of her shoulder or wrist or hip. My mind seemed to have emptied itself of all normal thought, making room only for the sensation of her touching me. I listened to Nirmal Babu's voice talking about the part of a stupa they had found near the Songarh ruin, about the crowds that now went to see it and scratched their names into the ancient stone, he almost regretted ever having unsettled it, he said; he talked about attempts to climb Everest, about his own old travels. His dog began whimpering a little in her sleep and he caressed her ears and then began again to discourse about fossils recently found in the Himalaya.

All the while my body waited for a touch from Bakul. My knees trembled with the effort of not edging closer to hers.

And then a stone shot through the darkness and fell at a little distance from us. The dog leapt up barking while Bakul sighed and said, "Time to go in!"

Another larger stone fell, this time in a clump of bushes by the gate. After a moment's pause, there was a strange crying sound, like a baby's or a cat's.

"What's happening?" I exclaimed, getting up in alarm and going towards the sound. "Who's there?" I yelled into the darkness, "Come on out, you cowards!"

"Sit down, Mukunda," Nirmal Babu said in a resigned, unsurprised voice. "They can't reach us here. They won't come in if they know we're sitting outside. And maybe they think we have a huge Alsatian."

"What d'you mean? I'm going to go out and find them. What's going on?"

Then, even before Nirmal Babu began to explain, I knew. These were Aangti Babu's men, my colleagues Bhim and Harold. Knowing what they were capable of, I could tell they were still just horsing around, had not yet really rolled up their sleeves. Their faces seemed to bob above the wall, gloating at my predicament.

"I'd thought we could spare you these tiresome details," Nirmal Babu said into the darkness in the same resigned tone, "but I suppose . . . sit down, Mukunda, it's no use pacing about."

I returned to my place next to Bakul but kept glancing at the boundary wall, wondering when the next stone would come. I could picture the cadaverous Harold intoning, "Look up at the stars, look, look up at the stars", as he searched for stones outside and pitched them through the night-sky into the garden.

"This is why Ajay could not let you in," Nirmal Babu was saying. "A few days ago, when Bakul had come with me to the doctor to get my blood pressure checked, two men came in claiming to be people from the electricity board. Ajay let them in and they went to the mains and cut off our electricity. When we came back, the house was in darkness. It took half a day's work for the electrician to repair it. So now Ajay has instructions not to let anyone in since he is too young to judge."

Nirmal Babu fiddled with his matches. The red tip of a cigarette returned.

"The reason you don't see Kamal and Manjula here is that they left Songarh. The business collapsed, Kamal was deep in debt despite selling all the assets – even the factory and some land for growing medicinal herbs. Their needs had changed too. Kamal thought he'd get a job and Manjula was never happy here anyway."

Nirmal Babu paused as if it was difficult for him to speak.

"Oh Baba! Don't make excuses for them!" Bakul exclaimed. "They were dreadful," she said, in a scathing tone. She turned to me. "One day we discovered that they had sold the house behind our backs, using some old legal papers Baba had given them in the years when he travelled all the time. They said absolutely nothing to us, just that we'd have to move, holding out some fiddly amount of money as a bribe."

"Not a bribe, Bakul," Nirmal Babu said, "just a share, compensation."

Another stone fell into the garden with a thud. A handful of gravel clattered onto the tin roof of the outhouse near the gate. Ajay came and took away the frantic dog.

"I'm sure we could have contested all this in court, but Baba . . . "

"I don't want to waste my life in a law court," Nirmal Babu cut in sharply, as if he had said this many times before. "There are other things to think about and do."

Bakul must have decided not to pick a fight. She took a sharp breath but said nothing.

"I can't see any way out, Mukunda," Nirmal Babu said. "I don't want to waste my life in law courts, especially fighting my own brother. I want to get Bakul married and then I'll move somewhere smaller."

Bakul snorted, but too softly for her father to hear.

"You know I was never one for relatives, Mukunda," Nirmal Babu said, forcing a smile. "But now I'm really having to cultivate them to find a suitable boy for Bakul. Tell me, is there anyone you know who might be a possibility? One of your friends?"

In the darkness I could not see his face and although his tone sounded jocular, perhaps he was half serious. After all Bakul was almost twenty-three, and at her age most girls were married. She did not think so, I suppose, and snapped, "Baba!"

"Well," sighed Nirmal Babu. "I just need some time, but the dealer who's bought this place is in a hurry, and he's set his goons on us. One night it's pebbles, another night it's our doorbell ringing repeatedly, some other night we find our well has rubbish thrown in it. We've never seen a soul, but these things have been happening the past fortnight or so."

He rubbed his hand over his eyes and then said, "For tonight maybe their activities are over. They must have run out of stones." He got up from his chair and stretched. "Stay here tonight, Mukunda, why return to the hotel when your own home's here?"

I got up too. "I need to go," I stammered. "I really have some work, some papers." I could not meet his eyes, even in the dark, knowing what secrets my own eyes hid.

"He doesn't want to stay, Baba," Bakul said scornfully. "He likes the comforts of his hotel."

"No, no," I protested. "It's not that, Bakul, the hotel is no good, but . . ."

"But this house is much worse?"

I could see her teeth shining in a smile in the darkness.

"Don't bother him, Bakul," Nirmal Babu said. "But will we see you again?"

"I'll be back," I promised. "Tomorrow."

* * *

I poured out a large rum from a bottle I had bought at a shop near the station. The water I mixed into it was lukewarm, and it was already late, but I took a long, scorching gulp. What am I to do, I kept repeating to myself, what am I to do? I could not throw up Aangti Babu's job and say to him, "I won't do your dirty work, take it somewhere else." What if he did? Everyone else would be more ruthless than me.

I could move them out gently, find them a nice place. But then, to think of that house, my home, going over to Aangti Babu and his henchmen, to be broken into, broken down, bartered away in parts, built over, forgotten. Impossible!

I had never thought the work I did would one day boomerang this way; its darkness had always been locked away behind the doors of other people's lives. It seemed out of the question that I should continue. Yet if I gave up Aangti Babu's work, what would I do? What other trade did I know? How would I feed my son? My wife?

I lay staring up at the ceiling, noticing the fan for the first time. Its bulbous centre was greasy and yellow. The grease was so thick and heavy, it did not look as if the fan could hold onto it much longer. It creaked through each rotation, so slowly I could see its blades were edged with warty soot. With each rotation a drop of dirt seemed to form and I waited for it to drop onto my open eyes.

My wife. What would she think of me flirting with Bakul the way we had all evening? And Tommy. Why were Bakul and he so comfortable together, so intimate? Were they lovers?

And if they were, why did it trouble me?

* * *

The sun shone straight on my face. It was already midday. I lay still for some moments, scratching the weal of a mosquito bite near my ear and listening to the muted sounds of the hotel. I got up at last, looking sourly at the half-empty bottle of rum, the glass next to my bed, and picked up my towel. The bathroom at the end of the corridor must be empty, I thought, and a long bath would do me good.

As I opened the door, I almost stepped into a leafy mass just outside. It seemed to be a bunch of flowers. I picked it up and returned to my room. There was just one large flower: it was pure white, some sort of lily with curling stamens. It had been uprooted together with its long, fleshy leaves. At the end of the leaves was the bulb, a large, whitish turnip-like thing with root-hairs sprouting out of the flesh, bits of the mud it had grown in still clinging to its skin.

I sat down on my bed holding the plant. There was something defenceless and infinitely vulnerable about the bulb, as if a heart had been torn out of a body and left out in the open for anyone to see. The flower reared out and away from its dumpy ordinariness, exquisite, perfect. I put the plant on the bedside table, but I could not look away from it. By turns it seemed enigmatic, pathetic, and even malevolent. I could not imagine why it had been left at my door, or by whom. Was it one of Harold's eccentric notions of a threat?

The hotel had begun to seem sinister and I left it as soon as I could. I had no appetite for hot, ghee-soaked rotis or the copious amounts of potato curry they were ladling out in the noisy dining room. Despite the waiter's anxious queries I left after a couple of mouthfuls and walked rapidly to the neighbourhood of my old school. There it stood, the same shed surrounded by scrub and straggly bushes, with the same group of hapless boys under the same banyan tree. I looked around for the master who caned us every day. I would have been glad to see him – anyone familiar at all, even the fishmonger or the samosa seller calling out, "Hey, Mukunda, is that you?!" I went up to a tonga standing by the tea stall – the same tea stall, but larger, and with different people – and asked to be taken to Dulganj Road.

We clopped off. The taste of the summer air on my tongue was warm and familiar, its dust and sun and lantana, its dry touch so different from the sweaty air of Calcutta. It seemed my duty to look around my old haunts, yet I felt no inclination to do so. I did not want to see the new houses that had come up in the fields we used to play in. I did not want to see my old abandoned fort with a ticket counter at its door and VIJAY LOVES SUNITA scratched into its walls.

I paid the tongawallah and went into Mrs Barnum's garden through an opening in the wall at the back. The trees around the lily pond had grown in height and now formed a canopy hiding most of the sky from view. The edge of the day's heat was blunted here by the cool darkness of the foliage. Large, purple water lilies floated in the leafy, scummy water of the pond.

Had we ever been little enough to swim in it? I lay on my stomach in the grass next to the pond, cradling my chin. In my mind I was in the water, among the weeds, Bakul was swimming by me, in and out of the murk. I was losing sight of her, trying to call out to her, the water muffling all sound. She swam up towards me again and I could see her clothes floating away from her, then clinging to her, only this time she didn't have peach breasts but grown ones. I thought I should not look, and then she swam up and through the water kissed me on the lips.

"Are you asleep? Mukunda?"

I opened my bleary eyes, shading them against the light. Then I realised the light had dwindled, and sat up with a start.

"How did you know I was here? This is like yesterday all over again!"

"I thought you would be, somehow. All day I thought you'd come, then you didn't, so I came here to look for you."

She sat down on the grass beside me in a sari the colour of a monsoon cloud and a sea-green blouse. It made her strange-coloured eyes look stranger still. She smiled, and I saw that crooked tooth. She was hiding something in her sari, bursting with suppressed excitement as she used to, even as a girl. Bakul could never keep a secret from me for long.

"Well, what are you hiding?" I asked her, lying back in the grass. She felt so familiar I could have said anything to her, and yet I felt immensely shy, all at the same time.

"Nothing," she said. Then, as if she could hide it no longer, she brought it out with a flourish and said, "Remember this?"

"The flute? *My* flute?"

"Your flute. The one you bought when we went to the mela, remember?"

I reached for it, felt its smooth polished surface, ran my fingers over the bits of string I had twisted around the ends to protect it. My flute from twelve years ago, a flute I had forgotten about. She had kept it all these years. I felt something inside me flip upside down. I held it out to her. I could not tell if she noticed the slight tremble in my hands.

"Don't you want it?"

I lay on my stomach again and dipped a hand into the water, running my fingers through it, feeling it resist.

"It's yours now," I said. "I'm sure I don't even know how to play it any more."

"Do you know," she said, "I learned how to play it. I don't just produce those . . . "

"Fart sounds?"

She burst out laughing, then put the flute to her lips and pursed them, but she began to laugh again. Exasperated, she exclaimed, "Now look what you've done, I can't play if I go on like this."

I said, "Let's think of something sad." I held my breath, bit my cheek and looked straight at her. I was thinking of her lips touching my flute where my lips had touched it once. A sentimental, stupid thought, but it pleased me nevertheless.

"You look as if . . . " she giggled again and I chuckled too.

"Now what is it? Can't you try to be serious, Bakul, for a minute? It's not as if we're ten years old and can't do without fits of giggles."

She put the flute aside and said, "I can't imagine laughing like that any more, can you? It seems so long ago. Can you imagine us being little enough to swim in this pond? Do you remember?" She waited for me to say something.

I lay back on my arms looking up at sky through the leaves, softer coloured now in the late afternoon. Birds had begun calling again, as if revived by the prospect of a cool evening. What did she remember? What did she want me to remember? Or had she forgotten everything and was just making conversation? Had anyone touched her after me, made her forget?

When she thought the time for an answer from me had passed, she lifted the flute to her lips and what I now knew to be Sibelius' flute melody floated out, limpid and heart-wrenching. Her notes trembled a little as if she was nervous, and one or two went wrong, but she

241

began again each time. She had shut her eyes. Her lips were pursed, and her cheeks hollow beneath her sloping cheekbones. I could see a small brown spot on her left cheek. In the evening breeze, her hair began to fly against her cheek. She shook her head to get rid of the hair. I did not want her to stop playing. I reached out and brushed it away, hoping I could do it without her noticing.

It was merely an excuse to touch her of course, and she stopped.

I had touched her though, and now I could not stop. I stroked her cheek. I traced the line of her jaw. I felt the shape of her eyebrow with my fingertip and the fragility of her closed eyelid as if I were a blind man memorising it for later. I twisted the gold stud piercing her earlobe and felt the petal-soft skin behind it.

I do not remember why the flute did not break between us, or when she put it aside, or how her sari fell away.

I remember how her lips felt, her tongue, her breathsmell like freshcut grass, and the way, despite my mouth on hers, she managed to keep saying, "Why didn't you come back? Why didn't you come back? I waited."

When we laid beside each other on the grass it was dark, and through the circle of leaves above us, we could see the stars starting to poke out one by one from behind the purple sky. From some distance, a rich old voice sang out the opening notes of a song that was popular then, "Babul Mora," the voice went, "Naihara . . ."

"Heard music is sweet, but music overheard even sweeter," I murmured, smiling into Bakul's hair.

"Terrible," she murmured back. "Is this what Calcutta has done to you?"

"Afsal Mian, isn't it?" I whispered. "He still sings."

She shifted so that her chin rested in the hollow of my neck and I did not need her to tell me she was thinking about that night we had run back from the old ruin together and then kissed each other in an empty dark meadow, stunned by starlight and the shooting star streaking through the black sky.

* * *

When we reached the house, Nirmal Babu was sitting at the far end of the garden in the darkness. The red point of his cigarette drew us to him.

"I have to go," I said to his starlit face as he patted a place on the swing next to him.

"What's the hurry?" he said. "Sit and smell the gardenia, how wonderful it is, and the raat ki rani . . . all my father's night-flowers filling the air. Won't you eat dinner and then go? Bakul, can't we . . ."

Before she could speak, I said, "I have a train to catch, I really must be going. But I'll come again when I can, and if you need anything from Calcutta – books? Music?"

"I never asked," Nirmal Babu said. "What was it that brought you here? You didn't just come to see us, did you?"

"I did," I smiled, not looking at Bakul. "Actually, I did come just to see you."

* * *

The train rattled me back to Calcutta and I sat sleepless again, but this time barely taking in the landscape outside. I could think of nothing but the way Bakul had clung to me, trembling, refusing to let go. To think after all these years that it was not I alone who had yearned for us to be together again! I had dozed off by that lily pond after we made love, and had woken to see her looking at me with fierce attention. "How could you go off to sleep?" she had said. "When we have so little time together?"

She ran her fingers over my face. She bent over and kissed my closed eyelids. It felt as if a bird had brushed past them. It felt all wrong and entirely right all at once.

"That tickles," I said, still drowsy.

"What are you thinking?" she said, in a voice barely audible.

"Nothing," I laughed. "I'm thoughtless."

She did not reply, but I could feel her eyes on me. I opened mine.

"What is it, Bakul?" I was half drugged with sleep.

"Haven't we done something wrong?"

243

"Do you think so? Are you unhappy?"

"No," she said vehemently. "Why should I be? I feel as if I had promised myself something all my life and now I've done it."

A curious serenity now gripped me too. I twisted a strand of her hair in my fingers and said, "Then why ask me?"

"We won't tell a soul, will we?" she continued. "I don't want you going and doing anything stupid. You have a wife and child."

"I know," I said, shutting my eyes again and pulling her closer. "I know. And you'll probably have a husband and child soon."

* * *

I now lay on my jolting train bunk, smiling happily into the darkness. After all these years I was sure we still felt a connection no-one else in the world did. Nothing else mattered, not even having to leave Bakul.

The other part of my brain was occupied with more mundane matters. I knew I had to face Aangti Babu. What would I say to him? I had not done his bidding. Far from intimidating Nirmal Babu, I had not even managed to mention the topic. I had not gone to meet Harold and Bhim or whichever hitmen were plaguing my old home, had not given them further instructions; they would certainly tell Aangti Babu about my laxity, or treachery even. Aangti Babu would suspect that I had struck some sort of deal with the inhabitants of the house. He trusted no-one in the end and had a shrewd hypothesis brewing for every possibility.

As the train took me closer to that world of wheeling and dealing and finance, and further away from Nirmal Babu, from Bakul and my old home, it became clear to me that I would have to think of something to subvert Aangti Babu's plans to throw them out and take over the house. But what?

I must have drifted into sleep, for I awoke with an idea that made me shoot up in the bunk, heart racing, an idea that was almost absurd in its simplicity.

FOUR

"You *didn't notice*," my wife pouted in the way she knew I found irresistible. "The little one is standing up. You should have seen the look on his face when he did it!"

It was the evening of my return from Songarh.

"Oh," I said. "It had to happen the only two days I was away."

I picked him up to place him in my lap and tried to pay attention to my wife, who was chatting on, providing me with news of all that had happened in my absence. The milkman's mother, a fat old lady in her sixties, had taken to delivering our daily milk and diluted it with more water than her son used to; the mango tree in the patch downstairs was finally flowering – how long had it been there? Forever, wasn't it? And, oh yes, a cat seemed to have littered in the back verandah. Is that meant to be a good omen or bad? Champa's mother says it means there will be more children in this house, isn't that funny?

I thought I was listening to her, but I must have been looking far away because she stopped abruptly and said, "Tell me, what did I just say?"

"You said 'Tell me what did I just say.'"

She frowned and said, "Don't be annoying. Tell me what I just said."

"Tell me what ..."

She went into peals of laughter and picked up a pillow and threw it at me. "No, I mean it," she said. "You weren't listening to anything."

It is true, I wasn't. I had been filled with a kind of wild elation since making love to Bakul and it was impossible for me to take in anything

245

else. I felt no guilt or self-loathing, I did not see it as any kind of unfaithfulness to my wife. Making love to Bakul was an inevitable and self-contained event, natural and obvious. I was wrong, of course, but my mind had no space or time for other thoughts that evening.

"I was, it's just that . . . " I said, sounding very contrite, but my mind was racing ahead. I removed my boy from my lap and continued, "I have been thinking on this trip. I had an idea. Tell me what you think."

She settled down with a grave look, understanding the seriousness of being consulted. I now think back with pity about that day. She was so certain all my decisions were made with a view to taking care of her and my son, that I would never do them the least injury.

"This house," I said. "As you know, it's not ours. It's been a long time, six years, and Suleiman Chacha has not returned, nor so much as written after the first couple of years. It is almost ours, but not really."

"Yes?" she said, looking a little worried.

"Perhaps Chachi and he are both dead. Who knows when some heir of his that we don't know of may turn up and claim it? I've learned enough of my trade now: these things happen all the time, and then out of the blue we'll be on the street. I want to start work on my own. We don't need such a big place, just the three of us. Let us sell this while we can and move somewhere smaller, and that way everything will be secure and I will have some excess money to put into a business of my own."

I waited for her to react.

"Has this anything to do with Songarh?" she said, suspicious.

In my years with her I had reminisced about the place, but my memories had always been well edited, or so I supposed.

"In a way," I said in a meditative voice. "It made me think. Look what happened there, one brother betraying another and leaving him homeless. Who can you trust if not your own brother? And here we are not related to Chacha, we are not even the same religion!"

"But I like this house. I like the verandah and my lemon tree. And what about Champa's mother and the neighbours? Where will we live? Somewhere strange and new and small! I don't want the money."

"It's not just the money. We may lose both the money and the house. Now that many years have passed since Partition and things are not so good for Bengalis in East Pakistan, some of them are coming back. I'm just trying to think ahead."

She lay down with a sigh and buried her face in a pillow. "I don't know what has got into you," she said in a muffled voice. "You go away for two days and come back with strange ideas. Why are you consulting me? Would you even listen if I said no?"

I knew she was crying inaudibly into her pillow at the thought of leaving our tree-fringed home, but I had begun to believe my story. Often, I told myself, events showed you the way. I had always been insecure about the house, living in it and not really owning it. Why should my life – and now my family's life – be spent in a house on loan? Now my dilemma was morally urgent too: how could I stand by as Nirmal Babu, who had brought me up, was made homeless?

* * *

I went to work the next day with some trepidation, wondering if Aangti Babu would agree to my plan. All morning I got up from my chair each time I heard someone enter the two-room office, but he did not come in until the afternoon. I waited by the door. He gave me an unsmiling grunt of recognition when he arrived and said, "Into my room. In five minutes."

He did not ask me to sit down this time. He busied himself extracting a paan from his box and then stuffing it into his already reddened mouth. Then, his mouth filled with betel juice, he waved me to the chair and mumbled sounds I interpreted as, "Sit down, tell me the news, are they out of the house?" Harold, Bhim & Co. were not back from Songarh, so he could not know of my perfidy yet.

I told him what in essence I had been inspired by in the train: I wanted an exchange. He could have my Calcutta house, far more valuable than an old house in a small town, if he gave me the one in Songarh. On condition that nobody knew of the exchange. It was to seem just a simple sale. And he would give me money to make up the

247

difference in value between the two houses, so that I would have the capital to start my own business. I spoke too fast, somewhat breathless, but what I said was lucid and my tongue did not get tangled up as my thoughts made their way into words.

Aangti Babu had been wiping his bald, sweaty head with his usual grimy handkerchief. He had been offhand rather than attentive when I began to speak.

But soon enough he was looking at me, a slow, cunning smile curling a side of his mouth. He gestured at me to stop, picked up his stained brass spitoon shaped like the face of a woman with her mouth open, aimed a stream of red spittle into it, then wiped his mouth. I looked away, queasy despite being accustomed to his habits. Two thin lines of red betel juice were now engraved into the wrinkles near his mouth. He scratched the back of his neck and then examined his nails as he spoke.

"So," he said, measuring out each word, "do I understand you right?" And he repeated precisely what I had said to him.

I wanted him to agree to my proposition, of course. But as his protégé I had thought, or perhaps just hoped against my better judgment, that he would have my welfare at heart. Even as I put my idea to him that day, I had expected him to dissuade me, to say, "Mukunda, don't be a fool. It's a stupid deal and I'm warning you off it because I have your interests at heart. If it were anyone else I'd have held my tongue and let him diddle himself."

But he agreed without hesitation and said, trying hard not to look crafty, "That's intelligent, Mukunda, very clever. You'll be getting a huge property, with lots of unbuilt land, and it'll appreciate enormously. And I've been thinking for a while that the time's really ripe for you to start off on your own. I've taught you all I can, you know. You'll go far, Mukunda, mark my words! As for this small old house in a Calcutta bylane that you're offering me, well, it is all so uncertain, no real papers, no deeds. Should I risk it? But perhaps I must, to help you on your way, the extra money will let you set up your own business, as you say."

The alacrity with which he agreed made me feel relieved as well as disgusted. Suleiman Chacha's house was in a prime location in Calcutta and he knew it. Possession was ownership as well as nine-tenths of the law, one of the tenets of his trade which he had instilled in me. And after six years, even if an absentee Muslim's heirs turned up, what chance would they have against Aangti Babu and his thugs? He would have the house sold and the money pocketed in two months flat. In exchange for this virtual certainty in his favour, from Aangti Babu's point of view I was taking on the opposite: risking possession of a disputed house in a provincial town that might never fulfil its grandiose prophecies. Aangti Babu did not want to know the reasons for my lunacy. He may have been curious, he may well have had his surmises. But he wanted the sale and exchange done before I saw the light and changed my mind. He was the embodiment of diplomacy, behaving as if I had just proposed a life-changing deal for myself. I had, but not in the way he thought.

Despite his haste, however, he managed to make me lower the amount I wanted for the Calcutta house, so that I was left with less than I had expected.

Any innocent belief of mine in his wanting to act out of some fatherly or mentoring impulse towards me was dispelled, but as I walked out of his room, what dominated my feelings was immense relief: Nirmal Babu and Bakul's future was in my hands. The ownership papers of 3 Dulganj Road would soon be mine. My childhood home was safe; it would not go to strangers to be broken down and built upon.

A few days later, when it had all been formalised, I sat down at the table I had along the corridor at Aangti Babu's office and began to compose a letter. "Dear Nirmal Babu," I wrote, "It is difficult to explain all this, but by chance I discovered I know the property dealer who bought your house from Kamal Babu and I have been able to persuade him . . ."

I redrafted the letter seven times. It was ready to be posted only at the end of the day. My letter made it clear that Nirmal Babu need not think about looking for other living arrangements for at least as long as I had a say in the matter, and that I expected this state of affairs to obtain indefinitely. He would be able to live on at Dulganj

Road without worry. By return of post there was a letter from him, alternately bewildered, grateful, curious, and apologetic, struggling to retain his dignity. He seemed to have believed and accepted what I had said in my letter to him. His reply confirmed the house was no longer besieged and expressed great gratitude to me, mixed with perplexity, that the days of harassment were over for Bakul and him. I felt sorry for him, and I put his letter aside without sending a reply.

* * *

Our move from Suleiman Chacha's house was not without trauma, even for me. My wife and I fought bitterly over what to take with us. I did not want to part with Suleiman Chacha's books, which had become old friends; my wife was determined to sell them to a second-hand dealer. Noorie had never endeared herself to my wife, who was not amused at being called names and sometimes pecked. But I shouted down her pleas to give the bird away or set it free. My wife wanted to take some heavy bits of furniture with us that she had been given as dowry, but I knew our new home would be too small for four-poster beds and enormous carved cupboards. All evening battle raged. If I gave in and said yes to a cupboard, I blackmailed her about Chacha's desk. We went to sleep silent and fuming and woke up sullen with stored-up rage.

Despite it all, I was intoxicated at being Bakul's saviour, knowing she was safe in her own home because of me, that even if absent I was looking after her. Those few hours with her in Songarh had changed me irrevocably and I knew I could not live the rest of my life as I had been living it the past few years. I felt something fundamental in my personality shifting and reshaping itself. I was now consoled by the thought that human beings were made to love many people. I did not try to explain it to anyone; I clutched at it almost as a kind of epiphany, some divine illumination that had chosen to shine on me alone. After all, did we not love our parents, our siblings, our friends, our spouses and our children simultaneously and in different ways? If at that moment my wife had announced that she loved another man as well, in addition to me, I was sure I would have been happy for it, because I was certain that I could – I *would* – love both my wife and Bakul in different ways. I saw it as my destiny. This was fortification against the guilt and sorrow that attacked me when I saw the pain I was causing my wife and the pain my son was too little to know I was causing him. I was never going to abandon my wife and child, of this I was sure. The thought of my world without Bakul may have become inconceivable, but equally the thought of life without my baby boy was a sterile vastness I could not bear to contemplate.

I did not want to buy a new house straightaway. Whatever money I had, I wanted to put it into a construction business, and because most of my money was locked up in the Songarh house, there wasn't much to spend. I was worried about how much money would be available to me once I started work on my own. All I could think about was economising, so I wanted to rent something small in an area we could afford. In the end I rented two rooms in a house in Shyambazaar. There wasn't space enough to swing a cat in there. It was a slummy area. Open drains, shared bathrooms which were dirty. We had to stand in a queue for the lavatory each morning. Then the men and children bathed at a tap in the courtyard while the women waited their turn for the solitary bathroom. There were about eleven tenant families. Street shops surrounded us. Right outside our bedroom a stall sold pakoras all evening, and the oil fumes smoked up our room if we opened our single window. By night there were crowds of drunken men milling about near the stall. Every day, from the chicken and mutton cutlet shop next door, we heard the terrified squawks of birds being slaughtered, followed by the smell of frying meat.

Then one morning my wife went into the lavatory and found that the child who had been before her had left a pile of mustard-coloured turds on the floor. My wife had squelched them.

"On the floor," she screamed. "What kind of children do people bring up that leave shit on the floor!"

"Ooooh," the mother of the child called out in a high voice, "my, my, aren't we lucky to have Queen Victoria herself staying with us! Used to a mansion, isn't she?"

"You watch what you say, Nakuler Ma," my wife yelled in a bellowing, heavy voice that I could hear from the first floor and did not recognise.

"And what will you do? Throw us out? Husband's a big landlord, isn't he? Runs a big business. Very high and mighty, aren't we now?"

Another woman joined the fray and said to my wife, "Come on, a child's leavings aren't impure. Haven't you heard? A baby's pee is pure Gangajal. You're a mother yourself, why should you mind?"

We moved house two weeks later, as soon as I had found another place, this time around Kidderpore. It was on a busy street slashed in different directions by tramlines. All evening and all day we could hear the clanging of trambells and the honks of buses below. Far into the night, when it was still and dark and even the trams had stopped, we would lie awake listening to the forlorn cries of a boy calling out for his drunk father. "Baba, Baba? Where are you?" he would call in a high voice that came from different directions as he walked the streets looking for his father. Then, long minutes later, he would stop shouting; perhaps he had found his father lying in a stupor somewhere and dragged him home. We would fall into tired sleep at last and wake to the sound of crows cawing and the trams clanging up and down once more.

It was one room, and a makeshift kitchen, but it was away from everyone else and there was a bathroom of sorts across the roof. I hung Noorie's cage on the roof, by the window. She seemed to screech less than she had in the poky Shyambazaar rooms. My boy could be put out on the roof on a blanket with his toys when there was shade. He gurgled with delight again. After what seemed a lifetime of never hearing the end of it, I found the new quarters had calmed my wife down a little, perhaps only because of the constant exhaustion to which our new life had subjected us, and I began to look for work.

* * *

The reprieve was brief. My wife had from the start been sceptical about the real reason for the sale of the house; now my father-in-law began to appear on our doorstep every few days to poke and pry and reinforce her qualms. The early happiness in my marriage began to dribble through my fingers as inevitably as water in a cupped palm.

Barababu had married his daughter to me because of my prospects. Despite my parentless background, despite there being no information about my caste, my father-in-law had liked – or accurately calculated – my property and prospects enough to hand her over. He did not like the change in our circumstances any more than his daughter did. "We may not be well off," he said to me more than once, "but we kept our daughter like a maharani. She's not used to all this hardship you're putting her through. And why?" It was latent hostility that I sensed in him more than puzzlement. I had long suspected I had been attractive to him as a prospective son-in-law more because of Suleiman Chacha's house than for any qualities in me.

"It's only temporary, while I set up the business," I said.

"But why should there be this problem with money? That's what I don't understand," he badgered me. "You've sold a big house in such a good locality, you should be rich! Instead you're stingy about food and I don't see you landing any contracts. Malini says you don't even buy fish every day any more!"

"I have the money from the sale tied up in certain investments," I said tight-lipped, turning away to put an end to the conversation. I began to find the very sight of my father-in-law, making his way up the stairs to our terrace room, wheezing and groaning, insupportable. Everything about him began to irk me: his overlarge nose with its hairy nostrils, his receding chin, his long-lobed ears over which he looped his dirty sacred thread when he washed his hands at the tap, and most of all the way his daughter and he spoke in whispers, darting looks in my direction. After he left and my wife repeated his questions to me as if they were her own, I said, "You don't understand about business, keep out of it and let me do what I think is right!"

"You're always shouting at me."

"I'm not shouting. And I'm trying to tell you something simple. Let me do my work. Don't interfere, don't bother me. Do I try to tell you how to cook or bring up Goutam?"

253

"It's not just this time," she continued as if she had not heard me. "I only have to *speak* for you to snap my head off. If I ask you to come and eat, you start shouting 'Can't you see I'm working, can't a man work in peace.'" She stormed out of the room muttering, "Since my speaking about *anything* annoys you, I won't speak, you wait and see."

Long silences would descend over the house, dense, tense hours broken only by the thin wail of the baby. I would leave in a huff and go and sit by the river on the Strand and watch the boats go past, emaciated boatmen pushing poles into the water to manoeuvre their old boats. Even they were happier, I thought. They knew what their work was, they earned their food and drink. Perhaps they were lucky and had no wives. At times I was racked by self-loathing at my duplicity, at the way I was making my family suffer, but I felt – I knew – that the course of action I had taken was the only possible one. Sitting by the river one day, watching the trams go past on one side and the boats on the other, I yearned with such intensity for the time I was unencumbered and light-hearted, walking the Maidan with Arif, talking of books and girls, that I almost walked into the river in despair. Arif's Lahore was in a different country now, as was Suleiman Chacha's Rajshahi. They were in the past – all my friends were. I was utterly alone. How had contentment deserted me? Why was I so overcome with dissatisfaction? Was it worth anything, this changed world in which I had lost a wife and gained only a longing for something so remote, so far in my distant past?

* * *

Six months passed without much change. My wife and I spoke, but we rarely talked. Her once-smiling face had assumed a rigid sternness. She lost her temper often. My child had become cranky. He had a long attack of some skin allergy that could not be diagnosed and I found it difficult to scrape together the money for his doctors and medicines. All night he kept waking up, wailing and sobbing and scratching patches on his body and scalp that went an angry red. To see him suffering tore my heart in two. The room on the roof was a heated box in summer and to sleep on the terrace was to have a symphony of mosquitoes around us. My father-in-law had been right; we could not afford to eat the things we had been used to.

It was not as though I had not been trying. I got little bits of work as an overseer as I waited for business opportunities that never came. Often, Aangti Babu handed me these odd jobs with a sarcastic, smug air. But now that I was in theory an independent contractor, I was without his monthly salary, and uncertainty clouded our days. In the weeks when I had nothing lined up, I would say I was going to work and leave the house to walk around the city, sleeping on the benches in the Maidan, eating jhaal muri and not much else. Around me, tall chestnut horses munched the soft, green grass and boys in whites ran about with ball and bat shouting to each other in breaking voices. I would feel myself uncurl a little, borrow some of the pleasure the horses took in their grass, the boys in their game. In the cool dark beneath a tree I would lie cradling my head in the crook of my elbow, looking at the world from beneath and wondering if it had a place for me.

Things had to improve, I told myself. Everyone said businesses took a long time to start up. I would soon save enough to make the kind of investments that would take me to where Aangti Babu was. At times I found myself fantasising about building a little house for Nirmal Babu and Bakul in their garden, and selling off the rest of the property. Surely they would understand my necessity. At other times, on the more miserable days, I would decide to sell the Songarh property back to Aangti Babu as anonymously as I had bought it. If he still wanted it. But then if I got a few months of work overseeing somewhere, I discarded that thought. Sometimes I got work as a subcontractor outside Calcutta, in smaller towns, and being away from home gave me some relief.

Every hour of every day through all those days, I thought of Bakul, the yearning yielding to calmer thoughts sometimes, at other times causing a frenzy made unbearable because it could not be spoken. I knew I had lost a wife, but I knew too that she was at home with my child and that all these contrary things together were now inescapably my life. It was the futility of it, I think, that prevented me even trying to write to Nirmal Babu or Bakul. The knowledge that they were safe because they were in my house sustained me through it all, but if I wrote to them, what could I possibly say?

* * *

When we had a little extra money some weeks later from these subcontracts, we took Goutam to a specialist for his skin allergy. My wife was more sullen than usual. We waited without speaking for the doctor to call us, knowing we would quarrel if we spoke. He was the kind of doctor who has magazines in his waiting room, and I picked one up. It had a picture of a beautiful woman on the cover. I turned the pages, not reading, not looking with any attention at the fantasy life its pages revealed. Then I stopped on one page at a small advertisement for cold cream. I looked at it closer, with disbelief. The face with the perfect pink complexion looked very like Bakul's.

Those days I often caught myself looking with hope and expectation at a particular back or shoulder on roads, buses, trams, when from a distance it seemed to belong to Bakul. When the woman turned and I saw the face of a stranger instead, my disappointment was disproportionate. This picture came closer than any of the others I had mistaken for her. It was not Bakul in every respect. The hair was too tidy. The skin was too pink, and she never smiled like that. I could not see her crooked tooth either, or perhaps it was on the other side of her face.

"What is that you are looking at with such attention?" my wife said in derisory tones. "Pretty woman, isn't she?"

"Oh, nothing," I said, turning the pages, feigning indifference. I had not realised my wife had been studying my face.

"Every woman is pretty when she doesn't have to sweep and swab and fill water all day. Then men think of them as apsaras."

"Come along," I said, impatient. "Can't a man even look through a magazine without criticism? Do you know how you sound?"

I had just returned from a fortnight-long, hot, wearying trip sorting out problems at a site for a government school, where I had stood for days on end in the blinding sun. I had come to the doctor's almost straight from the station. I felt unprepared for squabbles with my wife. But she was full of suppressed rage, having had to cope with our ill, cranky baby all that time alone. She would not stop.

"Hmph. Men turn strange at your age. I know that. Binu's mother was telling me she found bad pictures on her brother-in-law's shelf, under his clothes. And imagine, he is a forty-year-old father of two. Hari, Hari," my wife exclaimed. Then she shifted in her seat, moving the sweaty baby to her other shoulder. "I don't know how long we'll have to wait for this doctor. And what's the use? None of them have been any good."

"He's the best skin specialist in Calcutta," I said. "Where else can we go?"

In the flutter that occurred when the doctor popped his face out of his room and told us to enter, I managed to tear out the page from the magazine and put it in my pocket. Even if it was not Bakul, it felt as if I had her closer to me with that picture in my pocket. I could look at it at leisure.

After we returned home and put the exhausted baby to bed, I slid the picture into my cupboard beneath papers and bills where my wife would never notice it. I washed myself at the tap on the terrace and then, bare-bodied and refreshed, went to find something to wear. The cold mugfuls of water that I had poured over my body and head had made me regain my temper. "Is the food done?" I called out to my wife as I crossed the hot terrace on tiptoe, "I'm hungry, haven't eaten home food for a whole fortnight!" My few clothes, now looking quite worn, were in a washed pile at the foot of the bed. I tossed them aside one by one, looking for a kurta thin enough for the still, sweaty day.

My wife called out from the kitchen, "Are you there? The rice is done, come and eat." She was repentant after her earlier tirade, and solicitous.

But now I could hardly breathe, let alone reply. My hands trembled. I sat on the bed to calm myself, not noticing the pile of clothes beneath me.

I heard her say, "Just like you to take your time after forcing me to hurry the food, and now I am waiting with the hot rice, and me up since dawn and unslept half the night with this squalling child . . ."

Buried underneath the pile of clothes I had found a letter, put there by my wife while I was away. It was no more than a hurried scribble in Nirmal Babu's hand which said, "I'm sorry, this is sudden, but I hope you and your family can come. It won't be complete without you. There are still two weeks. We will talk when you are here, and I will tell you all the details."

The letter was folded around a stiff card printed in the obligatory red with the usual stain of auspicious turmeric on one corner.

It invited me to Bakul's wedding.

The wedding had taken place the day before, when I was on the train back to Calcutta.

I stared at the card longer than I knew, and though my vision had clouded over, what the card said was clear as daylight. Bakul now was a married woman.

* * *

A white heap of rice steamed before me, one side of it cascading with yellow daal, the other side still pristine. A bowl with one small piece of fish in a red turmeric gravy, a green chilli topping it, stood by my plate. My wife sat beside me, her fingers deep in her heap of rice, which was already half gone.

"What is it?" Her voice startled me out of my thoughts. "Home food not to your taste after all? I even managed to get fish." She looked hurt more than annoyed, and this shook me out of the stupor induced by the wedding card. I broke open my rice pile and began to mix a part of it with daal. In honour of my return, there was a vegetable as well. We never had all this at a single meal these days; she must have saved her household money over the period I was away.

"I'm tired," I said, putting the first bit of food into my mouth. "It catches up unawares. Hours in the sun, the chaos of travelling, shouting at labourers all day."

With my first mouthful I began to feel my throat stop. I had to cover my mouth with my palm to keep the food in and make it go down. My wife had turned her attention to deboning her fish. Her head was bent, and where she had sat cross-legged on the floor beside me before, now she adjusted her position to hunch closer to her plate.

"It's even worse," I said, "because I have to travel out again tonight. Not a moment's peace." I put my left hand on the floor to feel its reassuring stability and coolness as I spoke.

"What?" she exclaimed. "Out again, tonight? Where to? You said nothing about this before!"

In the minute I spent sitting on the bed after opening Nirmal Babu's letter, I had digested the fact that Bakul's groom was from Bombay: the card made that clear. That meant she would leave Songarh soon after her wedding. How would I ever see her again after that? I had to see her before she left – if indeed she was still in Songarh.

I had decided to leave for Songarh by the night train. I did not stop to work it through, to give myself a rational reason for going. It was an incontrovertible fact, a given: I had to go, I had to see Bakul once more before she left my life for good.

* * *

Going across the Hooghly that evening, caged by the soaring steel girders of the bridge, surrounded by a mass of strangers too busy to notice me, I felt as if after many months under observation I had been set free – of wife, child, parrot, home. For a while I was alone, a man who might do anything with his life. I looked at the river and allowed myself to linger over the memory of the pond at Mrs Barnum's. I thought of the saltiness of Bakul's lips, the cutgrass scent of her breath came back to me, the hard shoulder blades under her blouse, her hair which tickled my nose and made us laugh.

I had chosen an upper berth so that I could lie and think my thoughts in solitude. The train was surprisingly empty given that I was in a third-class compartment, normally packed to rubbing sweat on sweat. Today, there was only one other man in my compartment of four berths, a large, walrus-moustached man in a dhoti, with a folding table, a plant in jute sacking, two tin trunks, and a pink-eyed white rabbit in a hutch that he fed with leaves and sliced carrot as soon as he came in. I observed him for a while, then when the train gave a thudding jolt and at last pulled out of the platform – delayed by an hour – I closed my eyes, shut him out, and lost myself to Mrs Barnum's lily pond. If I tried hard enough, I could shut out the wedding card I had seen earlier that day and fill my mind with Bakul playing the flute, then kissing me on the eyelids as I protested. I could almost smell her hair, her soap and that talcum she had used the evening she cooked dinner for me.

But my compartment was pervaded by another smell, and now the moustached face was beside me saying, "You must be hungry, Dada, the train is late. Would you care for some poori and aloo and achaar?" He spoke in Hindi. The smell of the foods he mentioned permeated every particle of air in the cabin. The mustard oil of his mango pickle all but coated my tongue.

I refused and frowned, shutting my eyes again. I could hear sounds of the man's contented chewing and slurping. It must be past eleven, I thought, why is he eating now, on an overnight train? But of course people felt the need to eat the instant they got onto a train.

The thought occupied me for a moment and then the despondency that had overtaken me that afternoon had me in its grip afresh. I closed my eyes and saw Bakul's impish smile. I smiled sadly into the darkness. How must she have looked at her wedding in red and gold? Had she thought of me? Had she managed to tie her wild hair back so that she looked like a demure, conventional bride?

"Dada," the man was saying, his face bobbing near mine. "The lower berth is empty also, why not come down? I feel uneasy sleeping alone down here when the other berth is empty and the train is so empty."

"But I am in the same cabin," I protested. "Please go to sleep, you are in no danger."

The man beamed and said, "At least you are awake, that gives me some peace of mind. I tell you, I cannot sleep so soon in trains. I have to talk, for some time I have to talk. Dada, what is your name? What do you do?"

I looked at his eager face. He was leaning against my bunk, his elbows providing him support as he stood in the swaying train, his face only inches away from mine. Impossible to turn away and lose myself in my daydream again.

"I'll come down," I said. "If that makes it easier for you to sleep."

"And do you live in Songarh?" he continued, helping me to lay out my sheet on the wooden bunk next to his.

Without waiting for a reply, he said, "I've been there now for fifteen years. First I was in the timber trade, now I am in mica mining, you know mica?"

I nodded.

"During the World War, that was when I started, mica was in great demand then. Then it faded away when the British lost interest. But now after Independence, when we are ruling ourselves, we are exploring mining everywhere. The British did not care. Did they care?"

"They didn't care," I repeated after him.

"Panditji cares," he said. "He is nation-building – temples to modern India, mines, dams – all this he has promised."

He took my lack of interest for disagreement and said, "I know, you Bengalis are very anti-Panditji, you say Nehru is bad, and you say Gandhiji is bad. When Gandhiji was killed and the killer was Maharashtrian, I was amazed. Not a Bengali? See, you too are annoyed at the mere mention of these two leaders."

"I am not annoyed," I said. "Forgive me, but I'm very sleepy. I'll sleep now."

"Right, you are right," the fat man said, pulling a sheet over his head. "It's late, and we must sleep."

Air swept in through the window, cooler than before. All I could hear, now that the man had gone to sleep, was the clack-clack of the train rushing me towards the newly married Bakul – and her husband.

The man's voice said into the darkness, "Are you asleep, Dada? I am sensing you're not."

I sat up, resigned. He sat up too, and from his pocket dug out some sweet supari which he offered to me. He spoke about his wife and how she disliked Songarh. He spoke about their childlessness. "It is making me even more devoted to the Mrs, Dada, we have no-one else," he said. "But who will look after her when I am dead, who?"

"She may die before you," I said, touched by his sentiments, but wanting him to shut up.

"A few years ago, I almost died," he said, his voice less ebullient. "Shall I tell you the strange thing that happened to me? You know mica is not found deep in the earth, you do not have to drill mines, it is close to the surface. It is lying about all shiny and waiting, just a few feet below. I was camping in the middle of wild land not far from Songarh. What year was it, now let me think . . . can't recall, but maybe fourteen years ago, around 1940. I was camped there, wild emptiness all around me. No wonder my wife worries for me. All night I hear foxes and owls and strange sounds I can't place. My adivasi labour is all half drunk or doped, sitting or sleeping by their fire. It is late, but not very late. It is probably early evening, but we are very tired because we have just ended a day begun at dawn. I am resting in my tent before dinner and then, commotion! Commotion!"

"What happened?"

"I rushed out to see. My labourers were all speechless with fear, pointing at the sky. I look up, and what do I see, Dada? What do I see? It was a spaceship."

"A spaceship?"

"Space. Ship. That is it. Something strange flying in the sky. At that time we didn't know what it was. We wondered: was it a shooting star? Was it a problem of vision? But no, it was circular, it was glowing, and it was floating above our camp, coming down towards the earth."

He paused and chewed on his supari for a while.

"My labourers are praying and shouting. They will suck out our souls, these are people from heaven they say. I too, I am scared, the ship is now very low, and we can see it is neat and oval and it is not a star or anything like that. But I have to be the leader, say Calm down, men, calm down! All around us the forest has gone quiet. But everything is lit bright in white light from the spaceship. There is a low humming sound in our ears, like a vibration. At that time I knew no more about spaceships than my men, I thought it was a chariot from heaven that had come to take us." The man paused and, with glugging sounds, drank water from a bottle he held about four inches above his open mouth.

"Then?" I said, impatient to know.

"Then? Nothing. It floated near us for some time and then it rose and went away. I met many people later and asked them, Did any of you see this thing that we saw that night? Nobody, nobody saw a thing. People started to think of me as a little, you know . . . " He tapped the side of his head with a forefinger. "If my labour had not been with me and seen it too, I would also think I am . . . " and he tapped his forehead again.

When I woke up in the morning, the train had already been standing at Songarh station for a while. The fat man and his rabbit were gone. If not for the lingering odour of mango pickled in mustard oil, I would have doubted both his existence and that of the spaceship. Had Bakul and I seen what the man had seen that time, long years ago in the starry field? Was it as many as fourteen years ago? In my mind the image of that evening – the light in the sky, Bakul's proximity and our shared terror – was so vivid it seemed as yesterday.

* * *

Outside the station was the familiar rank of tongas, their horses and their drivers hooded with shawls. Although it was already hot and uncomfortable in Calcutta, here on Songarh's high plateau surrounded by forest it was only the end of a chilly spring, and I shivered when my tonga gathered speed and air on the slope down to Dulganj Road. I had decided I would not waste time going to a hotel first. What if I narrowly missed her?

The tonga turned the corner into Dulganj Road. It was empty in the half-light, with the sky still struggling between night and day at the western edge while the east was bloodshot. I was reminded of standing out on the terrace on a Saraswati puja dawn one cold January many years ago, waiting for Bakul and her relatives, not allowed to enter the puja room during the prayers. I paid off the tongawallah some distance from the house and heard it clopping away. I was alone on the road, but for two labourers huddled near a tea shop in mud-coloured shawls. I could almost hear the dew dripping from the leaves and grass in the profound peace of the dawn. Somewhere a tentative brainfever bird was trying out its voice, unused since winter. I noticed that the roadsides were piled at intervals with shining slabs of mica. Until my companion's discourse of the night before, I had hardly noticed it. I picked up a tiny sliver of mica and put it into my pocket as a charm.

I walked in the direction of the house. My feet dragged. I was not able to think any more of what I would say to Bakul when – if – I saw her. The man in the train kept winking and grinning at me, tapping his forehead. I reached the gate and looked in. There were no obvious signs of a recent wedding – no tent up in the garden, no piles of folding chairs, no rubbish from the feast. Perhaps the ceremony and the dinner had taken place elsewhere, not at the house.

I put my hand on the latch, and at the same moment a window opened on the first floor of the house, first one shutter and then the other. I could see a flash of orange as Bakul leaned out to open the second shutter. I thought I caught a glimpse of loose hair and a corner of her face. Something flashed in the first rays of sunlight that must have been gold.

Before she could see me, I wheeled around and hid next to the wall, my heart thudding against my chest hard enough to stop my breath. When I was sure she was gone from the window, I walked away, then half ran from Dulganj Road, past Mrs Barnum's house, past the new houses, past the tea shop with the peasants – now four of them, not two – past the corner where Nirmal Babu's office used to be. I could not think rationally about leaving without seeing her, speaking to her, when I had come so far. I had come to see her, but to encounter her as someone else's wife? I could not bring the journey to its logical conclusion.

* * *

There was nothing for me in Songarh, but I could not bear to go back to Calcutta. I stayed on in the cheap room I had booked myself into for the next couple of days, lying in bed, alternating between a dead, stunned doze full of troubled dreams and long wakefulness. I did not want to eat or get up. I felt as if I would not be able to move my body from the bed even if I tried, as though it had a separate, stone-like weight I would not be able to heave out. I did not want to bathe or brush my teeth. I did not care that, with barely any savings, I could scarcely afford to pay for a hotel. I was cold in Songarh without winter clothing, so I lay shivering under a threadbare quilt all day, refusing to open the window to let in the sun.

I felt as if, having been loved, I had now been cast into the dustbin of the unloved; out of the cool shade into the putrefying sun, out from shelter into the wilderness. I knew well enough even in that darkness and confusion that Bakul was blameless, yet I felt as if she had abandoned me.

* * *

I am not sure how long I stayed at the hotel. It felt an eternity of misery. Eventually I dragged myself home, too tired and disoriented to make up excuses to trot out to my wife.

When I opened the staircase door and reached our terrace, the first thing I noticed was that Noorie's cage was open and she was not in it. The terrace stretched out barren and empty in the sun without her.

The next thing I saw was that our door had its big brass lock on it. When I went down the stairs to the neighbour with whom we usually left the key, she gave me a strange look and handed it over with a note. She shut the door on me without a word, which was unusual. My wife and I always made fun of her garrulity.

"I am going home," the note said. No more. She had not bothered to seal the folded square of paper within an envelope to keep our neighbours from gossiping.

My wife could not have taken Noorie to the village with her. She must have thought that leaving the cage door open would allow the bird to fend for herself. But how could that tame parrot have found food? She must have stayed in the cage, cowering in a corner as she used to after Suleiman Chacha left, not daring to fly out, waiting for me to arrive with green chillies and fresh water.

I fiddled with the cage and looked around for Noorie, making the chucking sounds she responded to. I squatted in a corner of the terrace, feeling the baking midday sun burn the soles of my feet. I knew it was futile. There would be no familiar flash of green. No claws would dig into my shoulder, no beak would nibble my ear and search through my hair, consoling me with squawked obscenities.

Above me, in the dirty, grey-blue Calcutta sky, rapacious kites wheeled around and cawing crows hopped along the parapet mocking each other.

* * *

I let myself into our room at last, wondering what had made my wife go away like this. She was used to my travels, and certainly to trips as long as this one. Why should she have thought this time any different?

The room looked tidy and settled, as if she had taken her time over leaving. On the table by the window, in a neat pile, were Suleiman Chacha's books, our small, old radio, and the worn exercise book in which she kept conscientious household accounts, recording every matchbox and kilo of rice that she bought.

Within the account book was the picture I had torn out of the magazine at the doctor's that day, and Bakul's wedding card.

Later, from a clerk at Aangti Babu's, I came to know that my wife had visited the office in my absence. After all, he was a distant relative of her father's, apart from being my boss. I could not ask Aangti Babu what had transpired, but I supposed she must have been worried by my disappearance and gone to ask him when I would be back. What could he have told her that made her leave like this? She had never travelled alone before. Usually she went to her parents' once a year, at Puja, and I would drop her off at her village home.

Aangti Babu probably hadn't been able to resist the opportunity to be malicious when my wife went to him for news of me. I could imagine the scene: Aangti Babu twisting the blue- and yellow-stoned rings that cut into the flesh of his fingers, pumping my wife for information in his high voice. He must have deduced from her ignorance about Songarh that I had not told her of the house I owned there.

"My child," he will have said, "men are so terrible, they really think womenfolk don't need to know all this. Don't blame your husband, he's trying very hard to make his business work. It's a shame you're having to lead a hard life now, it will all change some day! This house of his in Songarh, which belonged, I discovered, to his old mentor and his young daughter, well, such a house is not easy to sell, is it? Sentiment! Doesn't that count for something? I met them, they are such estimable people, and such a beautiful, flower-like girl, you would have warmed to them instantly."

I was guessing all this of course. Despite my suspicions, I could not antagonise Aangti Babu. Too many of my contracts depended on him, and I had to continue taking on his overseeing work as if nothing had happened. He said nothing either. I may have been wrong. Perhaps he had tried to cover up for me, and my wife had jumped to her own conclusions.

When she had not returned after a fortnight, I began to miss my boy more and more. I wrote her a letter enquiring about her plans. Did she want me to come and fetch them in the next few days? After that I would be busy for some weeks with a new contract. The letter went unanswered.

* * *

It was a month or so later that I went out for a walk and actually took in my surroundings. The heat was less fierce. I could sense moisture in the light breeze that touched my skin. It was a soft feeling, like a passing feather, a breeze that made me feel as if I had a soul that could unfold and stretch. I sat on a railing by the footpath, in the shelter of a dilapidated bus shed. The day had darkened to an unnatural early twilight. The sky was low with purple-grey clouds that seemed too heavy to stay afloat. In a little while the expected deluge began and I closed my eyes in relief and gratitude as the thundering sound of rain drowned out the twittering of the late evening birds. The leaves on the roadside trees turned shiny green, and dipped and drooped with the water. For a little while, in the drumming rain, anything seemed possible.

The last few weeks had been the darkest time of my life: when I sat alone on that rooftop, day after scorching day, absorbing for the first time that Bakul was no longer mine. She was in a strange city, in a new home I could not visualise. In bed with a man whom perhaps she loved. When I managed to push this thought away, another would come to prey on me: I worried about Goutam's skin allergy and what care he would get in my wife's village. I longed for his milky, baby smell and piping voice. He must miss me so much, I thought, he must ask for me every day. When I pushed this thought away, yet another came to prey on me: Noorie, starving, being torn to pieces by other birds or cats as she tried to find me, find food.

I felt incapable of paying attention to anything else. The room on the terrace grew unloved and dusty, I threw off my clothes into a heap on the floor and wore them unwashed the next day. I must have smelled bad – there was no-one to complain save the milkman who came daily because I did not dare tell him there was no longer a baby who needed the milk.

When two months had passed without answers to my several letters, I went to my wife's town to try to persuade her to return. It was a pretty place, grown from village into town by virtue of a few large houses. One of these relatively large houses belonged in part to my father-in-law, Barababu. I had not told my wife I was coming. I had not known until I got on the train that I really would go. I was, to tell the truth, a little apprehensive about her mother, her loud-voiced, belligerent aunts, and her father.

I decided to walk from the station to her house, although it was a fair distance. It would give me time to settle my thoughts. Besides, I liked the walk through the emerald-lit, mango-fringed road. Parts of it were bordered by ancient terracotta temples set in groves of tall, old trees. The other side, halfway down the road, had a deep pukur as large as a small lake, filled with moss-green water in which you could, if you sat still, see the shadowy forms of fish gliding about.

My father-in-law lived in a jointly owned family home, a sprawling set of rooms connected higgledy-piggledy with verandahs, courtyards and walkways. In the early days I had often lost my way in it. As I approached the green door set in the lemon-coloured walls of the house I sent out a prayer to the gods in the temples I had just passed. The door opened into the first courtyard, a big one bordered by a wide, cool, shaded verandah on all sides, where the family's Durga puja was organised every year. I had seen it thronging with laughter, noise, incense smoke and people, but it was empty and quiet now, on a mid-summer morning.

My wife's family occupied rooms in the next courtyard, up a short flight of stairs. As I ascended the stairs, I came face to face with my wife's elder aunt. She shrank as if I were an assassin. I smiled and began to bend to touch her feet, but she hurried past saying as if to herself, "Oh Ma, the water tap must be open and flowing, I must rush."

When I reached the set of rooms belonging to my parents-in-law, I paused outside, removing my slippers. Through the insect-mesh of the door I could see my father-in-law reading the newspaper at their round marble table. I could not see my wife or son. I coughed and knocked on the door. He looked up. He saw me and did not smile, saying instead, "You've come?"

I walked in and sat down beside him.

"How are you?" I tried.

"Are you really concerned about my health?" he said.

"I wrote many times, to say I would come and pick them up, but got no answer," I said, deciding to set aside the pleasantries.

"What do you expect?" he said, heated. "My daughter finds out she has to live in penury because you are supporting another family, and you keep pictures of strange women in your cupboard, and then you expect her to come back? Which self-respecting woman would?"

269

"I am not supporting any other family," I said, trying to keep my voice calm. "I don't know what you have heard, but that's not true."

"Isn't it true you have bought a large property in another town?"

"Yes, but ..."

"Did you tell your own wife about it?"

"No," I said. "But ..."

"And isn't it true that this house belongs to some old family you know, with a father and daughter?"

"You don't understand ..." I began.

"Enough!" he thundered. "I understand everything! You locked up all your money in this house; you did not sell it, who knows why? Everyone says it is because you want to support this other family. And meanwhile, what about my daughter? She has to move from her own house, sell half the things we gave her for her wedding, and live in discomfort in rented rooms. What more do I need to understand?"

"Can I speak to her?" I said, my voice as loud as his by this time.

"Do you think she wants to speak to you?"

"Let her decide that."

"Come back once you sell that house," he said in clipped tones. "That is the only thing she asks. Meanwhile, there is no need to speak to her."

"My son," I said. "Where is my son?"

"Come back for him when you're fit to be a father," he said, and took up his newspaper as if I were no longer in the room.

I got up angrily from my chair and went to the door. As I bent down to put on my shoes I saw my wife standing at the side door of the room. She had been listening to our conversation. I started towards her, but she drew back, almost as if she were frightened. She opened her mouth to say something, but then a shadowy form passed the opened door beyond her and she seemed to jump. Quickly, she turned away, retreating into the other room.

I retraced my steps to the front courtyard. This time it was not empty. My son was playing on the verandah. With him was another little boy. They were about the same age, almost three. My son had a pebble in his little fist. He carefully laid it down and then got up and walked to the edge of the verandah, picked up another pebble from a pile and laid it next to the first.

I stared, mesmerised by the intricacies of the game which occupied him. I forgot the existence of the other boy and the servant woman who was sitting by them. My son looked up at me once and then went back to his game. I couldn't tell if he was sulking or did not recognise me. When one of his pebbles rolled off the side of the verandah, I stooped and picked it up. He laid out his tiny palm, pink and creased, the palm I had loved to hold to my nose, blow on, tickle.

"Golu," I said, wheedling, "Goutam, look who's here! Your Baba!" I smiled, holding out my arms.

"His name is Akshay," the servant woman smiled. "Call him Akshay and he'll come."

I placed the pebble in his palm and closed his fist. He looked at his fist with a frown and tottered back to his game.

I strode out of the courtyard, feeling loops and loops of barbed wire tightening around my heart.

I sat for a long time that day by the side of the town's pond, staring at the date palm and banana trees that shadowed the water at its edges, the steps which disappeared into the water, the two shiny brown boys who were splashing in and out at the other end. When it was time for the evening train, I got up, shook out my clothes and walked away.

FIVE

In the early days of my marriage, I found the idea of separation and solitude frightening. There was one particularly bitter quarrel my wife and I had – I forget the cause – and in the end I had stormed out of the house saying, "I'm not coming back". When I did, hours later, she was not at home, although it was late in the evening. I remember how a quiet pit of fear had opened inside me as I thought, This time she really has gone back to her parents.

Now that our separation was real, curiously I felt no fear, and after those first bad months I even began to feel a guilty contentment. I came back after work to the empty room on the roof. I cooked some daal and rice, and having eaten it, sat alone on the terrace feeling the city throb below me while I looked up at the stars from my little oasis, drinking rum, feeling the familiar languor spread by degrees to my fingertips. If I went to the parapet of the terrace I could see the trams moving like lit caterpillars, pinging the wires above, and the squares of yellow lamplight in the houses around me. Three floors down was the road, where I could see the busy shadows of anonymous pigmy people on errands I did not need to know about.

My solitude was absolute. I spoke to labourers and contractors and building owners during the day, but apart from professional talk I had no dealings with anyone at all. My neighbours side-stepped me, thinking me an evil man who had not only driven his wife away, but who also drank. This did not bother me. On the rare days I was overwhelmed by my solitude, I went to a crowded Muslim restaurant in Dharmatolla and ate rezala and roti, soaking in the clamour along with the grease.

Everything seemed to have become much simpler. I had the space to think or to daydream. I bought books again, after years, and began to read. On impulse, when I was walking past a market one day and saw some music shops, I went in and bought a bamboo flute with a rich, resonant timbre. I managed, after several attempts, to play the Sibelius melody on it. My terrace was immediately transformed into Mrs Barnum's garden and I felt as if Bakul were listening to me from some dark corner.

When winter came and the mosquitoes disappeared in the cold, I put my cot out on the terrace and lay there as I drank, looking up at the black, sooty, half-lit dome of the sky. One such night I saw a shooting star and returned in my mind to the flaming trail of light Bakul and I had seen in the sky years ago. What if it had been a spaceship? What if its space-people had touched her and me with their magic that evening, with their rays or vibrations? Changing us forever?

Perhaps I should go and surprise Bakul in her marital home in Bombay. But what would I say to her face to face? What if she looked cold and distant, as she sometimes did, and asked why I had come?

If she did, I would make an excuse, say work had brought me to Bombay.

She would make polite conversation and might even give me tea. We would talk about Bombay, the potato prices, her husband's job, then say goodbye. Her baby (she must have had one) would begin to wail. She would say she had work to do. Her husband would appear and ask her who I was.

I would go to Bombay on the train the next week. I would make an excuse, say work had brought me there, and Bakul, eyes dancing, would say, Lies! You came to see me! Admit it! I would pull her to me and it would feel as if there had been no years and no other people in between.

I would go to Bombay, and as I stood somewhere on the street trying to puzzle out where her house was, Bakul would tap me on the shoulder. I would start to say I've come to work and she would interrupt, I knew you'd come looking for me one day.

I smiled to myself in the dark and took out the sliver of mica that stayed with me in my wallet these days as a Songarh keepsake. I lit a match and watched the mica flicker in its flame, then lit my cigarette with it.

Downstairs, the forlorn son of the drunken man called out "Baba? Baba! Where are you?" as on every other night. His voice faded and then returned, faded and then returned again. And then stopped.

* * *

Two years passed this way. I was beginning to find more and more independent work. Aangti Babu, all said and done, had taught me the trade, and now I was a tough businessman. I could intimidate people into abandoning their houses. I could bribe government officials with ease. I could bully labourers into carrying more headloads than contracted. I could hold back payment from shrivelled-up, starving workmen if they missed a day. I developed a nose for buying and selling property and an ear for gossip about old mansions that had begun falling apart. I was making more money than I knew what to do with. I sent a generous monthly amount to my wife. Each month, along with the money, I wrote a brief letter: what work I was doing, the weather. For some time I had thought our separation would be temporary, and she would return, forgetting our last bad year. I had never intended driving her away, never imagined I would lose my son, and that she would be embittered enough to change his name. My letters were never answered. She had always been a diffident and reluctant writer, her alphabet round, childish, pressed hard into the paper. The thought also crossed my mind that perhaps my father-in-law, seeing I had ignored his ultimatum, was withholding both letters and money from my wife and she knew nothing of them. If that were so, my betrayal must to her have seemed too terrible for forgiveness.

* * *

I did not want to work with Aangti Babu, but I had no choice, for our work had become closely intertwined over the years. He, for his part, did not pass up any opportunity to taunt me. One day, as I left his room, he said, "So the house in Songarh did not, after all, come at a bargain price, did it?" Then he chuckled in that nasal way he had. "When will you put it to use, Mukunda? Are you a businessman? Or Mahatma Gandhi?" His eyes seemed smaller in a face that had become obese and pouchy. The years of betel chewing had stained his teeth and lips beyond redemption. He drew breath with a wheeze these days.

I thought it best not to answer him. The Songarh exchange was some years in the past now, and I had tolerated this jibe many times. Instead, I left him with a short, "I'll be back next week, have to travel." I stepped into the reception – Aangti Babu had prospered and made himself a reception area – and started collecting some papers from my former table that occupied one corner of it. The room's single, brown-upholstered sofa was occupied by a grey-haired woman who sat with her head in her hands. She had not been there when I had gone into Aangti Babu's room an hour before. She did not look up when I rustled my papers or chatted to the tea boy. When her head jerked downward in a sleepy nod, I realised she had dozed off. Despite being asleep, she kept a vigilant hand on a chipped purple trunk beside her. It was painted with red roses and green leaves, a pattern that I felt I had seen before – but then such things were common enough. I wondered what she was doing there; one hardly ever saw women in Aangti Babu's office. I stopped whatever noise I was making so that I would not wake her, and left the building.

Minutes after I had stepped out of the door into the elbowing, sweaty rush of the street, I heard someone calling and then a hand clutched my elbow. I turned with a protest ready on my lips to see a thin, elderly man in glasses. His clothes looked worn and the bag on his shoulder was an ordinary cloth jhola. His bald head gleamed with sweat. I thought he was a party worker of some kind, and said, "Dada, I am in a hurry." I did not want to stand there being told the benefits of being a leftist or a Congressman, not then, though such conversations often amused me.

"Don't you recognise me, Mukunda?" the man said with a smile.

The puzzle of his face melted into place. He had shaved off his beard and that made him look completely different, but now I knew.

"Suleiman Chacha!"

Even as I said the words, I wanted to turn and run, run as far away as possible from him, and from the little woman in the waiting room with the purple trunk.

"Shall we sit and have some tea somewhere?" Chacha said. "Your Chachi is so tired."

* * *

We did not want to talk in Aangti Babu's office, so we picked our way through the squalor of Bowbazar's street market in search of a suitable place. It was at its busiest: vegetables, fish, flowers, rickety chairs, birds in cages, trinkets and toys, all spilling at our feet, vendors shouting each other hoarse about the perfection of their wares. We kept losing sight of Chachi, then finding her again. I banged their trunk against people's knees in the crowd and pretended not to hear the curses that followed. Finally we found with relief one of those little restaurants that line the streets all over Calcutta, the ones with wooden benches and greenish glasses with bubbles in them. Three such glasses stood on the greasy table before us, steaming with tea. Chacha and Chachi were eating dhakai parathas, but I felt nauseous looking at food. Did they know what I had done? Did they know I had bartered away the house they trusted me with? That it was being demolished even as we sipped our tea? The thought was insistent, but I could not bring myself to raise the subject.

I barely heard the things Suleiman Chacha said about East Pakistan and how difficult life had been there at first, and how much he had missed Calcutta. "I remembered strange things, bhai," he was saying. "You know, the ships' horns at night in the docks, hooting in that spectral way. I had never really noticed them when I lived here and my ears ached for them there. And the school, the children. I had thought I was tired of their stupidity and the bullying of the older boys, but I began to wonder, did Monohar eventually clear his exams? Did Sudip

276

ever learn to spell Nizamuddin? Did Aslam migrate to East Pakistan or did he stay on in Calcutta? And that bookseller I went to on College Street, did he recover from his eczema? Nothing there seemed right, although if you come to think of it, Rajshahi is not that far . . . it's home, isn't it? It may be a hovel, but if it's your home then you can't stop longing for it."

We asked for more tea. I wondered when they would bring the topic up, or should I?

At last he said, "We went to our old house, of course." And after a bite of paratha he continued, "We went there straight from the station. Your Chachi was all agog, even though I kept warning her nine years had passed and things change."

Chachi said, "You look a grown man now, I would not have known you in the street."

I stared at my glass of tea. Chachi reached across the table and touched my cheek saying, "Look at you, so thin, your cheeks have gone in. And your clothes! Aren't you married? Doesn't anyone look after you? We wondered sometimes."

"You never wrote to me," I said. "Why did you not write?"

Suleiman Chacha smiled in the gentle way I remembered. "Arre bhai, Mukunda," he said. "You have no idea what was going on. Often your Chachi and I did not know where we were going to sleep that night, or where the next meal would come from. I tried so hard to get a job, but they didn't want schoolteachers there, especially of history." He laughed. "I've become an assistant in a watch shop. Still working with Time, you see, a historian of sorts!" He laughed again.

"What about your family?" I said, trying not to sound as if I resented him for returning, though at the time that was how I felt.

"What could we have expected," he said in a resigned voice. "Everyone told us to occupy any empty house whose owners had fled. But that didn't seem right. What if their owners returned, just as we thought we'd come home to Calcutta? We never thought we would stay there for good, so we kept living in rented rooms here and there. The family house turned out to be too crowded to give us space."

"Family house!" Chachi said with scorn and glared at her tea as she adjusted her sari in the righteous manner women do sometimes. "What family? What house? They looked at us as if we were usurpers ... even when we visited."

Chacha said, "We went looking for our house – and there is just rubble. The space looked so big, I hadn't thought the old house was so large." His eyes were too apologetic to meet my own. Although the crime was mine, it was as if he were the criminal and my sins had become his.

Chachi said, "The shopkeepers next door did not know about you, but they told us to contact this Aangti Babu. It's lucky you happened to come just now, we were about to give up."

"I waited a long time," I said. "But my letters got no replies ... "

"We had to move around a lot. I could get only little bits of work at first ... "

" ... then there was a financial crisis," I said, scrabbling around for something convincing to tell him, "and I had a real problem finding the money for the bills and taxes, and then there was a chance I would lose the house to a landgrabber ... "

"We've lost too much to worry about losing a house," Chacha said. "My brother, uncle and nephew were all killed in the riots, and I found out only a year later. I hunted for them for such a long time there. I heard they had been disembowelled, and then ... "

Chachi glowered at him and said, "Why go over all this now?" She was casting furtive looks around her, in case anyone had heard him.

"I didn't expect the old house to be there, only your Chachi did. She kept saying ... "

" ... All I had thought was that the house would have Mukunda's children playing about in it." She threw Chacha an angry glance. "Women my age want to be grandmothers to someone! That's all I said, nothing about the house. I know these years have been hard for everyone." She, like him, seemed desperate to make excuses for my wrongdoing.

" ... but never mind, these are futile things," Chacha said. "It's been so many years, a lifetime. What could we have expected? You have a life to live, could you have waited forever?"

"What will you do now?" I asked him. "Will you stay on here in Calcutta? I can find you work. You could work with me. If you don't want to work, it's all right, I will look after you. I have nobody else, Suleiman Chacha, let me! Come and live with me for a change!"

I was looking at their tired faces with desperate urgency. Nothing else seemed more vital for me now than to look after them. First I would take them to my terrace room and make their beds and cook them hot rice and daal. Then, after they had rested the night, I would look for a house with enough space for the three of us, like before. I would not let Chacha work, I would buy him books and music and watch him live a life of leisure. I would buy Chachi pretty saris and a harmonium. She had always wanted a harmonium. We would live together, as we had before. I would make it up to them.

Chacha looked at me with an amused smile. He stroked his bald head. "I don't know, Mukunda. I've just come, let me see. I have some people to see first, friends we have not met for so many years ... Bashir, you remember, who lives in Tollygunj? We have told him we're coming."

I looked down, disconsolate.

"Why do you say you have no-one?" Chacha asked with concern. "Have you not married? Don't you have any children?"

I rubbed my hands over my eyes and lied to them about my wife and my son: I said they were having to live in the village because I had to travel so often and Calcutta's climate was no good for my son's skin allergy. Chachi's eyes scrutinised my face so hard I had to turn away. "Once we are settled here again," she said, "I'll make some neem oil to massage the child with. This is no way for a young family to live, separately, and you looking so terrible."

The waiter in the restaurant began to give us exasperated looks, wiping our table every now and then to make us get up. Chacha sighed and stirred.

"It's quite late," he said, looking at Chachi with a raised eyebrow. "We ought to go, I am not sure I will find Bashir's house easily after so long."

I picked up the trunk with the roses when they got up to leave. They had a few other bundles that Chachi anxiously counted. She

279

looked up at me and touched me again on the cheek saying, "Don't blame yourself, what else could you have done? At least you waited all these years. There are those who sold homes while the pillows were still warm from their owners' heads."

We walked to their bus stop. The crowds had grown and the evening air was stewy thick and yellow with lamplight. I screwed up my eyes, peering into the distance, and said to Suleiman Chacha, "Let me get you a taxi. Don't go in a bus."

"Arre bhai, Mukunda, when have I ever taken a taxi?" Chacha laughed, "I wouldn't know how to direct one either . . . can't find my way about, everything so changed! What number bus should I take? Is it still . . . "

I saw their bus lurching over the cobbled tramlines in the distance, behind two others, and said, "It's coming. It'll take you straight to Tollygunj."

Chacha asked, almost shyly, "There was just one thing – I was wondering . . . about Noorie . . . ?"

Chachi said, "Come on, how long does a parrot live?"

"She was happy," I said. "She was happy and healthy, but would keep asking for you the way she did when you were here."

"And then?" Chacha looked at me with trepidation.

I began to confess before he could ask, "Chacha . . . I am . . . "

The traffic signal changed and their bus surged in our direction.

"It's alright," he shouted, making his way towards the bus. "She was happy with you! That's enough."

"Chacha!" I called out in the confusion, "What's Bashir's address? How will I find you? And you haven't taken mine either!"

He had begun to climb into the bus. Someone was pushing him. He wobbled dangerously, balancing a bundle, and Chachi, frightened, grabbed his arm.

"The address, Chacha! The address!"

Suleiman Chacha pushed his head over the shoulder of another man and tried shouting out the address. The man barked irritably, "Arre Dada, if you want to chat, get off the bus and let me get in!"

I heaved their trunk in after them and lost their faces among the

crowd of passengers pushing each other in their search for footholds
and handholds inside. The bus began to move forward in a cloud
of black fumes. I ran after it. I would climb in, go wherever they
were going, I had boarded moving buses all my adult life. The rear
doorway of the bus bulged with people. I managed to get a grip on
the steel rod by the door and hung from it as my feet searched for a
crevice on the footboard to jam in a toe. There were four other men
at the door, trying to haul themselves in as well. The bus gathered
speed, I felt the smooth rod slipping, I felt my feet meet the road at
a run and then stumble to a stop, my arms hanging useless by my
sides.

The bright lights darkened with the shadows of people who
blundered mothlike against me. I stood still in the middle of the street.
They milled around me, crowds of strangers who had friends and
family to go home to. Beyond this street were others, and beyond
those still others, a spreading web of streets, teeming with strangers,
hundreds, thousands, an infinity of strangers in a city where I no longer
had a friend, where nobody ever waited for me to come home.

* * *

I walked a long time that evening. I paused at Kalighat Bridge to
look at the river below, dark as buffalo skin in the night, the lights it
reflected struggling to wink on its scum-slicked surface. It was not
water any more, but greasy, stinking, rotting sludge. I did not know
why I had walked so far, all the way from Bowbazar to Kalighat. My
legs ached. Unexpectedly, I was reminded of the time I flew a kite
with my wife in the Maidan. It had been a winter afternoon a few
months before our marriage ended. We had had a long quarrel the
night before and I woke up determined to make amends. I thought I
would take my wife and son out for a day in the Maidan. They never
got out. I went and bought a few large kites and all the kite-flying
paraphernalia from a shop down the lane. I came home and, affecting
enthusiasm, said, "Come on, Sankranti is around the corner! We must
fly these kites! Up, up!"

My wife had looked at me bewildered. The quarrel the night before had been only one of many that had crowded the week.

"I'm tired," she said, "I've been on my feet all morning. Besides, when does a woman ever go running out to fly kites?"

"Oh come!" I said. "I'm trying to do something we'll enjoy. We'll get out of the house, take a tram."

We reached the Maidan. There was hardly a breeze. My son pranced about with delight, lisping, clapping with glee, looking at the other kites that dotted the sky, waiting for ours to join them. I told my wife to pick up the kite and set it aloft so that I could pull the string and make it fly. She could not get it right, though it was a simple enough thing to do. She would let it go too low, or too soon, or simply too lackadaisically. She kept adjusting her sari and saying, "Oh Ma! Is this something a woman can manage?" Or she would look around and say, "Everyone is laughing at me. Can you see any other woman here, doing this in public? This is terrible."

The kite would not fly. It would stay aloft a few seconds then begin its precipitous dip which brought it crashing down. Perhaps I too had lost the knack, but I got more and more frustrated and scolded my wife each time she made a mistake. My son lost interest and sat on the grass, picking at it and amusing himself. After many attempts, during which she managed to tangle up a kite in her sari and tear a gash in it, I lost my temper and shouted, "You're useless. Have you never done anything apart from housework in your life? There are women who climb trees and swim!"

I was struck with remorse as soon as the words had left my mouth and abandoned the kite string to go to her. She collapsed on the grass and began to cry. "I'm tired," she whimpered. "I've been working all day, my legs ache, I can't run any more, I'm tired."

* * *

I stayed up late that night, tidying in a frenzy. My cupboard had not been cleaned for years. I made a big bundle of old clothes so torn and filthy that I could not imagine a beggar accepting them. I threw in the few saris my wife had left behind. I paused some moments over my son's clothes from when he was newborn. He would be nearly six now, and I had not set eyes on him since he was three. But then I stuffed those into the bundle as well. The kitchen shelves were stacked with dusty, mouldy containers of greyed spices, damp papads stuck to each other, and unidentifiable powdery things in paper packets crawling with weevils. I threw them all out. Cockroaches skittered out from their long-undisturbed hideouts. I stacked all the utensils neatly in a corner and stood gazing at them for a while. There was the brass kashi my wife and I had bought together at a mela. The grinding stone I had had carved with a smiling fish especially for her. I put aside the silver jhinuk I had bought just after my son's birth to feed him milk with. We had hardly ever used it; he had gone straight from breast to glass.

I went to the other room and pulled all the books from the shelves onto the floor and began to sort them. Most of them were Suleiman Chacha's. He had read bits out to me from many of them, and all were annotated in his fine handwriting. Letters fell from a couple, a dried-up leaf from another. Stuck between books on the shelves were statements of accounts to Aangti Babu, across one of which I had scrawled: "Must tell him, we can get the old man out of the Dharmatolla house for less. Also, cheque for Sushanta may bounce." In one of the books I had written in English, "Dear Suleiman Chacha, with best wishes for your birthday, many happy returns, Mukunda."

Amongst the books, in a brown envelope, was my Intermediate exam certificate. And a letter from Nirmal Babu, his last before I cut off contact with him.

My dear Mukunda,

I am so very pleased to hear you have passed your exams. When I told Bakul about it she laughed, and wouldn't believe me until I showed her your letter. What are your plans now? I hope you will carry on and do a B.A. and then study further. Education is really the best thing life can offer. Now look, I am *lecturing you, but forgive me, I'm an old man. I've known you since you were a child. You were a bright-eyed, clever boy and now you're turning out to be an intelligent, well-read man. It makes me stupidly emotional to see you've reached this milestone in your life. I wish we could have celebrated it together, but I hardly travel now. Perhaps you will come to Songarh one day to see us all, and then we will talk of old times. Meanwhile, when you know where you are going to stay, send me your address so that I can visit you if I ever I come to Calcutta.*

My love and blessings,

Nirmal Babu

P.S. I am enclosing a little cheque, please use it to buy yourself something nice as a present. Why do you ask me to stop sending you money now and then? I do it out of affection.

I do not know when I finally slept that night, sprawled amidst the debris. My head ached, my eyes hurt, I wanted never to wake up again. But the cawing of the crows broke into my sleep as usual. I opened my eyes a crack and then sat up straight, wide awake.

I would give up my line of work. It was not too late, I could not have rotted all the way through, there was still time. I was not yet thirty. I would learn to make my living some other way, think of something else, even if it meant a few hard years. That very day I would go to Aangti Babu's to settle accounts and then call it quits. I would stop myself turning into him.

* * *

When I woke up the next morning and opened the door to the milkman, he was holding out a letter along with the milk. "It must have come yesterday, Babu," he said. "It was lying on your doorstep."

After the milkman left, I slit open the stiff, large envelope addressed to me in Nirmal Babu's hand. A night after I had re-read his old letter. We had not written to each other since he had sent Bakul's wedding card and changed my life forever. I wondered what new bombshell was enclosed in this envelope.

What first slid out of it was a photograph showing a large house, almost a mansion, that seemed to have a spacious verandah in its centre and rooms on both sides. The sides were framed by palm trees. Tall pillars of the kind that had been fashionable once upon a time towered right up to the first floor, reminding me of buildings like the town hall in Calcutta. Above was a folly of a roof. In the foreground was water: at the pillars, waves and eddies.

It was, I realised with a jolt, the house Aangti Babu and I had visited some six years earlier, the house by the river which he had tried to buy with fake papers. The house in . . . Manoharpur, that was it: I could visualise the name, black on yellow on that long-ago railway platform. It was the only time I had seen Aangti Babu lose money and face.

"The enclosed photograph is of Bakul's mother's old home, which is by a river," Nirmal Babu's letter said after a few lines of pleasantries. "The river changed its course over decades and finally flooded it in the year of Bakul's birth. My father-in-law tried many things to stop the disaster from happening, but to no avail. I read a lot on rivers at that time, and one writer who said: 'In a deltaic country, floods are inevitable; they are Nature's method of creating new land and it is useless to thwart her in her workings . . . the solution lies in removing all obstacles that militate against this result.' This was absolutely true of the house in Manoharpur.

"You may know some of this already: Bakul was born a month before time and nobody could reach the house with medical help because the house and the surrounding area were inundated. As a result, Bakul's mother died giving birth. After Shanti died, her father (my father-in-law) became a little eccentric; he insisted on staying in the house even though, each monsoon, the ground floor flooded and for several years he was marooned inside for weeks at a stretch. I am told people arrived by boat with food for him and he threw down baskets for them on ropes, but he wouldn't leave. People have strange

285

obsessions that nobody else can understand. They seem irrational, but to themselves these people make complete sense."

It was a long letter. I turned to the third page. It was as if he had embarked on an autobiography. He seemed to have been in need of someone to talk to who was familiar with his terrain, and I felt he was addressing me as he might a son. After my excoriating self-hatred the night before, the letter seemed a healing ointment that had come by post. It connected me, however tenuously, with a world in which a part of me existed, still untouched by later changes.

"A few years ago," the letter went on, "the government decided to construct an embankment further up the river. This was eventually completed, and all of a sudden, after the havoc of all these years, the river is tamed. Some other area must be inundated because of the embankment, but for the moment the house is safely out of the water and has been for a year or two now. (The garden would be a good place to find fossils.)

"To graver matters: we received some grim news a few days ago, which has prompted this letter to you. My father-in-law passed away, perhaps ten days or so ago, I cannot be sure – he died alone, away from family, but that's how he wished it, and I cannot pretend at this stage of my life that I was particularly attached to him. I had always blamed him, justly or not, for my wife's death. But the fact remains that he was Bakul's grandfather and she is emotionally attached both to him and to her mother's house. What I hear is that some others have collected at the house to lay claim to it – land and houses seem to bring out the rapacious in everyone. There is an old retainer who says the house is morally his, a neighbour who claims it as repayment for loans my father-in-law had apparently taken from him over the years, and a property dealer from Calcutta who has sent his men because apparently he paid some money for it in a fraudulent deal some years ago. They are all hunting for the original deed of the house, which my father-in-law seems to have hidden somewhere. Without this deed, none of them can claim the house."

My breath had quickened. I wished he would get to the point. I felt as if I had never read a letter so long.

286

"The house is Bakul's by right," the next page went on, "and she is the only person who knows where the deed is; her grandfather was extremely eccentric, as I've said – you know, he lived alone, trusted no-one, not even banks. Bakul remembers how he hid his house papers, almost as a game with her, on a visit we made years ago. I had no idea they'd done this because he swore her to secrecy, and she took – takes! – secrets very seriously. She's going to Manoharpur next week to try retrieving the deed and, if it's still there, to decide what she will do with her inheritance.

"Speaking for myself, I want to sell the house; I have never been attached to it – quite the reverse – to me it has always been my wife's tomb. I could not make myself return there for years after her death. Bakul has always resented this, I know, but I could do nothing about it. If she does decide to sell the house, I would appreciate your help. Once the sale money is in hand, we can begin to repay you – your generosity over this house in Songarh weighs heavily on me and I cannot rest until I have paid you back, though that would still not be enough to thank you for saving my home.

"Bakul would be extremely annoyed if she knew that I'd asked you for help. She refuses, as you know, to take help from anyone, even her own father. But to me you are like a son and who would I ask if not you? I'm writing this letter at night and will post it on my morning walk so that she doesn't know of it: I would be very grateful if you could go to Manoharpur, as if by accident, and help her through this.

"I have to be in Songarh: I have to stay here because of my dog – only other people as attached to their dogs will not think me irrational – but she cannot survive without me. Also, as you may have gathered, I'm hardly very practical in matters of land and money. But I am worried about Bakul trying to deal with this by herself. So I hope this letter reaches you in time for you to be there for her."

There were many things in the letter that worried me, but what occupied my mind to the exclusion of all else for the moment was this: what was Bakul doing at her grandfather's ruined house in Manoharpur? Where was her husband, and why had he not accompanied her?

Immediately my mind began to fly kites. Had the husband turned out an inept fellow whom nobody trusted? Had Bakul fallen out with him and returned home to her father? Whatever the situation, Nirmal Babu had thought of *me*, me and nobody else, in this time of Bakul's need. I clung to this simple knowledge – in his eyes I alone could help her. I would finally meet her, and she would be by herself, just as I had fantasised.

She would be there *by herself*. The thought also struck me with dread. Bakul in that secluded spot, that wilderness, with those sharks moving in? I remembered how far away the house had been from the shops and the railway station, how the grounds stretching around it shielded it from other people. If she shouted, nobody would hear. I tried not to think about that, but I knew better than her father how dangerously she would be out of her element. The dealer from Calcutta who had renewed his pursuit of the house could be none other than Aangti Babu, although there might be others too.

I plunged my arms into a shirt, took some money from the cupboard, and tore down the stairs for a taxi to the station. The letter was dated four days ago. Bakul might already have reached Manoharpur. I had lost a whole evening while the letter had lain overnight on my doorstep. There was no time to lose.

All that my mind could nonsensically intone as the train chugged out of Sealdah in the harsh ten o'clock sunlight was, "Look up at the stars, look, look up at the stars, look at all the fireflies . . ." I tried to remember the name of the poet, but the only name that came to mind was Harold.

* * *

When at last we drew into Manoharpur I leapt off the train before it stopped. The six-hour journey had seemed to me to take eight or ten, as the train stopped at every wayside station for passengers, tea, vegetable vendors and who knows what else. The engine wheezed and groaned and puffed through the landscape of ponds and greenery I usually found enchanting. On this journey I had leaned out of the

288

door, the wind in my hair, landscape rushing by me, as if peering into the horizon would bring Manoharpur closer.

The sign at the station was new, still black on yellow, but bolder and larger. The station had a concrete platform in place of beaten earth and its railings were now metal, not bamboo. There were more people than I remembered, and I got a cycle rickshaw right by the station gate. When I told the man where to go, he said, "Oh, to Pagla Dadu's?" He laughed at the surprise on my face. "Oh we always called Bikash Babu that, and he didn't care. He knew we thought he was half crazy."

He began to pedal and said, "I hear his house is for sale. So many people going to it these days!"

"Who?" I exclaimed. "Anyone you remember?"

"I just took a man there this morning, a tall thin fellow," the rickshawallah said. "But others have gone too I hear, Babu, what can you say of the greed people have? God save me from such greed."

He pushed at the pedals, his checked lungi riding up his thin, hard-looking legs. "So long as I have a little food to eat and some cloth to cover my body," he said. "I'll earn by my sweat, Babu, not other people's deaths, you understand, Babu?"

He stopped pedalling and, sitting on his saddle, wiping his face on the sleeve of his shirt, he turned to look at me. "The old man dies all alone, alone, you understand, Babu," he continued. "And now those very relatives who never took any care of Pagla Dadu in his lifetime, they want to sell his land and house and make off with the money."

"I'm in a bit of a hurry," I tried to edge in. "Could you . . . " I would have got off and walked to the house if I had remembered where it was. He turned back to the road with a sigh and pushed the pedals again.

"Human beings are vultures, Babu, take my word for it, you understand?" he panted. "That son-in-law of his – they say he was a good enough fellow – but can you fry and eat a good enough fellow? Did he look after his wife's only father when he was dying?"

"Didn't he?" I said, struck by this image of Nirmal Babu as a callous villain.

"No, he did not, you understand, not a bit! Poor Pagla Dadu even had to be cremated by his old servant's son, nobody from his family. Now tell me, is this right? Even if a man is a bit crazy."

I clutched the handle as the rickshaw crested a hillocky part of the dirt road.

"But what can you say, he only had that one daughter, and she's dead, poor girl. Even if she were alive, what good would it have done? Could she have lit his pyre? What's a man to do without a son? I'm telling you, Babu, I'm a poor man, not a landowner like Pagla Dadu, but God above has blessed me with two strapping sons. To throw me a handful of rice when I can't pull this rickshaw any more. To touch a flaming torch to my pyre."

We were approaching the same drive, now looking even more unkempt. The rickshaw set me down before the same deep front verandah that Aangti Babu and I had sat in. The same cane chairs stood in the verandah, and I could have sworn the brown discoloration on the verandah wall was the spot Aangti Babu's betel juice had splattered on. The rickshawallah took his money and cycled away.

Only one thing was different: one of the cane chairs was occupied by Harold.

* * *

He was dressed as usual: shiny old suit, narrow blue tie with bright yellow stripes, the trousers two inches too short for him, showing worn, black socks over thin ankles, despite which he looked respectable enough, more like an elderly schoolmaster than a thug. He looked up with a beaming smile when he saw me and exclaimed, "Oh, Mukunda, m' boy, I'm bloody glad to see you! Didn't know the boss was sending reinforcements."

He dropped his voice and said, "I tell you, m'n, this job's got me foxed. The boss said to go an' hunt for the deed – the old bugger who's kicked the bucket stuffed it in some hole somewhere in this whackin' big bledgy mansion of his. An' I've got to pose as a buyer and just look around like, and then find it! An' y'know what, m'n? For a change the

290

boss sez don't get rough, you got a girl here to work on, just find the dashed deed, he's already paid some bugger an advance for the house and he just needs the papers quick and quiet – but tell me how? Give me a straight job and I'll do it m'n, it's easy to beat the stuffing out of a man and make him cough up a bloomin' deed, but dealin' with dames? I wasn't brought up to bully the gentle sex, no, m'boy."

At this point Bakul came into the front verandah. I don't know if she had overheard Harold, but she gave no sign of recognising me. She gave me a quick, somewhat cold look and said to Harold, "If you and your colleague are ready . . . ?" She turned and walked back in without waiting for us to follow. Harold made a face behind her back, mimicking her frown, and motioned me to follow.

"The ground floor is a mess, I'm sorry to say," Bakul had begun, her voice echoing in the almost-empty room. "You see the river has been flooding it every year and there have been hardly any repairs, no upkeep. My grandfather lived upstairs till he died." She spoke with a measured politeness, a calm impersonality that confused me. Did she actually imagine I too had come to dupe her? Or was this part of some elaborate plan?

We went from room to room, Bakul providing explanations for each, with apologies for the all-pervading dust. She spoke in the same passionless, descriptive way, not pausing to let us respond. I recognised the mildewed portraits on the ground floor from my visit with Aangti Babu, and the chandelier he had been eyeing still hung from the ceiling, too grey with dust and cobwebs, surely, to make light. We passed through an enormous wood-panelled billiards room, the table piled high with legless chairs, broken boxes and pictures in frames. I wondered who had used it in the past – it was certainly never going to be usable in the future.

Harold was darting about like a long-legged insect, peering here and there. When he noticed Bakul's ironic gaze levelled at him, he said hurriedly, "Termites, ma'am, one can't be too careful, don't want to take on property with woodworm. If you'll excuse me . . . " He rapped a knuckle on the wood of a cupboard as if to make sure it hadn't rotted.

We went up a creaking staircase to the first floor. Upstairs, where I had never been, there was Victorian furniture, and everything was as if the occupants of the house had just gone out for a walk. There was a typewriter on a grimy rolltop desk, with a sheet of paper flapping in it. An empty cup and saucer, brown with dust, stood on a side table. I passed a huge framed mirror so opaque with dust that all I could see of myself in it was a shadowy form – it was like looking through the eyes of a half-blind man. We stepped through clouds of grime and cobwebs, passing ghostly chairs and tables, four-poster beds and sideboards, pictures on the wall that showed nothing but black fungus and dirt, and spiders' legs drifting streamers for a ghoulish party.

In one of the rooms there was a carved, glass-fronted cupboard in a corner, and Harold bent almost double to look into it. He gestured to me. "Bledgy hell, look at that, m'n, wouldn't the boss like that?" Inside the cupboard were five glass shelves, each containing delicate figurines of men, women and gods, children and animals, dozens of them, all in ivory. Even the wood of the cupboard was inlaid with ivory. Some of the figures stood upright, some had fallen on their faces in the dust that coated the shelves.

"Exquisite, aren't they?" Bakul's voice startled me. "And priceless. It shows the five days of Durga puja and all the different things that happen each day. Only, the key to the cupboard is lost, so when the figures fall, they remain forever fallen.

"As you can see," she continued, moving into the next room, "the upstairs is in better condition, structurally. I had planned to get everything cleaned before you came so things would look better . . . but never mind, you're earlier than I expected. The damage downstairs isn't as terrible as it could have been, considering the house had two feet of water in it every monsoon. Prospective customers are likely to know this from the locals – they call it the drowned house, so there's no point trying to hide the fact. Of course," she turned to me and Harold with a raised eyebrow, "your customers – or you – may not want to keep the house at all." She shrugged. "You may want to demolish it. If that's so, you're in trouble. This is a sturdy place. It won't go down without a fight."

By now we had rounded the corner of the wide verandah that ran the length of the house. Beyond it we could see hardly anything but trees, and only bakul trees. Soon they would be in flower and the air heavy with their scent. This part of the verandah appeared to have been swept and cleaned. It looked as if someone lived there.

"This is one of the upper bedrooms," Bakul said in a smaller voice than before. "There are four more."

The room was clean and smelled fresh, as if still in use. There was a single, green-sheeted bed with a simple headboard, an ordinary wooden cupboard and a dressing table with a long mirror. The window opened onto a tree whose branches almost came into the room. Another bakul tree. On the wall was a picture of Bakul's mother, Shanti. There was a thin, dried-up garland around the picture and the ashes of incense on the table before it. She looked exactly as Bakul had when we made love in Songarh that afternoon – her refusal to recognise me now made it all seem too far away to be true any longer.

For a moment Bakul and I stood in the room, not speaking, forgetting Harold. I remembered how she had longed for her mother all through her childhood, how she had tried to hide it. I felt wretched, but could do nothing. I could not hold her and tell her, "It's me, you can say what you like."

The moment passed. Bakul's voice returned, "I'm afraid the other bedrooms aren't quite so clean, but of course you must see them. The one that used to be my grandfather's has some spectacular carved cupboards and a very striking four-poster bed." Then she said, "What happens to the furniture? Is that part of the deal?"

"That's for you and your daddy to decide, ma'am. We've no preferences ... " Harold turned to me and said, " ... though the boss may fancy some of it, yeah? Likes a bit of good carved wood, does the boss. That ivory cupboard ... D'you fancy some of this for y'self?"

I walked quickly ahead, wanting to distance myself from Harold's predatory interest in Bakul's furniture. I went out to the verandah and took a deep breath, wondering, hoping this was some complicated game Bakul was playing. Sooner or later Harold would get tough, demand the deed, then begin his search – and how would she stop him? He would find it eventually. For all his languor and his poetry, I had never known him to fail.

Quite far from the house, from the verandah, I could see the river, a sluggish stream now. It had retreated some distance from its original bed. "There's a dam upstream now," Bakul's voice suddenly said next to me. "So this house is a viable proposition again. It once had two acres of garden, most of which has been under water all these years. Now it's surfaced again. There are a good many acres of fields as well."

* * *

We reached the head of the stairs, having completed our survey of the upper floors. Harold held back, saying to Bakul, "If you don' mind, ma'am, I'd like to look around alone, at leisure. Investment of this size, y'know. Need to take a good long look." He turned before she could say anything and ducked into one of the rooms.

I followed her down the stairs and into the front verandah. She was stalking ahead of me, as though hardly aware of my presence. Now that we were free of Harold for a few minutes, I had to ask her what it all meant: How could she really think I was here to wrest her house away from her? She had to know I was on her side, not Harold's. How could she possibly doubt it? I had to warn her that Harold was no innocuous or trustworthy buyer, that he was in there trying to find the property papers, that it was dangerous to give him the run of the house – she needed me, Nirmal Babu was right, and regardless of how she perceived me, she needed to be told this.

"Bakul," I began as we reached the front verandah, "I need to talk . . ."

The verandah was no longer empty, however. Sitting in one of the cane chairs as if he owned it as well as the house was a man about as old as Nirmal Babu. He had a prosperous face that shone with fat and sweat. He wore a crisp, white dhoti with a fashionably crinkled kurta that had diamond buttons twinkling in it. Next to him stood a shrivelled up, sorry-looking servant waving a palm-leaf fan over his master's balding head.

We stopped short. He got up when he saw us and said in a booming voice, "Namaskar, Shaheb! And you too, Bakul. You don't know me, but I know you!"

Bakul gaped at him.

"Your grandfather and my father were great friends, the greatest of friends! You must have heard. Ashwin Mullick was my father's name! And my own humble name is Rathin Mullick."

"I had not heard," Bakul said.

"Do sit down," the man said, inviting Bakul into her own verandah as though it had always belonged to him. She followed in a daze.

"Oh well, it's natural, how would you know me? You, poor child, have hardly ever come to this house! Strange," he said opening a silver paan-case and passing it around "No? Don't want paan? Well, as I was saying, strange indeed. You hardly know anything about this house, and I know every inch of it and all your grandfather's family and friends. I played here as a child, floated paper boats in the river, and in your ground floor when it started flooding. What fond memories! And the wonderful jackfruit dalna your grandfather's cook made! Even your mother . . . Shanti and I – for some years, we played together, in this very verandah! She was a timid sort. Whenever she lost a game she would burst into tears, floods of tears! Ah, but Rathin Mullick, stop, you must not use the word flood in this house, a bad word, a disastrous word! After what the house has been through!"

I was staring at the man dumbfounded. He sounded and looked like something out of a cheap film or jatra, laughable, yet somehow menacing.

Bakul was beginning to look impatient. In the crisp tone that I knew from years ago, she said, "How can we help you, Rathin Babu? This gentleman," she looked at me, "has come here on some work, so I'm sorry, but . . . "

"Ah, the young," he said with regret, "always, always in a hurry. I know why this gentleman has come, child, and why the other gentleman with him has come. And that is why I have come. Dear child, for years and years, my father had been telling your grandfather, 'Bikash Babu, sell this monster house, it will swallow you up, sell it, and if you like, I will buy it!' My father even gave him money for years as a downpayment, and Bikash Babu, your good grandfather, took it – otherwise how do you think your grandfather lived, eh?" The man sounded suddenly truculent. Then he softened his tone again, and continued, "My poor father, God rest his soul, looked after your grandfather, sent him food during the floods . . . and now I'm hurt, my trust in humanity is gone, my child! I hear – from other people – that this house is to be sold – behind my back! Behind my back, when my family has already paid lakhs of rupees for it! Can it be true, I asked, and came to see for myself."

A frog began to croak, and then a rickshaw's bells sounded. The withered servant, though half asleep, still stood behind his master waving the palm-leaf fan. Bakul looked as if she were trembling. She turned to me and said – and somehow the three words she spoke cleared the air as if a sharp gust of fresh breeze had blown over us – she said, "*Say something, Mukunda!*"

"I'm sure Bakul's father has no intention of cheating anyone, Sir," I said. "We know nothing about any understanding you may have had with Bakul's grandfather. Naturally, we need to see some documents, a contract between you and the property owner would be required for legal reasons . . . "

"Documents! Moshai!" the man spluttered. "When an old friend helps another over years and years for the whole of Manoharpur to see, with food, with money, with medicines, with servants, on an understanding between friends, are there documents?"

"Still," I said, with a new surge of confidence that came from all my years dealing with property. I knew that without papers he was a gnat I would brush off, a butterfly on a mill wheel. "I'm a mere agent for the seller, how can I do anything without the relevant papers?"

I could feel Bakul's eyes on me, different now, surprised and not edgy. Rathin Mullick's motive in arriving at Bakul's family home was no less predatory than Harold's, but his unexpected appearance had been my salvation, his intrusion had placed Bakul and me on the same side. He argued, alternating between threats and appeals to sentiment, and I let him. The longer he thrust, the more skilfully I parried, and the happier I felt at being able to wield my rapier – and before Bakul. I could not resist showing off a little, letting her know conclusively that I was on her side and Nirmal Babu's, that I was here to rescue her and save her old house.

We argued for what seemed like an eternity and then Rathin Mullick left, vowing that we had not heard the last of him. I knew that probably we had not, but the danger seemed to have passed even if temporarily, and it had served a purpose: I could talk to Bakul before Harold reappeared. Now, I thought, now I could explain everything to her.

"Bakul," I said, "I have thousands of times dreamed of us meeting again, but never like this. Listen to me now, we need to talk. There's no time to . . . "

"Well, life is always unexpected, isn't it? Nothing happens as we expect or dream it," she said, looking preoccupied. "Our chat will have to wait a bit – we should go in and see to that man – what's his name, Harold? What can he be doing in there so long? I can't believe a word he says, and he looks more sinister than anyone I've ever encountered. Mukunda, how can you work with such people?"

As if on cue, Harold walked into the verandah. He looked hot and irritable, brushing his hair and his tie free of dust. He had been ordered to find the deed or wheedle it out of the occupants and vanish with it, but given the size of the house this was a tall order, and he had obviously made no progress. Now he gave Bakul a belligerent look and said, "The place is a mess ma'am. I'm afraid it's in no fit state to be bought or sold. An' the papers, please. Show me the papers before I can say anythin' about our decision." Harold cast a glance in my direction for confirmation, saying, "Eh Mukunda, nuthin' goes further without the papers, right?"

As he looked to me for agreement and support, I had an idea in one of those flashes that seem blindingly obvious later. Why had it not occurred to me before! Harold was relying on me to back him up: we had been on many similar assignments together, too many to count! He trusted me and assumed Aangti Babu did too. If I convinced him I was better suited to extracting the papers from Bakul, that my familiarity with the house and its owners would work where his threats and blandishments had not, and that I would deliver the papers on his behalf to Aangti Babu, it might suffice for the moment and remove him from the scene.

"The deed is not here. I'm sorry I haven't found it," Bakul said.

"Maybe we can, ma'am, me and my friend here." Harold looked at me.

"You do need to show the deed to sell the house," I said to her, and then to Harold, "I know this lady's family. Aangti Babu asked me to follow up here because I inspected the property with him some years back . . . you know that. We couldn't seal the deal at the time . . ."

I looked at Bakul, carefully turning away from Harold so he could not see me signal to her with a look she knew from our childhood: "*Say nothing, trust me.*"

"Give me and my friend here a moment to discuss a couple of points," I said to her. "Then we can reach some suitable decision on how to proceed."

"I'll wait inside," she said. "For you and your *friend*."

I took Harold aside. "Either she really hasn't got the papers, or she doesn't mean to part with them," I said. "Whichever it is, we can't force the thing out of her. She's tough. I know how to handle this. We've got to take care. I know the family. I can convince her we're genuine buyers, but it'll take a while, she has to trust someone enough to fish out the documents. There's no point us both hanging on here, she'll feel even more intimidated and cautious than she is already. You go back and report to Aangti Babu. I'll get the papers out of her or her people over the next couple of days, I'm sure of it."

He looked doubtful for a moment, but the logic of the situation and of what I was saying, and the fact that I was Aangti Babu's blue-eyed boy, were sufficient. He had an agile mind and did not vacillate. "O.K., m'n, best of luck," he said, with a quick punch on my shoulder. "I'll push off and tell the boss, but play it carefully, m'boy, miles to go before you sleep." He waved me a goodbye and shuffled off towards the driveway. I followed to make sure he really was leaving.

I had done this kind of thing before in the course of my work, but

I had never had a personal stake in any of it. By the time Harold's leave-taking at the gate was done, I was exhausted by my arguing and trickery. My neck ached, and a spot behind my right eye throbbed with pain. I had almost forgotten that Bakul was waiting.

She had never liked to wait. As soon as she saw me approach, she said. "Have you managed to get rid of him? When did you learn to be so persuasive? Two men despatched inside an hour! Shall I call in the next buyer so you can work your charm on him too?"

"Can you be quiet for maybe a two-minute stretch?" I said.

She turned away, looking hurt. But I was too angry to stop.

"How dare you come here on your own? Yes, you can do everything, yes, you're not afraid of anything, that's how it's always been. But would it have hurt to bring your husband along? Just as a prop, even if you don't actually need him? Don't you know how dangerous all this is? Property disputes attract dealers and thugs. Why couldn't Nirmal Babu have come? Isn't selling his wife's home important enough? Staying back for a *dog*! What if Harold had hurt you?"

It emerged as a tirade. She cut me short. "Dealers and thugs like you?" she said with her crooked smile.

"You can smile, Bakul, because you don't know how rough it can get."

"Baba!" she said. "Of course! You must have come because my father told you to. He thinks I can do nothing on my own, doesn't he? I should have known it. I guessed something like this must have happened the moment I saw you, but you came with that other fellow and you looked like you wanted to buy me out! I wasn't sure how things stood until I saw you fend off that Rathin Mullick."

"Rathin Mullick is a lamb compared to Harold – the things Harold does – I can understand Nirmal Babu, he's never lived in the real world," I burst out again, "but your husband . . . I shouldn't say anything about him of course, but all the same Bakul, how could he?"

"Why are you going on about a husband, Mukunda? Don't you know . . . I mean, didn't Baba tell you?"

"Tell me? Tell me what?"

She looked at my face and threw her head back and laughed. "Did you *really* think . . . ?" she managed to say between bursts of laughter. "Oh, you look so . . . " I knew I looked confused and angry, sweaty, dishevelled and absurd. My impulse was to reach out and slap her face if she did not stop laughing. In the end she did.

"I have no husband, I never had one," she said. "Didn't Baba tell you the marriage was called off? I thought he wrote to you all the time! I thought you knew."

"Called off?" I repeated, almost in a whisper.

"Yes," she said, her impish smile back again. "They found out – that I'm not a virgin, that I slept with a married man – and they ran for their lives! The groom ran the fastest of all. I had only to swear one cousin to secrecy and tell her I had had an affair with a married man, and that was enough! With just seven days to go before the wedding, they called it off! I turned cartwheels for joy. Baba was livid; he muttered for weeks about what an archaic lot the groom's family were, and what an escape for me. He blamed himself because the groom was some history teacher Baba had thought would be perfect for me. I don't know why I ever agreed to the wedding – sometimes, living in Songarh with no change – such loneliness, such boredom, and no hope of release – sometimes I'd think anything would be better, even marrying a stranger. He looked pleasant enough and he lived in Bombay – but as the wedding day approached I felt I couldn't, I just couldn't. It all seemed too impossible and there was no other way of getting out of it but to spread the rumour and pray that it reached him."

"Why didn't you tell me?" I said. "Why didn't you tell me? I was there at that time: I came to Songarh! I was there knocking about in some miserable hotel room, killing myself thinking of you with another man!"

I looked at her smiling face. I was furious: how she could be so light-hearted about something that had almost wrecked our two lives? How could I have gone all the way to Songarh and not actually met her, thinking she was married? How simple it would have been if I had not run away that morning! And how could *she* have been so stupid, never telling me what had happened? All those wasted years since that miserable spring when I lost her and my wife and my child all at once. What if Bakul and I had never met again?

* * *

We walked in silence for a while in the grounds surrounding the house. The earth had a curious, bleached, aged look from having been so long underwater. There was all kinds of rubbish – bits of wood, dead fish, a dented enamel bowl – strewn around the grounds, as if thrown up by the tide.

Bakul sat down on the back verandah's worn steps, now exposed to air and light after years of drowning. The cloud-curdled sky was grey and white above us, making the light as soft as the evening's although it was still only afternoon. A short distance across a stretch of hard, dry clay that must have been the submerged garden, I could see water.

"My father's always done this to me," she was saying. "Don't you remember how he promised he'd bring us both here for a holiday, and then out of the blue sent you off to Calcutta instead? For years he never let me meet my grandfather, and then he brought me here just twice, once about two years after you left – that's when my grandfather hid the deed with me – and the next time when he was almost too old to know who I was. When we were here, Baba was so unfriendly, and both times we left within two nights after coming all that way."

I tried to pay attention to what she was saying about Nirmal Babu, but could think of nothing but this: she was not married, there was no husband. *Bakul had no husband.* She had never had a husband. After years of jealousy I had nobody to be jealous of. If she still wanted me (and how could she not?) then we could ... but what if she did not want me any more? She seemed to have everything on her mind but us.

"This terrible Rathin Mullick was right," Bakul was saying, meanwhile. "I don't know this house except from stories and pictures. When my grandfather was ill, I didn't get to know about it. When he died, we didn't know until ten days later! And now at last I'm here at the house, and there are strangers tramping all over it, measuring it up, assessing it, deal-making. I had wondered on the way here what I would do when I came. I was thinking perhaps I'd sell it. That's the most practical thing. What am I to do with this ramshackle old mansion far away from anywhere? But . . . " she laughed, "I must have something of my grandfather in me. I couldn't have sold it, I think, even if it was still flooded and as hollow as a coconut shell with termites. Oh, of course I showed it to Harold and all that – I couldn't very well not when I had agreed to meet him, but the thought of him – or anyone remotely like him – taking it over! Makes my flesh crawl."

When she spoke again after a pause, her eyes flashed. "Every room in this house makes me think of my mother. This is all I have of her. My father can't make me sell it, he can't!"

"Nirmal Babu . . . you know how he is, lost in his fossils and potsherds and stupas," I said. "He probably hasn't even realised you're attached to this house. He's just trying, for once, to be practical. He wanted you to have money to survive." I laughed in an effort to lighten the atmosphere, "And look how he blundered."

"You can laugh," she said, hardly able to keep the tremor out of her voice. "He's adorable, isn't he, so absentminded, so lost in his world of continents and kings. But he never had much space in his mind for me. He's always been concerned, but did he ever consider how I would feel if . . . " She stopped speaking for a while, then took a deep breath and said, "I'm just going on and on. Tell me about yourself. How is your son? Why have you given up your job?"

"What did you do with the house deed?" I asked her. "Have you got it safe?"

"I posted it, Mukunda, that's what I did the moment I knew I wouldn't sell the house. Just trusted the Indian Post and Telegraph with my life's wealth and posted it off to Baba! Three nights ago. I went straight to the place where the deed was hidden, found it, packed it securely and sent it as a registered letter to Songarh. You don't have to worry about saving me from your Aangti Babu. This house is mine now."

* * *

302

The relief of it made me garrulous. I sat on those steps and told Bakul about my wife and son, how I had not seen them after that brief glimpse when I went to my wife's village some months after she had left. I told her how I longed to see my son, still dreamed about him as I had seen him last, as a toddler, but my father-in-law was implacable and my wife never replied to my letters, and my son would not know me until it was too late.

I told her about the trips I had made to my wife's village over the years, hoping each time to be let into the house, and each time being turned away from their door. I had a child and yet I didn't have a child. How right that senile old astrologer had been!

I told her about Suleiman Chacha and Chachi coming back from East Pakistan. About the man in the train who had seen a spaceship.

In the end my throat felt dry. After years of living so much alone, I felt as if my voice was ringing in my ears. I stopped.

* * *

We walked across the clay to the placid water. It was no longer the wide river I had seen when I had come to Manoharpur with Aangti Babu. This was a flat, tranquil stream. How could it have flooded the house, caused Bakul's mother to die? It barely even disturbed the silt that disappeared into it, a smooth, silky, greyish black.

Bakul took off her slippers and walked into the wet mud. I followed, the cool mud oozing between my toes. She sat on her haunches by the stream, the edges of her sari growing damp.

It was quiet but for the call of a distant, monotonous bird. Bakul's chin rested on her knee, her hair shielding her face. She seemed sunk in thought. A long-legged insect made of straight lines trembled on the surface of the water. I touched it with my fingertip and it sprang away. I wondered what Bakul was thinking. Were we too late? Had her feelings changed? Had I said too much about my wife and child? Why did she seem so far away, trailing an idle hand in the water and looking out to the other bank as if she had forgotten I was there?

When at length a red flower came floating down the water towards me, I guided it to Bakul, hoping she would notice. She stopped hiding behind her hair and turned, and for the first time that afternoon she smiled at me in the old way. Her hand reached out for mine and our fingers found each other's beneath the water and intertwined.

The flower, the ruined house behind us, the two wispy-haired children staring at us from a mudflat across the river, everything receded. I could see and hear nothing with her hand in mine. I caressed each of her fingers until they slipped out of my grasp one by one. I heard the sound of water as she used her freed hand to push it back and forth. Far in the distance, a flat, dark country boat punted into view.

At last Bakul said, "Mukunda?"

I did not answer.

"How was I to know what to do? You were still married," she said, pulling at my arm. "What did you expect: that I'd write to you and say, Leave your wife, leave your child – come and live with me now, I can't go on this way, everything seems wrong, each day of my life seems only half lived without you . . . Is that what I was supposed to tell you?"

Somewhere far away a steamer hooted. Perhaps the real, wide river met the sea somewhere out of sight, but within our hearing.

I thought I had replied when all I was doing was staring at her and repeating her words in my head.

I felt as if everything had gone very still. The rushes had stopped nodding, the breeze had stopped blowing through our hair, the stream had stopped flowing, the curdled clouds had stopped drifting overhead, that bird had stopped its call, the two children on the opposite bank had frozen in mid-gesture.

The steamer hooted again, a little closer now, melancholy, hollow.

I noticed irrelevant things: that her sari was the green of a tender banana leaf, that its border had flecks of lemon in it, that she had tiny, fish-shaped gold studs in her ears, that the same thin gold chain still rode over her collarbone and disappeared into her white blouse. I traced the chain with the tip of my finger.

Our clothes were getting soaked in the grey river-bed, our feet were sinking in the mud, Bakul's hair had come loose, one of her gold studs had slipped off, the number of staring children on the opposite bank had gone up from two to seven, and they were leaping up and down, laughing and pointing and shouting things we could not hear. I took in none of this.

All I felt was that life had finally floated down the river and reached me.

FINIS

GLOSSARY

aanchal	one end of the sari, covering the shoulders and sometimes the head
achaar	pickle
adivasis	tribal people
almirah	cupboard
aloo	potato
apsara	divine beauty
arre baap	lit. "Oh father", exclamation of alarm
arre bhai	lit. "Oh brother", expression of affection
Baba	father
Babu	suffix added to men's names to show respect
bael	Bengal quince, *Aegle marmelos*; a hard-shelled fruit
Bahu	daughter-in-law
bathua	a wild spinach
beedi	a cheap, strong smoke
ber	a wild berry
bhoot	ghost
bhuttawala	corn-seller
Bibi	affectionate Urdu term for a married woman
biryani	richly flavoured rice cooked with meat
bonti	a curved blade mounted on a wooden stand
Boudi	older brother's wife
Bouma	daughter-in-law
brinjal	aubergine
bulbul	Indian bird with a sweet call

Chacha/Chachi	Uncle/Aunt
chappal	slippers
charpoy	rough, cheap string cot
daal	lentil curry
Dada	older brother
Dadu	grandfather
dalna	a light curry
dekchi	large cooking vessel
deodar	*Cedrus deodara*, a gigantic Himalayan cedar
dhakai paratha	paratha layered with egg and meat
dhoti	man's unstitched lower garment
Didi	older sister
doob	a fine, soft grass
duree	rug
Durga puja	an important annual festival worshipping the goddess Durga, who vanquishes evil
Durvasa Muni	a mythological sage renowned for his temper
gaandu	a term of abuse
Ganga	the Ganges, one of India's largest rivers, considered sacred
Gangajal	holy water from the Ganges
garh	fortress
ghat	steps to a river, bathing area
ghee	clarified butter
goondas	thugs
gotra	sub-caste
grihaprastha	one of the four traditional stages in a Hindu's life: the householder stage
gulli	alleyway
gulmohar	*Delonix regia*, a tree which is covered in bright-orange blossoms in summer
hakim	practitioner of traditional Islamic medicine
haraami	bastard; term of abuse
Hari, Hari	exclamation, something like "Dear God!"
havaldar	low-ranking policeman

huzoor	lordship
jamun	Java plum
jatra	folk theatre
jhaal muri	spicy puffed rice
jhinuk	a spoon for feeding babies
jhola	cloth bag
joota	shoe
juldi karo	"Hurry up"
junglee	savage [noun and adj.], used as mild, often friendly abuse
kachnar	*Bauhinia variegata*, a flowering tree with elegant purple or pink blossoms
kajal	kohl; black eye make-up used in the East
kanthas	thin, home-stitched quilts
kashi	large, flat-bottomed vessel with a low rim
khadi	rough, handspun cotton advocated by Mahatma Gandhi
khansama	cook and bearer
khurpi	humble garden tool for digging
kukri	curved Sikkimese knife
kurta	long, shirt-like garment
kutcha	unmetalled
lakh	one hundred thousand
lungi	unstitched lower garment worn by men
Ma/Mataji	mother
machan	a high, sheltered bamboo perch
madhabilata	Rangoon Creeper, *Quisqualis indica*
maulvi	muslim cleric
mela	fair/carnival
memsahib	originally, white woman; any upper-class woman
mishti	dessert; any kind of sweet dish
mofussil	small town
moong	green lentil
moshai	Sir; respectful form of address which can be used sarcastically

mulmul	soft, fine cotton
muri	puffed rice
namaskar	Indian greeting with joined palms and bowed head
neem	Margosa, *Azadirachta indica*, a tree with medicinal properties, whose twigs are used to clean teeth
nullah	drain/narrow canal
paan	an addictive concoction of betel leaf, areca nut, tobacco and other condiments, usually consumed after meals
pagli/pagla	crazy girl/man
pakora	salty fritter
papad	poppadum
paratha	fried, unleavened flat-bread
Parsi	Zoroastrian
payesh	Bengali version of rice pudding
peepal	sacred fig, *Ficus religiosa*
peon	office boy
phirni	Mughal version of rice pudding
poori	fried, puffed bread
puja	ceremonial prayer
pukur	open water tank, often large and used for bathing
purohitmoshai	priest
raat ki rani	*Cestrum nocturnum*, Lady of the Night
rezala	rich meat curry
riyaaz	music practice
rossogullas	a spongy, syrupy sweet
roti	unleavened, wholewheat bread
rui	a kind of carp
sarangi	a stringed musical instrument
Saraswati puja	yearly festival to invoke the Goddess of Learning
semul	silk cotton, *Bombax ceiba*, a towering, beautiful tree, almost leafless when it has its showy red flowers
shehnai	wind instrument usually played at weddings
shingara	deep-fried, triangular pastry filled with spicy vegetables or mincemeat

sindoor	red mark in the parting of a married Hindu woman's hair
stupa	Buddhist monument
supari	areca nut
swadeshi	a phase of the nationalist movement in India when people were urged to reject foreign goods in favour of those locally manufactured. Clothes made from imported fabrics were thrown into public bonfires as a mark of protest.
tanpura	a stringed musical instrument
Thak'ma	slang for "thakuma", i.e., grandmother
theek hai	"It's alright"
tonga	horse-drawn carriage for hire
tussar	luxurious, traditionally woven silk
vaid	practitioner of traditional Hindu medicine
zamindar	landowner

ACKNOWLEDGEMENTS

Christopher MacLehose – perfect reader, magnificent editor – has shown me all that it is possible for a publisher to be. His invisible ink is on every page.

Ravi Dayal used his considerable powers of persuasion to make me show him a draft when I was too uncertain to part with it; his acerbic pencilling in the margins became my last conversation with him.

Thanks to Shruti Debi for her persistence and her descriptions of crumbling old homes, some of which have entered the story; Laura Palmer for her reassuring combination of friendliness and efficiency; Nayanjot Lahiri for saving me from archaeological blunders; Katharina Bielenberg for being a last, super-fine sieve; Rohan D'Souza's writings for teaching me about floods, and Rajdeep Mukherjee for all the thrillers. The tribal song is adapted from one in Verrier Elwin's *Leaves from the Jungle*.

Friends (especially the B.M.C. and Ladeez Sangeet) and family made this book possible by just being there. Among them, Myriam Bellehigue, Kristine Witt-Hansen, Uday Roy, Manishita Das, Arundhati Ray, Sharmi Roy, Kavita Sivaramakrishnan, and Angela Smith have tolerated various ill-timed demands on their affection, which included the reading of drafts. Mukul Kesavan, Ivan Hutnik, Sikha Ghosh, Thomas Abraham, Prateek Jalan, and Ram Guha provided encouragement and insider info, and Uday Kumar space and supplies.

Thanks to Ma, Pa, and their bookshop for room in their lives and shelves, Chandra Dorai and Sukanta Chaudhuri for giving me the words, and Biscoot for making it clear that words are not anywhere as expressive as tail, eyes, and paw.

My mother for taking stories I scribbled into schoolbooks as seriously as she did drafts of this novel, and for making me believe I would finish it by simply repeating that I would.

In the end R – and not just for the optimal silences.